P9-ASM-514

Alligators May Be Present

Library of American Fiction
The University of Wisconsin Press Fiction Series

Alligators May Be Present

Present

A Novel

Andrew Furman

THE UNIVERSITY OF WISCONSIN PRESS
TERRACE BOOKS

BOCA RATON PUBLIC LIBRARY
BOCA RATON, FLORIDA

The University of Wisconsin Press
1930 Monroe Street
Madison, Wisconsin 53711

www.wisc.edu/wisconsinpress/

3 Henrietta Street
London WC2E 8LU, England

Copyright © 2005
The Board of Regents of the University of Wisconsin System
All rights reserved

1   3   5   4   2

Printed in the United States of America

Library of Congress Cataloging-in-Publication Data
Furman, Andrew, 1968–
Alligators may be present / Andrew Furman.
p. cm.—(Library of American fiction)
ISBN 0-299-20780-3 (hardcover : alk. paper)
I. Title.   II. Series.
PS3606.U757A79   2005
813'.6—dc22   2004024544

Terrace Books, a division of the University of Wisconsin Press,
takes its name from the Memorial Union Terrace, located
at the University of Wisconsin–Madison. Since its inception in 1907,
the Wisconsin Union has provided a venue for students, faculty, staff,
and alumni to debate art, music, politics, and the issues of the day.
It is a place where theater, music, drama, dance, outdoor activities,
and major speakers are made available to the campus and the community
To learn more about the Union, visit www.union.wisc.edu.

TO MY FAMILY,

FURMANS, DICKSTEINS,
AND DOOPANS

MAY 2005

Who is free? No one is free. Who has no burdens? Everyone is under pressure. The very rocks, the waters of the earth, beasts, men, children—everyone has some weight to carry. This idea was extremely clear to him at first. Soon it became rather vague, but it had a great effect nevertheless, as if someone had given him a valuable gift.

—Saul Bellow, "A Father-to-Be"

The moonlight froze on unknown bushes, on trees that had no name. An invisible bird gave a peep and was silent—perhaps it had fallen asleep. What kind of bird was it? What was its name? Is there dew in the evening? Where is the constellation of Great Bear situated? In what direction does the sun rise?

—Isaac Babel, "Awakening"

"Hope" is the thing with feathers—
That perches in the soul—
And sings the tune without the words—
And never stops—at all—
—Emily Dickinson

Acknowledgments

My deepest thanks to: Elisabeth Weed, who first glimpsed the potential of this novel; my agent, Mitchell Waters, for his continuing support and wisdom; Dave Keplinger, for his insightful reading of an early draft; Dirck Aumiller, for the beautiful cover art; Robert Mandel and the entire staff at the University of Wisconsin Press; my colleagues in the Department of English at Florida Atlantic University, especially my fellow fiction writers, Jason Schwartz, Wenying Xu, and Papatya Bucak; my students in the MFA program in creative writing, who continue to inspire me through their great talent and enthusiasm; and, finally, to my wife, Wendy, and my children, Henry and Sophia, who tolerate a hopelessly distracted writer in the family with great patience and love.

Alligators May Be Present

Does Everything
Have to Mean Something?

Matthew Glassman never anticipated that impregnating his wife would take so much . . . well . . . work. During the first eight years or so of their relationship, while they were seeking to avoid conception at all costs, Rebecca treated his semen as if it were the most potent of concoctions. Under no circumstance would she let a drop come into contact with her person.

"What, are you crazy?! They can crawl down through the skin!" she had admonished him while wiping off an opportunistic spec from her belly, a pearl he had carelessly let fly while peeling off his condom. Glassman teased his wife that she should volunteer her services to the U.S. military. If anyone could protect the troops from a toxic drop of Saddam Hussein's chemicals it was she. Becky had Glassman so wary over the ever present threat of fertilization—even while they used condoms laced with a special no-slip (and downright uncomfortable) adhesive, spermicidal jelly, and her diaphragm—that he couldn't help but think that merely one of his emissions sent along the vaginal tract, no matter how modest in volume, would yield a pregnancy during the very first attempt.

It discouraged Glassman that seemingly every other couple he knew who made an attempt at conception, no matter how avowedly lackadaisical the attempt was, succeeded with tremendous ease. Or at least this was the propaganda.

Screw all those couples who go on and on about how much fun the "trying" is. They're full of crap, Glassman decided after the sixth month of relentless and increasingly dispirited intercourse with his wife. He had always thought that the sex would get better once they were motivated by urges transcendent of the mere carnal. But this wasn't exactly how it was panning out. She was an irregular ovulator, a phrase Glassman hadn't heard of before his wife announced her gynecologist's prognosis. What this meant, in concrete terms, was that they were under strict doctor's orders to copulate as often as humanly possible.

Come on, big boy, time to do your duty, Becky would half-jokingly encourage her husband, just after their dinner and before either one of them could plea tiredness in the middle of a yawn, as much a rhetorical flourish lately as a sign of genuine fatigue.

Glassman obediently mounted his wife upon her instructions, and found the dependability of his sexual organ incredible. No matter how inured the rest of his body had become to arousal, the part of him that most counted invariably came through in the pinch. Millions of years of human evolution seemed to be on their side.

And, evidently, not on their side.

Glassman would have felt badly about his apathy were it not shared so wholeheartedly by his wife. She had begun to use their coital time to brainstorm their list of errands for the following day.

"Oh, we have to remember to call Crystal Pools about the filter," Becky had reminded her husband, working perfunctorily above her. "And," she continued, "did you pick up the cat litter liners at Publix?"

It was finally more than Glassman could endure.

"Honey! In case you haven't noticed I'm trying to concentrate here!"

"Oops. Sorry. Go ahead and finish up whenever you're ready," Becky replied contritely. Glassman, however, didn't know whether to interpret the soft pat upon his rump as a gesture of tenderness or impatience.

In any case, he had just about had it with the whole project. All things considered, they hadn't really been trying long enough for Glassman to have earned the privilege of his discouragement. Perfectly healthy couples could take up to a year to conceive, or even longer, Rebecca's doctor had informed her. Still, he couldn't resist the temptation to grasp for the larger significance of their reluctant reproductive systems.

We've made a terrible mistake! We're not really cut out for parenthood! Fair warning!

Glassman was beginning to oppress his wife with his gloominess.

"Why does it have to *mean* anything!?" Rebecca chastised him. "Does everything have to mean something?"

Of course not, he conceded.

But there were reasons, plenty of reasons, to take stock and reconsider while they still had time. For starters, Glassman wasn't altogether certain that his genes were such hot candidates for replication.

Here I Am

Glassman was fairly certain that he had the potential to screw up a child's life through inept parenting, through good intentions gone awry. But to doom a child to a life of suffering by the sheer act of creating that life. It was too horrific a possibility to contemplate, and Glassman tried hard not to yield to the temptation.

This, however, was especially difficult for him. For Glassman knew that he had inherited a legacy of suffering himself. Not the sadness normal people suffered, but a debilitating variant that was his birthright. Depression, people called it. A lame, limp word. The economy struggled through depressions; topographical and barometric depressions marked the earth's surface and atmosphere, respectively. The dip of a typewriter key was a depression of sorts.

Glassman suffered from protracted bouts of melancholy.

Bad genes. Tainted blood. He traced his inheritance to his grandfather, Abe Fishbein, and felt that his grandfather somehow held the Rosetta stone by which he might translate his otherwise inscrutable illness. But his grandfather was in no position to offer him this translation, and Glassman sorely felt his absence. It wasn't that Abe Fishbein was dead. At least not as far as Glassman knew. Just gone.

And not gone via any of the normal routes. His grandfather had eschewed all of the more conventionally scandalous modes of action for Jewish men in Lackawanna. He never gave even a passing thought to laying one harmful finger on Glassman's grandmother; he didn't run off with one of Teenie's best friends; he didn't gamble away all of their money on the ponies at Pocono Downs; to the best of anyone's knowledge, he didn't sire any illegitimate children, a crime for which Maury Luckman fled Lackawanna for fourteen years (because this, evidently, was the mandatory length of exile upon committing such an infraction); Abe didn't drink himself to death; he didn't defraud the IRS of any of the taxes he owed them from his moderately successful haberdashery. Rather, Abe Fishbein had simply disappeared. Disappeared without so much as a trace. On a Wednesday.

This was all very long ago, when Glassman was just seven years old. His parents hadn't even told him that his grandfather had vanished until he was ten or so, when it became fairly clear that Abe Fishbein would never return and that the FBI would never find him, alive or dead. Moreover, the length of his grandfather's business trip to buy rare hats in Belgium had grown suspiciously long, even to Glassman's young, gullible mind.

Even now, the details of his grandfather's disappearance remained sketchy at best. Glassman knew only as much as he could piece together from the isolated bits and snatches he had managed over the years to seize from his mother and grandmother, both exasperatingly reticent on the topic. The general circumstances seemed to imply foul play. Abe opened up the haberdashery as usual and put in a full day. Stanley Bassoff reported to the police and, later, to the FBI, that at four o'clock or so Abe had sold him a fine wool Cavanaugh and a silk paisley tie. Abe had even marked the transaction right there in his ledger beside the cash register. He had left the Pontiac in their garage. (Abe descended upon downtown each morning on foot from the hill district of cobblestone streets where they lived.) He apparently didn't pack a bag of clothes, nor did he seem to take, well, anything from their modest three bedroom duplex on Clay Avenue.

He didn't withdraw any money from their savings account. As far as anyone could determine, he didn't go through the Greyhound station or the Avoca airport. All of which suggested that Abe hadn't planned on disappearing off the face of the earth on that Wednesday so long ago.

To be sure, it perplexed the authorities that there was no sign of a struggle in the shop. That plenty of money remained in the register. They searched fruitlessly throughout Lackawanna for a malicious motive, and just as fruitlessly for Abe's corpse in the woods bordering town and even at the bottom of the black lake at the limestone quarry. But even though they hadn't tracked down any useful leads, the chances were that something untoward came of Abe.

"These things, ma'am . . . I'm sorry to say, believe me, but . . . well . . . you usually can't expect a favorable outcome," Investigator Stone informed Teenie in a nervous, halting cadence a month or so after Abe's disappearance.

Teenie looked up at the handsome young investigator with her piercing crystal blue eyes, suitably moist; she affected a solemn furrow across her prominent brow. Teenie knew that the earnest investigator, who thoughtfully wiped the mud off his shoes before entering her home, expected her to be the bereaved widow. Why disappoint him? But Teenie knew better. She knew, and was too ashamed to admit, that her husband hadn't been murdered or kidnapped. Rather, he had simply left. After Abe failed to return home by five thirty, after she failed to get through to him at the shop, she instinctively headed to the top shelf of Abe's walnut bookcase in the study. This was before she checked the garage to see if the Pontiac was still there. (It was.) Before she checked to see whether five pieces of their pea-green luggage could be accounted for in the basement. (They could.) Before she checked the closet to see if any of Abe's clothes were missing. (They weren't.) Straining on the tips of her toes, she grasped the too-light Bausch & Laumb case from the top shelf and immediately knew that Abe had taken his binoculars. A chill ran down her spine.

God in Heaven! Teenie cried. *Abe is gone!*

For as long as Glassman could remember thinking intelligibly about his grandfather's disappearance, the specific day of the week that he had vanished had always been the most curious detail to him. Wednesday. It didn't seem like a day for climactic action. The weekend, sure. Or even Monday. A fresh start to the work week, perhaps. But Wednesday? That his grandfather abandoned his former life on a Wednesday was one of the factors that convinced Glassman that a final nervous breakdown had somehow convinced Abe to pull up the stakes once and for all. His grandmother, apparently, felt the same way.

"To tell you the truth, Barb," Teenie had told Glassman's mother over the long distance wires to Los Angeles, "your father hasn't really been here anyway. Not for a very long time." And this was the last thing Teenie wished to say about the matter, or about Abe Fishbein period. For years she had been a good and faithful wife. Had done all she could for him. But he was the one who decided to stop seeing Dr. Pearl, and she couldn't force him to go against his will. He was a grown man, after all. So all Teenie could do was watch her husband withdraw further and further within himself. He brooded more and more, silently sulked throughout the house each night when he should have been sleeping. Whole weeks would go by and it would dawn upon her that they hadn't exchanged more than one or two desultory sentences over the breakfast table. He stopped playing golf at Willow Woods completely. Refused to go to shul on Saturdays. He began to spend practically all of his free time on his farkuckt birds. They were all he had time for anymore. On the weekends, he watched them with his binoculars at various undisclosed locales in the nearby Pocono woods. And to the consternation of all their neighbors, not to mention Teenie, Abe had discovered a loophole in the zoning ordinances and built an enormous pigeon coop in their small backyard. He tended to his homing pigeons early in the morning and late each afternoon until the purple twilight forced him inside. He exercised them frequently, and even built a special trap door through which they could enter, but not exit, the coop. The neighbors didn't care much for the incessant cooing, the white splatterings on their car windows and driveways.

One of the few tangible memories Glassman had of his grandfather was Abe standing in the pigeon coop, gingerly changing a befouled nest bowl. The acrid stench made Glassman wince, which was probably why he remembered the occasion, but his grandfather insisted that he remain there. Abe had something to show his grandson. The pigeon chicks—which looked fleshy and grotesque to Glassman in their sparse dusting of feathers, their still-blind bulbous eyes, and their oversized, crooked beaks—didn't seem to mind the way his grandfather scooped them from the dirty cardboard nest bowl, limp with their liquid waste; he arranged the two of them side by side in a stiff, dry bowl, and placed the bowl back into the wooden nest box. That task completed, Abe replenished the stainless steel bowls of water, various seeds, and brick-red grit that rested on the dirt floor of the coop. Then he raked up the droppings, leaving a neat design of ridges on the ground.

"It's important to keep the environment clean," his grandfather had advised. "Clean and dry."

After Abe vanished, Teenie somehow managed to track down a homing pigeon club in Milford, an hour or so away. An elderly representative from the club drove to her house in a dilapidated pick-up truck full of empty steel cages and efficiently retrieved all of Abe's pigeons. They were fine birds and would be well taken care of, he assured her. Henry, as he introduced himself, wore a ragged flannel shirt, dangled a dirty toothpick in his mouth, and unless Teenie was mistaken, sucked a wad of chewing tobacco that bulged from underneath his lower lip like a tumor. He struck Teenie as pleasant enough but uncouth, exactly the type of person who should have been raising pigeons. What business Abe thought he had with these birds she could never fathom.

These were fine birds, Henry opined, fondling the plump breast of one specimen with a visible delight that Teenie found unsettling. He promised that he would keep the birds in his breeding-only loft so she wouldn't have to worry about them escaping and flying back home, a possibility that Teenie somehow hadn't anticipated in any case. She breathed a sigh of relief after Henry drove off, and breathed another sigh of relief after the Gelb boys down the street came over later that afternoon and tore down the coop. For fifteen dollars, they dismantled it and hauled the splintered remains of wood and wire to the dump.

Well, that's that, Teenie mused. It had been easier than she had anticipated to rid herself of Abe's birds.

However, it didn't turn out to be so easy, after all. For just five days later, as she opened the back door to take out a half-full bag of trash to the tin garbage can, she had the dickens scared out of her by Abe's best bird. She immediately noticed him, standing there in the middle of the dirt patch where the coop had been less than a week ago. She suddenly heard glass shattering on the slate floor of their porch; she had dropped the garbage bag. Gathering her wits, she briefly entertained the possibility that this wasn't the bird, but there was really no mistaking him. Hercules was the loveliest pigeon in Abe's flock. Even Teenie could admire Hercules, primarily because he didn't look like an ordinary pigeon. He wasn't a dirty gunmetal gray, but mottled with chestnut brown and white. And, of course, he still had the shiny metal band wrapped around his left leg. He seemed nonplused standing there on the barren swath of earth. Teenie supposed, under the circumstances, he had every right to be confused. When Hercules finally noticed her standing there, frozen, he began to coo loudly and took a few steps toward her, stupidly cocking his head back and forth. Teenie retreated into the house, closed the door, and felt a bit foolish as she twisted the latch for good measure.

Over the next few days, practically all of Abe's pigeons returned to Lackawanna. There were at least thirty or forty of them loitering around the neighborhood by the end of the week. They spent their first day or two in Teenie's backyard where the coop had been, then gradually seemed to fan out through the neighborhood, as if they suspected that the magnetic particles in their brains had somehow led them astray but that their home had to be around there some-place. The neighbors began to complain. The fat birds just stood there stupidly in the cobblestone street, making it impossible to drive. They loitered in the front yards pecking at seeds, driving all the indoor cats wild. Marjorie Berger's orange Persian grew so frustrated helplessly watching the plump, tasty birds from the window that she destroyed all of their living room furniture with her anxious claws. The pigeons flew in a low, drunken formation throughout the neighborhood, nearly colliding with pedestrians. Miriam Goldfinkle famously dove into a holly shrub to avoid one near collision, suffering minor lacerations—an overblown maneuver, Teenie was convinced, executed by Miriam solely to garner attention. Still, she begrudgingly sent Miriam a tasteful arrangement of peonies from her garden.

"You know we feel terrible about everything that's happened, Teenie," Herman Berger mustered up the nerve to complain to Glassman's grandmother as she slouched to pick up the *Lackawanna Herald* from her driveway, "but we left New York just so we wouldn't have to put up with this dreck anymore."

Teenie sympathized with her neighbors. Truly she did. But what was she to do? She had called Henry in Milford right away, but he refused to retrieve the pigeons. They had somehow clawed their way out the bottom of his coop. He was sorry, but capturing forty-some-odd pigeons outside their loft wasn't exactly his specialty. They'd be okay, he assured Teenie. They'd figure out what was what soon enough and find another flock to join. Teenie abruptly hung up on him. The ignoramus. The mamzer. Still, as he predicted, Abe's pigeons began to disappear, one by one, after a few weeks or so. Teenie didn't know whether they were being preyed upon by wild animals—hawks maybe, or resourceful foxes—or whether they actually had decided to move on, to migrate north, south, east, or west in search of a new home. Either way, she couldn't say that she really cared. The point was that they were out of her hair. Good riddance! She gave Marjorie Berger a too-generous check to repair her furniture and that was that. No one in the neighborhood seemed to harbor any ill feelings toward Teenie for the fiasco.

The only thing that troubled Teenie was that she couldn't keep herself from pining, ever so slightly, for that last pigeon that stubbornly remained a week longer than all the rest. Hercules. She had resigned herself to the fact that her Abe would never return to Lackawanna. For the sake of her own sanity she refused to entertain such an unlikely prospect. But for the remaining twenty years or so that she lived in Lackawanna, she couldn't keep her eyes from scanning the juniper hedge-line in the backyard for Hercules each time she took out the trash.

The story of his grandfather's homing pigeons haunted Glassman. For he too wished that he could return to Lackawanna, the American homeland of the Glassman and Fishbein tribe, although there was nothing there for him to return to either. What was more, Lackawanna had never even been his home. Glassman had grown up amid one of the countless stuccoed suburbs of Los Angeles. It was a soulless, synthetic place, the San Fernando Valley, brimming with anonymous, uprooted citizens anesthetized by the sun, blinded by the smog. "Have a nice day!" The mantra of southern California, a land obsessed with the endless string of pleasant days to be enjoyed in the pleasant, dry heat. Community? Family? Judaism? How could these quaint notions compete with westward dreams of corporeal comfort and material plenty?

Glassman had never felt at home in Los Angeles. To his mind, he had endured a miserable childhood, which somehow seemed all the more miserable in retrospect. He blamed his parents for this. It was unfair of him, he knew. They had merely sought out a better life. At least what they had thought would be better, for themselves and for their children. What did Glassman have to complain about, anyway? His parents had kept him well-clothed and fed. Beyond this, he played Little League baseball and AYSO soccer. He was a Cub Scout. An all-American childhood he had enjoyed. In the larger scheme of things, there was something grotesque in continuing to blame his parents for the nebulous, visceral longings of his formative years. Yet he blamed them, regardless. To be a child, it seemed to Glassman, was partly to blame your parents for a whole host of your own failures, inadequacies, disappointments, shortcomings, etc., onto whom there was no one else to assign blame.

Glassman would have been happier, he felt, had he grown up in Lackawanna. But he only spent a few weeks there each summer when his parents took him and his sister, Sara, to visit their relatives. The way he viewed it, he had been in absentia for the first twenty-five years of his life soaking up the dry heat and the surf at Zuma beach three thousand miles away from landlocked Lackawanna, an ever-dying town built upon anthracite dreams in Pennsylvania's northeast corner.

Now he was there, even though there wasn't really there anymore, but hundreds of miles south. Florida, indeed, seemed as close as he could get to the town that his parents and, later, his grandfather, had abandoned. Practically everyone he had ever visited in Lackawanna was either buried in the fenced-off Jewish section of the cemetery, or living out the golden balance of their lives clustered together in carefully selected condos down south in Ropa Gatos, a town named with a catchy but fairly nonsensical Spanish phrase, or in various other nearby towns that ended with the word beach: Pompano Beach, Deerfield Beach, Delray Beach, Boynton Beach, or Highland Beach. He had taken to calling his grandmother's sprawling development Lackawanna-south, realizing full well that, for countless others, the same development might have been more properly called Buffalo-south, Syracuse-south, Pittsburgh-south, or Dayton-south. The country club dining room and the spa, the Loehmann's, the Bagel Boy, the Hair We Are, and the two-dollar movie theater all within a few blocks of one another on Powerline—these were the new, shared haunts of many a transplanted community. And Glassman had transplanted himself and Rebecca right along with these dwindling elders of these various clans, not least of all his own. For something in him knew that this was the only place where he could hope to find his footing.

He had rushed to his grandmother Teenie's doorstep, framed by scarlet bougainvillaea and painstakingly rectangularized, glossy-leaved ficus bushes, just after returning his gargantuan U-Haul truck to the Texaco station a few blocks from her apartment.

"Here I am!" he announced his arrival after she impatiently unlatched the chain-lock and twisted the three deadbolts to her front door, swung it open wide, and, standing on toe-tips, enfolded Glassman into her arms.

He was here now. At his grandmother's disposal, and happy to be of use, but hoping also to extract something useful for himself. There was something valuable here to mine. Exactly what he didn't know. He certainly couldn't have foreseen what he so readily found. Or rather, as Glassman would later reflect, what found him.

Hello, I'm Irving Shuman

Another crappy day in Florida," Glassman proclaimed sarcastically to Rebecca as he lurched out of bed, slid open the sliding glass door, and stepped out onto the cool chattahoochee stone floor of their patio. The morning sun, filtered though it was through the screen encasing the patio, bathed his groggy face in warmth. February. Not Glassman's favorite month, to be sure. He actually found it to be the most oppressive time of the year given the sheer concentration of human beings who, after sixty-five years or so of rootedness, managed to follow the migratory lead of the robins in their northern neighborhoods to escape the dead of winter for warmer digs. If they could afford it, these "shrivs" (as Glassman had heard the twenty- and thirty-somethings down in Florida refer derisively to the older folks living in the area) pulled up their stakes and congregated with one another to die in south Florida. Was this a phenomenon peculiar to America? It had to be. Their children had either abandoned them already for points west or didn't have much use for them. (These children with their twelve hour work days certainly weren't any use *to* them.) So good riddance! For the hearty and well heeled, it was off to the sun and the swap meets, bingo and bridge, the Pops, semi-retired borscht belt comedians—who still could tell a joke or two—three-day cruises to the Bahamas, day-trips on chartered buses to shop at Coconut Grove in Miami and to Naples, just a couple hours drive across Alligator Alley. He had actually taken to referring to them as "snow-birds," the year-rounders' semi-derisive referent for part-timers, who left their Florida condos vacant for long stretches of inexorable humidity. Their return migration, which hit full-swing just after Thanksgiving, ushered in months of gridlock on Glades (a treacherous six-lane gash through the center of Ropa) and hour-long seating delays at even the most mediocre of restaurants. February.

Still, as far as the weather was concerned, it was Florida's most glorious month.

"Ooo, don't let all that cold air in," Rebecca teased.

This was only their second winter in Ropa. That they could keep their windows open during the night with the overhead fan humming above their nearly naked sleeping bodies still made them giddy. After all, they had both suffered sun-deprivation (clinically, Glassman was convinced) at Penn State, where Glassman first honed in on Lackawanna before shifting strategies and heading south. The unfortunate residents of State College enjoyed fewer days of full-sun than the annoyingly prideful citizens of Seattle. Glassman had done his homework. It was right there in the Farmers' Almanac.

They met at Zeno's, a cramped, smoke-infused underground pub at Penn State that attracted, almost exclusively, foundering graduate students seeking to anesthetize themselves from the pain of their stalled dissertations. Zeno's boasted beer selections from a fair percentage of the world's industrialized countries and, by the fourth or fifth year of their project on Spinoza, or Shakespeare, or subatomic particles, most of the Zeno's regulars had taken at least a few turns around the beer universe.

Glassman and Rebecca had fared better than most. They were two of the more successful Zeno's alumni, having completed their degrees in closer to one year's time than ten: Glassman a master's in journalism and Rebecca a doctorate in English after breezing almost effortlessly through the program. So essentially they both attained advanced degrees that shielded them from all fruitful careers save for the most competitive and least remunerative that the country had to offer. "We're making hundreds and hundreds of dollars a year," Glassman had jokingly reassured his fretful mother, while in one of his better moods. In his worse moods, he made no bones about his disappointment that his chosen mate had neglected to follow a more practical route than his own.

Glassman knew that his looks weren't exactly the quality that first captured Rebecca's attention. His features, taken individually, were pleasant enough. He had almond-shaped, hazel-colored eyes ("nutty eyes," his mother would tease) that looked more or less green depending upon the light and the color of shirt he happened to be wearing, long eyelashes "women would die for," according to his Aunt Janet (a dubious compliment, he had always thought), ears no larger than necessary to serve their auditory function, a prominent but not ill-shaped "too-Jewish" nose (as his less fortunate sister continuously pointed out), orthodontically reconfigured teeth (once so overcrowded that Glassman couldn't keep his mouth closed without considerable effort), and a strong chin, squared and modestly cleft. At six foot three and two hundred pounds he was nobody's nebbish either.

The problem was that Glassman's pleasant features couldn't quite get along peaceably on his face. He was all askew. His eyes were set just a smidgen too far apart; his nose seemed grafted a bit too high on his face; his mouth too low. His left ear clung to a slightly higher spot on his skull than its cohort on the right. He invariably received lopsided haircuts from discombobulated barbers. Plus, acquaintances rarely believed he was an inch over five eleven. He just didn't *seem* tall. In sum, Glassman possessed the kind of middling looks that rendered dating a genuine possibility if he were willing or able to put much effort into the endeavor.

It was his aura of purposefulness, his intensity, that first attracted Rebecca to him. She had been able to tell right off from the way that his finger skated faster and faster rotations around the lip of his nearly empty glass (he hadn't imbibed, as far as she could tell, for the last ten minutes that she had been watching him) that Zeno's wouldn't be able to hold him. He would be off, like she, for bigger things soon. Either that or he was just plain crazy. Or both. Willing to take her chances, she wove her way through the throng of standing drinkers as if en route to one of the heavy wooden tables just beyond the one Glassman, in jeans and a wrinkled blue Oxford cloth shirt, was sharing comfortably with three strangers (it was just that kind of place) donning tie-dyed tee shirts in various shades of pastel. It was a tough ruse for her to pull off as they were seated at a corner table. She had to slow down almost to a stop—"because you were so goddamned oblivious," she chastised Glassman a few months later—before he finally lifted his head so that she could force eye contact with him. At which point she carefully feigned a double-take, took the two steps necessary to tower above the seated Glassman, and blurted out:

"You're the one who wrote the *Collegian* piece defending the paper's decision to print that Holocaust denial advertisement, aren't you?"

"How did you know?" Glassman replied, then sent the last wheaty-warm swallow of Yuengling Lager down his throat, more to mask his awkwardness than slake his thirst. He began carefully to refill his glass from the plastic pitcher. *Don't spill . . . Don't spill.*

"From your picture. It doesn't look anything like you, by the way."

He decided not to call her on the internal contradiction. Instead, he asked her what she thought of the piece, anticipating her praise. Why else would she have approached him in Zeno's?

"I actually thought it was pretty stupid," she replied honestly. She somehow hadn't foreseen that he would solicit her opinion, at least not so directly. She had just wanted to begin the conversation with a sexually uncharged comment. She wasn't just some slut who picked up men at smoky bars. Realizing, however, that she had struck a harsh note, she followed up:

"But I thought it was *written* really well."

She needn't have sugar-coated her response. It *was* a stupid piece. Glassman regretted having written it, had only recognized his blindness after the issue had gone to press. He had been sidetracked by sophistry, pilpul as a Talmud scholar would say. He missed the forest for the trees. *Fuck trees,* Glassman thought. *They were shrubs, weeds that clouded my vision.* He only hoped that his parents (who incessantly pestered him for clippings of his Wednesday editorials) wouldn't hock him about the skipped week.

"No . . . no, you're absolutely right," Glassman told Becky, staring down at his empty beer glass (had he really consumed the entire glass of Yuengling himself in the past minute?), and not even glimpsing how many times he would find himself repeating the very same phrase to her in the months, and years, to come.

"Do you think we should . . . you know?" Rebecca called from the bed.

Yes, Glassman knew. Mornings were often a woman's best time for conception, she had told him. Except when a woman's best time for conception happened to be at night. Or mid-day. It all seemed so imprecise. Maddeningly so. From the patio, Glassman glanced toward the bed, then back toward the pool, as if considering his options. Rebecca herself seemed rather noncommittal, leaning back on the bed, yet poised slightly upright on her elbows, as if ready to propel herself toward the shower at the first sign of her husband's unwillingness, or inability, to perform.

"Well . . . if we must," Glassman replied in a mockingly weary exhale, wondering as he strode toward the bed, as he slipped his boxers down from his waist and to the floor, how long he, how long they, would be able to maintain such good humor regarding their futile procreative efforts.

After performing the first of his morning duties, Glassman managed to track Troy down (largely by his musky odor) and led him out onto the sidewalk, leash in one hand and in the other a blue plastic baggie that had once contained the *New York Times* and would hopefully, without too much fuss, soon contain Troy's shit. Troy, a rotund black Labrador, hated the coarse St. Augustine grass in Florida (a variant of the crab grass that Glassman had "weeded" from his parents' lawn in California) and only gingerly stepped upon it when urination or defecation was absolutely unavoidable.

"Do your business!" Glassman instructed Troy. He had to do *something*, Glassman thought. He weighed nearly one hundred pounds ("so much for 'lite' kibble," Rebecca teased her husband) and hadn't taken a crap in three days. Did they manufacture laxatives or suppositories for canines? Glassman was beginning to wonder.

"Taking the dog out for another drag," his neighbor Chuck teased Glassman from across the street as he loaded up his van. Once again, he had caught sight of Glassman dragging Troy along the sidewalk. Glassman tried to resist feeling ashamed. The folks at PETA, no doubt, would see the scene as a textbook case of animal abuse. But what was Glassman to do? Troy, true to form, had tricked him and, instead of "doing his business," collapsed onto his side and refused to right himself. His meaty tongue made a water mark that nearly sizzled on the cement sidewalk. Troy was too heavy for Glassman to lift onto his feet. He had to get the dog going somehow. Besides, they had just gotten out the door. Troy couldn't have been suffering from exhaustion or dehydration. It was at least ninety percent petulance, he was convinced.

After fifteen frustrating minutes outside, Glassman successfully cajoled Troy into at least lifting his leg and deposited him back onto the cool linoleum in their kitchen. Glassman then entered Rebecca's study and kissed his wife good-bye. She was already immersed in her e-mail. Rebecca was always checking her e-mail, it seemed to Glassman, as if she were awaiting that one crucial message sure to arrive at any moment. She was constantly being invited over the wires to academic conferences where, on her own dime, she read the papers she assiduously wrote, between grading stacks and stacks of freshman papers, on Louisa May Alcott, Rebecca Harding Davis, Sarah Orne Jewett, or some other nineteenth century woman writer (all of whom seemed to have three names).

"Wait," Rebecca commanded after her husband turned from her. "You have shaving cream behind your ears you goofball." It wasn't unusual for Glassman, as preoccupied as he often was, to leave the house with generous dollops of Barbasol behind his ears, islands of bristles unshaven, his collar unbuttoned, his belt unlooped, or without a belt altogether. He entertained fears of one day leaving the house without pants. *It's warm enough here for me not to notice. Don't laugh Becky. It could happen,* he told his wife. Glassman took a silent step toward her. She reached up, wiped the creamy dollop from behind his ear and onto her robe where it vanished in purple terry-cloth. She kissed him good-bye.

Love manifested itself most purely, Glassman believed, in the smallest of gestures. A tender gaze, a soft approach, a reaching up of hands. Something there was in love that resisted more complex gestures, like words. He would be strong for Rebecca. He had failed her miserably in the past, had put her through the ringer with an unyielding bout of melancholy. He wished he could loop back in time and snap his former self to, not so much to alleviate his own suffering but to spare Rebecca. He couldn't change the past, of course. Yet he could renounce all future episodes. Yes, he could do this, he thought from his current vantage. It was the least he could do for his wife, far too young to be so long suffering.

The *Jewish Weekly Times* boasted its own one-story office building on Federal Highway in the heart of what locals unselfconsciously called downtown Ropa, even though it was only a mile or so stretch of store-front and strip mall. Only a few buildings poked their heads up here and there to look about. The regularly re-blackened asphalt of the strip, its ornate faux gas lights, its meticulously landscaped center islands—resplendent with live oak, gumbo limbo, banyan, scarlet and purple bougainvillaea, royal (not the sloppy native sabal) palm, and a revolving array of flowering annuals—and the conspicuous absence of automobile dealerships distinguished downtown Ropa from its more weathered neighbor cities just up and down the street. Most of the shops downtown, including Glassman's office, were also painted in the same color, an inharmonious intermarriage of salmon, peach, and pink. It was Ropa's Jerusalem stone.

No one was more surprised than Glassman himself that Sam Alten and the rest of his editorial staff, a group of yentehs and alter kockers, had hired him as their Weekly Books Editor. He was the sole full-time employee at the *Jewish Weekly Times* under fifty. He had promptly answered the ad that he saw posted on the corkboard in the main office of the Penn State journalism department. The word JEWISH on the rather nondescript black-and-white flyer immediately captured his attention. (It was among those few words—like SEX and ISRAEL and HOLOCAUST—that always magically captured his gaze even amid a sea of fine print.)

In and of itself, the job wasn't such a hot prospect. "Well, I suppose the market being what it is, you have to cast the net wide," his avuncular advisor at Penn State remarked once Glassman asked Professor Simmons to send off his recommendation letter. Glassman had, indeed, cast the net wide. He had dutifully sent off his packet of materials to papers in such backwater towns as Renovo, Pennsylvania, Orangeburg, South Carolina, and Plainfield, Connecticut. Sending an application to the *Jewish Weekly Times* actually ranked pretty low on his list of job searching indignities, notwithstanding his true motives for pursuing a position in south Florida.

What clinched the job for Glassman, he realized, was a series of articles he had run in his "My Opinion" column on the Great Jewish Novelists. He wrote the pieces primarily to atone for his misguided approval of his paper's decision to print advertisements denying the Holocaust (as if the First Amendment somehow required them to print every ad submitted, no matter how fallacious and caustic). In his atonement pieces, as he referred to them, he had meditated upon the "Importance of Saul Bellow," contemplated "What Drives Philip Roth," and breathlessly celebrated the arrival of a new group of Jewish fiction writers, who "had taken their place along the continuum of the Jewish literary tradition that began with the Bible, was taken up by the Rabbis in Talmud and Midrash, the Folklorists in their magical tales, the Yiddish writers of prewar Europe, and then arrived at them, the English language writers, steeped in Judaic values while simultaneously partaking of a modernist aesthetic."

The "atonement pieces" themselves were strong. In his very sentences—the clever turns of phrase, the idioms, the learned references peppered here and there—he recognized for the first time in his writing an unmistakable air of professionalism. His parents confessed that they couldn't quite follow all of the arguments ("if ineluctable means inescapable," his mother put to him over the phone, her tattered Random House Dictionary in hand, "why not just *write* inescapable?") but they got the gist of the pieces and approved.

The folks at the *Jewish Weekly Times* were enraptured by the articles. Etta Shlotkin, the paper's calendar editor, was downright effusive during the interview:

"It's so refreshing to see such a young man so immersed in yiddishkeit," she told him as she complimented him on his Saul Bellow article, a copy of which she flourished in front of her as if to underscore her enthusiasm. The sight of his article, between Shlotkin's plump fingers, unsettled Glassman. He felt exposed, as if it wasn't an article at all that she had there, but nude photographs of him that she had somehow unearthed.

Shlotkin escorted Glassman to the door after the hour-long interview. *Where had all the time gone?* Glassman wondered as he glanced down at his watch. *I haven't yet said a goddamn thing!* He suddenly recalled his mother's advice: "Just don't dress shlumpy, and remember to smile." *Yes, remember to smile.*

The hallway, to Glassman's mind, was a bit too narrow for them to negotiate comfortably side by side. Shlotkin, however, continually adjusted her jets to hold their wing-tip to wing-tip formation. At the door, she uttered conspiratorially, almost under her breath, "We really need a mentsh like you." By "we," Glassman wasn't sure whether she meant the *Jewish Weekly Times* or Jews worldwide. Who didn't want a piece of him? He managed to utter a meek thank you, grasping her moist palm just inside the too-frosty climate control of the office (he wouldn't permit her to endure the heat of the sun), at which point she pulled him toward her and planted a dry kiss just aside his mouth.

Sam Alten called him two days later to offer Glassman the job.

Glassman was relieved to find Mrs. Kreiser, the only full-time secretary in the paper's employ, on the phone as he entered the *Jewish Weekly Times* building. He thought that he saw her out the corner of his eye try to capture his gaze to gain his attention, but he had already decided to ignore her if he could pull it off without it being too obvious. She had been pestering him lately to contribute his obligatory five dollars, which she would put toward a suitable get-well gift for Saul Lippman, who wrote the "Some Lipp" column for the paper and recently suffered yet another minor bout of tachycardia. His fellow editors' maladies were beginning to cost Glassman a pretty penny. It was Kreiser's fault, really. She was out of control with her "get-well" gifts and cards. A real maven of misfortune. In Lippman's case, it seemed to Glassman that Kreiser should have figured out, at least by the fourth basket of cheese and fruit from the Cracker Barrel, that the "get-well" gifts simply weren't working.

In this instance, however, it didn't appear that Kreiser had wanted to capture Glassman's attention to hit him up for the latest Lippman fund. For he discovered immediately upon pausing at the doorway of his office what Kreiser had probably wanted to tell him, or warn him about rather.

Irving Shuman.

Somehow, looking at the back of the elderly gentleman's head—his loosely trimmed frost-white hair, his tanned, leathery neck—Glassman knew that he had to be this Shuman fellow who had left him a message a couple days ago. The old man seemed to be scanning the titles on the bookshelf. There was nothing incriminating on the shelves, but the Weekly Books Editor felt oddly violated nonetheless. Shuman's message indicated that he wanted to make an appointment to meet with Glassman. He had left his telephone number, but didn't mention why he wanted to see Glassman, or where he was from, what organization or publisher he represented. He had refused to leave any such pertinent information, which led Glassman to assume that he was just another one of their irascible, elderly readers who wished to complain to him about something he had read in the paper. Readers (yes, Glassman was constantly reminded, there were people in south Florida who actually read his "throw-away" paper alongside, or even instead of, the *New York Times,* the *Sun-Sentinel,* and the *Palm Beach Post*) were constantly ringing him up at his windowless office to harangue him about an article or review he had run, or had neglected to run. They kept him on the phone for several minutes; there was always one more thing to say; they wouldn't stand to have the connection broken. Glassman had never received an actual visit, however, and Shuman's unprecedented persistence annoyed him. True, Glassman was planning on ignoring the first message, hoping that Shuman would get the hint, but Shuman had no way of knowing this. For all he knew, Glassman was up to his ears in messages and just hadn't gotten around to returning the call yet. Glassman felt he had to nip this in the bud quickly. Receiving cranky phone calls was one thing, but he couldn't tolerate readers barging into his office out of the blue and demanding an audience. This wasn't in his job description. It was nowhere in his contract. He had too much work on his hands as it was . . . well this wasn't entirely true, but there was a precedent to set here. He couldn't just start taking on extra burdens. *Why me?* Glassman thought, right up until he stepped assertively into his office and took one look at Shuman's face.

The first features he noticed were Shuman's almond-shaped, hazel-colored eyes, his squared, modestly cleft chin. It seemed to Glassman that he was in some sort of time warp, gazing at his own visage sixty years into the future. The old man looked like one of those computer generated images of Glassman at eighty-five, made flesh and in 3-D.

"Uh . . . Uhmmm, uh . . ." Glassman sputtered incoherently.

His protracted moment of disorientation prevented him from introducing himself properly. He had to remind himself to close his mouth and swallow the saliva that threatened to drip down his chin. Finally, the elderly man sitting in the chair took the initiative.

"Hello, I'm Irving Shuman."

Glassman tried to summon a mental image of his grandfather's face in his pigeon coop, but couldn't bring one into focus. It was as if seeing this Shuman character had deleted the prior image from his mental screen. Judging from the man's seated pose, he was about Glassman's height, and still fairly well built. He had a slight paunch that puckered the buttons of his plaid, short-sleeved shirt. Meaty forearms coated with generous flames of white hair spread from his wrists only to end abruptly at callused elbows. His face wasn't excessively wrinkled, but it had to be the face of an eighty-five year old. Just about the right age, Glassman mused. Flesh flowed from underneath both brows just over his upper eyelids, obscuring the man's vision. Tiny purple threads decorated the tip of his generous nose.

Glassman knew that his own resemblance to his absent grandfather was uncanny. He had seen plenty of photographs. That is, before his mother, like his grandmother, finally packed up the photos of Abe in a cardboard box and spitefully (yes, spitefully, he was fairly certain at the time; but less so now) removed them from view. Moreover, Glassman could tell how his grandmother's friends from Lackawanna, now living at Cypress Ponds, always had to bite their bottom lips with their upper row of teeth to keep from mentioning the resemblance in front of Teenie. Could this actually be his grandfather, Abe Fishbein, sitting there in front of him?

No. There was no way this could be Abe. Glassman wasn't thinking straight. He had been brooding about his grandfather too much lately. Ever since Rebecca began insisting that they reproduce. So he must have been hallucinating. Any Jewish man over the age of eighty could have walked into his office this morning and Glassman would have mistook him for his grandfather. He had to get a hold of himself. He jostled his head quickly to clear his thoughts.

"Sorry to barge in on you," Shuman apologized, "but the nice young lady outside told me you wouldn't mind." *Young lady?* Shuman glanced out the door vaguely in the direction of Kreiser's desk. He supposed age was relative. It was then that Glassman noticed the sizable sheaf of paper on the old man's lap, its pages unaligned and held together flimsily by two rubber bands intersecting at right angles like window panes. He knew now where this was probably going.

"That's okay." Glassman, having gotten over his initial shock, introduced himself. He reached over the desk and shook Shuman's hand gingerly, grasping more knuckle than he had expected. He then took his seat, and immediately felt more in control of the situation. His chair had arm rests and the steel desk (which usually annoyed Glassman since he couldn't cross his legs under it) formed a welcome barrier between them. Glassman tried to resist feeling guilty for not having returned Shuman's call. It had only been a few days, after all. "I received your message. Sorry I haven't gotten back to you yet, by the way. It's been really hectic here," he lied.

Shuman dismissed the issue with a tilt of his head and a scrunch of his shoulders. He didn't care, Glassman deduced, that his phone calls went unanswered. He had managed to secure the audience of the Weekly Books Editor so the unreturned messages were now as irrelevant as irrelevant could be.

"You look so . . . young. How old are you, if you don't mind me asking?" Shuman tended, Glassman noticed, to punch—almost angrily—certain key words in each of his sentences. In this instance, "young" and "are" were the words that garnered not a small amount of bronchial exertion.

"Twenty-eight, and you?" The way he saw it, Shuman opened the door for the inquiry. Quid pro quo.

"Oy, twenty-eight. A real wunderkind they got here? Well, to answer your question"—Shuman paused to take a deep breath, whether for oxygen primarily or dramatic effect Glassman wasn't sure—"I'm eighty seven."

"Wow, you don't look a day over eighty." Glassman was taken aback by the disrespectful familiarity of his unfunny quip, but he felt awkward, and tended to resort to humor, however tasteless, in such situations.

Glassman decided to cut to the chase: "Well, what can I do for you Mr. Shuman?" Shuman, with a mild grunt, straightened himself in his chair as if preparing to answer the first question of a job interview.

"Well, you see Matthew, can I call you Matthew?"—Glassman nodded—"I've been writing journals . . ." As Shuman spoke, he began nonchalantly, almost reflexively, to unravel the rubber bands from the sheaf. Glassman took a rough estimate in his head. There had to be at least two hundred, no three hundred, pages there. "And I thought maybe you would like to hear some of it."

It was an awfully strange proposition. What, exactly, did this Shuman character have in mind? Did he want Glassman to collaborate with him on it, help him secure a publisher? If so, why not just come out with it? Why be so coy? Glassman felt his teeth clench cantankerously. He had a full-time job of his own to perform. Still, against his better judgment, he was curious about Shuman. A part of him didn't want the old man to leave just yet.

"Why do you want me to hear the journal, if you don't mind me asking, Mr. Shuman? You know, I'm sure there are a lot of . . . you know . . . clubs and stuff where people get together and read their memoirs." This was true. Various Jewish clubs and groups, including a memoir-writing club he was certain, advertised their meetings in the calendar section of the *Jewish Weekly Times*.

"Aaach." Shuman, Glassman gathered, wasn't so thrilled with the suggestion. "I don't want to read my journal to any of those yentehs." Shuman paused, groping to complete his response. "You're the one I want to read this to." Another awkward pause. "You know something about writing, yes? I really don't know much about writing. I was in the shmatteh business. You know what that is, right? You're Jewish, yes?"

The shmatteh business. The haberdashery. Close enough, Glassman reflected, then quickly admonished himself for so readily entertaining such outlandish thoughts once again.

"Just on my mother and father's side," he answered Shuman's query. Shuman managed to chuckle and clear his throat simultaneously—an admirable act of consolidation, Glassman thought.

"Anyway, I have several pages of just . . . well . . . moments, impressions. They're short. Most about a page or two long."

"Vignettes."

"Huh?"

"Well, it sounds like you're talking about vignettes." Glassman could almost see Shuman's hazel eyes light up. He shouldn't have opened his big fat pedantic mouth.

"Yes, vignettes. There, you see what I mean? You know about writing. I don't. I was just in the shmatteh business. Listen, I know you're a busy man. You have a job to do, yes? This I know. But can I possibly just read you a couple. Then you tell me what you think."

"You've got yourself a deal. Go ahead. Read me one." Glassman looked on as Shuman leafed a few pages into the manuscript toward what the editor presumed was a favorite section.

My father was a hard man. A violent man. My sisters and brothers and me. We were all scared of him. . . .

Shuman spoke in smoother cadences than he had before, and with a softer voice. This is his reading voice, Glassman thought.

He worked as a printer and had giant, muscular arms from lifting and setting the presses all day. He was up before dawn and off to work. When I heard the door creak and click shut, this is when I got out of bed. He was not a religious person. He didn't go to shul and neither I nor my brothers were ever Bar Mitzvahed. But he had his rules. The Tageblatt had to be on the kitchen table when he returned from work, or else it was a wollop to the ear for Lenny. That was his job. I remember he knocked me off my chair when I spilled a full bottle of milk. Klutz, I'll break every bone in your body! You pay for milk, then if you want you spill. My mother pleaded with him that it was an accident, but I needed to learn to be careful he said. We couldn't afford accidents. I was scared of him, but at the time I didn't think he was unfair or even very cruel. That was the way it was. It was what it was. But that's not what I want to talk about now anyway. My father started making more money. He must have because we moved to a bigger flat with a kitchen and a dining room also. He made plans to take us all on a train for a summer vacation in the Catskills somewhere. Where I don't remember, but that's not important.

He rented a kuch aleyn. This way mother could cook and we would save money on food. We get there, all the way on the train. It seemed to travel no more than twenty miles per hour the whole trip, and even broke down once, and we were stuck for two hours sweating. There was no air conditioning. So anyway we get there and we're tired. Rose is crying in mother's arms. She wet herself on the train. I didn't want anymore to sit next to her. I wanted to stand in the aisle, but father grabbed my puny arm in his grip like a vice and sat me back down hard in the seat. We're finally there. Everyone is unpacking. The room is crowded and hot, so I walk outside and into the woods. I hear a sad whistle that consists of two notes. The first one slightly higher than the second. Oh-mee . . . Oh-mee. *Then I saw the tiny black-capped bird in the cedar. It continued its plaintive call.* Oh-mee . . . Oh-mee. *I didn't know then that it was a chickadee, just that this mournful little bird somehow reached into the depths of my young soul. I had to wipe away a tear before going back into the cabin.* Oh-mee . . . Oh-mee.

Upon reading the last sentence, Shuman immediately looked up from his lap to gauge the expression on Glassman's face. The editor didn't quite know how to respond. He wiped away the pinprick drops of a cold sweat that had formed on his brow. Those last few sentences about the bird had stunned him. What was Shuman trying to tell him? How should Glassman respond? Was it time to make certain disclosures? Take certain risks? No, for the time being anyway, Glassman would play his hand close to his vest. He didn't trust his judgment.

But he had to say something. Shuman awaited the verdict: "Ummm, it's really, very, very interesting. . . . So, you like birds?" Glassman asked hesitantly, as if he weren't sure he wanted to hear the answer.

"Yes, boychik," Shuman answered, "I've loved birds my whole life."

Shuman rose from his seat abruptly, as if he had revealed more than he had intended. He had to leave, he explained. He had a doctor's appointment, and he had probably overstayed his welcome, in any case. Certainly the Weekly Books Editor had some work to do.

"No, don't leave yet!" Glassman spat out reflexively. He regretted the urgency of his tone as soon as the words escaped his mouth. "I'm just curious," he continued more calmly. "How did you find me anyway?"

"I'll tell you a story to answer that question. It's in here somewhere." Shuman tapped the sheaf of paper with two of his clamshell nails, but began his story extemporaneously. "When I was sixteen or so I had a job working at a hotel in the Catskills, bussing tables in the dining room. Now there's a tough job. You think *you* have a busy job?"—Shuman lifted his palm to the air as if to ask Glassman a question—"puh," he waved it down quickly. "Now what was I saying? . . . oh yes, my sister was working at another hotel near Monticello. It was about thirty or so miles away. I wanted to go visit her on my day off and managed to borrow a car from a friend. Now I didn't know exactly how to get there. The oil companies weren't really making those maps yet."

"Oil companies?"

"You know, gas stations. There were Standard and Gulf stations back then, if I remember correctly. They made the maps, but not yet." *No maps? Didn't they just come with the roads?* Glassman wondered. Shuman continued, "I knew it was seventeen miles between the two oil stations, and another eleven miles to the station in her town. Somehow I thought that I must have taken a wrong road because I knew I had gone farther than eleven miles. I was careless and forgot even to get her phone number. Finally, I reached an oil station"—three or four intakes of oxygen—"I knew it couldn't be the right one because I'd gone too far, but I figured I'd ask someone there how to get to my sister's. I parked the car and saw a woman sitting on the porch outside the station drinking a Coke. I figured I'd ask her. I walked right up to her and was standing just three feet away before I recognized that it was Dottie."

"Dottie?" Glassman inquired.

"Yes, my sister. There she was. Right in front of my eyes. Some mazel huh?" Shuman took a few rapid breaths before continuing: "You see? That's how I found you."

Shuman's eyes seemed glassy as he finished the story. Was he overcome by heartache? Loneliness? Regret? Or were his eyes naturally rheumy. Emotions aside, older people just couldn't hold their fluids as well as the young. Glassman's grandmother Teenie's eyes seemed ever on the verge of tears; his uncle Ben's nose was a rusty faucet that steadily dripped. Glassman was often priggishly repulsed by the sight of a mucus tear dangling precariously from between his uncle's bushy nostrils. Depend and Serenity undergarments, judging from the acreage of shelf space set aside for them at Publix, were bringing in big bucks in the south Florida area for the folks at Kimberly-Clark and Stayfree.

Yes, Glassman supposed it was time that Shuman left. For now anyway. He really should get to work. He had to proofread and edit two reviews before they were ready to go to press, and he'd probably have to get a hold of the reviewers to okay the changes; he had to break the news to Simon Glickstein about a review Alten had quashed; and he had three books Alten wanted him to send out to reviewers by the end of the day: a Sephardic Jewish cookbook, a children's story about Purim (that elided, as far as Glassman could tell, the final part of the story when Esther and Mordechai get a bit bloodthirsty), and some farkuckt self-help book with a Jewish motif. Oh yes, Glassman knew about writing. He was the Weekly Books Editor, and the pun was hardly lost upon him.

Shuman assured him that he would visit again soon. Glassman scooted out from behind his desk and walked Shuman the two or three steps to the office door. "Be sure to come back soon. Stay in touch," Glassman encouraged the elderly man. He suddenly felt himself overcome with emotion and tried to thwart the tears that threatened to embarrass him.

It's just the depression. Just the lousy depression.

While You Were Out

Glassman's encounter with Shuman had rocked him. He was in no condition to remain in the office. So when lunchtime arrived, he quietly slipped away and drove home. *Haberdashery... Haberdashery... Haberdashery....* Shuman's mention of the shmatteh business started Glassman thinking of his grandfather's haberdashery. He softly sounded out the word over and over again on the drive home until it began to sound nonsensical to his ears. But there was something unmistakably sophisticated about the name, as well. It was a word perfectly suited to the dignified tone that Teenie naturally assumed whenever she referred to the business. Not a chance she ever called Fishbein's Haberdashery a hat store.

Teenie had taken over the store after Abe vanished. What else could she do? Ever resourceful, she managed to maintain a decent business well into the seventies—long after the fashion currency of men's hats waned—by somehow convincing Lackawanna's male population that a real gentleman in New York and Chicago, despite unfounded rumors to the contrary, still wouldn't be caught dead in the street without a proper hat on his head. To remain afloat, however, she gradually expanded her line of fine shirts and ties, and took on a limited, but natty, line of wool sports jackets and suits. By the late seventies, Fishbein's Haberdashery was practically a misnomer as she carried only a fraction of the fine hats that Abe had once stocked. "I loved President Kennedy dearly," she told Glassman shortly after he moved to Florida. "All the Jews in Lackawanna voted for him. But I could have killed him when he showed up at his inauguration with a bare kop. He almost put me out of business!"

Abe was still in Lackawanna during the Kennedy years, and the way Teenie deftly elided his existence with a few choice words wasn't lost upon Glassman. Regardless, he would always think of Abe when he thought of Fishbein's Haberdashery. His grandfather behind the counter in the haberdashery was Glassman's second gleaming vision of Abe, a complement of sorts to Abe in the acrid pigeon coop. It was the off-season, as far as men's hats were concerned, during the summer when he and his family visited Lackawanna. So his grandfather didn't mind him messing up the displays as he donned all the fancy hats—Stetsons, Cavanaughs, Dobbs. He even let him try on the expensive handmade foreign hats, the Borsalino from Italy and some Austrian number made out of luxurious velour. The hats were so big on him that they rested over his eyes on the bridge of his nose and on the tops of his ears, partially obscuring his vision as he stood in front of the full-sized mirror aping the expressions of the few customers that visited the store. When he summoned the vision of his grandfather, he was leaning upon the counter just aside the antique register, looking upon him smilingly. But, unless Glassman's memory was playing tricks on him, his grandfather's gaze slowly grew absent, his smile fixed woodenly on his face long after he seemed to be thinking about something else just beyond Glassman's shoulder. And his grandfather's face—again, unless Glassman's mind was playing tricks on him—his grandfather's face was the face of Irving Shuman.

The hum of the automatic garage door opening thankfully interrupted Glassman's reverie. He and Rebecca had purchased a modest, white, two-bedroom house. It was built in 1970, which practically made it a historic landmark. Glassman was bemused to discover that any house built before 1990 was considered "old construction" in Florida. No matter. It was the architectural obsolescence of the ranch-style, low-ceilinged home that accounted for the successful outcome of their lowball offer. Their real estate agent, a genteel woman with one of the few southern accents Glassman had heard in Florida, only reluctantly presented the offer to the owners. She warned her "first time buyers" that this just wasn't the way things were done in Ropa Gatos. The owners were bound to be offended and would reject the "offer" outright without countering. She had almost convinced Glassman to up the offer by ten thousand dollars before Rebecca caught the drift of the conversation, ripped the phone from his hand, and told Ms. Evans that if she wouldn't present the offer to the Schneiders there were plenty of other agents who would.

It occurred to Glassman only later that they should have been at least a bit suspicious of the ease with which their deal went through. For it was becoming apparent that the previous owners had had the last laugh.

Or was it that every home rebelled against its new owners?

Practically every appliance, even the newer ones, died within a month after they had set up housekeeping. First, the motor in the new Maytag washer (machines touted, Glassman was fairly sure, for their hardiness) gave way, unleashing a foul smell of burnt metal that infiltrated every room of the house. "No use throwing any money at this thing," Chuck advised him after tilting the machine back and peering into its corpse from below. Within two weeks, the dryer — as if bereft over losing its mate — wheezed to a stop in the middle of a "Knit/Delicate" cycle. Next, the Rheem Air-Conditioning unit ground to a halt in the wee hours of an August night. They had awoken in the luminous darkness of early morning, minutes from one another, their foreheads moist with perspiration. Glassman, it turned out, had neglected to refill the oil in the unit (as if he was supposed to know that it took oil like a car!). The spanking new dishwasher shorted out next. It had evidently been installed improperly, a pleasant repairman from Sears informed Glassman, and then went on to explain, pleasantly again but firmly nonetheless, that the warranty only applied to the *original* purchaser. Even the light bulbs in their new home (Glassman never realized how many bulbs it actually took to illuminate an entire house) popped and dimmed long before their 750-hour potential had been realized.

To top everything, a water main sprung a leak in the front yard, transforming a coarse carpet of green into a shallow pond. The gumbo-limbo tree in the center of the yard, its bark sunburnt and peeling, stood in two feet of water. The new ecosystem attracted a flock of boat-tailed grackles that congregated to bathe, defecate, and noisily go about their mating rituals in the gumbo-limbo, beaks pointed skyward.

Glassman tried on one occasion to shoo the monstrous blue-black birds off his property. He rushed toward them all the way to the water's edge, wailing as threateningly as he could and waving his arms above his head as if he were trying to flag down a rescue helicopter off in the distance. But the flock barely budged. A few birds, or maybe it was just one, hopped a few paces away from him out of some obligatory sense of duty as a potential item of prey. It was as if they all knew he was bluffing. Or, perhaps, because there were so many of them collectively, not to mention their formidable size individually, they weren't altogether convinced that between themselves and the lunatic flailing his arms from the water's edge they should be the ones to flee.

Despite such aggravation, Glassman liked his new home, and he liked his new neighborhood. An aura of camaraderie prevailed, especially during the evenings when several residents sat on their folding beach chairs on some designated driveway. The smell of cheap pilsner and cigarette smoke wafted through the neighborhood at dusk. Which, somehow, was Glassman's first indication that the neighborhood wasn't particularly Jewish. Rather, it turned out to be the kind of neighborhood in which at least half the sons—several of whom buzzed noisily up and down the block on gasoline-motored scooters—seemed to be named Junior. As far as Glassman could tell from the surnames on the neighborhood watch telephone roster, he and Becky were the only Jewish family in Pine Lakes (and the only

Democrats, to boot, as he noticed by glancing down at the petition that a volunteer from the Sierra Club had persuaded him to sign). Pine Lakes. It was a curious name for the neighborhood. A modest swatch of oak scrub, it had been stripped in the early 1970s, Glassman learned, of every last live oak and Florida slash pine to make room for asphalt and three bedroom homes and the more conveniently placed and faster growing black olive trees, which generously dropped their crisp, wormy seedpods, leaving indelible rust-colored stains up and down the cement sidewalk. And, save for the temporary one on Glassman's lawn, Pine Lakes never had a lake as far as he could ascertain.

"I think you're crazy not to move into a young Jewish neighborhood out west. Mission Cove or something," Glassman's mother admonished him just after the Maytag malfunctioned. "I mean, they would know who you should call. There's a lot of fraud down there Grandma says."

What Barbara Glassman didn't realize (and what her son was slowly discovering) was that when appliances failed the young Jewish couples cloistered within their gated communities at Mission Cove et al., they wound up calling Glassman's neighbors at Pine Lakes. Repair and service people of every ilk lived in Glassman's new, gateless neighborhood. Chuck and his Chuck's Air-Conditioning van, custom built for added length and girth, lived just across the street; Robert Chadwick, a soft-spoken plumber with dirt encrusted finger nails and a lovely, blonde Cuban wife, lived around the corner in the only house that still sported a wood-shake roof; an eminently competent repairman with Friendly Appliance Repair and Service Contracts (whose armada-sized fleet of gleaming yellow vans roamed Dade, Broward, and Palm Beach counties, ever on call) lived just two doors down in the house with the manatee mailbox. What was more, Glassman's backyard adjoined Tom Murphy's, who owned and operated a swimming pool maintenance business, but curiously owned the only home in the neighborhood without one. Glassman hadn't yet the need to avail himself of a car mechanic, but when the time came he was fairly certain that Chuck across the street would be able to point him in the right direction just down the block. Indeed, Glassman couldn't imagine having neighbors who would serve better utilitarian purposes. They were only too kind to come over at a moment's notice and always granted Glassman what they termed, with a conspiratorial wink and a shot to the arm, the Pine Lakes Discount.

Glassman entered the house through the garage door and almost tripped over Troy, spread out like an oil spill on the cool linoleum floor. Troy had yet to adjust to the overwhelming heat of the semitropics; he much preferred the climate control of his new home to the humidity just outside the front door. Almost magically, it seemed, the move to Florida accelerated the canine's aging process. Renouncing middle-age completely, he evolved overnight from bounding puppy-hood to somnolent, flatulent old age.

"Honey, I'm home," Glassman announced his arrival before heading into the computer room. He knew that Rebecca had finished teaching her morning classes at Florida Southern, where she worked as a non-tenure-track lecturer, and would be hard at work at her desk. Glassman had considered becoming an English professor himself, but knew he wasn't cut out for it after spending two hours squinting painfully through articles on "discourse communities," "sexed subalterns," "hegemonies," "biological imperatives," "phallocentric tropes," "castration anxieties," and "vaginal 'spaces.'" So much attention to sex, and so oddly mind-numbing. The periodicals room had suddenly felt warm and claustrophobic. He gripped the turtleneck of his shirt and stretched it away from his throat. He couldn't seem to swallow enough oxygen and gasped for air. He abandoned the journals on the cold, hard reading table and fled through the turnstile, which whirled after him in three or four angry revolutions.

There was no point in Glassman becoming a lawyer or doctor or investment banker. His father had already done that, in a manner of speaking. It took only two generations for Stanley Glassman to realize the immigrant dreams of Matthew's great-grandfather Herschel, who owned a leather goods store in Lackawanna. (Shrewdly monogramming briefcases, valises, purses and wallets for free, Herschel managed to preclude any returns and earn a comfortable living for his family.) Glassman's father was a labor attorney, and Glassman knew he could never match his father's material success. Realizing this as a freshman at Penn State was oddly liberating. He was free to do something extraordinary, or at least interesting. So he eventually chose journalism, even though he initially considered it only a lark to write a column for the school paper, even though his parents had both insisted that law school would be a wiser, safer, more secure, choice. (He hadn't even the courage to tell them when he was kicking around the idea of becoming an English professor.) It wasn't that they felt there was something ignoble about journalism or the liberal arts. Financial security, however, far outstripped any other variable in their daily equations. It was something of a sickness, Glassman thought, how money dominated their consciousness, how they continued to scrimp and save, ever wary of some unforeseen fiscal crisis.

"I just don't understand why you would set yourself up for a life of financial hardship?" his father had challenged him when Glassman told him over the phone that he had decided to earn his M.A. in print journalism.

"With your grades I'm sure you can get into a fine law school," his mother, audibly concerned, chimed in on the other line. "You know Greg Himmelstein's going to law school at UCLA next year."

"Yes, you've told me, mom. It's just . . . I think journalism could be meaningful work."

"Meaningful," his father intoned the word softly in an apparent attempt to gain a greater grasp of its contours. "I think it was pretty meaningful to be able to put both of my children through college without any financial aid."

"I know dad. I'm sorry. Jeez, I didn't mean to . . . you know it's not that I don't appreciate—"

"It's just that we worry about you, Matthew. With your medical . . . uhh . . . issues. . . . We just don't want to see you have to struggle—"

"How were you planning on supporting yourself through this program anyway," his father interjected.

"I don't know. My savings, I guess. I might get a teaching assistantship too." Truth was, Glassman had assumed that his parents would support him, as they always had, but couldn't really expect that anymore, it seemed. This stung.

Things had turned out okay for him. He and Rebecca weren't exactly rolling in money, but they were comfortable enough. His parents, moreover, claimed they were proud of him. Yet Glassman knew they still worried about him, that they were still disappointed he hadn't chosen a more lucrative profession. He could never quite forgive them for this, for having disappointed them.

"Yes . . . yes, I'm in here," Rebecca called out absently. Glassman entered the room to see various colorful fish on the computer screen, animals which Glassman doubted actually existed in nature. In the middle of a complex thought, Rebecca's fingers often paused above the keyboard long enough that their screen saver popped up. She finally seemed to give up on whatever unformed sentence had been dogging her, and swiveled in her chair to face Glassman, who stood over her. "I didn't think you were coming home for lunch."

"Well, actually honey, I don't think I'll be going back in today. I'm not . . . I'm not really feeling too well." He didn't know exactly how much he should reveal to his wife and chose his words carefully. She had known, more or less, what she had gotten herself into when she married him. She had taken a risk, even though she insisted that she didn't see it this way at all. *There's always something,* she rationalized. Nonetheless, marrying him was a risk, Glassman knew, and he was grateful for his wife, who surely could have chosen a more solid mate. So for Rebecca he tried especially hard to keep the stitching in his mind sewn tight. He hoped to spare her Teenie's hurt, and the pain that his father too had suffered during his mother's episode so long ago now.

The last thing Glassman wanted was to expose Rebecca to his delusions.

Or expose his mother to his delusions, for that matter. Teenie was made of sterner stuff. She'd dismiss her grandson's dementia out of hand, quickly change the topic of conversation. Or at least he thought so. But his mother was more susceptible to her father's, and to her son's, contemplative somberness.

Which was why he never uttered a word about his grandfather in his mother's presence. And, perhaps, why she never uttered a word about her father to her fragile son. As a teenager, Glassman had mistaken his mother's silence for callousness, spite, even shallowness, perhaps. (Didn't she ever think of her father?) Until one day, having just returned home from basketball practice, he found her leaning over the sink, staring absently at a soapy dish in her hand, as if perplexed by its materiality.

"Earth to mom!" he had mocked her.

"Oh, hello Matthew," she greeted him softly. Her slender hands, he noticed, were wrinkled from the hot water. She glanced at him for just a moment, then lowered her eyes. He noticed that her eyes were glassy. He regretted having teased her.

"What's the matter, mom? Is everything okay?"

"Yes . . . yes. Sorry Matthew. It's just . . . just . . ." she exhaled audibly. "It's your grandfather's birthday today. That's all."

"Oh."

When people didn't speak of things, he realized then, you assumed that they didn't think of them, either. But this was untrue. After all, he didn't speak about his grandfather. Not to anyone, and especially not to his mother. He knew somehow that he shouldn't speak of him. Yet he thought about Abe constantly. Maybe . . . he had reflected after excusing himself from the kitchen that afternoon so long ago and fleeing to his bedroom . . . maybe it was what you refused to speak about that resounded most volubly to your inner ear. Still, if his mother didn't want to talk about her father, Glassman would honor her silence. And silent they remained. She hadn't mentioned her father again after that afternoon at the sink. At least not to her son.

Glassman only regretted that, to this day, he couldn't remember the date when he had intruded upon his mother, brooding over a soapy dish. The date of Abe's birthday.

"Do you have a fever?" Rebecca's tone grew concerned. She rose from her chair and placed a cool palm on his forehead. "You feel cool as a cucumber," she assured him.

"It's not a fever," Glassman explained. "Just a bit of a stomach flu, I think. I don't really have too many balls in the air today anyway, so I figured I'd just take it easy." Rebecca approved of his decision. She offered to make him some soup and dry toast as she strolled into the kitchen, but Glassman declined. He wasn't quite hungry yet.

"So did you have any more problems this morning with that obnoxious student of yours?" A young man had been pestering Rebecca about a grade she had given his first paper. It took Rebecca a moment to answer her husband. She had opened the refrigerator and was busy fumbling around for a drink.

"No, I think he's under control. I threatened to report him to the dean. You know, it's really frustrating. None of the male lecturers have any of the discipline problems I have. I don't know if it's just that I'm the only one who grades honestly, or if it's a woman thing. You know, maybe these male students can't accept the fact that I'm the authority figure in the class."

"Probably a little bit of both."

"That older man auditing my class, though, is really annoying me."

All Florida citizens over the age of sixty, Glassman had learned, could audit any class in the state system for free as long as there was a seat available. Most of the professors at the university thought they were, generally speaking, a pain in the ass. They monopolized class discussion, intimidated the younger students into silent submission, interrupted professors in midsentence to weigh in on the most picayune of matters. Still, Glassman (not having to put up with auditors himself) couldn't help but see something glorious in their endurance.

Some of these older folks were on their last legs. They weren't buying any green bananas. An auditor of Rebecca's once apologized to her for missing a month or so of class because she had to have part of a lung removed. (Rebecca told her not to worry about it.) On the precipice of death, they got out of bed and attended classes like British Romanticism, An Introduction to Philosophy, American Modernist Poetry, the History of the Middle East, Medieval Art. They read Trollope. This was no small feat as far as Glassman was concerned. Upon Rebecca's insistence, he managed once to get through almost half of *Doctor Thorne,* after which point he wasn't altogether convinced that Trollope read Trollope.

"The women auditors are great," Rebecca continued. "I love them. But I swear that Mr. Popowitz just sits there to look at my tush when I write on the board. Honest to God. He has a reputation for it. He only sits in on classes taught by female instructors."

Glassman sensed a small opening and debated whether he should proceed. "You know," he began reticently, "I had something of a run-in today with an older man. Well not so much of a run-in, exactly—"

"Oh? What happened?" Rebecca inquired worriedly. She had stopped her bustling about the kitchen and pivoted on her toes to face him. He noticed the furrow take shape on her brow. Her obvious concern, rather than elicit any further disclosures, silenced Glassman. It wasn't fair to put this on his wife. Not at this premature stage anyway. Not after what he had already put her through before they were married. . . .

Shuman was probably just a noodge who, for some reason, felt entitled to make what use he could of Glassman's literary expertise, such as it was. Or, worse, he wished to exploit the editor's (nonexistent) contacts with New York agents and publishers.

"Oh, it was nothing, really," he backtracked. "You know what honey? I think I could go for some chicken broth and toast now."

Glassman half expected Irving Shuman to be waiting for him again when he arrived at work the next morning. Instead, he entered his cramped office to find a pink "While You Were Out" slip curled like a comma on his desk. He recognized the plump, female script to be the youthful handwriting of Trish Rowan, their undergraduate intern from Florida Southern. Without adequate funds for more than one secretary, Alten had resourcefully decided that learning hands-on how to perform the day-to-day operations of a small-scale newspaper consisted mainly of secretarial work. She hadn't gone through the trouble of taking her SAT's, Glassman was fairly sure, so that she could play receptionist. So he was continually impressed that Trish (he had offered to call her Patricia, but she insisted upon Trish) performed her duties with such alacrity. For one thing, she was the only person he had ever met who filled out every line of the "While You Were Out" messages, which demanded an unreasonable quantity of information from the message taker as far as Glassman was concerned. The message troubled him:

To: Matthew Glassman
Date: February 21
Time: 9:47 A.M.
From: Grandmother
Of: your family
Phone: You know it by heart, she says
Message: Please call as soon as you get a chance. No hurry.
Please: See line above
Signed: T. R.

Now what the heck was he to make out of this? Teenie had yet to call him at his office. He, in fact, credited her for her forbearance. So Glassman's first instinct was to panic as he read "Grandmother" on the pink slip of paper. His heart jumped a beat and the hair on his forearm stood to alert. It had to be an emergency. But it said "no hurry," Glassman was relieved to discover as his eyes scanned hungrily down. He inhaled deeply and exhaled in a puff. It couldn't be an emergency. But if it was no hurry, why couldn't she wait until the evening to talk with him?

Glassman slid his chair out from underneath him and headed for Rowan's cubicle. He had to make sure of something. He approached her from behind and couldn't help admiring her kinky black shock of hair, tucked efficiently behind equally fetching ears.

"Trish, I have to ask you a question."

"Oh, good morning Matt. I haven't seen you yet today. That meeting must've been a real bear yesterday huh? You guys were in there for hours." *Shit,* Glassman thought. He had completely forgotten about the editors' meeting yesterday.

"Oh, actually, I was sick and had to miss it? How's everything with you Trish?" Glassman forced himself to back up and greet Trish appropriately. When he had his mind on something, he tended to neglect bestowing the requisite niceties upon his colleagues. This was a bad habit. Etiquette was important. There was no doubt about it. His mother drilled this into his head during his childhood and continued, in fact, to extol the virtues of good manners. No need. A year in Florida was enough to convince her son, once and for all, of all her arguments. Without etiquette, things did tend toward the anarchical. Why else did his local bank have to place that ever so subtle sign at the entrance to the teller's line: "We Are Ladies and Gentlemen Serving Ladies and Gentlemen." Things, evidently, were getting out of hand.

"I'm doing great, Matt. I love that tie. I'm working on that project you assigned me right now. It's really a lot of fun. The Penguin page is totally cool."

"That's great. There's no rush. Just take your time on it. Get acquainted with the sites." Glassman had asked Trish to check out the web pages of several key presses to see if there were any books they weren't sent, and that he had overlooked, that she thought they might be interested in reviewing. Not that Alten let him run too many reviews of books Glassman actually found worthwhile. "You gotta think of our audience kid," Alten had advised him. "You're not working at the *New Yorker* you know." Yes, Glassman knew.

In any case, Glassman assiduously scanned the web sites himself for interesting titles. There was no need for Trish to duplicate his

46

efforts. But he felt guilty that Alten charged Rowan with such mind-less tasks.

"Listen, Trish, do you remember taking that message from my grandmother this morning?"

"Oh yeah, of course. It was just twenty minutes ago . . . maybe a half hour. She was really nice. She sounded so young too."

"Well, she's getting up there, but listen, did *she* say that it was no hurry whether I called back, or did you just get that impression somehow and write it down?" Glassman realized how ludicrous this all must have sounded to Trish. It sounded ludicrous to himself.

"No, she definitely said no hurry . . . well, maybe she said no rush, but you know six of one, half dozen of the other, right?"

"Yeah, right." Glassman chuckled. He never quite understood that expression. "Thanks Trish." She flashed him her brilliant smile for an answer. Even though she drank copious amounts of coffee—a paper Starbuck's cup (the chain had just infiltrated Ropa) was always within her grasp—her teeth remained almost preternaturally white. *Bleach?* Her upper lip was slightly larger than her bottom lip, and this curious physical quirk had a disconcertingly powerful effect on him. Glassman envied the blissfully, guiltlessly lubricious, but knew he could never count himself among them.

He retreated to his office and stared at the phone for a minute, which quickly became two minutes, then three. He felt himself on the verge of crossing a dangerous threshold, but it was ridiculous to just sit there brooding.

Oh hell, be a mentsh! Glassman chastised himself.

He stabbed at the buttons on the phone with his forefinger and lifted the receiver to his ear. His grandmother picked up the phone in the middle of its first ring and said hello. He visualized her sitting next to it on her floral print chair, her feet upon its matching otto-man. She had been waiting for him to call. He was certain of it.

"Hello grandma. It's me. I called you back as soon as I could."

"I know you did dear." Was she being kind, or letting him know what she expected of him?

"So, what's up?"

47

"Oh, I feel terrible calling you like this, Matthew, but I'm in a bit of a pickle."

"What is it?" He wasn't sure whether or not to be worried.

"Well, I have an appointment with my dermatologist today at one o'clock for a procedure that I need to have done. Ruth was planning to take me, but she's feeling under the weather."

"Ruth!? You were going to let Ruth drive you?"

Ruth Spitz, one of Teenie's oldest friends from Lackawanna, was possibly the most dangerous driver in south Florida. Glassman had been a passenger of Ruth's once on the way to brunch and resolved never to be her passenger again. She had overlooked, or at least misinterpreted, a concrete median while making a left turn—"horribly marked," she would claim later—and neglected to drive around it to the actual right side of the four lane street. Instead, she began driving down the left side of the boulevard, hugging the median to her right, and would have been none the wiser were it not for Rebecca's frightful gasp from the backseat.

"Now don't you get started on Ruth. She's a perfectly safe driver. She's just been having some vertigo lately. She's not having a great year altogether, poor thing. The doctors can't figure it out. Anyway, can you come down?" Glassman heard his grandmother's chair groan as she fidgeted. She didn't like asking favors of him; it made her uncomfortable. "I was going to cancel the appointment, but I just hate to do that at the last minute, and I don't know when they would be able to schedule me again. He's highly sought after."

"What's the procedure?"

This came out wrong. He sounded as if he was planning to base his decision upon the severity of her infirmity.

Melanoma? Be right down. Wart? No way José.

But he had already decided to come down, not entirely for unselfish reasons. New questions now burned in his mind, the answers to which he hoped would squelch, once and for all, his irrational yet unshakable suspicions about this Shuman character.

"I mean, I'll come down and take you, of course," Glassman

continued before giving his grandmother the chance to reply. "I'm just concerned."

Which he was. There were an increasing host of maladies that his grandmother endured, and, for the most part, didn't share with her grandson. And this was the 1990s. No disease of any kind or intensity, physiological or psychological, malignant or benign, chronic or ephemeral, seemed taboo anymore. Everyone wanted to talk about what ailed them, or publish a book about it. But his grandmother operated under an older dispensation. It seemed to Glassman that she thought there was something mildly shameful about illnesses, the serious ones anyway. They were something to be endured stoically, not dwelt upon.

Small wonder that she never flew out west during her daughter's brief crisis, or during Glassman's own, that she refused to answer her grandson's queries regarding his grandfather's own shadowy mental problems. She parried Glassman's every thrust. Outright prodding never worked. It invariably took careful, circuitous verbal maneuvering to unearth even the sparest of details about Abe. So he had long ago decided to be patient, to wait for the opening to present itself. But there was more at stake now that Rebecca had her heart set on reproducing. Now that Shuman had visited him.

Glassman knew he had his work cut out for him if he were to extract any useful information from Teenie. He only found out about most of his grandmother's "procedures" through his parents, who relayed the information to him. *Just so you know.* In addition to her "regular" doctor, she routinely visited separate doctors for her skin, heart, sinuses, gums, thyroid, joints, ears, eyes, and throat. He had kept a tally of her procedures. In the months since he had arrived on the scene, his grandmother had undergone two colonoscopies, arthroscopic surgery to repair a torn ACL, had at least two potentially malignant moles excised from her nose, and (most frighteningly to Glassman) had laser surgery performed on her eyes. He was horrified to hear that the doctors zapped both her eyes during the same visit, so cocksure they were about the infallibility of the technology and their own dexterity. The surgery was a success, supposedly, but still didn't improve her vision quite enough to satisfy the Department of Highway Safety and Motor Vehicles. Hence, her need to have someone drive her to the dermatologist.

And these were just the conventional medical procedures. He didn't even try to keep up with the goings on at her homeopath, acupuncturist, and chiropractor, all of whom she managed to see even more frequently than her "real" doctors. She ingested any number of pills and powders directly from skinny, clear plastic vials. "Touching them with your fingers harms their potency," Teenie had explained upon reading her grandson's bemused expression. She wore magnets in her shoes and in undisclosed locations beneath her clothes. "Everyone uses them down here. They're very popular," she insisted. "Stop making faces." Even when she was feeling well, she had the suitably Asian Dr. Lee stick her with three needles at her "general wellness points," somewhere on or around her ring finger. It all seemed bizarre to Glassman, and probably a waste of good money. But he supposed it wasn't so unusual that the middle-aged woman he saw in his parents' home films (recently converted to VCR format and dubbed with classical music to incongruous effect) chasing him on his tricycle pfff-pfff-pfff-ing away the evil eye hovering somewhere above his three-year-old head would, in old age, seek medical recourse beyond the AMA's parameters.

"Oh, it's really nothing too, too serious. Just another"—it took her a moment to find the right word—"blemish that the doctor wants to biopsy. Just to be sure. It shouldn't take long. We can have lunch maybe."

Just to be sure . . . Just to be sure.

"Oh, grandma, you don't have to take me for lunch."

"I know I don't *have* to buy you lunch. I'd *like* to is all. But if you don't have time, I certainly understand." Her voice had cracked as she finished her sentence. Had he hurt her feelings? Her voice was prone to cracking in any case, so it was tough to tell.

"No, no, that'll be nice. I'll be right down. . . . Oh, grandma"—a question suddenly occurred to him—"why did you say that it was no rush in your message?"

"What, you should worry?"

Glassman grabbed up his Italian leather briefcase (a gift from his mother she picked up on the cheap in Florence that smacked too much of lawyer-hood he thought) and sped past Kreiser's desk. She, thankfully, was on the phone. He wasn't so lucky as to avoid Lippman, however, who swung open the glass front door from the outside just as Glassman reached down for the horizontal handle-bar from the inside.

"We missed you at the meeting yesterday, kiddo," Lippman gruffly accosted his young colleague.

"Yes, I apologize. I was ill," Glassman explained politely, albeit curtly, as he dashed by Lippman to the parking lot. He harbored no great enmity toward his fellow editor, but felt that Lippman could have done more to make him feel welcome at the paper. He greeted practically every suggestion that Glassman proposed, no matter how innocuous the suggestion was, with impatient condescension.

"If it's not broke, why fix it I say," Saul Lippman had growled after Glassman suggested that they revisit the paper's uninviting lay-out. It was a maxim, Glassman immediately knew, that the cantankerous Lippman had milked for years too long when it came to his own person. It troubled Glassman to think that, regardless of Lippman's demeanor toward him, he might have been kinder toward his senior editor had it not been for his near grotesque appearance. The flesh on Lippman's face was variably blotched in patterns of pink and bone-white and taut as if it were a mask stretched too tightly to fit over his nose and cheekbones. Glassman wondered whether he had been scarred in a fire, or if decades of blissful, filterless smoking had been the culprit. In any case, his visage bespoke deformity beyond mere aging, a sort of Tithonus-like deformity, the deformity of those cursed to immortal life without everlasting youth. It got worse from the neck down. Folds of cellulite billowed from his sides, pushing his arms out ever closer to horizontal. Said arms swung outward dangerously as he walked. An enormous stomach hung like a half-empty sac well below his waist. And still Glassman had caught him munching macadamia nuts from a glass jar atop his desk ("It's okay, I'm on the Atkin's diet," he muttered defensively to Glassman, who expressed his concern). One mention of Seth Goldblum, the former editor of the paper who "thought he was the Czar!" (as Lippman put it), and Lippman's face went from blotchy to full pink. Worse, his inhalations and exhalations, laborious undertakings anyway, intensified to an uninterrupted wheeze at two frequencies. Glassman wasn't about to have Lippman's corpse on his conscience, so he invariably deferred to him at all of their editors' meetings. It was really no fair arguing with the man.

Glassman opened the door to his Toyota and was blasted by a torrent of hot air, as if he had just imprudently peeked his head into an oven set at broil. Glassman, as Rebecca continued to remind him, had yet to purchase the requisite aluminum foil sun shield that Floridians placed inside their windshields to fend off the sun's searing semi-tropical rays. He usually circled parking lots several times in search of the preferred shaded spots, usually under ficus or oak. But the ficus trees in the *Jewish Weekly Times*'s lot needed a good five or so more years before they would serve any such utilitarian function. There was no getting into the car for at least a few minutes. He opened all the doors, rolled down the windows, and twiddled his thumbs.

Set on scan, his radio repeated its cacophonous medley at least ten times up and down the dial as Glassman slowly made his way south on the interstate. It took him longer than usual to reach his grandmother's development. He didn't anticipate traffic on the 95 in the middle of the day, but there had been an accident. Not such an unusual delay, really. Accident sites dotted the highway like random sobriety check-points every ten or so miles. He occupied himself by taking inventory of the bumper stickers. In addition to the countless "JEB" stickers, there was one that read PREPARE FOR MOSHIACH, and another he hadn't seen before on a station wagon: ONLY HALF OF THE PATIENTS IN AN ABORTION CLINIC COME OUT ALIVE. There wasn't much else to look at from the highway. Just several of the odd trees—some kind of pine, his neighbor Chuck informed him—that jutted out of the impossibly flat landscape like enormous green bottle brushes.

Lippman would bad mouth him at the office. Glassman was certain of it. He could imagine Lippman's very words to Alten. *First he misses an editor's meeting. Next day he makes tracks before ten o'clock. Where does he get off?* Glassman gripped the wheel tightly, his palms wet with paranoid perspiration. Well, what was he to do? What choice did he have? His grandmother needed him. And he, of course, needed her.

Alligators May Be Present

"Matthew Glassman for Teenie Fishbein in Banyan North, 104 D. I'm on the permanent guest list," Glassman advised the security guard, somewhat impatiently. The guard looked eighty years old himself. Was he really up to protecting grandma? Glassman wondered. His white uniform was too white and the creases on his short sleeves too crisp. Glassman realized it was a minority view, but he always believed such over the top neatness betrayed inefficacy. Anyone with his head in the game would always be just a bit shlumpy and unkempt, no matter what that game happened to be. Finally the guard handed Glassman his parking pass, clicked the remote control attached to his belt, and Glassman drove inside the stuccoed wall.

Walls. Glassman pondered the irony. These Jews knew walls. Not a few of them, he was sure, had been imprisoned behind walls over there. *Over there.* He would have thought that they wouldn't tolerate walls anymore. But this wall was different. It wasn't concrete block or barbed wire, but stucco with a flourish of color, a pastel blue band near the top. A wall of privilege. It kept undesirables out. It didn't imprison those inside. At least this was the logic.

Despite the urban blight that continued unchecked outside its perimeters, Cypress Ponds managed to continue on unbesmirched thanks to costly neighborhood association fees. The result: Cypress Ponds looked increasingly out of place amid its environs. It was as if a sizeable swath of Brentwood or Santa Monica had been magically removed and plopped down in the heart of Watts.

The word neighborhood didn't quite do the place justice. Boasting its own zip code, it was more like a small city unto itself. Once inside the gates, each of the four possible routes to his grandmother's took Glassman over five minutes as he drove past high rises of various heights, two-, three-, and four-story condos, and even small homes. While it was difficult to find a spot of green outside the walls of Cypress Ponds, the neighborhood itself was ever verdant, eerily so. A formidable team of landscapers kept the grounds impeccably manicured. Impatiens, nasturtium, salvia, geraniums, petunias, and periwinkle were deposited in the soil in intricate patterns of color and shape, then culled and replaced at the first sign of a drooping petal or wilted leaf. Glassman learned that several mutant varieties of annuals were continually being developed to withstand the sweltering heat and satisfy the aesthetic demands of the "snow-birds" accustomed to northern standards of flora.

Curiously enough, there were few Cypresses on the property. In their place were less bedraggled looking members of the arboreal race, a cohort only slightly more native to south Florida than their human neighbors in their condominiums. Ficus, scarlet hibiscus, pink, red, and white oleander, royal palm, purple jacaranda, and bottle brush each had their designated locales from which they weren't permitted to stray via sloppiness or their reproductive efforts. They were furiously trimmed into neat geometric shapes; their seed pods, stray leaves, flowers, and branches were devoured by a herd of enormous motorized beasts, not quite sit-down mowers and not quite vacuum cleaners, but something in between. They looked suspiciously like the surreal machines Glassman was certain he remembered from a Dr. Seuss book.

All the landscaping in Cypress Ponds was for the now. The residents evidently believed that after years of enduring long, drab winters they were entitled to year-round technicolor. After all, who knew how long they had left? Why should they pay good money to look at immature trees or withering flowers? Close to death, they demanded robust life on every side. Well, Glassman hoped that they were happy with their lush surroundings, and supposed that they were. But every inch of artificial nature irked Glassman. He found it eery and forbidding. Everything pulsed with life at peak bloom, and lifelessness was the result. The advanced age of the residents, who regularly exercised along the Cypress Ponds Fitness Trail (an asphalt sidewalk really that ran along the murky canal bisecting the development), only underscored the synthetic aspect of the life over-brimming in every direction.

Crossing the canal overpass, Glassman read the wooden sign, a green octagon with white block letters, one of the many such signs that warned walkers every hundred yards or so along the canal that ALLIGATORS MAY BE PRESENT. These signs, scattered throughout south Florida, always captured Glassman's attention. He had only lived in Florida for a year or so and was far from inured to the reality that dangerous prehistoric reptiles lurked in such close proximity to their human neighbors.

After parking in one of the guest spots, Glassman rang the bell once and waited patiently. It usually took a bit of time for Teenie to make it to the door. Glassman had a key, but was reluctant to use it as his grandmother had yet to insist upon it. Her last knee operation never truly "took," as the doctor explained (no doubt in the appropriate regretful cadences), and she had been forced ever since to keep an aluminum walker by her side at all times. Glassman had stored it in the trunk of his car on several occasions and had become eminently familiar with its specifications; it sported a hand-brake, folded into near invisibility, and couldn't weigh more than a few ounces. It was actually quite an impressive contraption. Top of the line.

Most people in his grandmother's condition, with adequate means, had already made the move to assisted living residences, and there were plenty of nice ones in the area. Cypress Ponds even had a special assisted living section at its eastern perimeter. (And a nursing home, impractically located at its western perimeter, perhaps to reassure those in assisted living that their final stage of life was still far off, as if miles were months; hourly, yellow and blue Cypress Ponds shuttles transported wives in assisted living to visit their husbands in the nursing home, and husbands to visit their wives.) But Teenie wouldn't hear of it. The Cypress Ponds shuttles already transported her daily to her friends' apartments, the Winn-Dixie, the restaurants, the two dollar movie theater, and the beauty parlor. They even made special trips every few days or so to "the Flea" on Sample Road, bingo at the Seminole reservation, local plays, museums and such. So the way she (somewhat illogically) saw it, she didn't need any assistance. "I've lived without anyone's help for eighty-five years," she insisted to her daughter. "I suppose I can do the same for a few more. Now you just quit hocking me about it, Barb!"

A few more, Glassman had thought when his mother told him about the conversation. *Is this how she sized up her present circumstances? She had a few more years to live? Or a few more until assisted living? What did she mean by a few? Did she have a number in mind? Two more years? Three? Four? Ten?*

Teenie, Glassman knew, was lucky that she lived in a first floor apartment for she could no longer negotiate more than a few stairs at a time. Or, as his grandmother insisted, luck had nothing to do with it. She knew perfectly well what she was getting into, and was ready to fight the association tooth and nail against paying her share for an elevator they had voted on installing.

His grandmother finally opened the door without asking who it was first. He hoped that she checked to see it was him through the door's peephole. "Hello dear," she greeted him. Glassman wondered if there was an exact moment in the past year or so when the tone of his grandmother's greetings shifted irreversibly from the elation of novelty to the spiritlessness of routine.

"Hi grandma, how are you feeling today?" This was never exactly a rhetorical question. Teenie's answer, depending largely upon her gastrointestinal system and her knee, varied between three pithy responses: "Good," "Okay," and "Not so good, you?" Today was a "Good" day, Glassman was happy to hear.

There was too much time to leave for the doctor's office right away, but not quite enough time to have lunch, so Teenie decided that they'd relax for a while inside. There were always several issues of the *Sun-Sentinel* and an assortment of glossy magazines—*Lears* and *People* were always conspicuously present—lying around within arm's grasp of the floral print chair. He had to move an issue of *People* over to sit in his favorite corner of the sofa. Teenie was an aficionado of the *New York Times Magazine* crossword (she used a pen!), and Glassman could always spot one of the magazines somewhere around the house. There were usually ten or so vacant squares of that elusive last clue or two. But the magazine was nowhere in sight now. Probably in the bathroom, he figured.

There was just enough reading material strewn about to make the apartment look willfully disheveled. Teenie had long been relieved of the tidiness imperative that still dogged Glassman's mother. *I've straightened up for seventy years,* he imagined his grandmother thinking. *Genug Shoyn! Enough already!* It wasn't that the place was dirty. Messy was one thing, but Teenie wouldn't countenance a spec of dirt. She had her "girl," Maria, come every week to vacuum, disinfect, dust, and deodorize.

"It took you a bit longer than usual to make it down here." Teenie scrupulously timed Glassman's commute. It seemed to him that she sought reassurances that the trip really wasn't too long and held him somehow responsible when it took longer than was appropriate.

"Oh, yeah, I suppose so. My car was too hot to get into right away, and I ran into some traffic on the highway."

"I don't know why you just don't take Powerline. It's *just* as fast you know. Everyone says so." Glassman couldn't help chuckling. She took it as a personal affront that her grandson had decided months ago to spurn her navigational advice. He secretly enjoyed ruffling her feathers in this small way. But, the fact was, Powerline wasn't nearly as fast as the 95. At least not usually.

"I've tried Powerline, grandma, but I'm always getting stuck behind . . ." He managed barely to hold his words in check, but he might as well have finished his thought.

"Behind *old* people." Teenie finished her grandson's thought for him through curiously twisted lips that betrayed the offense she had taken, but also an unmistakable glee of the *you-can't-get-one-by-me-I'm-not-farmisht-yet-you-little-pisher* variety.

"Behind slow drivers," Glassman feebly attempted to dig himself out of the hole.

"You and your *old* people," Teenie admonished him. "It's as if that's all you notice about people anymore," she continued to chastise him. "You can't just lump me in with everybody else over seventy you know. I was always a perfectly fine driver."

This wasn't exactly true, Glassman immediately thought. Behind the wheel, Teenie was a woman who never met a curb she didn't like.

Glassman decided to change the subject with his grandmother, but didn't feel the time was ripe yet to ask the questions that seemed to rise up from his throat and press against the inside of his mouth. As if to release the pressure, he asked an unrelated question.

"So, how's Ruth doing, anyway? Is it just dizziness she's dealing with?"

"Well," Teenie conceded, "she just can't seem to lick that pneumonia she got last year, either." Teenie said this all rather matter-of-factly, but it must have been difficult for her, Glassman thought. To see all her closest friends on the wane, dead or dying.

"How's Rebecca doing?" Teenie changed the subject. Glassman told her she was doing fine, that she was enjoying her classes, which wasn't exactly true but seemed like the right thing to say.

"Do you two have any . . . plans," Teenie, somewhat cryptically, inquired. He knew what she meant, though. It wasn't like Teenie to ask questions of a personal nature, which was probably why she had done so so clumsily.

"Well . . . no." Glassman wasn't quite ready to confide in his grandmother about this sensitive matter. "We figure we're in no hurry. Rebecca's still young. There's plenty of time to have kids. If we even want them." Rebecca's period, with brutal punctuality, had just arrived that morning.

"Kids?" Teenie replied, scrunching her nose. "Who said anything about kids? I was just wondering whether you were planning on taking a vacation soon."

"Oh . . . ummm . . . no," Glassman attempted lamely to regroup. "We've been kinda busy."

Teenie nodded her head slowly, silently. He could almost see the wheels spinning in his grandmother's head. Through his knee-jerk defensiveness, he had inadvertently revealed more about their reproductive plans than he had intended. An uncomfortable silence permeated the room.

"Hey, have you heard from mom or dad lately?" he sought to steer the conversation onto smoother terrain.

"Yes, I just talked to your father last night. He sounded good. He's been working very hard, though. He was tired." Despite his grandmother's worried tone, Glassman knew she wouldn't have it any other way. She admired her son-in-law's work ethic. It amused Glassman how much she seemed to like him. Their relationship was utterly uncomplicated. He aptly performed the one essential function, it seemed to Glassman, of the son-in-law. He worked his ass off at the firm and provided amply for his family.

"What was mom up to?" Glassman inquired.

"Oh, she was with her Russians." *Her Russians.* Teenie uttered the phrase with derision. His grandmother, it increasingly seemed, disapproved of her daughter in a hundred small ways. Glassman's mother, for her part, had always complained that Teenie was "impossible." Where his Aunt Janet figured in all of this he hadn't the foggiest idea. She had pretty much checked out, herself, just a few years after Abe disappeared. From what he could gather, his mother and Teenie kept track of Janet, and vice versa, but you couldn't exactly say that they kept in touch. Glassman's mother and Teenie, by contrast, spoke on the phone regularly, but his mother rarely visited Teenie in south Florida and Teenie's knees, his grandmother claimed, weren't up for transcontinental flights. Glassman wondered whether being in each other's presence somehow magnified Abe's absence; whether that was the real reason they had more or less avoided one another all these years. Perhaps his mother and grandmother had always blamed one another for Abe's disappearance. *If only Barbara hadn't moved three thousand miles away from her poor father. . . . If only mom had been more patient with dad, warmer. . . .* Had all this blaming caused them to disappear from each other, as well?

While his mother never came right out and said it, Glassman knew that she couldn't understand why he had moved to south Florida. It was as if he, unwittingly, had chosen sides in some undeclared war. Perhaps she thought he had not so much joined his grandmother as run away from his mother and father. And perhaps, he reflected, there was some truth to this. Wasn't this exactly what his own parents had done, moving out to California in the first place? Glassman liked to think that he had rejected his parents' choices, their priorities. That's what moving down to Florida had meant to him. But, in reality, was he merely repeating their flight pattern?

Whatever Teenie thought about her daughter, she didn't approve of the Gittlemans. This was clear enough. They were recent immigrants whom Glassman's mother had met through the synagogue. B'nai Torah set aside a generous amount of money each year to help Russian Jews, like the Gittlemans, become productive citizens of the United States. In addition to the plane fare and a modest stipend for a while, the Russians lucky enough to be sponsored by the synagogue could count on congregants like Barbara Glassman to teach them Jewish rituals (of which they were horribly deprived, Glassman's mother lamented) and to help them fine tune their English. Barbara had to admit to her son that she was disappointed that the Gittlemans seemed almost completely indifferent when it came to learning the Jewish rituals. They fidgeted impatiently through her explanation of the Sh'ma and the Shehekhiyanu, the Passover Seder and Purim. What they really wanted was to learn English, which they knew enough of to communicate to her loud and clear. So Barbara relented. She devoted the two nights a week she visited the Gittlemans in their modest Chatsworth apartment solely to English instruction.

But this wasn't why Teenie didn't care for the Gittlemans. For it gradually became clear that they expected even more from her daughter than English lessons. They began to call at all hours with a whole host of requests. *Could Barbara fill out their DMV forms since she knew how better than they did? Could Barbara drive them to Venice Beach on Saturday since they weren't exactly certain how to get there? Could Barbara call the Bank of America and find out what the rate of return was on CD's? It was so hard for them to understand the woman on the phone.* These were just minor nuisances. Things that, to Teenie's mind, the Gittlemans could have done on their own if they weren't so lazy. She had met them when she traveled to California for Mother's Day last year. Their English was fine. Not brilliant. But fine. She didn't raise her daughter to be anyone's servant.

The "Gucci purse incident" (as it would be remembered in family lore) was the final straw. As Teenie related the story, Bea Gittleman fawned over the purse so effusively that Barbara had no choice but to offer it to her. *Oh, if only she had such a nice purse. She and Lionel could never afford such a beautiful purse, what with all their expenses as new immigrants, and with Lionel's modest income at the Cigar Shop. The Jet Propulsion Laboratory was where he really should be.*

From his mother's perspective . . . well, it wasn't a brand new purse anyway. So she decided to give it to Bea. And she had felt good about it. Right up until the moment, just two weeks later at Ralph's, when she ran into Bea in the canned fruits and vegetables aisle. As she approached her Russian friend to get her attention, Barbara couldn't help but notice another Gucci purse, newer than the one she had given Bea, resting on Bea's shopping cart. She could have sworn that Bea blushed upon finally seeing her, and glanced down nervously at the purse. Barbara only reluctantly shared the information with her mother.

"Chutzpeh! That's what it is!" Teenie barked afterwards at Glassman over the phone. "They're taking advantage of her. I don't know why your mother lets them get away with it. Why don't you try to talk some sense into her?" But Glassman didn't know what to say to his mother. He knew that his grandmother had a point. He was exasperated by the culmination of events, if not by any single event, as well. But he also sympathized with his mother's perspective. Just a few generations ago, after all, the Fishbeins and Glassmans were under the czar's thumb. *It was all downhill after the czar was killed,* his great-grandfather Herschel Glassman had tersely explained his reason for leaving Poland. Glassman eventually learned about the pogrom in Warsaw, and the thousands of Russian-speaking Litvaks, who began emigrating to Poland to escape the brunt of the terror under the new czar's regime. They made things even more difficult for Herschel and his fellow Jews already living in Plock. The Poles weren't so crazy about them before all their foreign cousins flooded into the region. It was time for Herschel to leave.

And now, now it was time for Herschel's descendants to aid and assist their brethren. The latecomers. Yet another in a series of obligations to be dutifully performed. If after you had died you could break down all the hours of your life, Glassman began to speculate, how many hours would you have devoted toward yourself, and how many hours toward all the others clawing at your knees? Was there some sort of balance to be struck? A corresponding itinerary or game plan to follow? Or were you simply done for once you even started looking at it this way?

Glassman brandished his arm like a sword in front of his grandmother to help her into his Corolla. It was invariably an awkward moment. The car seat was a bit too low for Teenie to settle down into easily, but not so low that she couldn't do so herself without her grandson's help. Half the time, she released her grip from her walker and used his arm for support. And half the time she waved him off, as if mildly insulted by the offer. It seemed to Glassman that she was just feeble enough—physically at any rate—to need help with doors, stairs, and other obstacles most people took little notice of, but just well enough to resent any such help one was likely to offer. What was he supposed to do? Not offer his arm?

The drive to Dr. Adler's office was a short one that crossed Powerline en route to Federal. Out of the corner of his eye, Glassman noticed his grandmother's gaze following the path of the pedestrians in the crosswalk. She appeared to be watching a tennis tournament in slow-mo, for there was plenty of time for her eyes to gaze north then south, north then south along with those passing the hood of the car. If you missed a light in south Florida, you could count on a long wait.

"Am I crazy," Teenie suddenly asked, her eyes fixed on a black woman in tight jeans crossing the street, "or are their tuchuses higher than everyone else's?" To emphasize her point, Teenie affected a lifting movement with two upturned palms.

"Well, grandma, I'd never say you were crazy, but I'm not sure you could accuse black people of having higher tushes than the rest of us." He decided to pursue an analogy. "Do we have bigger noses than everyone else?"

"Acch," his grandmother snorted at him, and swatted down his challenge with a swipe of her palm, as if it were a pesky airborne insect buzzing between them. "I'm not blind, I'll tell you that. You can't tell me their tushies aren't higher than ours."

"Well, *hers* is," Glassman conceded. "I'll give you that much, grandma." Teenie, resettling herself in the bucket seat, seemed content with the compromise.

While his grandmother underwent her procedure, Glassman mechanically flipped the pages of a two-month-old issue of *People*— Brad Pitt purportedly had body odor—and eavesdropped as one of the elderly patients complained to the receptionist. It was difficult to hear, but he gathered that it had something to do with a miscommunication between the man's HMO and Dr. Adler's office. "The left hand doesn't know what the right hand is doing," the man complained without much heat. He had dealt with too much aggravation of a similar ilk to get too worked up over it.

The next thing Glassman knew, his grandmother was writing a check at the receptionist's window. As he approached her, he noticed the small, circular, flesh-toned bandage near her left temple. He hadn't even thought to look at her "blemish," as she called it, before it had been removed.

Glassman had been patient at his grandmother's apartment, and he had been patient in the car, as well. At lunch he would make his move. Upon Teenie's suggestion, Glassman drove to the Bagel Boy, a bright, clamorous Jewish delicatessen adjacent to the Cypress Ponds perimeter. One thing Glassman enjoyed about south Florida was the abundance of Jewish delis. A corned beef or pastrami sandwich on rye (real rye with caraway seeds), matzo ball soup, kreplach, knishes, nova, whitefish, bagels *and* bialys, were never very far away. Eating Jewish food reminded him of his childhood trips to Lackawanna where at least one meal at Morris's Deli, which suspiciously burned down and was refurbished off the insurance money at least once every seven years, was a given. A meal at Angelo's, for that matter, was also a given, where a glossy sheen of olive oil coated the pizza's plum-red tomato sauce, which Angelo lovingly applied above rather than below a paper-thin layer of cheese. At Angelo's, Glassman could also order a Herschel Salad, a chef's salad without ham named after his great-grandfather.

When the young hostess greeted them at the Bagel Boy, Teenie said hello and lifted her walker clear off the ground with both arms, pointing its rubber stoppers and wheels toward the table next to the window where they would sit. She often powerfully wielded her walker in this manner, as if it were an extension of her index finger. Her upper body, clearly, was still strong. Glassman only regretted that his grandmother couldn't distribute some of that excess vigor below her waist to her aching knees and ankles.

They gazed over their menus.

"What's flanken, grandma?" Glassman had somehow never heard of this item, purportedly prepared either "In The Pot" or "On The Plate."

"What's flanken? Ahhhh . . ." Teenie moaned as if Glassman had uttered the name of a passionate lover from her past whom she had nearly forgotten. "Osso Bucco . . . everyone makes such a fuss over it. Well, flanken is just as scrumptious. No," Teenie corrected herself, "more scrumptious. It's like a short-rib. You can eat it dry, or in a broth. I don't know how else to describe it."

Glassman took his grandmother's opinions concerning food with, pardon the expression, a grain of salt. She may have been a gourmand, but she was certainly no gourmet. Her mandel bread ("Better than biscotti," she insisted) was igneous; her brisket was tasty but a formidable challenge to the musculature of the jaw; the jam-pastry ratio of her rugelach was invariably out of whack.

Despite Teenie's culinary allegiances, she decided flanken was too heavy for lunch. Instead, she ordered a turkey sandwich. "It *is* off the frame, isn't it?" she asked their waitress. She had ordered the same sandwich at the Bagel Boy countless times in his presence, but liked to make sure. She wouldn't tolerate the slimy, processed turkey meat they tried to foist on her at the Winn-Dixie deli counter.

"You got it hon'," the waitress set Teenie's mind to rest. Her name, Glassman recognized from the pin on her Bagel Boy T-shirt, was Claire, and she was from Pittsburgh, Pennsylvania. For some reason, a number of south Florida restaurants compelled their employees to advertise their home towns, perhaps to encourage an affinity with customers hailing from the same locales.

"And hot water, with lemon," Teenie finished her order.

Glassman ordered what he always ordered, corned beef on rye and a Dr. Brown's Black Cherry, and proceeded to inhale three spears of Ba-Tampte Half-Sours; Teenie quietly nibbled at the wet cole slaw, toppling its ice-cream scoop outline. For some reason they called it health salad at the Bagel Boy.

"Here, eat some chopped liver," Teenie suggested as she slid the small bowl toward her grandson. There was no need for her to coax. Glassman relished the chopped liver at the Bagel Boy. It wasn't over-blended, but contained discernable chunks of liver and egg. Glassman applied a thick, pasty coating of the offal to a slice of rye bread and gobbled almost half the piece down with his first bite. It gave his grandmother naches, a special prideful joy, to see him eat, and this was one area where he was fairly certain he'd never disappoint her. It made her happy, especially, to see him eat the delectable foods (e.g., real chopped liver) that she had been forced reluctantly to forswear years ago. The eggs. The organ meat. It was strictly off-limits to all of Glassman's south Florida relatives, each of whom seemed to be battling unfavorable HDL/LDL ratios and an overabundance of triglycerides. Besides which, it was "gouty," according to his Uncle Herbie (who then had to explain to his grand-nephew what gout was) and to be avoided at all costs. Instead, his relatives prepared an ersatz, green pea concoction for gatherings which, if nothing else, reminded them of how scrumptious real chopped liver had once tasted.

"How is it?" Teenie asked.

"Oh, it's okay." It was actually delicious, but no reason to rub it in, he thought. "I probably shouldn't eat too much more."

"Oh, don't be silly. Nosh a little. You can afford it." This wasn't altogether true. At least by Glassman's standards of fitness, he was slipping. His sister, on the corpulent side by the time she was sixteen, had warned him (and secretly hoped?) that his metabolism would slow down eventually, and eventually had arrived, not quite in thunder, but as a light shower. The modest band of cellulite that for years had staked out the territory just under his belly button had begun recently to acquire additional territory above his belly button. Still, Glassman was reluctant to start regulating his diet. He had heard that eating large quantities of food kept one's metabolism high and he didn't feel like fighting news that encouraged his inclinations. What he really needed to do was start exercising more than the one day a week playing basketball.

Claire soon brought out their heavy plates. It was now or never, Glassman knew. He would go slowly, make the most benign inquiries first and see where they led him.

"You know grandma, I've been noticing all these ads in our paper for Kutscher's Country Club and the Concord, and half a dozen other places up in New York, and I was wondering . . . did you used to visit the Catskills?" *Oh-mee . . . Oh-meee,* a chickadee whistled plaintively in Glassman's ear.

"Sure," Teenie answered nonchalantly. She was busy weeding out with her fingers the fatty pieces of turkey from her sandwich. "We all went to the Catskills. . . . Well," she reconsidered, "we started to go to the Caribbean instead eventually, but we visited the Catskills several times."

He was just about to ask who she meant by "all," by "we," but was interrupted by a vaguely familiar red-headed woman wearing enormous glasses with cream-colored frames, who suddenly towered over them.

"Matty Glassman, right? Do you remember me?"

He and his grandmother never got through a meal at the Bagel Boy without at least one former Lackawanna resident approaching to inquire as to his lineage. He usually answered the familiar question he had just been asked with his stock answer, *yes-I-think-I-do-you-look-really-familiar,* but the query annoyed him this time so he uttered a less generous, albeit more honest, response.

"I'm sorry, I'm afraid I just don't." By now Teenie had laboriously turned her head over her shoulder and said hello to their visitor, whose name, apparently, was Mildred.

"Well," the apparently unflappable Mildred continued, "I'm Mildred Weiner. I was very close to your Grandma Pearl, may she rest in peace. She was a gorgeous lady."

Glassman could have sworn that he noticed Teenie roll, or at least half roll, her eyeballs. He sympathized. It was difficult for her to compete against the constant kudos bestowed upon her long-dead rival, and she resented it. Grandma Pearl's kuchin and rugelach tasted sweeter with every passing year; her kindness swelled; her beauty tripled!

"Thank you. Yes, I remember how beautiful she was." He did remember, but just barely, and the memory of her face was receding, or at least mutating.

"How are your folks doing?" Mildred continued. Glassman told her that they were both doing well.

"Will you tell both of them that Mildred Weiner says hello?" And once more, slowly, for emphasis, "That's Mildred Weiner. Would you please do that for me?"

"Of course I will." He made a mental note.

"Bye Teenie. See you at the spa tomorrow." And Mildred Weiner was off with a lithe pivot of her heels. No knee trouble there.

"So, what's new with Uncle Ben and Aunt Edith?" Glassman asked his grandmother. He figured that this question would open the door so that he might inquire about additional relatives. Namely, did Grandpa Abe have a sister named Rose? And another named Dottie? Was his father a printer? Had they all lived in New York before moving to Lackawanna? Glassman felt foolish for not knowing the answers to these basic questions, but such inquiries had always been off-limits to him. He knew that his grandfather had some siblings, but Teenie had cut herself off from them after Abe had disappeared. Or else, perhaps, they had cut themselves off from her. Glassman couldn't remember who had blamed whom for Abe's disappearance, or whether they had all blamed one another.

Ben was Teenie's closest surviving relative (a double-cousin; reader, figure it out) and lived in Cypress Ponds also. Teenie had had six siblings who Glassman barely knew. One died of a brain aneurism when he was less than five, and the others died young of cancers that originated in various locales—kidneys, prostates, lungs, breasts. Glassman's grandmother and Ben had won the Fishbein-Trucker cancer gene lottery. Or else genes had nothing to do with it and it was something in the Lackawanna air or water, Glassman thought. And hoped. The radon, perhaps, flushed out of the ground and into the air during years of relentless anthracite mining; or, more likely, the toxic gases from the mountain of slag that had somehow caught fire and smoldered for forty years until federal funding finally came through to extinguish it. Along with the rock bluff nearby at the Delaware Water Gap that looked just like an Indian's profile (*I can't see it!* Sara would complain), "Fire Mountain" had been a magical part of Lackawanna to the young Glassman. When he could summon Grandpa Morty's image in his mind, who died just a few years after Abe disappeared, it was always his profile, not unlike the Indian's on the mountain. He is sitting alongside his grandfather on the enormous vinyl bench seat of the Pontiac. It is past his bedtime. Morty is taking him (Sara isn't interested) to see Fire Mountain aglow in fluctuating patterns of blue, green, and violet, smelling like rotten eggs. Lackawanna's sulfurous eternal flame.

"Ben and Edith are doing well. They're going on a short cruise next week to Jamaica on that new *Norwegian Two* ship, or something like that. Ben says they haven't heard from you in a while. Are you and Rebecca going to make their brunch? You should really call and let them know as soon as you get a chance." Teenie uttered the advice rather coolly, but Glassman grew defensive.

"But I just talked with them on the phone last week. . . . Okay, maybe the week before. I could have sworn I told them we'd be coming," he prevaricated. He had forgotten about the brunch.

Since he and Rebecca had moved down to Florida, a seemingly endless string of commitments needed to be made months in advance. Where he and Rebecca would be spending their Passover Seders, by about mid–January, was of utmost importance within his circle of relatives. Glassman was certain that intricate and sensitive negotiations regarding his physical whereabouts on these two particular evenings were carried out at his grandmother's Tuesday mahjong afternoons, or at Wednesday pinochle, or at Thursday bridge.

You know, Teenie confided in her grandson during one of their now nightly telephone conversations, *I don't really enjoy mahjong. I just play because the girls need me. If I dropped out the whole game would fall apart!*

"Oh, don't worry about it," Teenie now assured him. "They get plenty of phone calls. Just give them a quick ring to let them know about the brunch." She took another bite of turkey, staining the rye bread in a thin C of ruby red from her painted lips. Teenie was always quick to allay his guilt when it came to his keeping in touch with Uncle Ben and Aunt Edith, or, for that matter, with any of his other south Florida relatives, and there were suddenly plenty of others. First cousins once-removed, second cousins, great-aunts and uncles, and people who simply claimed to know his great-aunts and uncles from Lackawanna all came out of the woodwork once Glassman and Rebecca moved to south Florida.

He was slowly beginning to suspect that she didn't necessarily want him to stay in touch with others besides herself. Having been abandoned by her husband (presuming he wasn't murdered), having distanced herself, and vice versa (and for whatever reason), from her children, Teenie seemed intent to hoard those relatives who remained. Her grandson was a natural resource, *her* natural resource, that could be depleted by overuse. She was his closest relative in the area, and thus laid a definite claim upon him. No one from the Glassman or Fishbein tribe, whose bloodline traveled along a more circuitous route before meeting Glassman's, would think of launching a preemptive invitational strike when it came to Pesach, or Rosh Hashana, or Yom Kippur Break-Fast, or Thanksgiving.

It put Glassman just the slightest bit on edge that his social plans were constantly being made for him behind the scenes. He was tempted to refuse all first invitations, if only to assert control over his and Rebecca's lives in this one small way. But instead he tended to balk, only to relent at the last minute. He couldn't muster up the nerve to say no to his grandmother, or to any of his older relatives. He invariably went with the flow, and dragged his often irritated wife downstream with him. Dinner plans with friends from her department were constantly being rescheduled, and then rescheduled again. Weekend trips to Sanibel Island or the Keys that Glassman had promised to Rebecca were repeatedly postponed for one family-related reason or another.

"Oh, grandma, you know I was wondering, did you guys all live in New York before settling in Lackawanna?" Glassman tried as best he could to betray a casual, off the cuff nature to the inquiry, but knew that he had failed miserably.

"Of course. For a short while. Who didn't?" his grandmother answered laconically. She had grown impatient with his questions. He could tell not only by the sharp edge of her voice, but by the way she bit down almost angrily into her sandwich, more a rhetorical gesture, Glassman was convinced, than an act of legitimate hunger. She never liked it when he dredged up the past. He didn't quite know how to proceed, so was relieved to see Mr. Kravitz approaching their table to say hello. Sam Kravitz was a permanent fixture at Banyan North for as long as Glassman could remember (and he started visiting his grandmother during his spring breaks in high school). He had seen Kravitz on several occasions swimming laps in the too-hot pool. Tall and slender, with a caved-in chest and visible pacemaker bulging from beneath a patch of taut skin on his shoulder, Kravitz seemed all angles to Glassman. His bony knees and ankles seemed perpetually flexed at around a hundred-and-fifty-degree angle, as if he feared hyperextension. Glassman also never saw him without an Ace bandage wrapped around his left elbow.

Kravitz was repeatedly, and currently, Banyan North's elected representative to the Cypress Ponds Neighborhood Association. He loathed having his constituents embarrass him at the biweekly meetings and, consequently, ran a tight ship. To many a tenant's dismay, he could sniff out kitty litter through the ventilation and contraband barbecue grills on screened-in patios like a Miami International Airport Drug Enforcement dog could sniff out cocaine stashed in suitcases. He had even caught Teenie grilling Specials (*They're better than Hebrew Nationals,* she repeatedly insisted) one evening years ago and marched right on over to issue a tactful warning.

Glassman pictured the delicious moment vividly in his mind: *Teenie, we have the place surrounded! Now don't do anything foolish! Just drop the tongs and step slowly away from the hibachi . . .*

"How're you doing boychik?" Kravitz asked him. "Teenie." He uttered her name as a statement more than a question. Teenie said hello neither enthusiastically nor curtly.

"Fine Mr. Kravitz. How are you? You look well." The same was really how he looked, which was well given the fact that he must have been pushing eighty. It seemed to Glassman that Kravitz had reached about sixty-eight, and managed to stall the aging process somewhere right around there. All that policing kept him spry.

"Nice of you to visit your bubbeh."

"I have a *very* nice grandson," Teenie assured her elected representative in a tone that almost sounded to Glassman like a challenge.

She stabbed another forkful of health salad. Teenie, for the record, had voted last year for Ruth Spitz, who, evidently, had yet to live down her complicity in the tree trimming fiasco during her last term six years ago. The jacaranda outside Teenie's door was still only a skeleton of naked branches. It was probably dead, although Teenie insisted, for Ruth's sake, that it was merely dormant and might flower again at any time. Teenie had forgiven Ruth. Why couldn't anyone else?

"Goodbye folks. Remember," Kravitz advised Glassman with a tap of his fingers onto the formica table, "be good to your bubbeh. There's nothing like a phone call."

Once Kravitz left, Glassman couldn't summon the will to ask his grandmother any further questions. He knew that he had somehow exhausted her limit for the day. She was on to him, he was certain, and wouldn't tolerate any further prodding.

After Teenie paid the check, he drove her to her apartment as she fiddled with the air conditioning vent in front of her. *Too much air? Not enough? What did she want?* He retrieved her walker from the trunk, unfolded it, and helped her to the door. He thanked her again for the lunch. She again said that he was welcome. He opened her front door for her with his own key. She held it open with her walker, turned toward him and said goodbye. He said goodbye back and, before he knew it, the cream-colored door was between them. At some point in the past several months, she had decided—or perhaps they had decided mutually—that the goodbye kiss was an extraneous gesture. They would be seeing one another again soon. He wasn't flying back to L.A., nor was she flying back to Lackawanna. No need for emotional farewells.

Their relationship was gradually morphing, he realized, into something new, something he couldn't quite bring into focus, a vessel a mile or so off the coast obscured by layers of gaseous heat above the ocean. Whether it would approach the shore or recede into the distance he didn't know.

A Change in Altitude

A week passed, then two, and Glassman still hadn't heard so much as a word from Irving Shuman. He should have been relieved that he had somehow shaken off the nuisance. But relief was not what Glassman felt. Rather, he felt frustrated and ever so slightly lonely with each passing day. For the editor's initial suspicions about Shuman—suspicions he had nearly convinced himself to dismiss—began to bloom in his mind once again like a once dormant flower. After all, if Shuman were merely the noodge Glassman took him to be, surely he would have shown himself again by now, especially since the Weekly Books Editor had foolishly encouraged him to stay in touch, as if he were a long-lost friend. But, instead, the old man had mysteriously vanished.

Glassman blamed himself for not asking for Shuman's telephone number, but he had been certain at the time that he would see the old man again soon, that Shuman would drop into his office as he had promised. Whether he was his grandfather or not, it was incredible that he would simply disappear. Could it be that he would never see Shuman again? How could he not have asked for the man's number?

His carelessness was a sore tooth he troubled with his tongue.

He wouldn't just sit around waiting. After the second silent week passed, Glassman dialed information in various nearby towns—Delray, Boynton, Deerfield, West Palm, Fort Lauderdale, Hollywood, Jupiter. There were two listings for an Irving Shuman. He nervously called both numbers, and was disheartened to hear aged voices, utterly unlike Shuman's, greet him impatiently over the line. Both strangers were convinced that their young caller wanted to sell them something. That Shuman, his Shuman, apparently didn't exist provided some evidence, scant though it was, that the old man may have used an alias, that he, in fact, was Glassman's grandfather. The Weekly Books Editor took little pleasure in such reflections as it rendered the old man's disappearance all the more agonizing. The most likely scenario in any case, he decided, was that Shuman's number was unlisted. Simple as that.

Glassman rehearsed their brief encounter countless times in his mind, hearing anew the cadence of each of their sentences, the timbre and pitch of each word exchanged. Eventually, however, he began to suspect that he had been embellishing upon their brief exchange with each of his revisions. The sentences began to seem more and more surreal, a distant echo of any conversation that could have actually transpired between two people. And so finally, after a month passed, Glassman decided that he must have imagined the whole thing. No one, not least of all Abe Fishbein, had visited him in his office. That he had successfully refrained from burdening his mother, Teenie, and Rebecca with his delusions offered him some small comfort.

He and Rebecca, at any rate, had more pressing concerns to occupy themselves. Mucus test. This was the activity to which he and his wife had been reduced. From what Glassman could gather, Dr. Arias needed to ascertain whether Rebecca's secretions provided a conducive environment for the seminal commute. Ergo, she needed to observe his semen in action. This was the plan: Rebecca and he would conjoin at seven in the morning and Dr. Arias would peer into Rebecca by eight to observe the post-coital goings on. Mucus test.

The timing was crucial. She had to have Rebecca in the stirrups within an hour after ejaculation. Glassman's ever pragmatic wife seemed to have no problem with the procedure. She had established a rapport verging on the sororal with Dr. Christine Arias. But it all seemed a bit too voyeuristic to Glassman. Next thing, Arias would want to observe them in sexual congress itself to make sure he was performing adequately; he was fairly certain that Becky would invite her over without hesitation.

No, not like that. Arch your back for crying out loud. Ándale. Ándale. You call that thrusting Glassman?

"Hurry up, honey," Rebecca urged him. "I have a nine o'clock today. Wait, are you still hard?"

Just barely. The thought of Dr. Arias gauging the hospitality of his wife's vaginal environment within the hour—and no doubt sizing up the volume of his contribution as well—sort of killed the moment for him. Glassman chalked up shy testes along with his shy bladder. (He often sat through professional sporting events and airline commutes in agony.) Perhaps, Glassman mused, this mucus test mumbo jumbo was just a ruse to procure a semen sample. Becky had already warned him that this was the next test "they" would have to undergo. Dr. Arias's prescription, as a matter of fact, a mercilessly transparent vial awaiting its viscous contribution, stood erect in the kitchen cupboard next to the juice glasses. He had been balking. There wasn't a lab close enough for him to harvest his sample at home. He would have to masturbate at the lab, feigning inexperience to some nurse.

"I'm okay, honey. Can you just, I don't know, lift your knees up a little?" He squeezed his eyes shut and used his imagination. Just ten or so months ago—well into his seventh year of blissful, near daily sex with Rebecca—he was still conjuring up images of nuns and professional wrestlers to forestall climax. Now, he found himself summoning up images of nubile friends and acquaintances just to maintain his turgidity.

"Oooo." Becky registered her husband's progress.

"Good boy. Okay. I've gotta run. You don't have to get up. You're walking Troy, right?"

"Yeah, sure. But wait, maybe . . . you know . . . we should wait a few minutes and try again. I'm not sure I . . . gave you enough."

"Oh don't be silly. I'm sure it's fine zinc boy," Rebecca teased him. Fifty milligrams he'd been taking daily based upon a rumor he'd heard somewhere about zinc and increased sperm production.

Rebecca was dressed and out the door in record time. He almost couldn't believe she was actually gone. Had she even brushed her white, femininely rounded teeth? Combed her auburn hair? For years, he had enjoyed watching from their bed as she prepared herself to face the day. After her shower, Rebecca remained nude much longer than was absolutely necessary. She knew that he enjoyed watching her, and being watched, Glassman gathered, probably did something for her, as well. She sat, nude and erect, on a cushioned wrought iron chair. She applied make-up only sparingly and fleetingly, but spent several minutes applying copious amounts of high-end moisturizer—one of her few cosmetic indulgences—to almost every inch of her flesh. She started with her arms and made her way to breasts and abdomen. Glassman shivered with delight when her hands finally ventured lower than her waist to lather her lithe inner thighs. It was a highly charged moment that had only recently grown, well, less charged. Somehow studying his wife in those moments just before she put on clothes, usually without a word passing between them, seemed as intimate as their lovemaking the night before.

Deprived of her morning bedroom routine (had he dozed off?), he listened carefully, hopefully, from the bed for her kitchen sounds that would reveal her presence: the disposal devouring coffee rinds (decaf now), the *New York Times* slipping out from its plastic, the kiss of the refrigerator opening, the steely *brring* of the toaster oven announcing the end of its cycle. But all he heard was the rhythmic snoring of Troy, who slept on the rug floor at the foot of the bed.

Glassman felt utterly alone.

Grief suddenly threatened to engulf him. It announced its presence physically, in the pit of his stomach. Not exactly a punch. More like a sudden change in altitude. An airplane bobbing in turbulence. It was an all too familiar sensation. His chest tightened as panic threatened to consume him. He had to remind himself to breathe. He inhaled deeply, then exhaled deliberately. Then inhaled again.

Just focus on the little things. Breathe. Yes, that's it. In . . . out . . . in . . . out. Breathe, Glassman reminded himself. *Relax.*

It would be a bad day.

Glassman knew that he had to get out of bed. This was of utmost importance. His very life depended upon it. His disease often attacked him while he was idle. Like any predator, it pounced on its prey fiercely, unrelentingly, while its victim lay prostrate.

Within a couple months after meeting Rebecca, he was stricken by a severe case of bronchitis and forced into bed for over a week. By the end of the third day in Rebecca's room (it was that or the infirmary at Ritenour), it had developed into the worst case of bronchitis that Rebecca had ever seen. Glassman couldn't eat even though he admitted he didn't exactly feel nauseated. He simply had no appetite. Just a week ago he was still too shy to shower with her without blushing (which Rebecca found endearing), but he suddenly lost all of his inhibitions and lay naked above the sheets, onto which his scrotum sagged like an old man's. His eyes seemed perpetually welled up with tears. He wouldn't speak more than a few somber words at a time. As long as he was drinking juice, eating some dry toast, and wasn't running a fever, the infirmary nurse advised Rebecca, he would do better under her own care. Who knew what other illnesses he'd catch at the infirmary? Yes, Rebecca had heard how opportunistic germs tended to be in hospitals. But if Matthew didn't turn the corner in a few more days, she would have to take him to Ritenour. It would be the only responsible thing to do.

Rebecca could tell that Glassman was depressed, but just assumed it was the bronchitis that had him down. He was used to playing basketball every day, not lying around in bed watching reruns of

Gilligan's Island and ads for any number of vocational schools in Altoona and Pittsburgh. No wonder he was so down. She didn't entertain the notion that the bronchitis only exacerbated a preexisting condition.

Glassman had managed to call the infirmary himself when Becky was at her Virginia Woolf seminar. Perhaps, he vaguely hoped, the antibiotics were the culprit. *Did Erythromycin cause depression in any patients. . . . No? Were they certain?* He was unable to will himself out of the doldrums. He was slipping, slipping, and he knew it. But if he knew it, could it have been so bad? He took a small measure of solace in the thought that if he were truly, clinically depressed, he wouldn't have been able to render his own diagnosis.

He and Rebecca endured like this for a few more days. And then magically, as suddenly as the fog rolled in, a brisk Happy Valley breeze cleared the skies and he could see and breathe again. He had lost a pound for each of the ten days he was bedridden, but managed somehow to emerge, to function again.

Never again, he had told himself. The next day he remained in bed for over fifteen hours would be the day he drew his last breath, and no sooner. Plus, he decided to stay away from Erythromycin. Just in case.

It would be months before Glassman would tell Rebecca the truth. That his episode during the bronchitis wasn't exactly unprecedented. She had the right to know. She'd put two and two together sooner or later anyway.

"It happened during the summer of my sophomore year," Glassman dutifully began to explain. They were in Pittsburgh for the weekend, at Point Park, celebrating their one year anniversary. He couldn't wait any longer to tell her; he shouldn't have waited as long as he had. It had been selfish of him. They sat on a concrete step next to the fountain, a safe distance away from where a large group of children, mostly black, splashed and frolicked. Gazing across the wide stretch of brown water where two placid rivers joined to create a third, Glassman told Rebecca about Saint Vincent.

It all happened so quickly. His descent. There had been little warning. He had enjoyed a perfectly normal childhood. Soccer, Little League, Boy Scouts, karate, piano lessons. He performed admirably, if not exceptionally well, in all of these childhood endeavors. By all accounts (and, after Saint Vincent, his mother consulted practically all of their close family friends to receive their accounts) he had been a happy child, if a bit moody from time to time. He earned B's and A's in school, and scored an eminently respectable 1150 on his SAT's. So who could have predicted the summer of his sophomore year?

Glassman couldn't handle going to work that Thursday so he called in sick. Everything seemed so . . . pointless. His job waiting tables, happy-hours at El Torito every Friday with the same crew of high school friends. Were they as sick of him as he was of them? Guzzling down mediocre beer just about every night after his shift and scoping out women at the restaurant for a good hassle-free lay . . . and thinking and thinking and thinking and thinking about all this crap! It was the constant thinking about everything that was torturing him. His brain felt like a walnut in a vice. At any moment his skull would burst under the pressure. Somehow, somewhere, he had lost his way and didn't have the vaguest notion of how he would find his way back, or where back even was. By the weekend, he was lying underneath his bed to get away from it all. This seemed perfectly normal to him. He felt better there. But this was about all that his parents could stand.

"How can you do this to yourself? Please come out from underneath the bed," his father pleaded, lifting the dust ruffle. "Don't you love yourself?" Of course he did, Glassman wanted to explain, but couldn't summon the words from his throat. How could he explain that it was almost like he wasn't even the person under the bed. He could see him there squinting and sobbing. He loved this person, and wished he didn't have to go through such torture.

Next thing he knew he was at Saint Vincent Hospital, but he didn't actually remember very much about those four weeks because of the shock treatments. Dr. Abramson called it ECT, not shock treatments, but Glassman didn't see any reason to mince words. The medications alone—the drugs that wouldn't permit him to sleep and made his hands tremble furiously—simply weren't working. So Dr. Abramson recommended ECT. She assured his parents that the procedure had come a long way. They used a very low "dosage," and would only shock one side of his brain, "unilateral" was the term, so that he wouldn't suffer any long-term amnesia.

Regardless, most of his stay at Saint Vincent was a blur, which Glassman supposed may not have been such a bad thing. Gazing out across the murky Pittsburgh rivers, he told Rebecca what he remembered: a list on the wall of Negative Coping Strategies and Positive Coping Strategies written on butcher paper with messy purple marker. He remembered Walter, who wore a hockey helmet and face shield, because he had blackened both his eyes and broke his nose with savage blows of both fists. He remembered Berthea, so drugged up that she didn't even know where she was. It tore Glassman up when her husband brought their child in for visits. He remembered the smoking breaks in the fenced off yard of grass out back. The doctors actually encouraged them to smoke; there was something curative about the nicotine, at least for mental cases. The only problem was that Glassman didn't smoke, so he just lay there out back and stared up into the vacant, pale blue sky. He remembered his sister, who had flown in from Seattle, sitting next to him impassively on the stiff-cushioned sectional in the common room, unsure of what she should say; they both stared silently, vacantly, at the television. He remembered his mother telling him how lucky he was that it was the summer so they could take care of his illness at such a good hospital before he went back to school, that he wouldn't have to drop any classes and his grade point average wouldn't suffer, even-though-that-wasn't-the-most important-thing-in-the-world-just-then-he-should-focus-upon-getting-well-of-course. He remembered his parents, striking their typical pose outside the ward's door each day just before visiting hours. His mother with her hand on the knob, waiting for the buzz like it was a starter's gun. His father just behind her, slightly dazed. He remembered the hard impatient steel click of the door latch opening.

His parents had been as supportive, as loving in their own way, as parents could be under the circumstances. Glassman knew this. Yet rather than bring him closer to his parents, he withdrew from them after he was released from the hospital. Not malevolently. Or even consciously. But discernibly all the same. They had seen him at his worst, what would hopefully be the absolute nadir of his existence; they had stepped up to the plate, had seen their son through his crisis. But for some visceral reason that eluded even Glassman . . . shame? blame? hate? love? . . . he couldn't bear to be in his parents' presence for sustained periods after their shared ordeal. Something about the way they looked at him, or at least the way he thought they looked at him, their eyes shaking in their sockets as if they feared he might vaporize at any moment.

Every so often, Glassman read the ten or so loose pages he kept tucked away underneath his socks, the surviving remnant of the journal he had been encouraged to keep at Saint Vincent as some sort of cathartic exercise for want of more rudimentary artistic skills with blunt-tipped colored pencils and waxy crayons. He had written these particular pages near the end of his ordeal, when he was slowly gaining ground thanks to the ECT. This fragment of what he had written in those twenty-four days had somehow survived, had refused to be expunged. And now they were the only tangible relic that remained of those dark days and darker insomniac nights on the annoyingly loud, plastic-coated twin mattress at Saint Vincent.

Glassman had taken no special care to preserve the pages in those first few weeks after his "incarceration," as he referred to it at the time. His parents, who, silently and industriously, did his packing for him both to and from the hospital, were the ones who must have stuffed the notebook pages into his blue canvas backpack. He wasn't even particularly careful about preserving them once he returned home. Indeed, it wasn't so much that he saved them, but that he somehow couldn't bring himself to discard them in the frayed wicker trash basket in the corner of his bedroom. As if under their own volition, they had found their way to his wooden dorm-room desk once he returned to Penn State for his sophomore year. But still,

Glassman didn't read them, or even take much notice of the envelope that often covered the staples, paper clips, and return address labels for which he often groped. It was only two or three years later, while a graduate student, that he rediscovered the contents inside the manila envelope and began to read his journal deliberately, regularly. He deciphered the manic, nearly illegible, handwriting during his strongest moments—after receiving an A on an exam, or after a glorious performance on the hoops court at the IM building—to guard himself against getting cocky, against letting his defenses down. And he read the journal during his most fragile moments when he felt that he was most in danger of slipping. And sometimes he just read it. He didn't know whether this was a wise thing to do. It probably wasn't. But reading the journal, he felt, offered him a cautionary glimpse at the almost-stranger he had been, and could be again if he weren't careful, whatever careful entailed:

> They tell me I'm crazy so this probably wont make any sense and if it doesnt its not my fault anyway. Well they don't really say I'm crazy actually everyone here the doctors the nurses even the security guards are awful careful not to use that word here which I'm sure is pretty tough I mean think about how many times you use the word in a day. What they call me is bipolar but that's just a fancy phrase they use for crazy. I've been here for almost five weeks now at least that's what my parents tell me I don't sleep much despite the pills they give me so the days just sort of bunch together I probably shouldn't even ask them what day it is cause it just upsets my mom she stiffens in her chair just after I ask as if shes getting ready for me to punch her in the gut or something sees my confusion I guess as proof that I've lost my marbles. Fact is I've been having a tough time remembering much of anything over these past few five? ten? A hundred!!! days ever since they've been giving me shock treatments of course they don't call it that. They call it ECT. It stands for something with about twenty syllables so everybody just calls it ECT for short it's really no big deal. I never saw that wacked out movie with Jack Nicholson that everybody keeps talking about here so I wasn't as scared the first time as a lot of people seem to be I wasn't even awake for it. They put me out just like they did for my wisdom teeth a few years ago and when I woke up I was a lot less sore

and it was the most sleep Ive gotten in weeks also but heres the problem I've had about six treatments now and dont seem to remember much about the past few months including why I'm stuck in this place to begin with which I suppose might not be a bad thing but still. Dr. Abramson told me that they were only frying one side of my brain though she used the term "unilateral" so that I wouldnt suffer any longterm amnesia, but I'm convinced that I'm forgetting a lot even stuff from a long time ago which isnt supposed to happen. It's tough to tell though I mean how do you know what you don't know anymore????? But it seems like I cant remember anything important. Like the first line, anything, of my Haftorah hours with that thin green book with the red plastic spiral binding and the tape recorder listening to Chazan Turndorf singing it. I memorized every lilt in his voice the words are easy for me to read but its those cadences that are so hard to copy and the cadences are important they mean something it's not like random. It takes me months but I was ready when the time came boy without a hitch I stand there in front of everyone and chant my portion and I'm not even too nervous because I'm like you know taking in the moment looking around the synagogue and I can see grandma Teenie kvelling in her seat and my friends fidgeting toward the rear and Mr. and Mrs. Goldstein beaming smiles toward me. They never knew I had this in me I'm the athletic Glassman kid to them just like their all-American kids with their crew cuts every summer and bad grades in non-honor courses even though I don't have a crew cut and get good grades in honors courses but I sing the Hebrew now as if I understand every word I'm saying which I don't of course so why can't I remember even a word of my Haftorah today or come to think of it that word my Grandma Pearl who never lived to see my Bar Mitzvah used to call me. I know it's something special that she doesn't call my sister she just calls her by her name which means as far as I'm concerned that I'm her favorite who she bakes pan after pan of ruggelach filled with homemade preserves every time we visit from out west. It's my favorite dessert so why can't I remember what she used to call me? There's a lot I can't remember about Lackawanna and it seems important now cause I know that the recent stuff will come back but I feel like it's now or never for my Lackawanna memories and I want them back at least the good memories anyway and it seems like it's only the good ones that I've forgotten and I haven't forgotten any of the bad stuff like Aunt Janet turning her lips away from mine offering me only a cold powdered cheek because mom tells me later that Aunt Janet who usually smothers me with hungry kisses is angry at mom for scheming to get grandma and grandpa's silver and there was something about their place at Lake Lenape too but I don't remember. Mom thinks she's full of shit which is exactly what she said and she usually says sugar when she means shit so she must have really been mad but who knows maybe Janet has something there there's two sides to every story but somehow I guess loving me got a lot tougher for Aunt Janet although mom and she have supposedly made up things can never be the same and I don't care if I never see her again and I bet she senses it. The most pathetic thing is that she still sends me birthday cards a few weeks late and without a check each year and I bet mom hasn't even told her I'm in here and I hope not. Even the small bad Lackawanna memories won't budge like my Uncle Sol's mucousy eyes just a hint of blue in the irises that scare the crap out of me every time I see him and the gloom that hangs in the stale air of Aunt Sylvia and Aunt Marta's nearly light-less apartment my mother's spinster relatives the odd women out in Lackawanna and Aunt Roses yellowy buck tooth that I feel against my tightly pursed lips each time I do what mom says and greet her appropriately and if it were up to me we wouldn't visit any of these relatives but my mom makes us since a mentsh wouldnt dare visit Lackawanna without visiting every Jew who can claim an ounce of common blood but why can't the good memories come as clearly to me as Aunt Janets swiveled head and pinched lips? There's a zoo grandpa Morty used to take us I'm sure of this that it's close to the house the house mom grew up in because we always walk there on the sidewalk that I'm always tripping on because it's so warped by the big roots of the Oak and Sweet Gum trees no one probably ever thought would grow so huge. Grandpa's strong and he's handsome yeah I remember seeing him this way with dark, curly hair just barely receding and a large but nice nose that I squeeze and he goes Honk Honk and he lets me punch his solid thighs like steel as hard as I can and he seems well-tanned and healthy. I'm convinced that this is what kept the doctors those fucking numb-skulls from figuring out until far too late that angry cells were munch-ing away at his bones but what I can't remember is the last time I saw him cause all the memories I have of him are years before he got sick but I must have seen him sometime later. I'm hoping Doctor

Abramson isn't screwing with me and that this stuff will all come back soon after I'm out of here. She's been hinting that it won't be too long before I'm discharged and the way I see it Ive outstayed my welcome since only a few pathetic cases can claim theyve been here longer than I have. Poor Walter I'm not sure they'll ever let him out. Can he ever be me Christ I hope not and I hope that doesnt sound mean. In some ways I might miss this place you know cause I'm really popular with my peers and most of them seem to be girls my age or maybe a bit younger and I wonder what that means that I'm like the only guy my age here so maybe I'll finally meet a nice Jewish girl here mom. Ha. That'll get her. Being populars nice but I suppose the preferences of my particular friends here shouldn't really count for much since Lester hasn't taken his hand off his dick for the five days he's been here and Berthea's totally wasted. It's a good hour or so before visiting hours mom and dad of course are going to be here and stay the whole time until eight-thirty so I guess what I'll do is try to remember some of the stuff I have a pretty strong suspicion Ive forgotten since Dr. Abramson even said that this would be a good thing to do positive coping is what she actually said which is better than negative coping on the wall in purple marker maybe I should write it down here for later 1) Yelling 2) Ignore Problems 3)Abuse, Physical/Sexual 4) Contemplate Suicide 5) Self Mutilation 6) Negative Thinking and the positive coping 1) Seek Help 2) Be Open-Minded 3) Draw. Since these are the only three options Im hoping they just haven't had time to finish the list. For one thing I stink at art and can't draw to save my life and I never could but they won't believe me and keep telling me that my indeci- pherable chicken scratches are a product of my deep-seated anxieties a manifestation of my illness as doctor Abramson explained to my folks as if I weren't even there and my goddamned mother won't dig up my FUCKING PATHETIC FIRST GRADE CRAP that I know she still has in a box somewhere so that I can prove it to them Christttt!!!!! I swear if you're going to go crazy you better know how to finger-paint it should be some kind of frigging prerequisite. It's really her fault that I'm in here in the first place not that I really believe I'm as screwed up as they keep trying to convince me that I am but if I am it's her fault cause I get it from her from her side of the family cause everyone knows about Grandpa Abe being crazy and disappearing maybe getting killed who

86

knows which doesnt mean he still wasnt crazy so I don't know why she has to always deny that he was totally wacked out and I know there's something something SOMETHING important they're just not telling me. Something that has my mom really scared and makes her ask doctor Abramson a million questions and even every nurse on the floor so how does Matthew seem to you today? Better? Yes? Why? How? In what sense? Since my sisters fine I guess it was just the odds that screwed me over.

The journal chilled Glassman to the bone each time he dipped a toe into its icy waters. It wasn't the content so much as the sloppy grammar that, to his mind, betrayed how sick he had been. Run-on sentences, missing apostrophes and commas . . . he was usually far too fastidious to write such horrendous prose. He assiduously proof-read his greeting cards—birthdays, Mother's and Father's Day, thank you's, what have you—often scrapping them and starting over with a fresh card when he judged them to be irreparably marred. Most of the journal seemed to be written by a stranger, or at least by an acquaintance Glassman could scarcely remember. But reading certain sentences elicited a jolt of recognition that traveled painfully down his spine. Still, Glassman took a small measure of comfort in reading the journal because he did remember most of the things that he had temporarily forgotten. Even his Bar Mitzvah Haftorah if you could believe that. (After that first elusive line came to him, the remaining lines flowed almost hauntingly from his tongue and lips, as if some mellifluous dybbuk had possessed him.) *So three cheers for shock treatments and the ephemerality of its associated amnesia!* But the drugs. No way he was taking those drugs anymore. The lithium had turned him into a zombie in those several weeks during and after Saint Vincent's, never asleep but also never quite fully awake. Drugs were out!

His illness, he explained to Rebecca, was his birthright. The odds had it, he had gleaned from a study on depression conducted on the endogamous Amish, that roughly one third of Abe Fishbein's descendants would be stricken with some form or another of his disease. His sister, Sara, was fine, so it was just the odds that did him in. About his grandfather, or his illness, he couldn't remember much. He remembered more about his mother, who was doing fine now thanks to her perfectly honed doses of lithium and God only knew what else. It was something he would never forget, the first time he heard and saw what he couldn't deny was proof that his mother just wasn't right. It didn't matter how many times they shocked his brain at Saint Vincent. That memory wasn't going anywhere, he told Rebecca. He was lying in his bed, clutching his stuffed but emaciated bear, Oscar. The first thing he noticed was that it was too dark in his room for him to be awake. The birches outside the window were still making frightening shapes against the walls. And the wind was still whistling against the shutters. But that wasn't the sound that really frightened him. What scared him and what must have awakened him was the sound of crying up and down the hall outside his door, cracked just so to let in a sliver of light. He was relieved when the sobbing seemed to recede but then it got louder, then subsided again, then got louder. It was high-pitched and wheezy, with nonsensical mutterings mixed in. It wasn't a crying that he recognized, but he knew that it had to be his mother. Who else could it be? He told himself that he must have been dreaming and pinched his eyes shut, but the same wheezy crying wouldn't stop and let him have a different dream. So he just lay there frozen in bed, eyes wide open, waiting for someone to do something.

That's what he heard. What he saw when he finally couldn't stand it anymore and crept to his door to look through the crack was his mother naked, pacing up and down the hallway fending off his father's advances, not letting him wrap his brown terry-cloth robe around her shoulders. What scared him the most wasn't her nakedness, but the panic in his father's face. He didn't go out into the hallway. It wasn't a place for him to go. He stumbled back to his bed. When the morning light finally sliced through his shutters and woke him, he made his way to his parents' room across the hall to see his mother lying in bed in her long purple cotton nightgown, the one with little white flowers that she wore so much that it was all faded and pilly. She lay completely still and her eyes were wide open, but she didn't seem to be looking at anything. Sara was standing over their mother just staring down at her, perplexed. Their mother just wasn't the type to be so . . . motionless.

"Come here Matthew," his father instructed him softly from the closet. "Help me pack your mother's suitcase." It was that he called him Matthew, not boychik or kiddo or Matty or all of his other nicknames, that frightened Glassman. He was just a kid. He wasn't supposed to be Matthew yet.

He refused to help his father rearrange the messy clump of clothing in the suitcase. Instead, he asked of no one in particular—and Glassman would never forget this—"What's for breakfast?"

"It's okay," Rebecca had assured him, covering his tightly interlaced hands on his lap with a soft one of her own. "You don't have to say any more, Matthew. It's okay. We'll work through it. There's always something. And besides. I love you."

Love made certain unyielding demands, it seemed to Glassman. And this was a good thing. For it was his love for Rebecca that impelled him now to lift both legs off the side of the bed as if he were a paraplegic struggling to his wheelchair, to lumber toward the bathroom mirror. He was a frightening sight. His eyes were bloody yolks and his beard seemed to have grown at a preternatural rate over night. Had he forgotten to shave yesterday? How Rebecca managed to tolerate him on top of her at seven this morning he had no idea.

Just do one thing at a time, Glassman instructed himself. *Just concentrate on the little things.* First, he brushed his teeth for a full five minutes in circular strokes, taking care to stimulate his gum-line with the medium-hard bristles. The ADA recommended at least five minutes on the activity, which was actually quite a long time to brush your teeth, Glassman had discovered. It seemed too long a time to devote solely to the activity, and, to compromise, he often sat on the toilet to complete both tasks simultaneously. But today he would force himself to relax. After brushing his teeth, he flossed fastidiously, drawing blood from the gums beneath his back molars, which he usually neglected. After rinsing his mouth, he coated his face with a generous foamy beard of Barbasol, Sensitive Formula, and proceeded to scrape in long, even rows, rinsing the bristles, dead skin, and cream off the disposable safety razor under a stream of cool water after each swipe. His skin always felt less irritated after a cool, rather than warm, shave. It took him nearly fifteen minutes to perform the ritual as meticulously as he felt he should perform it this morning. He went over the elusive locations twice: the narrow band just below his nostrils, the stubbornly pubescent locale on his neck just out of sight beyond the curve of his squared jawbone, the tight horizontal flesh underneath his modestly cleft chin. After his fingers were satisfied with the smoothness of his face, he cupped his hands together as if to hold an injured fledgling and doused himself with handful after handful of cool water. He wouldn't be leaving dollops of shaving cream behind his ears today. That was for certain. After about the ninth handful of water, he felt himself slowly coming out of it. He didn't exactly feel well, but he didn't feel like collapsing back onto the bed either.

Rebecca, however understanding she had been in the past, would have been upset and angry to see him like this. Mostly angry, he knew. Her patience with him was just starting to wear thin when it came to his depression. It was his aversion toward seeking treatment, rather than the depression itself, that had her riled up.

"What if I had cancer and refused to undergo chemotherapy?" she had reasoned with him. "Wouldn't that be selfish?"

"The analogy isn't precise," Glassman argued, even though he knew that his wife had a point. It was ridiculous for him to be in pain, and it *was* pain she insisted. Physical pain. She had seen him during some of the worst episodes. The dichotomy (as Rebecca put it) between mental and physical illness was what was imprecise, not her analogy. His brain was sick, she insisted, just like his heart or kidneys could be sick. It was just another organ, yes?

There was no need for him to endure such pain, she insisted. She had done some research at Florida Southern's Tuttle library, pulling down titles one after the other in a dimly lit aisle of the fourth floor stacks. There were plenty of new antidepressants and mood stabilizers out there. Lithium and those antiquated tricyclics, which had turned him into a "zombie" and a "raving lunatic" respectively before she had met him, were only the tip of the iceberg in the 1990s. Forget Tricyclics. Now there was Prozac and at least half a dozen other Selective Serotonin Reuptake Inhibitors worth considering: Paxil, Zoloft, Serzone, Luvox, et al. And if he didn't want to take lithium, he could try Depakote, an anti-seizure medication that now doubled as an impressively effective mood stabilizer. New drugs in new combinations could offer him real help.

Of course, there was no simple recipe. It took time to find the right medications, the right combinations and dosages. It was all about "levels." But doctors couldn't predict yet with any real certainty which drugs would have the most ameliorative affect on which people. They didn't even know, from a biomedical standpoint, exactly how most of the drugs worked, just that they did, indeed, work. So they essentially experimented with the proven commodities first, waited the weeks and sometimes months that it took for the drugs to work their way through the bloodstream, and then just took their cue from the patient's response, or lack of response, to each new course of treatment. It took time and patience and, yes, perhaps some unfortunate reactions until the most favorable result was achieved. But wasn't it worth it in the end? The new drugs, Rebecca had tried to convince her husband, wouldn't change him into someone else. They'd just ease his anxiety, take the edge off.

Why screw with depression in the 1990s for God's sake?

This all sounded well and good. However, Glassman reasoned with Rebecca, when they were *your* anxieties being calmed, *your* sharp edges being sanded away, it tended to make you see things a bit differently. Didn't his experiences—however painful—*mean* something? Wouldn't erasing the texture of those experiences somehow erase him, as well? Besides, he didn't have any terribly malicious symptoms. He was just sad from time to time. Fine, melancholy. But maybe a good dose of melancholy was what everyone truly needed. People were *too* functional in south Florida. That was the problem.

Some sadder, brooding, pensive citizens was just what the place needed.

Glassman wasn't sure he believed all of these arguments, but, nonetheless, they tended to hold sway. He hadn't seen a therapist since the time at Saint Vincent, and he had remained thoroughly, resolutely, and unwaveringly unmedicated. No Prozac. No lithium. Not even any dropper-fulls of that frippy homeopathic St. John's Wort concoction that everyone, even the blissfully chipper, seemed to ingest these days.

He couldn't argue much with the results from the ECT. The seven treatments did manage somehow to jump-start his brain. Plus, as Dr. Abramson promised, Glassman did manage to recall most of the things that he had temporarily forgotten. But drugs were out!

He would just do the best that he could. Like so many. Like so many Jews. For there was something about Ashkenazic Jews and depression, Glassman was convinced.

His mother was not: "Don't be ridiculous Matthew. Illness doesn't discriminate based on race, religion, or gender. If you still feel depressed, please . . . please see someone, but don't frighten yourself into thinking it's fate."

"But what about you and grandpa? What about Aunt Janet?" He only reluctantly brought up the topic of his Aunt Janet. Five years or so after Abe's disappearance, his aunt enacted sort of a half-assed disappearing job herself. First (as he was to learn later), there was the petty spat with his mother about the cabin at Lake Lenape. He had forgotten who wanted to sell it and who didn't. Then, her phone calls grew less frequent, then ceased altogether. Next thing everyone knew, she had moved out of her East Stroudsburg apartment. Barbara's birthday card to her sister appeared in their mailbox just a week after she had sent it with a crooked blue stamp at the bottom, ADDRESSEE UNKNOWN. It was six months before Janet contacted Glassman's mother, from Erie. She still spoke with Teenie and Barbara about every few months or so for three or four awkward minutes. *She's just not Janet anymore,* Glassman remembered his mother saying after one of these conversations.

"I've been fine, Matthew, just fine. For a while now. You know that, don't you? You're not worrying, are you? I just take a very low dosage of medication. And your Aunt Janet's problems have nothing to do with depression." Her tone shifted here, grew suddenly harsh. "Can't people hold stupid grudges without being mentally disturbed? Does there have to be a medical explanation for everything?"

Glassman didn't challenge his mother further, but her arguments seemed uncharacteristically, and perhaps willfully, asinine to him, especially given her own personal history. First of all, there was no way his Aunt Janet wasn't clinically screwed up. Normal people just didn't act that way. And what did she mean illness doesn't discriminate? Had she ever heard of Sickle cell anemia, Tay-Sachs, Gaucher, osteoperosis, Cystic Fibrosis? Disease, if it was anything, was politically incorrect. Aside from a few egalitarian variants, it specialized in the young, the old, the Black, the Jew, the Native American, the Amish, and Irish. Every day, it seemed, there was another report about a special deleterious gene that some race or ethnic group possessed as its very own.

Glassman carefully measured out five heaping tablespoons of coffee and waited patiently for the machine to announce its completion with a gurgle. He poured himself a cup and sat with the paper. Rebecca, evidently, had taken the front page for Dr. Arias's waiting room, so he was left with the Living Arts section, his favorite section in any case. He couldn't concentrate on more than one sentence at a time, however. He was too distracted. Too depressed. He didn't feel like eating either. This wasn't the depression, he thought. He rarely felt like eating early in the morning and often forced a half bagel and some orange juice down his gullet only to mollify Rebecca. But he was free to fast today. He decided to make a list. He often made lists. Lists, not Prozac, was what eased his anxiety. He still had one elongated pad of paper with an unflattering photo of their platinum coiffed real estate agent on top of it. Well, it would do:

Things to Do

1. Call Grandma to see how she feels (thank her for lunch too)
2. Quick call to Ben and Edith from work, who I know I called last week but whatever
3. Get Becky to get Ropa Pops schedule at school for Bea. She asked for it two weeks ago!!!
4. Call Simon Glickstein about his killed review. Throw him a bone. Maybe that new Kamenetz book to review. Do we give a kill fee? Better check with Alten first
5. Thank you card to Aunt Ellen and Uncle Herbie for Sunday Brunch at the Hilton. Becky's never going to do it
6. Give Troy a bath
7. Reply to Herbie's e-mail joke. Just say thanks and be done with it
8. Coordinate good date with Becky to invite Edith and Ben to dinner. They've had us out three times already. Do we invite grandma too? Better think this through
9. Get Sara birthday present. Don't forget this year!
10. Call Grandma

General Goals for February

—Get into work earlier and stay later
—Stop eating out so much
—Start saving more in Janus. Automatic Deposits? Look into it
—Fun, have

Glassman immediately felt relieved, as if a great burden had been lifted. As if he had already completed the tasks he had just jotted down, and then some. He put the list in his breast pocket, then took Troy for his drag. The German shepherds were in their yard today. He could hear them barking from afar. Behind their chain link fence, the fierce dogs could discern his and Troy's presence while they were still a block and a half off. Lovely dogs. He had been amused to learn that German shepherds, as a breed, were prone to hip displacia and detached retinas. They could expect five, maybe six, good years. The perfect canine complement to the master race.

Chuck crossed the street to greet Glassman as he and Troy approached home. *Not now. I can't deal with Chuck's rambling now,* Glassman thought.

"So, Matt, did you hear about that fuckin' Haitian high school girl with tuberculosis who disappeared?"

"No." Glassman avoided the local news at all costs. It was just one case of horrific child abuse after another. Not only the garden variety beatings. The authorities were constantly summoned by neighbors to rescue malnourished children imprisoned in homes stacked wall to wall in reeking garbage. People were twisted in south Florida. More twisted than elsewhere. He was convinced. Maybe it was the heat. The most recent story topping every broadcast and plastered all over the papers—Glassman simply couldn't evade it—involved a Palm Beach Gardens high school teacher named Mandelbaum (MANDELBAUM!), who had been arrested for imprisoning a ten-year-old boy from Nicaragua in his home. His own personal sex slave. A real credit to the race, Glassman had lamented to Rebecca.

"She's a goddamned illegal," Chuck continued. "That's why she's disappeared. If we didn't let all these frigging illegals in, we'd only need three new schools in the area. Now we need twenty."

"Oh," Glassman murmured. He was in no mood to challenge his neighbor and wasn't even convinced that Chuck was entirely wrong. How many more people could they squeeze into south Florida? Still, he knew that the Haitians lucky enough to make it safely ashore took on the least palatable jobs, jobs no one else seemed willing to perform. Glassman regularly noticed several of these especially dark Francophiles walking their paler, aged wards up and down the sidewalk outside the nursing home located just beyond the perimeter of Pine Lakes. The elderly residents there were quiet and unobtrusive. *Good sedatives make good neighbors.* Glassman couldn't help noticing that the Asian elderly were the only patients who were regularly accompanied on their walks by people he presumed to be their younger relatives, sometimes three, four, or five of them at a time. He was moved by these doddering Asian caravans that made their way two-by-two on the sidewalk, and wondered whether his way-ward tribe of Jews shouldn't take note. Take his own family, for instance, which had willfully scattered themselves across every quadrant of the continent. All the same, he wasn't about to head on over to one of the homes and volunteer his services. He was no saint and didn't fool himself into thinking otherwise of himself. So humanitarian interests aside, if Chuck had his way and they deported all the "illegals" tomorrow, who else would change the soiled diapers of the aged? Had anyone thought of that? Rather than pursue a debate, Glassman told his neighbor he had to get to work.

BRRRING! The phone pealed just as Glassman entered the house with Troy. He wasn't certain whether he had caught the first ring. *BRRRING!* Another angry complaint. Should he wait for the answering machine to kick in? Probably. But somehow he could never bring himself to screen his calls. When his number was called, he had to pick up.

"Hel-*lo*." Glassman attempted always to lace his greeting with just a modicum of hostility to discourage the hordes of salespeople who had been calling incessantly since they had moved into the house. These salespeople played by altogether looser rules of etiquette in south Florida.

"Good morning Mr. Glassman," a woman's too-friendly voice greeted him. "Allow me to congratulate you on the purchase of your new home on behalf of Quality Water of South Florida." Glassman was immediately suspicious, but the name of the company sounded quasi-official. "Mr. Glassman, we have a team of hydrologists in your area right now, and we were wondering whether you'd be interested in having your water tested absolutely free of charge." Upon hearing the word free Glassman was fairly certain that there was a catch, but he was curious. The tap water in his house did taste as if it were siphoned from his swimming pool.

"What do you test the water *for*?"

"Well sir, an incredible number of harmful things. Bacteria, lead, chlorine, copper, cryptosporidium, fecal matter . . . my, any number of contaminants. Do you want me to keep listing them, or would you like to talk to the experts directly when they arrive? I can have them out to you within an hour."

"Ummm . . ." The saleswoman's directness caught Glassman off guard. "Well, what do you really *want*?" he finally managed to ask. The woman's voice lost a bit of its friendliness as she replied. She seemed the slightest bit disgusted. Glassman had breached the protocol.

"We don't *want* anything from you sir. We'll just perform this hundred percent accurate water test at absolutely no charge and no obligation to you, and, depending upon the results of the test, our hydrologists might recommend a water treatment filtration system to suit your needs."

It was all finally becoming clear to him. He should have simply said no thank you and hung up. But he had suffered through too many of these calls lately not to engage in a little verbal sparring.

"And so your hydrologists will recommend a reliable company to install such a system, if, in fact, my water just happens to be contaminated?"

"Well, sir, Quality Water of South Florida will be happy to install our patented reverse-osmosis system for you should you need water filtration and purification."

Glassman marveled at the saleswoman's persistence. Or was she just slow on the uptake? Could she possibly believe that a sale might still be a real possibility? Glassman was slowly growing angrier. He looked down at the clock on the oven. 8:47. She had robbed him of five minutes of his life!

"No, I don't want your free test. You know, I'm really sick and tired, to tell you the truth, of being bothered at all hours of the day and night by you people. Damnit!" Glassman was suddenly enraged.

"Sir, I really don't appreciate your abusiveness," the saleswoman replied acidly.

Glassman heard a click. *Dial tone.* He had never been so aggressive over the phone to a salesperson and relished the moment for just a second, as if he had been the one to hang up the phone first, as if the woman on the other end of the line really cared a fig about what he had to say, as if he didn't have to hustle now if he was even to stand a chance of making it to work before nine.

BRRRING! The blaring phone, still in his hand, sent a jolt down his spine. These damn salespeople, salespeople of every ilk, were driving him crazy. Were they certain they didn't need a water purification system? Window tint that would keep the electric bills low? Steel shutters to protect them from hurricanes? Their lawn mowed? Their carpets cleaned? Their outside painted? Their pests controlled? Glassman was constantly playing defense against such aggressive solicitations. And now his morning tormenter evidently decided that she wasn't quite through with him.

"What!" Glassman viciously demanded.

"Yes, um, I'm sorry, but is that Matthew Glassman there?" a tentative voice inquired, a breathy voice that Glassman instantly recognized, as if he had heard this voice each day of his life. He felt his heart skip a beat. He never expected Shuman to call him at home. He hadn't given the old man his home number, had he?

"Why haven't you called?" Glassman jumped ahead in the conversation. *Careful!* he warned himself. He wished Shuman hadn't caught him at such a bad time, when his defenses were so low. Glassman couldn't afford such effusiveness; he needed to keep his emotions in check. He suspected that his desperate tones at the conclusion of their first encounter had caused Shuman's temporary withdrawal. He didn't want to frighten him away again.

"I mean," Glassman continued, "I've been a bit worried about you is all."

"Oh, don't you worry about me, son." *Son?* "I'm perfectly fine. I just didn't want to impose on your time once again so soon." Glassman told him that it was no trouble. That he enjoyed their first meeting. This seemed to encourage Shuman.

"You seemed pretty interested with the section of my journal about the birds." Glassman assured him that he was, in fact, intrigued by that particular section. He asked him whether he wanted to drop by the office and read more to him.

"Well, to tell you the truth," Shuman answered, "I got the impression with all those books on your office shelves that the last thing you need is to have me read you another one. You don't get outdoors very much, do you?"

"No, I suppose I don't," Glassman confessed. He anticipated before moving to Florida that he and Rebecca would at least go to the beach from time to time. But it hadn't quite worked out that way. On the weekends, there were always innumerable chores to do around the house, his grandmother and other relatives to visit.

"Now, you'll tell an old kocker if he's being too forward . . . and tell me if I'm wrong . . . but I figured you might like to meet me at the Everglades sometime . . ."

Meet the Wood Stork

Glassman, upon Shuman's instruction, arose from bed at the crack of dawn Sunday and headed to Loxahatchee, the last surviving remnant of the northern Everglades. Just who was this Irving Shuman character? Rebecca asked him the night before as they lay in bed. They had just dutifully coupled so as not to miss that crucial window of ovular receptiveness. Glassman explained to her, elusively, that the old man was just someone he had met at the *Jewish Weekly Times,* which was true enough, and she seemed satisfied with his sparse response. Still, she thought he was out of his mind to get up so early on the weekend and instructed her husband to refrain from waking her if he could manage it. So Glassman crept stealthily out the garage door, his car keys in one hand, a green spray can of insect repellant in the other.

The road taking him west at six thirty was nearly empty, almost eerily so given its usual congestion. Glassman marveled at the change in scenery as he made his way past the strip malls and condo complexes that were so familiar to him. It didn't take long to enter utterly unfamiliar territory. In less than fifteen minutes of westward driving on Atlantic, stuccoed walls, security fences, and shopping centers gave way to open farmland and flat-bed trucks. Not many trees, though. Mostly the large sloppy pines, non-native aggressors planted years ago as fast growing wind-breakers, Glassman had heard, by myopic developers; the droopy, dusty looking trees had been busy ever since muscling out their arboreal competitors.

Neither he nor his relatives knew anything about this place just minutes from their homes. It was much farther away, Glassman mused regretfully, than its proximity suggested. He noticed dark men and women in the fields, some wearing round, straw hats, others with just some loose pieces of fabric covering their heads. They were crouching between tall cane breaks, plucking fruits or vegetables. Tomatoes, Glassman thought. Or maybe they were red peppers.

When he reached the 441 he noticed a mini-mart on the corner and stopped to pick up a drink. He parked his Toyota next to a dilapidated bus, a retired school bus Glassman figured that had probably dropped off its workers between fields to pick up some food and drink. Stepping out of his car, he read the large blue words painted on the white stucco:

Food
Groceries
Beer
Mexican Food
Bait & Tackle

ENVIE DINERO RAPIDO, he noticed in smaller, hand-painted white script as he swung open the glass door. The terse Spanish phrase, he suspected, said more about Florida's "illegals" than any of Chuck's rantings. On the way to the refrigerator at the rear of the store, he scanned the items on the shelf: bags of Ever-So-Hot Rancheritos, Churritos y Limón, and some strange dried peppers he was fairly certain he had never eaten—ancho, pasilla, and guajillo. He also noticed giant cans of chipotle en adobo, serranos, and jalapeños. Now jalapeños he knew. Rebecca grew up in Pennsylvania's Dutch country on a curious admixture of Jewish and Dutch cooking, high in starch but low in spice. After years of pickled eggs, kugel, apples and cabbage, brisket, creamed chipped beef, chicken corn soup, and shoo-fly pie, she couldn't quite fathom the use of the jalapeño as a food item (*Why eat something that hurts your mouth?* she had asked Glassman, who had dragged her to her first Mexican restaurant), but Glassman loved their flavor and heat. He wondered about the potency of the other peppers he was only just discovering.

Standing at the glass window of the refrigerator, pondering the beverage selections, Glassman was suddenly conscious of two burly workers (Mexican? Guatemalan? Honduran?) on either side of him, also peering into the refrigerator. They were a bit too close for comfort. He felt the hair on the back of his neck stand on end. Then, suddenly, they opened the doors in front of them, selected a drink and departed, leaving Glassman in peace and ashamed.

Along the 441, he noticed several black people fishing in the canal, in between the solitary great blue herons, one of the few birds Glassman knew by name. There were plenty of other birds fishing in the canal as well. A solitary, prehistoric looking white bird with a fleshy, featherless head particularly caught Glassman's eye. It swung its large shoe-like bill back and forth, half submerged in the water, apparently groping for food. Glassman had to swerve back onto the highway after hearing the crunch of loose gravel and dirt under his tires. He wished the bird luck, but couldn't imagine that eating the fish could be too safe, for the people or for this bird, given the murky run-off from the fields that gushed into the canal from enormous rusty pipes every mile or so.

At the refuge at last, Glassman parked the car at the visitor's center, as Shuman advised, and ambled across the road to the Marsh Trail where Shuman said he would meet him. Glassman squinted as he walked the short distance. The sun, just above the nameless, fragrant shrubs to the east, seemed to have doubled in intensity since he stepped out of his house less than an hour ago. It seared the left side of his face. It was, in fact, turning out to be an unseasonably hot winter. *Like stepping into someone's mouth,* Teenie had once described the mugginess in Florida. An apt description. Mosquitoes shouldn't be a problem this time of year, Glassman figured, but given the heat, who could tell? He paused in the middle of the dirt road and sprayed himself generously with the medicinal smelling repellant. He then smeared the excess all over his face, neck, and ears. For as long as Glassman could remember, mosquitoes dined on him as if they had sworn off all other sources of nourishment. For the few weeks that he visited Lackawanna each summer as a child, his parents enrolled him and his sister at the Jewish Community Center day camp twenty minutes outside town in the Poconos. Sara returned on the bus each day unscathed, while Glassman scratched feverishly at nickel-sized crimson welts behind his knees and on his ankles, often forcing trickles of blood to ooze down his leg. Little wonder that Glassman had stayed pretty much clear of nature as an adult.

Shuman was already waiting for him near the trail. Glassman recognized the old man sitting on a single wooden bench facing a shallow body of water. His face, weathered from some combination of age and sun exposure, was shaded by two intertwining trees ten feet away and the khaki, wide-brimmed hat he wore at a slight sideways slant. He held a pair of binoculars between both hands but didn't appear to be using them as Glassman approached. Rather, he gazed quietly, almost statue-still in his seated pose, toward the various birds that busily swam and waded before him.

"Hello, Mr. Shuman," Glassman softly greeted the elderly man. He only reluctantly announced his presence. For some reason, he felt as if he had interjected in the middle of a conversation.

"Oh, hello Matthew," Shuman replied as he turned to face his young companion. He gestured toward the space on the bench next to him and Glassman quietly, nervously, sat down. Learning the rules of etiquette had been a salient feature of Glassman's childhood. He always knew which fork to use on his salad, how to properly greet his elders, when to send thank you notes, etc. etc., but felt particularly awkward now at Loxahatchee with Shuman. He knew that certain rules obtained for bird-watching, but wasn't familiar with the protocol. Should he speak or remain silent?

"Here," Shuman broke the ice, "take these binoculars." *Binoculars.* He handed them to Glassman, who obediently accepted them.

They felt solid and substantial in his hands. "You can hand me the repellant. I'll put it in my bag. You don't need it anymore. Lord knows you've sprayed enough on." Shuman good-humoredly fanned the medicinal air between them. Glassman sheepishly handed over the canister and the exchange was complete.

"Besides my insect repellent, it smells pretty nice out here . . . spicy," Glassman observed.

"Yes, it's the wax myrtle," Shuman explained. "They're growing all around the saw palmetto and cabbage palm." Without turning around, he raised his elbow and pointed over his shoulder at the healthy shrubs and stubby trees that Glassman had just walked past on the way to the bench. The editor surmised that the abundant dusty green fans growing aside the shrubs were the leaves of the saw palmetto or cabbage palm.

"These trees are pretty interesting," Glassman added, pointing above them at the complex network of intertwining branches. "One of them's a cypress, right?"

"Yes, very good," Shuman answered, again without looking toward the foliage in question. "The other one is just a strangler fig living up to its name."

Glassman had originally entertained a harmonious vision of the trees, a couple locked in a passionate embrace; he quickly adjusted his vision to accommodate the parasitic nature of the relationship. The fig's smooth, muscular arms were suddenly tentacles that smothered and choked.

Shuman suggested that Glassman take some time to look at the various birds with the binoculars. Glassman obeyed, and was dumbfounded by the number of different birds that shared the same "lake." It was actually an impoundment, Shuman explained. The Everglades, officially, were just over the canal a half mile or so to the west. The Fish and Wildlife Service controlled the water levels scrupulously in the impoundments along the Marsh Trail bordering the Glades to provide a suitable habitat to a wide selection of resident and migrant birds—mostly herons, egrets, ducks, sandpipers, ibises, and rails. Glassman didn't even bother trying to ask the names of all the birds. There were simply too many.

After scanning the entire impoundment, Glassman lowered the glasses. He had suddenly grown impatient. He possessed, in fact, a rather impatient, frenetic personality, and couldn't stand to be idle for more than a few moments at a time. He wasn't used to sitting still. Just the other day, Rebecca had admonished him for brushing his teeth while he sat constipated on the toilet. But he couldn't help it. He couldn't stand wasting time. It occurred to him that he probably wasn't cut out for bird-watching.

"Do you ever, like, bring a book out here to read or something?" Glassman asked. It seemed incredible that Shuman just sat there on the bench for hours at a time.

"Here," Shuman instructed, picking up the binoculars from the editor's lap. With a trembling hand, he placed them in front of the young man's eyes. Glassman raised his hands to steady the glasses and looked out once again at the birds swimming amid the reeds and lily pads. "There," Shuman announced. "You're reading. . . . Why don't you tell me something about the book."

Glassman inhaled deeply and let out a long exhale. Somehow, with this single breath, he managed to banish from his mind all that lately consumed him: his and Rebecca's fruitless attempts to conceive, his tenuous relationship with his grandmother, his mother's subtle, yet palpable, remoteness, his frustrations at the *Jewish Weekly Times,* even his curiosity regarding whether or not the man sitting next to him was his grandfather. Somehow, he simply let it all go. He felt the tension around his eyes relax, and realized that he must have been squinting. What a tightly wound knot he had become. What a wreck of a human being!

Looking out at the water, Glassman knew what the old man had meant. It wasn't just a lovely portrait before him, as he had initially thought, something static to admire briefly before moving on to the next room of the museum. Rather, it was a rich, dynamic text worthy of study. He told Shuman what he read. A dark, duck-like bird with a white bill dipped its head in the water for nourishment and came up again and again chewing on spindly green plants. Two smaller brown birds dove underneath the water for long stretches, then bobbed energetically atop the surface like buoys. A heron, blue and mottled at the throat in chestnut and white, stood patiently at the shoreline just twenty or so feet from Glassman; it caught small, glistening fish every few minutes or so by darting its long bill into the water. A similarly shaped white bird with black legs and yellow feet, like golden slippers, hunted in the same manner from its precarious perch on a dead tree limb, which stretched out of the water like the desperate arm of a drowning man. A turtle, its shell barely visible beneath the surface, jutted its hog-like nostrils out of the water to breathe. An entire flock of white birds, with splashes of buff yellow on their breasts, back, and head, suddenly took to the air in a fast-moving cloud, which circled twice before disappearing from the atmosphere.

"You're a good reader," Shuman complimented him. "But what about the sounds?"

Sounds. Glassman hadn't even thought to register the various sounds that whistled through the air. Almost completely inured to the traffic noise that bore inexorably down upon him in Florida—the growling engines, the screeching tires, the constantly blaring sirens—Loxahatchee had actually struck him as blessedly quiet. However, sitting there next to Shuman, closing his eyes and concentrating upon what he heard, Glassman registered innumerable sounds. They emanated mostly from the impoundment, but also echoed from the cypress swamp nearby. It was anything but quiet. Duck-like birds with the red bills and foreheads screeched alarmingly at one another; frogs, or toads probably, belched loudly from the reeds; small songbirds above them in the cypress with yellow underneath their tails *chip-chip-chipped;* an insect rattled somewhere in a bush; a woodpecker in the swamp off into the distance hammered loudly at a tree. A pileated woodpecker, Shuman explained. Another bird clinging to a nearby tree trilled rhythmically, repetitively. A red-bellied woodpecker, he learned.

"Well, perhaps now we can take a shpatzir Matthew. A little stroll." Glassman had been looking forward to taking a walk around the trail, and wasn't certain whether they ever would. It was entirely possible that Shuman couldn't take more than a few steps at a time.

He stood up quickly, reached his hand toward Shuman, and helped the man to his feet. He was delighted to observe how gamely Shuman managed to walk ahead of him toward the mouth of the wide trail that circled the impoundment. At the trail entrance, Glassman noticed a metal sign affixed chest high to a wooden post. No "Alligators *May* Be Present" signs here. Alligators, apparently, *were* present at Loxahatchee. The paragraph in white block letters underneath the likeness of a rather corpulent alligator (emblazoned there, perhaps, for the benefit of the hordes of German tourists, many of whom couldn't speak or read English), alerted visitors to their immovable presence.

ALLIGATORS ARE PRESENT ON THE REFUGE GROUNDS. THEY ARE AN IMPORTANT PART OF FLORIDA'S ECOLOGY AND MAY BE FOUND WHEREVER THERE IS A NATURAL OR MAN-MADE BODY OF WATER. THEY HAVE A NATURAL FEAR OF MAN, BUT MAY LOSE THAT FEAR, ESPECIALLY IF THEY ARE FED. WHEN THIS HAPPENS ALLIGATORS CAN BE DANGEROUS. FOR THIS REASON IT IS AGAINST THE FEDERAL LAW TO FEED, MOLEST, OR ENTICE ALLIGATORS IN ANY WAY.

16 USC 668dd   50CFR27.51

"We're not in any . . . you know . . . danger or anything, are we?" Glassman timidly inquired. He had heard somewhere that alligators were actually much faster than they appeared.

"What, from the alligators?" Shuman replied. He seemed mildly amused by Glassman's trepidation. "They're harmless creatures. Make no mistake, I wouldn't get too close to one, but if you don't bother them, they won't bother you." This sounded fair enough to Glassman, who proceeded warily after his elder.

They passed several bird-watchers on the trail, who seemed fairly experienced to Glassman, primarily because of the costly looking scopes on padded tripods through which many of them peered. About halfway around the loop, they stopped ten feet or so away from five or six other bird-watchers to observe a large group of shorebirds wading in the shallows. The members of the group were taking turns looking through a large scope encased in green canvas. Glassman read the brand name on its side, Kowa. "So," Glassman heard a separate man begin to inquire as he approached the group, "what do you got out here? Anything interesting?"

"Nah, just the usual suspects," the woman currently behind the scope answered. A long, loose braid flowed down her back, keeping three mousy strands of hair from interfering with her vision. "Some black-necked stilts, moorhens, coots . . . a few limpkins."

Glassman knew which birds must have been the black-necked stilts. They were elegant black and white birds with long, slender bills. They seemed less patient than the herons he had observed, as they stepped lightly on red legs back and forth across the shallows, gazing down all the while in search of their next meal.

"Those black-necked stilts are gorgeous," Glassman quietly opined to Shuman, standing impassively beside him, some fifteen feet away from the other birders.

"Yes . . . yes they certainly are," Shuman agreed. Glassman asked him whether he wanted his binoculars back, but the old man declined. He didn't need them just then.

It appeared to Glassman that his elder was a bird-watcher of a different stripe from the ones who congregated around the scope. He couldn't quite put his finger on it, but there was something intrusive, even vaguely mercenary, about their approach. Perhaps it was the way they aimed their giant scope like a canon at the raft of birds, the way a few of them fired off several rapid exposures at a time with their hand-held cameras, the way they hungrily rifled through their identification guides to verify or dismiss possible sightings; or maybe it was just their casual banter about "usual suspects," "possible 'lifers,'" and "hot spots" that made Glassman recoil. Whereas Shuman's approach was introspective and humble (yes, Glassman thought, humble was the correct word), they were aggressive, competitive.

They continued their slow walk. As they reached one large bush, a wax myrtle, Glassman thought, Shuman began *pish, pish, pish-ing* a bit, not too loudly. "Now you can't do this too noisily," Shuman warned. "One of the most important birding rules is to avoid chasing or repeatedly flushing birds." In any case, his soft *pishing* was enough. For, suddenly, a small bird popped up from the dense blanket of green and showed its black bandit's mask, its lemon throat and breast. A common yellowthroat, Shuman told him. As they continued around the trail, Shuman spotted countless birds without the benefit of the binoculars. He seemed to know exactly where to look, as if he had somehow prearranged their perching and wading spots. Red-shouldered hawk, palm warbler, redstart, smooth-billed ani, grebe, tri-colored heron, snowy egret, great egret, purple gallinule. . . . The young editor tried hard to memorize the names, to keep the fifty or so birds he was seeing for the first time straight in his mind.

Three or four people they passed inquired whether and where they had seen 'gators. One man, stout and pasty looking with curly locks of red hair that peeked out beneath his black Harley-Davidson baseball cap, advised them exuberantly that they could see an alligator around the next bend. It was sunning on a log about fifty feet from the observation tower. Shuman thanked the man benignly for them both.

"You must get really sick of all these people making such a fuss over the alligators, eh?" Glassman asked. After all, they didn't seem to care about the birds that mattered so much to Shuman. Reptilian scales covered their eyes.

"No, I don't mind," Shuman surprised him with his answer. "It's all one nature, Matthew. The birds need the alligators. They clear out the sawgrass and make broad water holes. The holes are good hunting spots for the birds; and, of course, alligators hunt the birds in kind. So, you see, the alligators need the birds. All one nature.

"You see these rusty butterflies all around us?" He lightly waved one from his field of view. "The flowers they feed on?" He pointed to a hardy looking plant with a thick stem and white broccoli floret.

"The grasses beneath our feet? The rocks? The soil? All demand closer inspection, don't you think?"

Glassman agreed that they did.

They arrived in view of the enormous alligator just in time. Glassman actually heard it thrashing in the shallow water off the trail before he saw it. It was much closer to the trail now than the man implied, if, indeed, this was the same alligator. Glassman jumped away alarmingly while turning his head toward the noise just in time to see the alligator take one more gnashing chomp at the turtle it had captured. "Relax," Shuman advised. "We're safe here."

The turtle's shell that up until then had protected its tender meat was now jagged shards stubbornly attached to the flesh underneath. Perhaps spotting them and not wanting to share or lose its hard-earned meal, the alligator descended into the murky water and was gone. A few blades of bobbing sawgrass indicated the direction toward which it had fled with its prize. Glassman tried to keep from wincing. It was nothing to wince at, after all. It was just nature. Stark, competitive, deathly nature, "red in tooth in claw," as Glassman remembered the English Poet Laureate bewail, his faith in God shaken.

Around the last bend of the impoundment, still a bit shaken by what he had witnessed, Glassman spotted an unusual looking hawk with a mottled, pale-rust chest perched atop a cypress tree, festooned with Spanish moss and pink bromeliads. (Shuman had earlier identified the tropical plants for him.) It took Glassman only a moment to figure out what was unusual about the bird. It had only one eye. A lazy lid on the left side of his face covered half of an empty socket. Through the binoculars, Glassman watched the hawk busily preen its feathers some forty feet off the ground.

"Is that hawk okay?" Glassman inquired. "Should we do something? Report the injury to someone?"

"No, he's fine," Shuman assured the young editor. "He's a red-shouldered hawk. I've seen him here for the past several years. He was probably born that way. A birth defect. Pesticide-induced maybe. But it's okay. Birds are fairly amazing that way, Matthew. They find a way to endure."

Yes, Glassman agreed. This was an amazing quality, one worthy of emulation.

As they neared the mouth of the trail once again, where they had started from an hour or two ago, Glassman suddenly remembered to ask Shuman about the giant white bird he had seen in the canal on the way to the refuge. He described it the best he could. It was prehistoric looking. It had a fleshy, wrinkled face and a shoe-like bill, not narrow like a heron's bill. And it might have had some black on it somewhere. He was driving at the time. It was tough to tell. He almost swerved right into the canal.

"Ahhh," Shuman answered. Yes, he knew the bird Glassman had seen, but wouldn't tell him its name right away. Instead, he somewhat mysteriously instructed Glassman to sit down once again on the bench. They sat there, silent, for five minutes, ten, then twenty. *What?* Glassman wondered. Wasn't he worthy yet of knowing its name? How long would he have to sit there and wait for Shuman to respond? He found himself growing impatient once again.

Then, suddenly, Shuman pointed toward the west, low in the sky. "There," he announced.

"Where?" Glassman asked, mildly irritated. He was hot and sticky, not to mention thirsty. He was ready to return to the car where he had left his bottle of water. Then, Glassman saw them. They were just a faint, dark line off into the horizon, but a line that grew gradually larger and larger, gradually curved into a V. Soon they were nearly overhead, flying in squadron formation. Thirty, maybe forty, of them. They were large with broad black and white wings, like piano keys. Their fleshy, dark heads jutted straight out and bobbed slightly with each flap of their wings. Before Glassman knew it, they were directly over their heads, and then gone, gone east toward the ocean.

"Oh, my god," he marveled. "That was incredible! *Those* were the birds! How did you know they'd be coming?"

"Patience . . . patience," Shuman replied, raising a single finger. The old man was relishing the moment, it occurred to Glassman, as if he didn't fully expect things to work out so nicely. Then, just a few moments later, he pointed over the cypress swamp to the north. The birds, apparently, had circled back. The young editor saw all of them soar slowly down toward the impoundment; they nearly slowed to a stop in midair before splashing down just thirty yards or so in front of them. Glassman could hear them clacking their bills as they walked about heavily in the shallows like . . . yes, he decided . . . like stooped elderly men with their hands behind their backs.

"Matthew Glassman," Shuman announced rather formally. "Meet the wood stork."

They sat quietly and watched the birds feed for a while, swinging their broad bills back and forth across the shallow water, half-open he could now tell, groping for food. Shuman explained that the snapping reflex of their bills was much faster than an alligator's jaws. The fastest of any vertebrate, in fact. Before they departed, Shuman revealed to his young companion how he knew, or was fairly certain anyway, that the wood storks would be descending upon the refuge. A flock or two flew in practically each morning. They fed in the impoundments during the day and, as dusk approached, gathered themselves up in a mighty *whoosh* and headed back west to their nesting colonies deep in the Everglades in the sulfurous mangrove swamps and in the few remnant stands of old-growth cypress. Their numbers had been steadily declining, especially since the Army Corps of Engineers tampered imprudently with the natural water-flow of the Glades by building a web of concrete canals. It was all about levels. The water levels now in the Glades throughout the year were either too high or too low for the wood storks to hunt successfully. Still, a few colonies managed stubbornly to endure. Like many of their human counterparts, they had become reluctant but perseverant commuters. Each and every day, without fail, they flapped and soared miles and miles to acceptable foraging habitat, then tiredly returned home each evening.

"I can see why you enjoy bird-watching," Glassman observed. He felt mildly intoxicated by the story of the wood storks, by the whole breathtaking morning. "It's great to escape. To get away from everybody once and for all," he heard himself blurt out. He had promised himself before leaving this morning that he would do his best not to frighten Shuman off once again. And he truly didn't mean now to provoke his companion sitting next to him into any disclosures. The words had simply escaped his lips. It *was* nice to get away from all the craziness of south Florida, all the craziness of his family. Only after he rashly uttered the words did Glassman realize the way they might have sounded to the elderly man sitting next to him. He apprehensively awaited Shuman's response, which didn't appear to be forthcoming. Unless Glassman was mistaken, the old man slumped his shoulders; he seemed to withdraw into himself like a turtle receding back into its shell. Finally, Shuman spoke.

"Yes, son, there is something to be said for getting away from it all. That's true. . . ." Shuman took a moment before continuing. He seemed to be gathering his thoughts. "But you see these birds." He gestured toward the wood storks with a dramatic sweep of his loose fist from which an index finger poked out slightly. "They're fascinating and miraculous creatures, worthy of serious study and reflection. I believe this with all my heart. They've offered me peace and serenity at times when I've needed it most. But they can't . . . they can't love you," he uttered wistfully, as if he had only recently arrived at the unfortunate conclusion. "Truth is, they couldn't care less about you. Or me. Only people, Matthew, can love you. It took me a long time to figure that out. Too long. It was already too late. You don't want to make the same mistakes I made."

They were nearing the edge of a dangerous precipice. Glassman knew he should step only lightly. But he couldn't keep himself from stumbling forward. "Mistakes?" Glassman echoed Shuman. "We all make mistakes, I suppose. What kind of mistakes do you mean?"

"Acch." Shuman shrugged off the question. "There's really not much to tell. Let's just say I've done fine by the birds, but I could have handled my human relationships . . . better. But enough already!"

Now Shuman was the one who grew impatient. Glassman knew that the morning, magical though it was, had reached its conclusion. His companion had grown tired. He wasn't a spring chicken anymore, Shuman explained. He couldn't do too much in one day. It was time to return home for a shloof, a rest. So they walked slowly back to their cars.

"Think about what I said," Shuman instructed the Weekly Books Editor at the lot. He needed to go inside the visitor's center to use the restroom before leaving. "We'll see each other soon, boychik," he pronounced as he turned from Glassman on the asphalt. Glassman stood there for a moment, transfixed, as he watched Shuman lumber slowly up the concrete walkway to the wooden building.

"Ouch!" Glassman shouted, just before opening his car door. He futilely slapped the back of his neck. A mosquito had bitten him. The repellant, he gathered, had worn off.

Only people can love you, he softly uttered to himself in the car, tasting the words in his mouth.

Glassman returned home from the Everglades to find his front lawn freshly shorn, and Chuck preparing to do likewise across the street. Their division of the domestic labor was a curious one, one that didn't likely earn Glassman many points in the neighborhood. Mowing the lawn, after all, was something of a fraternal exercise in Pine Lakes. All one had to do was start up his Briggs and Stratton and, within minutes, the revving of various horsepower pitches could be heard throughout the neighborhood.

"Some deal you've got there," Chuck teased Glassman as he poured gasoline from a red plastic dispenser into his (professional grade) Snapper mower. "Rebecca works like a dog pushing that cheap mower of yours." Chuck, Glassman realized, probably thought that he didn't do a damn thing around the house except walk their pain in the ass dog. Rebecca was the one he saw mowing and edging the lawn, replacing the sprinkler heads, and pruning the palms. Chuck took it for granted, most likely, that she took care of the inside chores as well. That Glassman was the one who ran the wash, vacuumed, cleaned the dishes, and did most of the cooking was something that Chuck probably couldn't fathom. Glassman didn't believe it would necessarily up his masculine stock any in the neighborhood to disabuse Chuck of his misconceptions.

"Yeah, Chuck, I won't argue with you there. I did pretty good for myself. . . . Hey Chuck . . ." Glassman just remembered what he had been wanting to ask his neighbor. He made his way across the street. "So do you think we better go ahead and order hurricane shutters?"

"Naah, I don't think it's worth it. You're talking about five thousand dollars to do the whole house. Worse comes to worse, I'll help you put up some plywood."

"Are you sure? What about the last hurricane just before we moved in? Didn't that cause some damage around here?"

"Shit, you mean Jacques? You think a Euro-fag hurricane like that could do any damage?"

Glassman supposed not.

"Oh, by the way, I finally got around to tuning up that condenser for you," Chuck uttered as an afterthought just as Glassman turned to head inside. "It's in fine shape now. Those Rheem 12 Seers are quality."

"Oh, gee Chuck. You didn't have to do that. What do I owe you?"

"Nothing. It's no big deal." Glassman didn't quite know what to make of Chuck. It frustrated him.

Glassman entered the house quietly through the garage. Rebecca wasn't in the kitchen, where he expected he might find her reading the paper. Perhaps she was in the shower. He headed down the hall, entered the bedroom, and was surprised to find her at her desk, still in her tattered work clothes, crouched over an open book. She didn't seem to realize that he had entered the room, and something told Glassman not to startle her. He approached slowly and heard her muttering words that he thought for sure he recognized as Hebrew.

"Rebecca," he intoned softly. She flinched, then turned to face him with glassy eyes. He wasn't used to seeing her on the verge of tears. "Sorry, I didn't mean to frighten you, honey. Everything okay?"

"Yes," she answered, "I'm fine. You just startled me."

"Were you . . . praying?" Glassman asked his wife. The prospect worried him, as he had never seen Rebecca pray before, at least not outside a synagogue.

"I know it's silly, Matt. I just saw the prayer book on your shelf and started thumbing through it. I found a prayer for a couple who fear that they may be infertile. I didn't even know we had a prayer like that. . . . I don't know, I figured it couldn't hurt any. Like I said, I know it's silly . . ."

"No, sweetie, it's not silly." Rebecca, Glassman realized, yearned for a child more deeply than he had fathomed. Her calm and measured approach to their problem—like her approach to any and all such obstacles that arose before them—had obscured her pain. But the pain, he now realized, was nevertheless real, and profound.

He recognized the prayer book. It had been sent to him by the publisher, who hoped that the *Jewish Weekly Times* would run a review. But Glassman, as a general rule, didn't run reviews of straight liturgical texts. The audience was too narrow and, besides, he had his literary pretensions to honor. He hadn't so much as cracked the book's spine, and felt suddenly ashamed.

"Here, why don't we read the prayer together," he proposed. He placed his hand on Rebecca's shoulder and gazed down at the open page. They read the prayer in Hebrew first, laboriously, clashing over the pronunciation, then read the English translation more smoothly:

Our God and God of our ancestors . . . We say these words with sadness, for we feel the pain of our ancestors, Abraham and Sarah, who were childless many long years. We feel their yearning and know their despair. We know, too, that they were blessed with a child after all hope had disappeared. As You blessed them with a child, we pray that You will bless us with a child. Guide all who seek to help us. Enlighten and bless our physicians and nurses, our family and friends. Whatever lies ahead, sustain us with Your love and Your mercy. Strengthen the bonds between the two of us so that whatever may result from our endeavors and our prayers, our hearts will always be filled with love, one for the other. Amen.

They kissed and migrated to the kitchen to eat breakfast. Glassman prepared an omelette with cheddar cheese and mushrooms, a favorite of Rebecca's. He could feel her mood lighten as she ate her eggs and slowly slurped her tea.

"So how was the Everglades, anyway?" she asked.

"Interesting," Glassman answered. "It's amazing how many birds live out there." He regretted giving such an utterly inadequate account of his trip, but he was wary to disclose anything further. His wife already had a rough enough morning.

Besides, Glassman, somewhat inexplicably, found himself distracted just then by stirrings that seemed to originate in his belly, spreading southward.

"Rebecca, sweetie, what do you say we wash up and do our duty?"

"We don't have to," Rebecca shared the good news with her husband. "We just did it twelve hours ago."

"Who said anything about have to? You know it turns me on to see you *daven* in work boots." He was being facetious, of course, but did find himself curiously aroused. Maybe it was the caffeine. At any rate, the way things were going, he didn't see any reason to waste any erections, prayers or no prayers. "Let's do it right here in the family room," he continued. "On the floor."

"Here?" Rebecca asked incredulously. Glassman figured they needed to shake things up a bit. The most wild thing they had done to spice up their efforts was order one of those how-to videos advertised on a near weekly basis in the *New York Times Book Review*. Rebecca simply wouldn't allow pornography past her threshold. It was exploitative. Rebecca was no Dworkin, but she knew where to draw the line. The rub: watching pasty, plump, middle-aged people fornicating, while perhaps more socially acceptable than watching *Debbie Does Dallas* (available, Glassman knew, at any number of sleazy "adult" video stores never more than a mile or so from any given south Florida location), didn't prove to do much for either one of them. Thus, Glassman's family room floor proposal.

"We've got to do something Rebecca. We're still in our twenties. We're too young to be doing it like were fifty."

"Can I at least shower?" The bargain had been struck.

"Here do my back?" Rebecca asked him as she handed her husband a soaped sponge and turned her back to him in the shower. He scrubbed in careful, circular strokes, as if cleanliness was really the priority that Rebecca had in mind. As he reached her lower back, she arched her posterior. It affected him powerfully.

"Come on," he urged. "Let's rinse and get out of here." He would have liked to have commenced activities right there in the shower. Their present orientation would have done just fine. But he knew that she wouldn't permit it. Sex in the shower or bath, or while submerged in any body of water for that matter, was strictly off limits. It interfered with the requisite lubrication. Whether she had learned this from a book or from some unpleasant B.G. (Before Glassman) experience, she didn't share. And Glassman, in any case, preferred not to know.

"So impatient," Rebecca chided playfully, leading her husband out of the shower by the hand.

Brrrriiing. Brrrriiing. Brrrriiing. "Don't answer it," Rebecca turned her head to instruct her husband. "It's just a salesman. Keep going." But he was already distracted.

"What if it's somebody important?" Glassman asked. "The phone is right here anyway." Glassman, against his wife's wishes, squirmed free and answered the phone next to the bed in the middle of its fourth ring.

"Hello?"

"Oh, hello Matthew." By "Oh" he recognized his grandmother's voice. "I was just about to hang up. Are you in the middle of something. You sound winded."

"Oh, I do? Well . . . I . . . just ran in from mowing the lawn. Why were you going to hang up anyway? You weren't going to leave a message?" Rebecca could sense, by the tone of his voice, he realized, that it was Teenie, and knew that her husband would be on the phone for a while. She vigorously wrapped her robe around herself, a reproachful gesture, and strode out of the bedroom.

"Oh, I don't like leaving messages on those . . . machines," Teenie answered.

Glassman suddenly felt a wave of guilt sweep over him. He had managed not to think of his grandmother for almost the entire weekend. An accomplishment. He always felt more guilty about not seeing or calling Teenie on the weekend. During the week, after all, he had work. So did Rebecca. But they didn't work over the weekends. There was nothing really keeping them from Cypress Ponds, and his grandmother surely knew this.

"Well, I'm glad I heard the ringing from outside. I was going to call you when I finished as a matter of fact. What's up? Anything?"

"Nothing. Not a thing. I just thought I'd call to see what you've been doing."

What could Glassman say? *Well, I just spent the morning bird-watching with grandpa, I think. I was shtupping Rebecca when you called. How 'bout you?*

"Oh, nothing," he replied instead. "It's pretty slow here. We just have, you know, a zillion house chores to do this weekend. What did you do last night?"

"I had an okay night. I went to see that Kevin Costner movie with Ruth Spitz." Glassman could tell by the tone of Teenie's voice that she didn't like the movie much.

"You didn't like it?" he asked

"No, it wasn't so good. There was just so much foul language. What do they think they have to prove by cursing so much? Is it supposed to be cool or something?" The word "cool" coming from Teenie's mouth sounded funny to Glassman.

He decided to play devil's advocate. "Well, I'm sure they're just trying to be realistic."

"Oh come on Matthew. People do not curse like those people in that movie were cursing. Now I am *not* old-fashioned. You know that. But it was distracting. Ruth and I would have walked out if we hadn't already bought a popcorn to share."

"Well, I'd have to see it. . . . Anything else going on?"

This was the torturous part of his conversations with Teenie, the waning moments of the conversation when it was time for him to tell her when he would make it down to see her once again. Teenie rarely asked him to come down outright, but he knew she expected an E.T.A. But he'd hold out this time. He wasn't up to the visit this weekend. He just needed to relax. Visiting his grandmother could be many good things . . . interesting, eventful, even entertaining. But it was rarely relaxing. He managed somehow to say goodbye to Teenie, tell her that he loved her, which seemed to catch his grandmother by surprise, and return the phone to its cradle.

Someday You'll Talk about Me Like This

For the next week, Glassman remained in bed slightly longer than usual once he awoke in the morning. It wasn't that he was depressed. Rather, his morning at the fringe of the Everglades with Shuman had convinced him to seek something of a greater wakefulness before rising from the sheets and joining Rebecca in the kitchen. He lay in bed and listened. The first thing he heard was the grating din of Ropa that he usually tried so hard to ignore: the piercing whistles of the Florida East Coast trains lumbering up and down the coast, the perpetual low murmur of cars on the interstate just a mile or so from the house, the intermittent roar of jet engines taking off from the private airport nearby. . . .

By the end of the week, he began to hear other sounds, sounds that echoed not from above, or even from below, the clamorous noise of the city. They played on a different frequency entirely, one that Glassman had somehow learned to access. He heard the staccato trills of red-bellied woodpeckers, the cardinals' bright chirping, the rapid whoosh of mourning dove wings, the competitive cackling of blue jays, the rapid Morse-code twitterings of chimney swifts. Somehow, these few species, and one or two others that Glassman had taken the time to observe while walking Troy, managed to make a go of it in Glassman's neighborhood. Like the one-eyed red-shouldered hawk at Loxahatchee, they found a way to endure. They seemed to beckon for him as he lay there listening.

But they weren't capable of love, Glassman knew. What had Shuman told him? *They don't care a fig about you. Only people can love you.*

So when Sunday arrived, he stirred from bed somewhat more quickly, and readied himself for his Aunt Edith and Uncle Ben's brunch. Time to be with people, his people. Who knew what he might discover at Ben and Edith's? He invariably learned something interesting, often entertaining, about his family at every such function. Perhaps he could make certain inquiries this morning, elicit certain disclosures.

Leaning above the bathroom sink, he carefully scraped two day's worth of stubble off his face as Rebecca slept. She worked terribly hard, harder certainly than he worked, so he would let her sleep as long as possible. Who knew also how beaten down she was from their reproductive frustrations? He decided to be a more considerate husband, less obsessed with his own burdens. In the spirit of his little pact with himself, Glassman dragged and fed Troy, changed a sprinkler head that Rebecca must have shredded to bits with the lawn mower (on Troy's walk, he had seen torrents shoot from it in a geyser), started his coffee, and put an English muffin in the toaster for Rebecca to hold her over once she woke up.

Scanning the *New York Times* headlines in the kitchen over his second cup of coffee, he waited patiently for Rebecca to emerge, patiently insofar as he didn't pester her from the kitchen to get her tush in gear, but instead glanced repeatedly at the antiquated digital clock on the oven that announced each passing minute with a click followed by the whirring of gears. He braced himself to arrive a few minutes late to Ben and Edith's without feeling guilty about it.

But they couldn't arrive a half-hour late.

"Come on, honey. You need to get up now. I made you a muffin." Glassman, in the bedroom now, proceeded to pare moon slivers from his fingernails at the foot of the bed, gathering up the remnant shards in a small pile. It was a superfluous exercise; he had just trimmed his nails a few days ago.

"Who has brunch at nine in the morning?" Rebecca complained as she rolled off the mattress and stumbled to the sink, wiping the sleep from her eyes. "They haven't earned the *unch* if you ask me. Do they all have big plans this afternoon or something?" she added sarcastically.

The traffic was light on the interstate so they arrived at Cypress Ponds pretty much on time for the brunch. Glassman parked the Corolla in one of the guest spots at a fairly remote distance from Ben and Edith's ("We shouldn't take up the good spots just in case a few people are still coming," he explained to Rebecca, who rolled her eyes) and knocked on the door.

They exchanged kisses with Edith in the foyer. Glassman shook hands with Ben. As always, he noticed the bedraggled cluster of bearded, aged men on the small, dusky canvas over Ben's shoulder. The men, painted in coarse brush-strokes, stretched laboriously up from their chairs to argue over a tractate of Talmud at the center of a table.

"Nice shoes you got there Uncle Ben."

"These old things?" Ben replied jokingly as he strained to peer downward over his paunch. (In the months that Glassman had been living in the area, Ben had taken to tying his belts at least six inches higher on his torso.) Ben had owned a men's shoe store in Lacka-wanna, selling it just two years before the downtown mall was built, which would have "finished him" anyway, he liked to explain. Before turning over a fistful of keys to the new owners, Ben had apparently relieved them of the entire stock of Floresheims, Dexters, and Cole-Hahns in eight-and-a-half DD.

The most distinctive feature of his uncle's appearance were his dramatic eyeglasses that he had worn for as long as his great-nephew could remember. Glassman could clearly see them resting halfway down the bridge of Ben's nose as he summoned his most distant memory of him—Ben showing off one of his polished and pristine remote-control airplanes to his awestruck great-nephew in his dank, dimly lit Lackawanna garage. The dark tortoise-shell frames were bulky and of an odd shape, nearly rectangular, with thick lenses behind which Ben's eyes seemed to grow larger and larger through the years as his vision deteriorated hypermetropically at a rate, as far as Glassman knew, acceptably commensurate with a fairly long life expectancy. There was something decidedly feminine about the frames, or at the very least androgynous, but his uncle had evidently found a look that worked for him and he was sticking to it. An inordinate proportion of Ben's identity, it seemed to Glassman, hinged upon a paltry few ounces of plastic.

"So, when are you going to give that talk to one of our havurah groups?" Ben predictably cajoled his nephew. "Isn't it about time you let your uncle show you off?" Glassman's uncle had fashioned himself into something of a macher at his synagogue. He was president of the Brotherhood and had been pestering Glassman ever since he had moved down to give a talk on Jewish literature to one of Beth Sholom's many havurah groups. He was the Weekly Books Editor of the *Jewish Weekly Times,* after all. Glassman had been balking, but assured Ben that he'd select a date soon.

Glassman eventually migrated into the living room and surveyed the scene. It was a small get together. Good. Glassman spotted Teenie, Herbie and Ellen, Ruth Spitz, Mildred and Nat Siegel, and a couple he didn't know. They all balanced drinks in front of them with personalized blue cocktail napkins. *The Truckers.* Teenie, sitting at a far corner of the sectional with her Dewar's and water, casually waved and said "Hello kids" rather than get up. In this way, she flaunted the privilege of her familiarity with the young guests. Or else she was just fatigued. Or both.

"You look well," Glassman lied to Ruth Spitz after kissing her. Truth was, she looked worn and pallid. The skin on her face seemed drooped, as if the muscle scaffolding underneath had grown tired of holding up the flesh and had suddenly collapsed. His grandmother had predictably downplayed the severity of her friend's condition.

"So do you, you little marshmallow," she replied. "I look at you, I see . . . well . . . you look marvelous." Ruth, Glassman knew, barely managed to refrain from mentioning his resemblance to Abe.

While Rebecca exchanged pleasantries with Ruth, he shook Nat's hand and dutifully kissed Mildred's heavily perfumed cheek. A dark plum outline bordered her lightly glossed lips, to near grotesque effect in Glassman's estimation. "Hello gorgeous!" Mildred shrieked, and insistently planted her painted lips dangerously close to Glassman's mouth. Mildred was his grandmother's most garrulous friend, something of a drinker from what Glassman could tell, and tended to put him on the defensive. Rebecca finally made her way over and greeted the Siegels, as well. They had been trying intermittently to take him and Rebecca out to dinner ever since they had moved down to Florida, but something else always seemed to get in the way of the proposed dates. Glassman finally forced Rebecca to admit that she was just inventing excuses, putting the Siegels off because she couldn't tolerate Nat Siegel. "He's so touchy-feely," she had explained. "He gives me the creeps Matthew."

"Come on, you're being silly," he had insisted. "Nat and Mildred have known my grandma since they were in elementary school in Lackawanna." Glassman knew Rebecca probably had a point, but he wasn't entirely confident in Rebecca's judgment concerning the propriety of affectionate gestures. He had only seen her hug her mother once in all the years that he had known her. It was a stiff, laborious gesture. Her father she never hugged. Glassman wondered mutely whether the gentle, rolling farmland of the Susquehanna Valley, the blankets of green corn and golden wheat, had somehow smothered the filial warmth of her Jewish family.

Aunt Edith, their hostess, approached them with the couple Glassman didn't think he recognized. "Matthew, Rebecca, these are the Birnbaums. Ida and Leonard. Ida and Leonard, Dr. and Mr. Glassman."

"Very nice to meet you," Glassman said to the Birnbaums, and began to shake their hands. Rebecca did the same.

"The pleasure's all ours," Leonard answered as he gripped Glassman's hand. It may have been Glassman's imagination, but it seemed as if Birnbaum held his grip a bit longer than was normal, as if bent on inspecting him closely. Glassman averted his gaze just before Birnbaum released him.

"Matthew you might remember the Birnbaums. They lived . . . or live I should say . . . on Ash Street a few blocks over from where your grandma used to live on Sycamore." *Live on Ash Street?* Was he hearing correctly? He didn't think anyone still lived in Lackawanna.

Matthew was relieved when Mr. Birnbaum took the pressure off of him. "No Edith, he would never remember us. The last time we saw him . . . it must have been at Sara's Bat-mitzvah in Lackawanna."

Sara's Bat-mitzvah in Lackawanna.

Glassman remembered the somber occasion only vaguely. Grandpa Abe was long gone, destined already to be only the memory of a memory to his grandson. The indomitable Herschel—unable to outlive a third wife—had only just passed away a year before. Grandma Pearl had passed away only a few months ago. So it wasn't scheduled in Lackawanna for their benefit, or for Teenie's benefit either, but for Grandpa Morton's (Teenie could have traveled to Anchorage on a moped for the Bat-mitzvah). It was now Morton's turn to battle a cancer diagnosed long after it had metastasized. The whole family's attention, including Morton's, was too focused upon Pearl's illness to recognize his symptoms earlier. At any rate, he was too frail to make the trip out west. Rabbi Zilversmit, a redoubtable figure with a thick neck constricted by his tight collars, and a red, enraged face, had generously agreed to monitor the progress of Sara's Maftir and Haftorah via tape recordings that they mailed from the opposite coast.

Sara performed beautifully at the service, but it was clear to everyone that Morton was failing, both mentally and physically. On the walnut bima, he bent over the Torah painfully as if it were a lead weight he had strained to carry his whole life and had just set down. *Barchu es adonai ha . . . ham . . . eh . . . ham . . .* He could barely muddle his way through the aliya, the aliya he must have recited in front of his neighbors from behind the bima at Beth Israel dozens of times. Heck, Glassman could already recite the aliya by heart.

Rabbi Zilversmit, who purportedly once yanked Glassman's father off his wooden chair to the ground by his ear during Hebrew School, mercifully helped Morton finish: *Hamvurah.* Glassman remembered that the congregation joined in much louder than usual: *Baruch adonai hamvurach lai'olam va'ed.*

I saw him last . . . no I saw him last . . . no I saw him last. Glassman remembered the morbid debate with his sister just weeks later in Los Angeles, after his father received the telephone call.

He had seen Grandpa Morton last. His grandfather didn't want to come downstairs to say goodbye. He hugged his sister and him tightly, one after the other, from his bedroom. The coarse bristles of his salt and pepper beard scraped Glassman's cheek, and would have made him laugh if something didn't tell him to stifle his laughter. *You two go on now with mommie and daddy.* Sara lingered behind, then bounded ahead of him down the staircase steps of creaky wood and worn carpet, forcing him to hug the weak railing. He turned back up the steps. *There was one more thing to say.* He walked slowly down the hall to the bedroom, but stopped in his tracks before reaching the light emanating from the open door. *Muffled sobbing.* He should have been in the car already. He shouldn't have been listening to his grandfather behind the bedroom door *(that's called* ease-dropping *Sara says).* It wasn't someplace for him to be. He turned slowly, quietly on his heels, and crept back down the steps. But only after peeking into the room with one eye, seeing Grandpa Morty crouched over the edge of the bed, his face hidden underneath hands.

Glassman's parents barely spoke during the entire long drive to Newark Airport. Sara and he remained quiet, as well. Somehow they knew not to bicker. His mother, Glassman noticed from the back seat, rested her hand on top of his father's thigh, and kept it there for a long time. Her father had already disappeared, and she had survived. Now her husband's father was leaving, and she would help her husband survive. Glassman studied his father's reflection in the rear view mirror. His father didn't even once take his eyes off the road to glance at Glassman's mother, or to fiddle with the radio or heat. He just kept his eyes fixed on the monotonous highway that stretched out before them. And drove. Throughout the trip to New Jersey, Glassman watched the rear view mirror for a tear, or the sign of a tear. But Stanley Glassman refused to cry.

"How's your sister doing, Matthew?" Mrs. Birnbaum inquired.

"Fine. Just fine," Glassman answered, returning from his unpleasant reverie.

"And your folks? I remember your mother when she was a baby. She was an adorable baby, with great big chubby cheeks." Mrs. Birnbaum filled her lightly rouged cheeks with air to illustrate her point. Glassman hadn't spoken to his parents in a few weeks, which was a long time for them to go without at least a short telephone conversation. Discussions with his parents, however, especially with his mother, had grown more difficult since he had moved to Florida— more stressful than he felt (however uninformed and unfair the judgment) that conversations between parents and their children should be. Beneath their innocuous sentences and phrases—*how's work? are you enjoying the weather? have you seen much of your grandmother?*— lay a subtext of . . . what? . . . worry? disappointment? betrayal? None of these things, it occurred to Glassman. Just a nebulous and dispiriting distance, accented by the salty static of the long-distance line. It was somehow easier simply not to talk. His parents, perhaps, felt the same way. In any case, he assured Mrs. Birnbaum that his folks were doing quite well also. Pathologically well, Glassman thought. It was unfair.

Uncle Herbie and Aunt Ellen approached and he and Rebecca exchanged kisses with them. In his day, Glassman's Uncle Herb was a biomedical researcher, who helped develop a drug, so family lore went, that alleviated the itching and burning of several dermatological maladies. It was a mysterious ingredient still purportedly included in all the major anti-itch creams. Herbie always insisted on kissing his grand-nephew on the cheek and Glassman deferred to his wishes. *Your great-grandfather Herschel kissed Morty and me on the lips until the day that he died, may he rest in peace,* Herbie had once explained, and repeated for emphasis: *On the lips!*

Out of consideration to his Glassman blood, Teenie and Edith began inviting his Uncle Herbie and Aunt Ellen to all of their functions (brunches, Rosh Hashanna dinner, Break-Fast on Yom Kippur, etc.) even though they didn't usually make the cut before Glassman had arrived on the scene. It wasn't that Teenie and Edith didn't like Ellen. They still traveled in the same Lackawanna-south circles, were in the same Thursday card game, and even went to the Flea with her from time to time. Ellen was one of the "girls." But Teenie and Edith (and several of the other "girls") begrudged Ellen's baking prowess. Ellen didn't keep her recipes a secret. Not exactly. All of the recipes in Jewish Lackawanna (at least the good ones) were shared among the group as a matter of unwritten policy. All the Jewish wives in Lackawanna had everyone else's recipe for mandel bread, rugelach, honey cake, tzimmes, brisket, varnitshkes, lokshen kugel, spatzle, kreplah, macaroons, chocolate roll, and poppy-seed hamantaschen, which they sloppily transcribed on index cards around the pool at Willow Woods. But Ellen's kuchin had the audacity of somehow tasting better than anyone else's. Was it the coconut she procured? The chocolate? The nuts? It couldn't be. Teenie had tried all the possible combinations.

I just know that she must be using lard! Teenie had confided to Glassman recently in conspiratorial tones—after he had mischievously brought up the subject—and repeated the malicious accusation: *LARD!*

"What do you have for me, Herbie?" Glassman offered his uncle his usual greeting after their kiss.

"Well," the diminutive Herbie began, "not much kiddo. Let's see . . ." Herb, deep in concentration, lowered his head and scratched his bald pate lightly as if to stimulate his synapses. "Oh, I have one!" he suddenly remembered. "A woman at the nursing home is . . . well, let's just say she's very large. Beyond zaftik. One morning she walks up to all the men sitting around playing checkers, holds out her fist and says, 'I'll sleep with anyone who can guess what I have in my hand.' Now, as you can imagine, none of the men know what to say . . . they don't want to guess the correct answer. One of the men, a mentsh, decides to take a guess to keep from hurting the poor woman's feelings. 'It's an elephant,' he safely guesses, and the woman replies, 'CLOSE ENOUGH!'"

"HAAA!" Glassman shouted, howling with laughter. Rebecca had to shush him he was laughing so loudly. Glassman suddenly experienced a flash of insight. No matter how much he viewed these family gatherings as cumbrous obligations, even chores, beforehand, he invariably had a wonderful time once the festivities were underway.

His relatives were interesting. They had *lived*. They had stories. They had jokes. What's more, they knew how to have a good time, period. He noticed the photograph resting on a glass table next to a pink recliner. Several of his Lackawanna relatives and their friends, many of them now dead, stood in a wavering drunken line for the picture, martini glasses in the air. They seemed to challenge Glassman from their graves:

Top this!

Most of them lived short lives, but managed nevertheless to carve out a great measure of joy in Lackawanna: Fourth of July clambakes at Willow Woods; summer weekends at cottages on Lake Lenape twenty minutes away in the Poconos; Huckleberry picking around the Lackawanna Reservoir (*Huckleberrisa! Huckleberrisa!* the Spanish Huckleberry woman called temptingly, sensually, as she strolled up and down Lackawanna's hilly cobblestone, brick, and macadam streets, an enormous straw basket of berries balanced atop her head); lovers' strolls at Mulberry Park along the snow-lined trail through the zoo, the creaky carnival rides, and past one of Lackawanna's many abandoned coal mines now within the park's border, three rusty coal cars parked just outside the gated mine entrance; "parking" on the bluff overlooking downtown, dotted with ocher streetlights; swimming in the frigid water in the abandoned limestone quarry just above the rusty skeletons of abandoned cars and far below the steel bridge from which the Erie-Lackawanna trains roared every other hour, making the black water tremble; Saturday morning shul; veal scallopini at Mario's; wafer-thin pizza coated with a delectable sheen of oil at Angelo's, at least when Angelo didn't have his Mafia friends over and agreed to make you a pie. If Glassman, if they all, could only return to Lackawanna . . .

You're romanticizing it! Teenie would have argued. *It wasn't that nice. The winters were brutal. The spring was only a week long and the summers were as humid as Florida. Our mosquitoes were bigger and nastier. The city buildings were black with soot. The whole downtown was dying as early as the forties after the anthracite was all gone. And once they built the interstate and traffic from Binghampton and Philadelphia started bypassing downtown altogether . . . forget about it. Kaput! That horrendous junk yard that the Billoti kids still own, those chazzers, stretches for five miles alongside the 81 now. The burning slag heap made the whole city smell like rotten eggs when the wind blew in the right direction. It's an ugly place. You should go back and see for yourself. Blackawanna. Your parents were smart to get out when they could. Florida is a hundred times more beautiful. Why do you think we all live here?*

She would have a point, Glassman conceded. After all, if Lackawanna was so nice, why did Abe leave?

But in his mind he also envisioned his other grandfather, Morty—who lived in Lackawanna his whole short life and never saw Florida—coughing up blood, wrecked by the radiation and chemotherapy, telling Glassman's father from his narrow hospital bed, just days before his death, "Life . . . Stanley . . . life is . . . sweet. It can be sweeter than honey. Remember." A gift to his son from his deathbed.

"So, what golf tournament's on?" Glassman asked his Uncle Ben, who had finished serving him his Bloody Mary and Rebecca's virgin version (who knew when she might conceive?), and was standing in front of the television watching.

"I'm not sure. But Arnold Palmer's doing pretty good. He's just two shots down."

"Arnold Palmer," Teenie repeated the name venomously from her position on the sectional, her left eyebrow raised high above her right one. "You know he's an anti-Semite don't you, Ben? Years ago at one of the tournaments down here . . . the Honda Classic or the Doral . . . I don't remember which one . . . he was asked *not to return* because of something he said."

Not to return. Could anyone punch a phrase like Teenie?

"Oy gevalt, don't *tell* me Teenie," Ida Birnbaum pleaded. "He always seemed so nice on the Johnny Carson show. Here he's a shtunk and I've been rooting for him all these years?"

"What did Palmer say grandma?" Glassman was curious. Did she know what she was talking about? Did she have evidence? His relatives could be pretty quick to accuse people of having it in for the Jews.

"Oh, that we're tight, or loud, or vulgar, or have ugly noses. What else would he say?"

"Well, as far as I'm concerned," his Aunt Edith chimed in, "he's still better than that . . . that Corey Pavin. I'll take mild anti-Semites over self-haters any day. You know, if you're going to become a born-again, that's your business. But don't go on interviews and talk about how wonderful Jesus Christ is and how much better Christianity is than Judaism. It's improper. Past nit! His parents must be mortified. *Ab-so-lute-ly* mortified."

Glassman never knew that Corey Pavin was Jewish to begin with, just as he had never guessed that Matt Lauer from the *Today* show was Jewish, which, as far as his Aunt Edith was concerned, was exactly the point. *It's like he's ashamed of his heritage!* Edith had vented to Glassman and Teenie at the Bagel Boy a few months ago when she was busy "outing" Jewish television personalities. Teenie, to her credit Glassman thought, had replied, *Honestly Edie, what's he supposed to do, wrap tefillin on the air?*

"It's that Tiger Woods I don't like," Ben added. "Don't get me wrong. I think it's great that he won the Masters. The kid's a hundred pounds soaking wet and he can drive the ball to the moon. But it's obscene the millions of dollars he's making in endorsements. And only because he's black. Talk about past nit."

"Oh Ben," Herbie countered, "the blacks have been kicked in the teeth enough. If they're going to pay him to be black for a change, let him rake it in, I say."

"Kicked in teeth," Mildred mockingly reiterated Herbie's comment. "Have they had a Holocaust? I don't think so. The blacks don't know from kicked in the teeth as far as I'm concerned. I'm sorry Herbie, but I'm just sick and tired of hearing about how racist America is and how hard it is for the poor blacks. It might not be a nice thing to say, but maybe if they weren't so lazy, they'd be doing better for themselves. You should just see, Herbie, how slow those girls are behind the deli counter at the Winn-Dixie. You can barely even get their attention."

Glassman rolled his eyes. Perhaps he should mention the plight of the Palestinians and the Siegels could get all their hate-mongering over with before the bagels were served.

"Well," Ruth added from her seat on the sectional next to Teenie, "he does seem like a very nice young man. I've seen him being interviewed and he's very polite."

"Yes, yes you're right Ruthie," Ida Birnbaum seconded her friend's opinion. "And when he hugged his father after the Masters . . . well I almost broke down and cried myself."

"Me too," Ellen added a fourth voice to the pro-Woods lobby.

"Me three," said Mildred Siegel as she devoured a candied pecan. "Ruthie is this drink yours or mine?"

"Could be," Ruth replied. Glassman stifled a chuckle.

"Well, which is it? *Yours* or *mine*?" Mildred asked impatiently. Glassman had noticed that the older folks he fraternized with rarely gave one another a break when it came to momentary disorientation. Possibly afraid of succumbing to senility themselves, they were constantly in attack mode against any and all of its incarnations.

"Oh, no, he's not so polite. I think he has a big head," Edith countered the pro-Woods sentiment in her midst. "And his father . . . as

133

long as we're talking about his father, did you all know that his father left his first wife and child, and here he's cashing in on his reputation for being such a wonderful father and family man. He's laughing at us all the way to the bank. *Feh!*"

Glassman glanced toward Teenie to register her reaction to Edith's comment, but his grandmother remained unmoved. Perhaps she had grown inured to such remarks regarding wayward husbands, had managed in the last twenty years to achieve a certain critical distance from the general issue of family abandonment. Then again, perhaps there was something to be made of Teenie's sudden and uncharacteristic silence, as well.

Apparently, his grandmother had yet to develop her take on Woods. The conversation went back and forth between the Birnbaums, the Truckers, the Siegels, the Glassmans, and Ruth Spitz for several more minutes at a dizzying rate. Glassman had difficulty keeping all the arguments straight.

Palmer an anti-Semite? Pavin a born-again Christian? And a Jew before that? This was all news to Glassman. He should have known better than to expect a conversation about a golf tournament to have anything to do with the golf itself, the way the greens were playing, the tightness of the fairways, or the aesthetic beauty of the trees, flowers, and shrubs on the course. He still didn't even know the name of the tournament they were watching. What he knew instead? Palmer, Pavin, and probably Tiger Woods, wouldn't be welcome at any of the Truckers' or Fishbeins' Sunday brunches.

Bad for the Jews.

"Hey, have you heard the one, Matthew, about the old Jewish man at the goyishe country club?" Leonard Birnbaum asked. All the golf talk must have sparked Birnbaum's memory. Glassman told him that he probably hadn't heard the joke.

"Lenny's a wonderful golfer," Edith remarked, apropos of the general topic of conversation.

"Well, it's amazing what a hole in your pocket does for your lie, eh Lenny?" Ben needled his old friend.

Glassman wondered whether Mr. Birnbaum was as good a golfer as Abe had been in his prime, before he abruptly gave up the sport entirely, traded in his weekend foursomes for the forest and his birds. As far as Glassman knew, his grandfather was the only member of Willow Woods to hit a hole-in-one twice at the same hole (the tenth, its tee situated propitiously just below the luncheon deck). Glassman's mother had given him one of Abe's three silver trophy-cups engraved with the lines, ABRAHAM FISHBEIN, GOLF CHAMPION, WILLOW WOODS COUNTRY CLUB, 1952.

The cup rested on the mantel in Glassman's family room and desperately needed to be polished. Or, as Becky insisted in her Dutch country dialect, "needs polished."

"So this old kocker," Birnbaum began his joke, "walks right up to the goyishe golf pro and challenges him to a game of golf for a hundred clams. The pro doesn't want to take advantage of the ferkrimpter man—"

"What does ferkrimpter mean?" Glassman asked.

"Crooked. Bent over," Birnbaum explained.

"So, anyway, the pro tells him he doesn't want to take away his money, but the old man insists. 'Don't worry about me boychik. I still have my stroke. I just have a little trouble getting out of the traps.' So the strapping young pro asks himself, why not take some of the Jew's money off his hands? and accepts the challenge. Through seventeen holes the old man amazes the pro by how well he plays. His short game . . . his long game. Both beautiful. As the old man tees up on the par-three eighteenth, he's one stroke up, but then hits the ball right into one of the traps next to the green. The pro figures he has a good shot of winning the match, given the old man's difficulties hitting out of the sand. But, as he watches from the green, the old kocker hits the ball right out of the trap and into the hole. 'I thought you said you had trouble getting out of the traps!' the pro asks the old man furiously. 'I do,' he answers feebly, lifting his outstretched hand toward the angry pro. 'Can you give me a hand?'"

Finally, Edith set down a platter brimming over with various fishes, a basket of bagels and bialys, and a noodle kugel, and informed her guests that it was time to eat. She didn't have to tell Glassman twice. A glance at the fish platter and he began salivating like a Pavlovian dog. Glassman and Rebecca took the two seats at the card-table extension to the dining room table. By the time they were forty, Glassman figured, they'd graduate from the kiddie table, but would anyone present, besides themselves, be alive? While he waited for the platter to get around to him, he complimented Edith on the large white table cloth, with its decorative center design and border stitched in blue and yellow thread. It covered both tables.

"Thank you, Matthew. You're a dear. I made this years ago," Edith informed him.

"We *all* used to make table cloths like that," Teenie added, as if her pride had just been mildly threatened. "I'll make you one, Rebecca, if you'd like."

"Isn't it difficult?" Rebecca asked.

"Nah," Edith answered for Teenie. "I want to make one for Melanie. We'll make them together Teenie," she said excitedly. Teenie nodded.

"Well sure," Rebecca said. "We'd love one, grandma, if you don't mind going through the trouble."

"What trouble?"

"Would you take a look at this beautiful platter," Leonard Birnbaum beat the rest of the guests to the punch.

"It's magnificent," Teenie added, an uncharacteristic hyperbole from her quarter.

"Well you know where I got it from?" Edith posed the question to her guests. "I wasn't crazy about Irving's last time so I went to the Lox Maven on State Road 7. It was twenty dollars cheaper than Irving's and would you look at this platter? Look at what you get."

Glassman was looking. The nova on one end of the platter was sliced thin and sweating fine drops of oil. Thin striations of fat would add silk to its taste. Kippered salmon, its flesh pale and looking moist (it was prone to drying out), was stacked at a corner.

Paprika-dusted sable quivered at the other corner of the platter. Glassman could never quite warm up to its raw texture. At the center of the platter rested a large smoked whitefish with coppery scales. A brittle tail hung over the platter onto the table cloth. Its moist meat was already nudged just off its bones and, in place of its swim bladder, heart, and liver, whitefish salad filled its cavity. Glassman tried not to look impatient as Mildred Siegel, sitting beside him, took her time scooping glossy, grayish nonfat cream cheese off the platter and onto her plate. He nibbled at the Corn Flake–encrusted kugel on his plate. It was sweet and tasty (Edith, Glassman had learned, favored the variation of the Lackawanna kugel recipe that used apricot preserves), but not the main attraction.

"Lox Maven," Edith insisted, "is the only place that includes the whitefish salad along with the whitefish. And it's very tasty. They don't dilute it with too much mayonnaise, egg, or celery."

"That's how they get you," Teenie warned the table.

"Well, I went to the Lox Maven last year," Mildred announced, pursing her lips as if she were biting into a lemon, "but I wouldn't buy a thing. It looked . . . dirty."

"Well what did you expect out of a kosher market?" her husband Nat chided brightly. "They're *always* the filthiest."

"Nat!" Ida Birnbaum admonished her old Lackawanna friend, whether for his backhanded dig at Edith or his denigration of kosher markets Glassman couldn't discern. He was surprised that the Siegels would carry on so rudely. Granted, from Glassman's limited shopping experience, Nat may have been right about kosher markets. But still . . .

"For your information," Teenie finally weighed in, "the Lox Maven is not dirty, Mildred. I was just there last week and it was perfectly clean. I don't know *what* the two of you are talking about." Here Teenie waved her butter knife toward both Siegels accusingly. Glassman was glad that his grandmother stood up for Edith, who seemed unfazed by the discussion anyway.

The conversation slowed down a bit as everyone consumed their bagels and fish. There was an amicable debate over which of five local bagel shops boasted the tastiest bagels. All seemed to agree that personal taste played a large role. Bready or doughy, slightly crisp or soft, gigantic or small enough to fit in the bagel guillotine.

Amid intermittent moans of delight, Edith apologized and asked if anyone wanted eggs. Everyone, predictably, declined. Glassman wondered whether she even had any eggs to begin with, or just cartons of egg whites infused with yellow colorant.

On his second bagel, stuffed with nova and whitefish, and shmeered with whitefish salad for good measure, Glassman listened intently as Teenie explained to Edith and Mildred (for the, what, twentieth time?) the distinction between second cousins and first cousins once removed. "Now listen Edith. Just listen. When two first cousins have children, their children are second cousins to one another. Now a *child* of a first cousin is the first cousin once removed from the other first cousin. Take me and Solly—"

"I thought it was the other way around," Mildred interjected.

"Yeah, I think I did too," said Ida Birnbaum.

"Nope," Teenie set them both straight, poking out the side of a cheek with the tip of her tongue for good measure. "I'm positive."

"That's always stumped me," Rebecca added to the conversation. "Thanks Grandma Teenie."

Glassman suddenly picked up the thread of a separate conversation at the other end of the table:

"So Lenny and I are at the slot machines at the casino, and after just three or four quarters, we win the jackpot. Quarters are shpritzing out of this machine, bells and whistles are going off all over the place, and we're more than a little bit nervous, let me tell you, cause this is Biloxi, Mississipi. It's, you know, the sticks. Who knows anything about these people?"

"So what happened?" Glassman asked from the other end of the table, only mildly concerned for the Birnbaums given Ida's smile and jocular tone.

"So this old lady comes right up to us after we collect all the money. We piled it in tin buckets once some man working there brought them over, but before he came over we were stuffing the

money into our pockets, in our shoes, in my bra . . . it was unbeliev-
able. So this little old lady in a purple leisure suit rests her hand on
my arm and says in a southern accent, 'You know, shugga', I was
playing that very same machine for an hour befo' you started playing. The good Lord must've known that you needed the money
more than I did.'

"'Yes, Jesus loves us,' is what I was about to say. I would have
been the queen of the casino if I would have just said that. Jesus loves
us. They would have carried me through the casino on their shoulders! There would have been an Ida Birnbaum day in Biloxi!"

What the heck the Birnbaums were doing in Mississippi Glassman had no idea. But the story was amusing. Everyone laughed.
Glassman's belly ached, whether from laughing or eating too much
fish or some combination of the two, he didn't know. Individually,
his relatives were, well, old. But get them in a group, put even just
two of them together, and the years dissolved like the Equal in their
decaf. A little repartee and they were in the spring of their youth.

The conversation quieted down. No one seemed to have a joke
or story to top Ida Birnbaum's.

Amid groans inspired by distended stomachs, everyone slowly
migrated toward the more comfortable seating in the living room,
where they would recline and digest their food. Glassman followed
his aunt to the kitchen and offered to help with the dishes. Edith
told him not to be silly, she could handle it, but if he wanted to
make himself useful, he could carry the garbage bag out to the
dumpster. It contained all that remained of the whitefish—its coppery skin and skeleton, and the few tattered morsels of flesh that
stubbornly clung to the frame. It would be best to dispose of it immediately, Edith explained, lest it stink up the entire apartment.
Glassman promptly lifted the liner from the plastic can, knotted it
shut, and headed toward the door.

"Wait up," he heard Leonard Birnbaum command from behind,
just as his hand grasped the cool, steel doorknob. "I'll join you. I
need to walk off this meal anyway." Birnbaum gingerly patted his
modest belly with the fingertips of both hands.

"Sure," Glassman answered agreeably. The short walk to the dumpster would hardly offer Birnbaum any exercise to speak of, but he figured he simply wished to take a break from the women for a while.

"You know . . . you look just like him," Birnbaum proclaimed matter-of-factly just after Glassman heard the front door click shut behind them. At the instant of registering Birnbaum's comment, he could feel the hair on the back of his neck stand straight up. *Amazing,* he mused. Amazing, the effect of a few innocuous little words, strung together in a sentence.

"Like who?" he inquired casually without turning around. The sun, higher now in the sky, made his eyeballs ache. Of course, he knew the answer to his question but, for some reason, wanted to hear Birnbaum—wanted to hear anyone—say his grandfather's name.

"Like your grandfather. Abe. I'm sure you must know. You're the spitting image. A dead ringer. It really takes me back, I tell you." Birnbaum emitted a rueful sigh, as if he wished mightily that he could, indeed, unravel his long yarn of years and walk the thread of his twentieth, thirtieth, fortieth year.

"What do you remember about my grandfather?" Glassman asked as he swung the white trash bag over the lip of the green dumpster; it landed with a metallic thud. "I don't really remember much about him you know. I was only five or so when he . . ." Glassman groped for the proper word . . . "disappeared."

"Oh boy. That's a tough one kiddo. I remember quite a bit about him. Where should I begin? He was a fabulous golfer, I'll tell you that. Always had soft hands. He had kind of a softness about him in a lot of ways actually. He was a quiet guy. And something of a luftmentsh too. His head always seemed to be in the clouds. He—Oh!" Birnbaum interrupted his own train of thought. "I have a story for you Matthew. Let's walk a bit further. No need to head back just yet."

No need at all, Glassman agreed. His scalp tingled with anticipation, but he tried not to betray his fevered state, as if Birnbaum was a talking horse he might carelessly spook. Upon Glassman's suggestion, they started around the short block that bordered one of the

140

Cypress Ponds golf courses. Glassman heard the thwack of an iron making sweet contact with a ball in the fairway, the plaintive coo of a mourning dove; he smelled the near nauseating ripe greenness of freshly cut grass clippings and felt the zig-zag trickle of a sweat tear down his back. All his senses seemed to be operating at high alert.

"We were at Penn State," Birnbaum began. "I'm a year older than Abe so was already a brother at the fraternity when your grandfather decided to pledge." *I'm a year older.* That Birnbaum used the present tense wasn't lost upon Glassman. "All the Jewish boys from Lackawanna at the time joined one of two fraternities, and ours was the best one, so it really wasn't much of a choice.

"We really put those greenies through the paces. Did some pretty despicable things when you think about it. Can't say I'm terribly proud of it in retrospect, but we were young back then and boys will be boys you know."

"Yeah, sure, I know what goes on at fraternities . . . the hazing." Glassman sought to assure Birnbaum that he needn't be so defensive. He wished that his elder would cut to the chase already.

"Yes, well, anyway, Penn State is pretty much in the middle of nowhere, even more so fifty years ago before there was the interstate or much of a population out there in the middle of all those woods. Just a few farm towns, not even any light industry to speak of. Well, one of those podunk towns out there, just a half-hour or so away from campus, Yeagertown . . . what do you know, I can even remember the name . . . well, they had a huge pigeon-shooting festival every year. Probably still have it for all I know. It was a pretty backwards place."

"Pigeon-shooting festival?" Glassman asked. His ears pricked up at the mention of pigeons.

"Yeah, to mark the beginning of the hunting season, or some such malarkey as that. You know, hunting's a pretty big deal in Pennsylvania." Birnbaum paused for a moment on the sidewalk, apparently both to rest and to emphasize his last point. "Okay, off we go," he instructed. Glassman took care to slow his pace. "Anyway, they'd cram thousands and thousands of those pigeons into steel cages. All the men would squat behind some hay stacks with their rifles and shoot the birds down as they opened the cages one by one, fifty birds or so at a time I suppose. The women and children would cheer like it was a Penn State football game. There was music and dancing . . . a pig roast. It was a real big deal for them. Like the Fourth of July clambake at Willow Woods. You remember that right? I remember your folks used to take you when you all visited."

"Yeah, of course I remember, but what does this have to do with Grandpa Abe?" Glassman was beginning to grow impatient.

"Hold onto your horses. I'm getting to it. You see, not all of the pigeons . . . in fact, not even most of them . . . were killed so cleanly. Often they were just winged or something and lay there on the ground trembling or thrashing about. A pretty grisly sight." Birnbaum shivered as if from the cold, which was an odd gesture given the eighty degree heat. "But it didn't seem to bother the townspeople too much. Funny what you can get used to I guess. Anyway, the children, those too young to do the shooting, were assigned to do the clean up work. After each round of shots, they'd scamper out onto the crisp yellow field, collect the fallen birds and wring the necks of all the pigeons that weren't quite dead yet. They seemed to like it too. It was a real treat for them. An initiation of sorts, I suppose."

"Sounds pretty disgusting to me," Glassman couldn't help but vent his disapproval.

"Well, to us too, but I can't say we were any better. Disgusting was the point. You see, this is where your grandpa comes in. We used to make our pledges run out there with the little boys and do that dirty work also."

Birnbaum must have caught the incredulous expression that Glassman couldn't keep from his face.

"Oh, I know it was a horrible thing to do. I'm not defending it. You wanted to hear a story about Abe? I'm telling you one." Birnbaum's nostrils flared and reddened at the edges. He seemed annoyed.

"No, go on, Mr. Birnbaum. I'm listening. It just seems a little bit odd that they'd let your fraternity . . . you know . . . do that."

"Oh, to tell you the truth, I think the town got a kick out of it. To see the big shot university boys, Jewboys at that, crouching over the pigeon carcasses like scared little children. That's why we made the Froshes do it too. To shame them. Even frighten them. It was the last thing a Jewish kid from Lackawanna could see himself doing. Yeah, it was a horrible thing to make them do. The whole event was barbaric. Like I said, I'm not proud of it."

"So . . . what? . . . grandpa Abe did this too. Is that what you wanted to tell me?" Suddenly, Glassman felt anger well up in his belly. So, his grandfather was terrorized by his philistine fraternity. By Birnbaum. Is this what the old man wanted to share with him?

"No, no, just listen, will you?" Birnbaum sternly replied, his own tone shifting dramatically.

"Abe was outraged," Birnbaum continued. "We never told the pledges where we were taking them. It was a surprise. But nothing like the surprise that your grandpa had in store for us, or for Yeager-town for that matter. Once he figured out what was what, he walked over to the cages. He didn't run. I can still remember it like it was yesterday. It was a cool fall day. He was wearing a green wool toggle coat and a gray wool cap. He had a goatee in those days too. Anyway, he just walked over there silently, casually, as if he just wanted to check on something. Then, without any warning, but again, not hurriedly, just deliberately, he began releasing the metal catch on all the cages. He just walked down the line releasing the birds. The men hadn't even loaded their rifles yet. And they couldn't really shoot anyway. It wasn't safe. People were milling about all over the place.

"'*That fuckin' kike!*' I can still remember one of those rednecks shout. Your grandpa caught everyone completely by surprise!" Birn-baum was relishing the story. Increasingly so as he told it, as the de-tails of the event blossomed once again in his mind. Glassman could tell by the faraway smile on his face that grew broader with each sentence.

"It was an amazing sight, I'll tell you. Thousands of pigeons in the sky." Birnbaum flicked the back of a hand high above his head to emphasize the point. "I can still remember the way it looked as they streamed from the cages in an enormous gray funnel cloud. And the sound . . . the *sound*. That whooshing. It was deafening. I think the whole town was in awe at the spectacle, actually. They weren't used to seeing so many birds in the sky all at once. Eventually, the pigeons separated into three or four enormous flocks. It was like there were three or four rapidly moving rain clouds above head flexing into different shapes and patterns. They actually darkened the sky and cast shadows on the ground. They circled higher and higher, way out of range of gunshot. There were a couple stray firings that made me jump in my boots. I remember that vividly. And then the flocks suddenly vanished."

"Wow," Glassman replied.

"Yeah, it was pretty amazing. You have to appreciate the kind of guts it took to do something like that. I mean, the whole town was carrying rifles, after all."

"It's amazing he wasn't shot right then and there."

"I know. But it was such an awesome spectacle that I think most of the people had to remind themselves to be outraged. One of the sheriffs there, who had planned on taking part in the pigeon shoot, took Abe into custody. Your grandpa didn't resist. I remember that. He raised his hands high in the sky just after he unlatched the last cage. Quite a vision. He was invisible for several moments as the birds whooshed all about him; thousands of beating wings surrounded him. Then we saw him, both his arms outstretched in the sky, his fingers splayed, his neck tilted back, as if reaching toward the birds flapping away above his head. It was kind of unclear, actually, whether he was giving himself up or reveling in the spectacle he created."

"So, what happened after that?" Glassman asked. The sweat on his forehead had grown cold with excitement.

"Well, they were planning on keeping him overnight at the Lewistown jail. But we called the Penn State provost and explained what had happened . . . the only sensible thing we did all day. He drove right over that afternoon. Four of us brothers waited at the station while Abe was in the cell. We were real worried about him.

Who knew what they were going to do to him back there in the cell in that hick town? He pretty much ruined the whole festival. They used to feed the dead birds to the hogs, so I'm sure they weren't thrilled to lose all that feed. And I think the shooters had to pay an entrance fee, so they all had to be reimbursed. Someone lost a good chunk of change.

"Anyway, Provost Schmidt . . . he was a real cool customer, dapper with a freshly pressed suit and a leather briefcase out there in the middle of the sticks, an operator, you could just tell . . . he must have known what buttons to push, because he managed to get Abe out of there within an hour or so. I think he had him pay some fine or something and that was that. He gave us a real talking to, back at campus. The fraternity was put on probation for the semester. Of course, we never took part of the Yeagertown pigeon-shooting festival ever again."

"So what happened to grandpa when you all got back?" Glassman asked. "Did Abe wind up joining the fraternity?"

"That's an interesting story in and of itself," Birnbaum added excitedly, as if Glassman had jarred his memory. "We wanted *him*, of course. It took brass balls to do what he did. But he didn't want anything to do with us, as I guess you can imagine. I still remember exactly what he said to us. Twenty or thirty of us, nearly the whole house, went to his dormitory room that night to check in on him and grant him his status as full brother. But he didn't even let any of us in the room. He just stood there in the doorway and calmly told Sid Shifmann 'I don't care to fraternize with you.' He didn't curse or anything like that. In fact, I can't remember him ever cursing as long as I knew him—"

"Yes, I've heard that about him."

"'I don't care to fraternize with you,'" Birnbaum intoned once again. "He just shut the door quietly and that was that. We didn't even try knocking. I think we pretty much knew that it was no use pressing him. Your grandpa wasn't exactly ambiguous about his intentions. And he wasn't really the fraternity type anyway, to tell you the truth. He'd much rather be off by himself hiking somewhere in the woods . . . like . . . well, I'm sure you know enough about him to know that, right?"

"Yes. Right," Glassman answered softly, puzzled. What was Birnbaum about to say? *Like* . . . what? He considered posing the question, but he had a separate, more pressing inquiry that he wished to make. There wasn't much time. They were nearly back at the apartment, just a few yards from the parking lot entrance. "I know grandpa was quiet. But do you think he was ill?" he asked his elderly companion. "You know, mentally? Manic depressive or bipolar or something?"

Birnbaum contemplated the question for a moment, inflated his cheeks with air as he exhaled in a puff.

"Well," he began, "I really couldn't say. I'm not a doctor. He did seem a bit sad from time to time. But manic depressed . . . bipolar? We didn't really think in those terms back then. A lot of us were depressed. It was cloudy and rainy in Lackawanna for about nine months of the year. Blackawanna, we used to call it. None of us were exactly dancing in the streets."

"What do you think happened to Abe? What do you think really happened?" Glassman pressed on. "Grandma and mom think he just took off. I mean, I think that's what they think. They don't talk about it . . . or him. But do you think he could have been . . . you know . . . murdered?"

The question visibly pained Birnbaum. He stopped in the middle of the parking lot and placed his hands at both hips, thumbs forward, as if to support an aching lower back. He began to shake his head slowly and raise his shoulders slightly to his ears, his body anticipating the sentence he had yet to begin. "Well, boychik, the truth is, I do. I think everyone does, really. Even your grandma, though she wouldn't admit it I'm sure. It's easier for her to think he ran off. Easier in a way, I mean. Easier to remember him as a bastard than . . . well . . . you see what I'm getting at?" Glassman, who didn't know *what* to think any more, simply nodded.

"I used to think he just disappeared," Birnbaum continued. "That's what I thought right after it happened. But as the months went by it seemed to make less and less sense to me. To take off without a trace? With all those FBI guys looking for him all over the country? More and more it just seemed like wishful thinking that he fled Lackawanna.

"One time, you know, I even imagined that I saw Abe. It was five years or so after he disappeared when Ida and I took that trip to Florence. Right on the Ponte Vecchio I thought I spotted him. He was leaning over the bridge gazing down at the Arno. The son of a gun looked just like Abe, with that strong, squared chin. Just like yours. And, of course, standing there alone gazing down at the muddy river and the plain-looking ducks with all that beautiful gold jewelry up and down the bridge . . . it was just such an Abe Fishbein thing to be doing. I walked over to him slowly, sweating bullets, leaving Ida to hondle with some shopkeeper about the price of a scarf she was admiring. But just as I reached him, at the moment that he turned toward me to find out what I wanted, I could tell that I had made a mistake. 'Come sta?' I asked the fellow to save face. 'How are you?' It was one of the few Italian phrases I knew. . . . You see, it was just a hopeful delusion of mine. I decided right then and there to say goodbye to your grandpa. No point in courting the dead."

Glassman could almost feel the color drain from his face. Birnbaum must have noticed, as well. "Hey, listen, I hope this isn't upsetting you. Maybe I shouldn't have been so direct."

"No, that's all right," Glassman assured Birnbaum as they continued to the door. He took a deep breath and began to regain his composure. He would take Birnbaum's opinion for what it was. An opinion. A compelling one, perhaps. One to keep firmly in mind. But hardly irrefutable. "Thanks for telling me the story, Mr. Birnbaum. Both stories. Thanks for telling me something about my grandfather. It was very kind of you."

Birnbaum told Glassman that he was welcome at the door, then opened it. A vision of whooshing wings fluttered in Glassman's mind as he was greeted by a gust of too-cool air in the foyer.

"Well, there you two are," Edith announced from her enormous sofa. "We were about to send out a search party." Glassman sucked in a nervous intake of air. He glanced instinctively toward his grandmother, apparently unfazed by Edith's remark, a careless, insensitive remark, it seemed to Glassman. He scanned the room. No one else seemed the least bit perturbed, either. What did this say about them? he wondered. What did his own, perhaps outsized, reaction say about him?

"We just took a little walk," Glassman explained defensively. Needlessly. He sat down on the sectional between Teenie and Rebecca.

"In this heat?" Mildred Siegel cackled rhetorically from the opposite end of the sofa restoring Glassman once and for all to the paltry present. Birnbaum told her that the heat wasn't too oppressive.

"We were just talking about that new breast cancer gene that they isolated in Ashkenazic Jews?" Ruth Spitz informed them. She was seated on the recliner beside the sofa. Glassman had noticed the cover-story in the *Jewish Weekly Times* a week or two ago, and even CNN had aired a story about it. He had been paying close attention to such news lately in any case, given his recent Tay Sachs test. It had come back with favorable results in bold, large caps: NEGATIVE FOR COMMON JEWISH MUTATIONS. *Sure,* he had cynically thought, *they just don't know all that they should be looking for yet.* He was fairly certain that, in addition to Hexosaminidase A, there were plenty more Jewish mutations to go around. Other genes in cahoots with specific cancers, heart attacks, strokes. And, of particular concern, chemical imbalances in the cerebrum. There were two kinds of Jews, Herr Nietzsche had opined, obnoxious and melancholy. An anti-Semitic barb, sure. But also an apt diagnosis of bipolar disease well ahead of its time.

"I think it's just horrible!" Teenie answered, throwing Glassman for a loop. "It's like these scientists think we're diseased or something. Well there's nothing wrong with us! We're not diseased!"

"I'm with you, Teenie," Edith seconded Teenie's arguments. "I don't know why they come out with these studies anyway. They just change their minds the next day. It's ridiculous."

Glassman was perplexed. It was good news that scientists were beginning to isolate the genes responsible for Jewish diseases, wasn't it? Treatment, perhaps, would be right around the corner. *Good for the Jews.*

"Ida and Leonard," Edith began. "As long as you're both here, you can help us catch up on a few other people. Mildred, Ruth and I were going through all the people that lived on our blocks between Sycamore and Lemon Street when we were children and we couldn't remember what happened to a few of the families."

"Go ahead. Shoot," Leonard told Edith.

And so Glassman learned all about Sid Greenstein, the taciturn plumber who, in his spare time, could fix almost anything, including Nat Siegel's grandfather clock (which he somehow recalibrated with lead fishing weights); he learned about Rae Appelbaum, who purportedly used to climb a ladder to trim her crab apple tree every other day just so she could peek into the Bergers' backyard; and he learned about the noodge, Minnie Popowitz, who once tracked down her recalcitrant husband, Arthur—"who God forbid was enjoying a movie downtown," Birnbaum remembered—by taking a flashlight right into the theater and shining it on practically everyone's face until she found Arthur cowering in the front row. "When poor Arthur became ill," Ida reflected ruefully, "she wouldn't let him take a break. 'You're not so sick Mr. Smarty Pants!' she insisted. He never could quite convince Minnie that he wasn't faking it. He had to drop dead to win the argument!"

"They know *everything* about each other," Rebecca silently mouthed to her husband, who nodded. Yes, Glassman reflected, they know everything about one another. Almost everything.

Edith, Mildred, Ruth, and Teenie pretty much remembered what happened to everyone else between Sycamore and Lemon Streets. The Feldmans moved to Allentown; the Hodens both died in that terrible car accident on the way to Penn State before they built the 80 when it took six hours to get there; Myrna and Simon Katz ended up renting the bottom story of their house to an Italian couple once their kids moved to Denver. "It was the best decision they ever made," Edith opined. "That Italian girl was an absolute saint to Myrna after Simon passed away."

The Gelbs . . . the Mandels . . . the Wolfs. . . . Glassman listened as his elders recounted the fates of a fair percentage of Lackawanna's Jews.

"You know Matthew," Teenie told him through glassy eyes, finally breaking her silence, her warm hand resting upon his, "someday you'll talk about *me* like this."

On the way home in the car, Glassman was mute, lost in amorphous thoughts. Rebecca broke the silence by asking him what Mr. Birnbaum and he were up to for so long outside. "Nothing special," Glassman laconically assured her. Rebecca, he knew, had enough on her mind. Apparently content with his reticence, she reminded him to stop for gas at the Citgo station.

He obediently filled the tank and paid the cashier behind the bullet-proof glass. While his Visa card was being scanned to ascertain his credit worthiness, he stared blankly at the covers of various hard-core pornographic magazines. In minutes, silent minutes, they were on the interstate headed north.

The Yeagertown pigeon-shoot. He would sear this precious vision of Abe into his memory. Abe and his pigeons. Perhaps this was where his fascination with pigeons, with all birds, lay rooted. In this disgraceful small-town ritual of blood and gun smoke. In this stupid fraternity stunt. He couldn't get the image out of his mind. His grandfather at twenty or so with a goatee, his hands splayed and outstretched, surrounded by a funnel cloud of whooshing birds. He catalogued this image along with the two other images of Abe he had somehow retained in his mind. Abe at the haberdashery. Abe in his pigeon coop. For nearly the entire drive home, he thought of his grandfather.

And he thought of Teenie. His grandmother was right. Glassman would talk about her. He was sure of this. Only a split second after his mind formed this thought, his stomach inexplicably sunk. Glassman marveled at his body's capacity to register certain feelings seemingly out of thin air; his thoughts were constantly playing catch-up to his inner organs. He wove his way home through the increased congestion, gazing absently above from time to time at the puffy cumulus clouds creeping slowly westward from the ocean to the Everglades. Then suddenly it came to him. The reason why his stomach had dropped out from under him. Who? Glassman wondered . . . who would sit around a table eighty years from now and talk about him?

Think of How Lucky
We Are

The serenity Glassman first glimpsed at the Everglades somehow gave way to a nebulous melancholy. So the Sunday after the brunch with his relatives, he spirited himself away to Loxahatchee, hoping, expecting even, that Shuman would be there waiting for him. He tried to imagine the old man on a crisp autumn day wearing wool, a green toggle coat and a gray cap. His fingers splayed high above his head toward the spreading funnel cloud of pigeons, a legion of birds, the sky and earth darkened beneath their wings. Pigeons. He would talk to Shuman about pigeons today.

But Glassman arrived to find the wooden bench vacant. He sat for a while, hoping at least to see the wood storks fly in, but he waited in vain for over an hour. Apparently, they had found a more suitable foraging habitat for the day. The prolific duck-like birds with the red bills and foreheads—moorhens, Shuman had told him—seemed to mock Glassman from the sawgrass with their human screeching. A giant turtle lumbered lugubriously across the marsh trail, moss stubbornly clinging to its shell. It descended quietly into a separate impoundment of water and reeds. No, this wasn't helping, he thought to himself. Rather, the solitude only exacerbated his inexplicable despondency. He returned to his car and fled.

He would stick to his routines, banish idle time, those most treacherous minutes. In this spirit, he laced up his high-tops later that week and headed to Patch Corral Park to shoot hoops. In the first game, he promptly collided with a young, wiry black player and injured himself. His adversary had lunged to make a steal and unintentionally butted Glassman's forehead with his own. Not too hard a blow. It didn't even hurt, really. But the black player's head struck Glassman at his most vulnerable spot, the bony bridge of his brow. Glassman reached up alarmingly with the tips of two fingers, felt the trickle of warm blood, then gloomily inspected his crimson fingertips.

Glassman stanched the flow of blood with his sweaty T-shirt on the sideline while the game continued without him. A short park worker in a polo shirt suddenly appeared and handed Glassman a plastic bag of ice. It was time to deal with the swelling. Before Glassman could apply the ice, the employee inspected the cut and broke the news to Glassman that he would probably need a few stitches.

"I don't have to tell you not to take a nap on your way over to the hospital, do I?" he asked rhetorically. Glassman assured him that he didn't.

He decided to have the stitches taken care of before heading back home. It wasn't that Rebecca wouldn't have been sympathetic, but he didn't want to alarm her. Plus, the worse shape she saw him in, the more vigorously she'd continue her anti-basketball lobbying efforts in the future. Since he had met her, he had lost an incisor (he now wore a mouth guard), busted his left ankle, sprained his right one on countless occasions, twisted a knee, and, on a weekly basis, sustained any number of bruises from knees and elbows and scratches from untrimmed fingernails.

I don't know why you keep playing that stupid game! Rebecca regularly berated him as she smeared antibacterial ointment on fresh wounds before bed.

Ropa General was a good hospital, built in the 1960s by the sheer will of the community after a young girl in Ropa, who had swallowed something toxic, expired in the ambulance en route to the nearest hospital five miles north.

"Yeah, mi hijo, you're going to need four or five stitches," the nurse told him as he examined his head with gloved hands.

"Oh," Glassman softly replied. His sadness had suddenly given way to outright gloom. Too suddenly! It wasn't normal. Were his eyes beginning to well up? He knew it wasn't the prospect of stitches that rocked him. He had already counted on those and adjusted his psyche to the reality. He wasn't sure it was anything concrete. That was the problem.

He did know that something about all those latex gloves irked him. When he was playing on the basketball court, his body had been in direct contact with his opponent from one end of the court to the other. Contact. It was a contact sport, despite what most people thought. And the contact invigorated him. He was never low on the hoops court.

But the moment he was bloodied, everyone scattered, or stood their distance. Even his friend Glen had remained a yard or so away from him at all times. Bloodied he was suddenly a pariah. The only one who would touch him was the park worker, who had inspected the wound through two layers of latex. Everyone was worried about AIDS. Did they think he was a heroin addict? Gay? Or just heterosexually promiscuous? *I don't have AIDS!* he had wanted to scream to the players, standing in the shape of a half-moon ten feet away. *I won't contaminate you! You don't have to run away!*

The current, conservative dispensation was prudent, Glassman allowed. But still, there was an associated loss. A human loss. There was no use in denying it. He remembered the time, the horrifying time, when he slipped on the slick blue floor of the children's pool at Willow Woods in Lackawanna. He had fallen flat on his nose and had broken it in two places. The foot-deep water and the inflated orange pillows wrapped about his arms did little to break the fall. Blood had gushed from his nose down his chin, onto his chest, and into the pool as if from a fountain. He couldn't remember whether he or Melissa Kornblatt, frolicking in the pool with him at the time, had screamed first. But this is what he did remember: before he could even think to run to his mother, sitting nearby at a glass table under an umbrella playing cards with her old friends from Lackawanna High, a flurry of hands—hands belonging to Fishbeins, Glassmans, Dicksteins, Hodens, Gelbs, Goodmans, Kornblatts, Truckers, Spitzes, Bassoffs, Wolfs, Dinners, and Bergers—were reaching out toward him, pulling him from the pool, wiping away his blood to survey the damage; an enormous, pendulous breast had slipped free of its suit and swayed in front of his awestruck eyes, quieting him. It wasn't a time for modesty.

He never thought he'd be sitting in a hospital in south Florida, looking back on the experience fondly. Did parents still shower such attention, such love, upon other people's bloodied children? Upon their own? He hoped so. But doubted it.

There were all kinds of exotic illnesses floating around south Florida (*It's those goddamn illegals,* Chuck had argued once). Tuberculosis and hepatitis were even making auspicious comebacks. As a result, most Floridians operated on a prophylactic credo. But Glassman hungered for a human touch. Why else did he relish those few minutes every three weeks or so when the Haitian shampoo-lady scrubbed his scalp. They never exchanged a word. Glassman didn't even know whether she spoke English. For ten minutes, she vigorously, even a bit painfully, massaged Glassman's scalp with the strong tips of all ten fingers. Contact. The haircuts were expensive ($25!) and not even very good—which Glassman was used to, given the slightly askew placement of his ears—but he continued to frequent the salon for the shampoos. It was only a matter of time, perhaps, before his shampoo-lady began wrapping her hands in latex herself. In the meantime, he kept his hair short.

After having a modest patch of his hair shaved and receiving his stitches (seven!), Glassman drove home, scripting in his mind a version of the day's events least likely to stir Rebecca, his parents, and Teenie into a conniption.

As Glassman feared, the blow to his head somehow knocked him into a melancholic slough from which he struggled desperately to escape. For the next couple weeks, he managed, more or less, to navigate through a thin haze. He reported daily to his windowless office at the *Jewish Weekly Times.* As he put it to himself, he "showed." Which was something. He exchanged terse, but not curt, greetings with Mrs. Kreiser. He managed to socialize a bit with the rosy-lipped Trish. He got his job done, though not in any spectacular, or even mildly creative, fashion. Alten had entered his office one day and asked him, feigning concern, if everything was okay. If there was something they could do to improve his current "situation," as Alten somewhat mysteriously put it. Was he as happy at the paper as he had hoped to be? The clear implication: the paper wasn't so elated with him. His boss had meant to put him on notice. This would have occurred to Glassman had he cared enough to ponder the implications of Alten's remarks.

Outside the office, he began to handle himself rather more disgracefully, setting a new, frightening precedent. First, he accosted the Japanese-looking young employee at Crystal Clear Pools. It always took Glassman several months before bringing his pool water in for the free testing, and each time he did so he was forced shamefacedly to bear the disapprobation of the eighteen- or nineteen-year-old employee, who just couldn't countenance Glassman's lackadaisical attitude toward pool maintenance.

The young man began, at his usual breakneck speed, to pour the pool water sloppily from Glassman's tupperware container into several long, narrow-lipped vials. Then, seemingly out of thin air, he brandished eye droppers of red, yellow, and green liquid. From pinched fingers, two veritable trickles descended simultaneously into their designated vials. How could he count the drops? Glassman wondered. He was going too fast! There was going to be a spill!

As the water in the vials began to take on hues of various shades, the employee began clucking his tongue and shaking his head disapprovingly. The grinning, toothy Indian on his baseball cap even seemed to mock him. Glassman felt his face turn gradually hotter.

"You're like, *real* low on your stabilizer, calcium, chlorine *and* alkalinity," the kid rendered the diagnosis while raising both eyebrows, a gesture that betrayed surprise and at least a trace of disgust. "You have, like, a yellowish-green film on the side of the pool, don't you?" the chemical expert predicted mysteriously.

"Well, yeah, maybe a little," Glassman replied, impatiently rather than sheepishly.

"You know you really gotta get in here more often," he advised Glassman while peering at his computer screen. "It's been four months since your last water test you know."

It was one more sentence from the employee than Glassman could bear.

"Listen, kid, do you have any idea how low on my list of priorities the alkalinity level of my pool is?"

"Huh?"

Glassman had, evidently, caught the employee off guard with his brazenness.

"I'll tell you what, just give me the fucking reading, would you please!?"

The employee silently did as he was told. He ripped the computer printout along the perforation and handed it to Glassman, who folded it into quarters, shoved it into his front pocket, and was on his way. He'd buy his chemicals at K-mart.

At work later that week, he received an unsolicited e-mail, one of several such variants he had been receiving since beginning his job at the *Jewish Weekly Times:*

From: Yerushalayim@web.access.com
Subject: Appeal
To: mglassman@weekly.com

Soon, it will be sixty years that my entire family, my brother, my sisters, my parents, and six million men, women and children from Germany, Poland, Holland, Italy, Greece, Rumania, France and other European countries who were brutally murdered for the crime of being Jewish. There Ashes are scattered in the Death Camps, and not even one Star of David is there to identify that they were Jews. As a Jew, you have amoral and Religious obligation to demand a Jewish Star be put at all the Death Camps in Europe. Other-wise, your committing a religious crime by using the Holocaust for personal profit in the pages of your magazine/newspaper/journal.

Do not Desecrate the memory of the Six million. Tell your Senators and Congressmen about the need for a Star at all the Death Camps.

Yerushalayim.

The message, like its countless cousins slung at him from cyber-space, repelled Glassman. Just the other day he had received (and managed to ignore) a separate e-mail from one of these ubiquitous defenders of the faith urging him to "Send this message to everyone you know who's Jewish. If we reach six million screen names we'll show g-d that we're still here and still Jews!" *Terrific,* Glassman had dimly thought before clicking the delete button. *That'll show God.*

Against his better judgment, he clicked on the reply window this time. He couldn't help but reply to such wrongheaded vituperation, however disembodied the censure was:

From: mglassman@weekly.com
Subject: A Response
To:Yerushalayim@web.access.com
Dear Yerushalayim,

I'm sorry for your tragic losses. Really I am. And I think it would be great to place a Jewish star at all the Death Camps in Europe. In fact, why stop there? Why not hit Barcelona, Seville, Lisbon, Cairo, and Medina while we're at it? But accusing me of exploiting the Holocaust for "Personal Profit," and, worse, committing a "Religious Crime" for my complacency on this matter? Is this really the way to go about things? I know, I'm probably taking it too personally. I'm too defensive. It's a weakness of mine. You sent this message to hundreds, maybe thousands of folks. But you DID send it to me also and, all things considered, I think I've done all right by the Six Million without lobbying for Jewish Stars at the camps (and, fine, if I have to get right down to it, I don't think lobbying for Jewish Stars is really the most productive place for you to be devoting your considerable energies in the first place). Those of us who devote our energies elsewhere certainly aren't committing a "Religious Crime." As for "Personal Profit," you should just see one of my pay stubs!!

Glassman.

He regretted his reply as soon as he hit send. He had overreacted.

He couldn't go soft. He had to stick with his routines. So he checked in with his grandmother as soon as he got home.

"Hello grandma, it's me."

"Well hello Matthew."

"Just calling to check in. How was your day?"

"Oh fine, just fine." She began to chortle. "I went with Ruth and Edith to the Seminole's. You know I don't care for bingo but we just had to see Edith. She's what they call the queen for the week."

"Queen for the week?"

"Yeah. They somehow picked her last week, so she gets to sit right up there on the stage with the announcer and play as many cards as she wants for free. It's all week. You know she plays forty cards." His grandmother uttered this last sentence pridefully, as if she were boasting an estimable skill in the possession of her double-cousin's wife.

"Well, how'd she do?"

"Aaach, she hasn't won much yet. And she's getting pretty pooped too. It's like work shlepping out there every day to play."

"That's funny. . . . Well, anything else new."

"Nothing. Everything's fine."

"Well, not much going on at this end. I'll talk to you tomorrow, I guess, or the next day."

"I hope so dear."

I hope so. Glassman hung up the phone.

Even the mildest of admonishments from his grandmother—not even an admonishment, really—wounded Glassman deeply. He could feel himself slipping. Irretrievably slipping.

And where was Shuman? Gone. Vanished. Vanished once again.

Rebecca was growing worried. He didn't have the State College clouds anymore to blame for his funk. They were living in sunny Florida. He needed to go and see someone. Just to talk, she urged. He wouldn't have to take any drugs.

"Ah, but that's just where it all starts," he told her. "And what about applying for life insurance or health insurance in the future?" he continued. Have you ever been under a doctor's care for mental illness? Do you suffer from clinical depression? Are you currently taking any antidepressants? Have you, or anyone in your family, been diagnosed with a mental illness? If so, please specify."

These were questions, Glassman knew, that they asked on such forms. He could fudge some of these answers, but once he started "seeing someone" the jig would be up. He couldn't lie flat-out about his own condition. Should something terrible happen, they could do some snooping and the contract could be voided. If he started taking antidepressants, his blood-screening would reveal it anyway. Bye-bye affordable insurance. Hadn't he and Rebecca been talking just recently about investing in a whole life plan?

He was doing fine, he insisted. He wasn't missing any work. He wasn't agonizing through fitful, sleepless nights, nor was he having trouble rising from bed in the morning. He could continue to "show." But for how long was anyone's guess.

And then . . . then . . . SUCCESS!

Rebecca hadn't even told him, when she slipped away from the family room futon after their dinner (microwaved burritos), that she was planning on aiming a yellow thread of her urine onto the last plastic wand that came in the pregnancy test three-pack they had purchased months ago. She didn't want to set him up for yet another fall, she told him later. He was depressed enough as it was.

"Matt!" he heard her scream from the bedroom. "Matt, get in here!" It wasn't a sound from his wife's lungs with which he was familiar. He rushed to the room, anticipating the worst. *She had slipped in the shower and fractured her leg. Troy had choked on his rawhide, was dead, laid out on their comforter, his tongue purple and distended.* He always assumed the worst, whether depressed or not. The phone, ringing even slightly outside the appropriate time window to which he had grown accustomed (nine-thirty A.M. to ten o'clock P.M.), was surely bearing tragic news about his family in California or Florida or Washington, where his sister lived. There had been a car accident. A stroke. A heart attack. He was only an infrequent flyer, but was certain that it would be his airplane that would plummet to the ground one of these days; he only hoped, sardonically, that the tragedy could wait until the return flight so he could at least enjoy one final vacation. Why did he entertain such horrific thoughts? What great tragedies had he suffered thus far in his blessed life?

"What!? What's the matter!?" Glassman asked his wife, who appeared just fine standing in front of him. No sign of Troy, to his relief. Her mouth was in the shape of an o, suddenly silent, as if ineffable emotions or thoughts (whether bad or good) occupied her attention. Finally, he saw her inhale, gathering her wind to speak.

"I'm pregnant!"

"You're what!?" She had to have been putting him on. They had only made love once, maybe twice, in the past month or so. Through a silent agreement (for how could they have articulated it to one another?) they had decided to give it up, decided to stop trying. Or at least that was what he had thought.

"You heard me, Matt. I'm pregnant." To underscore the point, she brandished the white wand between them. He saw two red lines, one fainter than the other, against a yellow backdrop. Evidently, this meant his wife was pregnant.

"But one's fainter than the other," he protested.

"That doesn't matter, Matthew," Rebecca answered excitedly. "The box says it doesn't matter how faint the second line is. All that matters is whether you can *see* it or not." She was positively beaming. "Think of how lucky we are!"

"Yes," Glassman agreed. "That's incredible, honey. Really." Glassman waited for his own elation to arrive, to seize him like an electrical current. But he was grounded, subdued, pensive.

After about an hour or so, the news finally jolted him.

"Oh my god!" he bursted out, slightly startling Rebecca. She was sitting next to him on the futon, holding his hand, lost in her own thoughts. "I'm going to be a father!"

We've Come All This Way

If the collision at Patch Corral Park had been the blow that jostled Glassman's wiring, blurring his mental screen with snow, Rebecca's announcement was the flat-handed smack that cleared the snow away. There was too much to think about, too much to do, for Glassman to be despondent. There were magazines (e.g., *Parenting, American Baby, Fit Pregnancy*) and books (e.g., *What to Expect When You're Expecting, Dr. Spock's Baby and Child Care*) to read. Rebecca and he were nothing if not diligent about their homework. There were special diets and exercise regimens to contemplate, a whole new host of web sites to visit and bookmark on their computer. From one of these sites, Rebecca had printed a special nine-month calendar that would keep them up-to-date, daily, on the development of their sweet pea (as Rebecca began calling the baby). The calendar, Glassman thought, contained slightly more information about the changes going on in his wife's body than he cared to know. *Excessive saliva. Flatulence. Enjoy,* he teased his wife.

Rebecca's first appointment with Dr. Arias went well. "I heard the heartbeat!" she exclaimed to Glassman as she kicked off her sneakers (*ah, the wardrobe of the professorate,* Glassman mused enviously). He was busy testing the texture of a strand of pasta between his teeth that he had plucked from a pot of boiling water. "Boomboomboom-boomboomboomboom." In her best baritone, she imitated the stac-cato rhythm she had heard through a microphone. Then she fished into her pocket and handed him what felt like a folded fax sheet, which he promptly unfolded.

"There . . . there's the little sweet pea," she pointed to the black and gray image with her pinky. Glassman struggled to assign human attributes to what looked like a slightly curved spec, a comma nes-tled against the inside wall of a lima bean. The first baby picture. He put it inside his wallet and promised Rebecca he wouldn't show it to a soul until they announced the pregnancy in three months or so.

They were both relieved when Rebecca's "tri-screen" (as Dr. Arias called the blood-work) came back saying all the right things. No sign of Down Syndrome or, as the results read, "any other disorders for which defective genes or chromosomes are responsible." But what would they do, Glassman pondered for a moment, if there *were* signs of Down Syndrome or "other disorders"? Could they do anything in utero for such things, or did the doctors simply recommend abor-tion? What would he and Rebecca do if presented the option at ten weeks, twelve, fourteen?

Just as long as it's healthy, couples cooed, congratulating them-selves for their hip, gender neutrality. But what if it wasn't healthy? What then? Nobody seemed to talk about this. Sitting there with the results of Rebecca's blood-work in his hands, Glassman remembered painfully the time when his childhood friend, Robbie Gelman, told him that he had an older brother. He was retarded—*like, really really retarded*—Robbie had explained, and lived in an institution. Glass-man rushed home and found his mother in the kitchen. She was cry-ing over onions, which always bothered him. Crying was crying as far as he was concerned. He told her about the Gelman's secret. *It's okay, mom,* he insisted, *he's like, retarded. Really, really retarded.*

No Matthew, Barbara Glassman uttered calmly through her tears. *It's not okay. He should be home. Everyone can feel love, Matthew. Everyone.*

If you were out you were out. Good for you. But if you were in you were in. There wasn't an in between. Was this what his mother had been trying to tell him? Is this what she would tell him now if he were sitting over less positive results from Dr. Arias's lab?

Glassman didn't dwell upon such somber thoughts, and chastised himself for entertaining them without any good reason, for allowing himself to be held hostage by such dusty, gray childhood memories.

Caught up in generally buoyant spirits, Glassman found himself acting more generously. He spent hours teaching Trish how to search the web most efficiently for information using Yahoo. As he sat, she leaned over his shoulder to watch the screen; he was intoxicated by her Tea Rose and the loosely coiled curls of her dark hair that brushed teasingly against his neck. So it really wasn't such an unpleasant pedagogical exercise. But he also dallied at Mrs. Kreiser's less enticing desk in the mornings before entering his office and listened intently as she unloaded herself of her burdens. Occasionally, he offered a humble opinion. *Well, it doesn't seem right to me either that your daughter spend her entire vacation with her husband's family in Scarsdale, but, then again, I'm not a parent. What do I know?* He accepted Alten's "suggestions" of books for the paper to review without protest, and began working longer, harder hours. Glassman also made of himself the most innocuous presence at the weekly editor's meetings, approving wholeheartedly the proposals of his peers and keeping his mouth shut when it came to his own brainstorms and preferences.

"You've been a real mentsh lately Matt. A real team player," Lippman complimented him between wheezings as they stood from their chairs after one of the meetings. Glassman had, just minutes ago, agreed that it would be a great idea for the paper to pay fifteen hundred dollars to sponsor one of Lippman's right-wing cronies (whose name Glassman couldn't even place from the pages of *Commentary, The Forward, Midstream,* or *The New Republic*) to give a talk for the community. Glassman wasn't sure of the role compliance and obsequiousness played in team sports, but he bit his lip and accepted the compliment.

Alten also complimented his young editor, poking his head into Glassman's office one day on his way out for the evening.

"I was worried there for a while boychik, I don't mind telling you now. You were a bit too excitable, even brash. Then just plain old gloomy. But you've settled into a groove. And you've finally developed some patience. Some zitsflaish."

Glassman's generous mood, while earning him points at work, left him susceptible to any number of solicitations. He finally relented and invited a hydrologist over to conduct a test (from one of the scores of water purification companies that had been calling), after which he bought one of their middle of the line under-the-sink units for almost five hundred dollars. "You don't want the baby to be drinking impure water, do you?" he reasoned with Rebecca, who thought it was a waste of money. What's more, he began donating large sums to callers from the Sierra Club, the World Wildlife Fund, Blind Citizens, and the American Cancer Society. He sent Disabled Veterans a check for a hundred dollars after they sent him a pack of sharp little return address stickers for the sixth or seventh time. He began purchasing waxy chocolate and rolls and rolls of wrapping paper from the hordes of neighborhood schoolchildren, who evidently needed to foot part of the bill for their (public) education. They had figured out fairly quickly that a shnook was among them.

Rebecca threatened to take away his credit cards. "What are you doing?" she asked him as she pulled her hair out at the dining room table over one of their statements. "We give plenty to the United Way and UJA already! Control yourself. We've got the sweet pea to think about now." Thinking of the sweet pea herself, she could scarcely manage to get (to say nothing of stay) angry at Glassman, who promised in the future to keep his wallet under his shoe whenever he answered the phone or front door.

He began calling Teenie twice, sometimes three times a day (*everything's fine, just fine,* she would assure him by the second call), and visited her at least one evening a week, usually on Wednesday evenings so they could watch her favorite television program, *Law & Order.* It aired too late for Rebecca to want to join them. *Why can't the*

two of you choose a show that starts sometime before ten? she asked. On
the way to Cypress Ponds on *Law & Order* night, he would stop at
the Sam's Club to pick up one of the apple or rhubarb pies that Teenie enjoyed. Before leaving her for the evening, he changed the lights
that had popped and dimmed over the course of the previous week,
took out the trash and recycling, culled the dead leaves from her Silver Queen plants, rearranged tables and chairs for her Thursday gin
game, and, standing atop a lucite footstool, retrieved any canned
goods from the upper reaches of the kitchen cabinets that Teenie anticipated she might want to use over the next few days. Garbanzo
beans, crushed tomatoes, tuna fish, fruit salad, artichoke hearts. . . .

As long as I'm here.

On his way home, usually around 11:30 or so, he would hand a
piece of pie to Leon, the appreciative, aged security guard at the gate.

Glassman was spreading himself thinner than ever, but somehow
felt less pressured, less stressed out, than he had felt when he was dil-
igently guarding his time. He was doing better than merely "showing." Everything was running smoothly now, as if he had somehow
managed to shift up after being stuck in too low a gear.

So when Glassman finally received Shuman's telephone call at the
office—it had been weeks since he heard from the old man—it came
as little more than a pleasant surprise. He had been so preoccupied
with Rebecca's pregnancy that he had, frankly, given little thought to
Shuman over the past few weeks. Little thought to his grandfather
and the pigeons whirring above his head.

Shuman apologized for his long silence, but he had been quite ill
with viral pneumonia, which set in just after they last met at the
Everglades. He had been in the hospital for nearly a week. Glassman
suddenly felt badly for not having worried about Shuman, for not
entertaining the possibility that the old man might have fallen ill, for
not having scanned the obituaries. As Shuman himself put it, he
wasn't a spring chicken.

"You know I did go to the Everglades a few weekends ago to find
you," Glassman explained guiltily. "I was upset when you weren't

there." He felt his defenses weaken as he remembered that gloomy morning. "I was going through sort of a rough patch. I really wanted to talk with you, but you didn't give me your number. You're not listed in the book."

"Yes, I'm sorry Matthew. I live in Fort Pierce," he somewhat cryptically explained. What was he sorry about? For not giving Glassman his number? For not calling sooner himself? Or, simply, for living so far away? Glassman, in fact, was surprised to hear that he lived nearly two hours north. He had just assumed that the old man lived somewhere between Ft. Lauderdale and West Palm. There was so little that he actually knew about Shuman.

"Are you all right now, son?" Shuman continued worriedly. *Son?* Glassman heard his voice waver at a higher frequency than usual. He wondered what thoughts currently occupied Shuman's mind. He was tempted to play the scene out. See where it led. No, he would say. He wasn't all right. He was chronically depressed. Every day was a struggle. Could Shuman be of any use?

But it would be self-indulgent to unload all of this upon Shuman, recovering from an illness of his own. Besides, Glassman happened to be doing okay now. Better than okay. "Yes," he assured Shuman, "I'm doing very well now, actually. I have some good news for you."

He wouldn't tell Shuman about Rebecca's pregnancy over the phone, though. He would be breaking the three-month rule in telling Shuman at all, but knew that he would be powerless to keep the news from the old man. He had already suppressed so much, so much that he wished to say to this Shuman, whoever he was. Now seemed his first chance to share something real with the old man. Something essential. Surely it was time now to unstop his throat. So Glassman resolved to tell Shuman about the baby at Loxahatchee that Sunday, where they arranged to meet once again.

It turned out to be an unlovely, overcast day, so dark it was impossible to discern exactly where the sun hovered in the sky. A gray blanket covered the Everglades in oppressive warmth. It wasn't raining when Glassman exited the car in the lot, but the very atmosphere was saturated with moisture. A nearly visible steam sealed itself around every square inch of his flesh, invading his pores and making it difficult for him to breathe.

Shuman, once again, had arrived at the refuge before Glassman and was waiting for his young companion on the same bench, underneath the intertwining branches of cypress and strangler fig. Something about the way Shuman sat, his stillness, gave Glassman the impression that he had been sitting there all his life. He was somewhat surprised that the old man looked pretty much the same to him. A part of him, he realized, had expected Birnbaum's story about Abe and the Yeagertown pigeon-shoot to transform Shuman in his eyes.

"Are you sure you want to stick around here?" he asked his elder as he crouched to sit next to him. Just about everyone else thought better of any plans they might have had to go to the Everglades this morning. There were only two other cars in the lot besides Glassman's Toyota, a gargantuan sport utility vehicle (all the rage in south Florida) and a rusty Subaru wagon, the latter of which Glassman assumed was Shuman's.

"Of course I want to stay," Shuman answered. "We've come all this way."

Glassman wanted to stay also, but worried about Shuman's pneumonia. The heavy, drenched air couldn't be good for his lungs.

They sat for a while once again before walking the trail. The flat landscape seemed stark and foreign now to Glassman, only scarcely recognizable as the radiant vista he had glimpsed twice before. Against the most diffuse rays of sun, the sawgrass—which Glassman remembered as slender, brilliant green spears—took on the grayish hue of canned peas. Before, the water in the impoundment had been clear several feet below the surface, where Glassman had spotted countless submerged turtles and gleaming silver schools of fish. But now he couldn't see any signs of life beneath the surface, black and opaque. The birds were drained of their color, as well. The once blue and green herons were a gunmetal gray; the snowy egrets seemed

dirtied with urban grime; even the purple gallinules, usually irides-
cent in several shades of green, blue, indigo, and violet, seemed un-
spectacularly wan. Glassman was relieved that a much nicer day had
greeted him a few weeks ago, when he visited alone and in poorer
spirits. Now he was doing well, and felt almost impervious to the
gray.

"So, don't keep an old man waiting, Matthew. What's this news
you have to share with me?"

"Oh," Glassman responded somewhat dazedly. He hadn't
planned on telling Shuman about Rebecca so soon in the morning.
He didn't want the news to overshadow their morning of bird-
watching, and figured that he would tell him on the last leg of the
trail. But seeing as Shuman asked . . .

"It's just that . . . that my wife, Rebecca . . . you know I don't
think I've even mentioned her to you . . . she's pregnant. We're going
to have a child," he added redundantly, as if to reinforce his point.

Shuman remained placid. He bobbed his head slowly once or
twice, taking a few moments to register what his young companion
had just told him. Glassman heard a red-bellied woodpecker trill in
the distance. Something unseen plashed quietly where the reeds met
the water. A toad, Glassman surmised.

"Ah," Shuman finally responded. "There's no greater blessing in
the world than children. And what naches, what joy, you will give
your parents." Glassman was certain he detected an air of wistfulness
in Shuman's voice. Emboldened by stronger spirits, the young editor
decided to press on. "You mentioned that you made some mistakes
with your family. At least I think that's what you said. What happened? Please tell me."

"Oh, you don't really want me to put a damper on your good
mood, do you?" Glassman told him not to worry about his mood.

"Well, boychik, I did make some mistakes, mistakes I should
never have made . . ." Shuman paused rather than vent more intimate details . . . "Let's just say I left. I fairly abandoned my wife, and
by the time I realized how stupid I had been, it was too late."

"When did all of this happen? How long ago?"

"Oh my, nearly twenty years ago, but to tell you the truth I was gone a long time before that. She was probably relieved when I left."

"I doubt that," Glassman opined tersely.

"The thing is," Shuman continued, "solitude ruins a man. No matter how pleasant it is in the beginning. Yes, you see, that's where the danger begins. It's easy to slip away. It feels good to be free of your family, to be free of everyone and everything. At first. Then, suddenly, empty is all you feel. But here's the worst part. By the time you realize what a shell of a man you've become, what a poor excuse for a human being, you're ill-suited for the world of the living. You've simply spoiled, like so much bad fruit."

"What do you mean?" Glassman inquired. He wasn't sure he was following the old man.

"You can't tolerate people anymore! That's what I mean!" Shuman answered sharply. He seemed to grow more impassioned as he spoke. "Somehow, you lose the ability to coexist with others, as if it were a language you refused to speak for too many years. You're one of the very few people I can tolerate, Matthew, and you see how frequently I've managed to call you." Glassman tried, and failed, to resist the sting of Shuman's comment. Injury, however, slowly gave way to impatience, impatience with Shuman's self-serving philosophy toward which he had obviously devoted a great deal of thought.

"Maybe you just can't let yourself off the hook so easily. Maybe you have to force yourself back home. Maybe you have to force yourself to speak the language, as you call it, even if you have to learn it all over again." Glassman startled himself with the words that came gushing from his mouth. He had never spoken so frankly to an elder. Shuman seemed taken aback, as well. Glassman noticed the old man take a deep intake of breath. He exhaled in a sigh.

"Yes, you have a point, Matthew. I'm not saying I haven't been selfish. Lord knows I have been. I'm an old man. Alone as a stone. Just me and these birds. And you see, the worst part of it all is that ninety-nine percent of the time I wouldn't have it any other way. So, yes, I've been selfish. That's exactly my point. Solitude, as I said, ruins a man. It devours you. Like a cancer, from the inside. Don't forget that. Especially now that you're going to be a father." Glassman assured him that he wouldn't.

"Come on." Shuman stood abruptly, a dramatic gesture to indicate that the conversation was over. Over for now, anyway. "This weather brings the bugs out. It's good for warblers and other insect-eaters," he continued in a suddenly spirited voice, his bird-watching voice, Glassman gathered, unperturbed by the world of the living. The human living, anyway. He followed Shuman to the trail and they began their walk.

"Are you sure we're not going to get rained on?" Glassman asked.

"No," Shuman answered laconically. "I'm not."

He proceeded up the trail and Glassman followed. There wasn't much to see, at least not to Glassman's mind. It seemed as if the animals, as well as the people, had decided to lay low on such a bleak morning. But whereas the people could stay indoors, where did all the birds hide? As they silently walked, he scanned the few trees that bordered the impoundments—bedraggled looking cypresses weighted down with blue-gray moss, mahogany with innumerable pale green leaves curved and narrow like fingernail shards, sea grape generously clothed in a foliage of green discs—but couldn't locate any birds slouching in the branches, no feathered dartings within the various green canopies.

Halfway around the marsh trail, just as they reached the wooden observation tower, Glassman noticed a family a short ways off, probably the owners of the expensive sport utility vehicle in the parking lot. The parents held one another's hands while they watched their blonde son (five or six, Glassman figured) running back and forth below them along the canal. Glassman was cheered by the scene of domestic harmony. In the three times he had been at the Lox, this was the first young child he had seen. He immediately resolved that he would introduce Rebecca to the Everglades, that they would take their child to visit regularly.

Suddenly, Glassman noticed a brown fluttering emerge from where the child was romping; it settled back down in the privet about fifteen yards up the canal, fifteen yards closer to where Glassman and his elderly companion momentarily watched. The boy was chasing a sparrow, or perhaps it was a warbler. Glassman still couldn't identify even half of these small songbirds, passerines as Shuman called them. The bird and the boy seemed mutually engaged in the game. The boy again crept stealthily amid the wax myrtle and privet, then pounced, whereupon the bird lazily fluttered away to land ten or fifteen yards down the canal. The parents laughed simultaneously at this latest attempt, at two separate pitches. The game seemed harmless enough. Glassman only worried about the alligators as the boy frolicked dangerously close to the canal.

He wondered whether they should warn the parents about the gators. Perhaps they were from out of town? Perhaps they didn't see the signs? He was just about to consult Shuman, but suddenly the old man was bounding ahead toward the family in surprisingly swift steps. Glassman raced to catch up, holding his binoculars to his chest to keep them from flying up into his face.

"Stop . . . STOP . . . *STOP*!!!" Shuman cried breathlessly in a voice Glassman scarcely recognized—a foreign timbre—both hands extended in front of him, his elbows locked, his fingers splayed, as if he were a blind man groping for a wall. The two parents looked toward the old man with furrowed brows. What was it? Glassman wondered, as did the parents, he was fairly certain. Did Shuman see an alligator!?

"Stop flushing that bird! The boy must stop! He must stop! IT'S AGAINST THE LAW!" Shuman shrieked as he reached the perplexed couple.

IT'S AGAINST THE LAW!

The words—no, more than the mere words, their syntax, cadence and pitch—jarred something buried deep in Glassman's mind. He halted dead in his tracks, skidding ever so slightly on the dust beneath his feet, paralyzed by a horrible vision that took shape in his mind. The black and white film began rolling and he was powerless to stop it, not that he would have done so even if he could.

A young boy, five or so, and his grandfather, stride through Mulberry Park, both of them thickly wrapped in winter clothes: a wool toggle coat and corduroys on the grandfather, a puffy down jacket, an oversized wool hat with ear flaps, and mittens on the grandchild. Both figures breathe smoke into the gray atmosphere. The brown, frozen grass crackles beneath their feet, especially the grandfather's heavier feet, which the grandson stares down at as he struggles to keep pace. His grandfather's high boots, leather from the ankles up to his calves and rubber at the feet, somehow seem clownish and make the child chuckle. He is excited. Despite the freezing weather, the amusement park is open and his grandfather is taking him to ride the bumper cars.

Suddenly, though, the grandfather stops short and tightens his grip. Inertia being no match for such a grip, the grandchild is jerked backwards and nearly falls to the ground. Ow, grandpa! *he complains.* Let's gooo! *he demands with the petulance of a five year old. He tugs his grandfather's arm impotently.* Come on, I'm getting cold! *The child, growing frustrated, stamps both his feet in succession, but he cannot elicit a response from his grandfather, much less get him to move. The grandfather's steely eyes seem fixed at a point off into the distance, his bushy brown and gray eyebrows knitted together in concentration, or maybe anger. The child follows the angle of his grandfather's gaze toward the large frozen pond about a hundred yards away. A solitary, drab duck, black and gray with a long bill, bobs at the thawed edge where the creek trickles into the pond.* What is it, grandpa? *the child asks impatiently. The cold now burns his ears, which poke out against the wool flaps.* QUIET! *the grandfather silences the boy's whining in a pitch completely alien to the child. He begins to cry.*

Rather than soothe his grandson, he commands him to stay put and wait for him. NOOO! *the child begs, afraid now, as he feels his grandfather's hand slip free of his own. The cold penetrates his suddenly free hand. The child looks down upon it and realizes that his grandfather has ripped his wool mitten right off his hand.* Grandpaaaa!! *the child wails, thick tears streaming down his face, clear mucous from a single nostril flowing saltily into his mouth.*

The child begins running toward the pond in the direction of his grandfather. He sees the dog now. A lanky dog with long hair and a thick tongue that droops heavily out the side of its mouth. He sees the man several feet away from the dog, an amused expression on his face, a leash folded like an electric cord in his grip. The dog, barking stupidly, bounds freely ahead toward the duck. Auurf . . . auurf . . . auurf . . . auurf. *The child sees his grandfather arrive at the scene just after the duck begins to thrash its wings violently against the water, then the ice, finally managing to take flight.* Kwuk . . . kwuk . . . kwuk, *it croaks angrily as it flees the pond.* Kapow! *The grandfather lands a powerful kick to the dog's ribs, taking his grandchild, who stops dead in his tracks some twenty yards away, completely by surprise. The dopey dog lets out a squeal and retreats to its owner, its tail between its legs. His grandpa loves animals. He raises homing pigeons in his backyard. So why did he kick the dopey dog.* Hey there! What the hell you think you're doing buster?! *the dog's owner leaps to the animal's defense. The grandfather doesn't shrink from the confrontation. He strides deliberately toward the man and his dog, cowering between its owner's legs.* No, grandpa, please don't kick the man too, *the child silently begs from afar.* You must collar that dog! *his grandfather demands imperiously, his face inches now from his shorter antagonist. The boy can see saliva shoot from his grandfather's mouth, the dog's owner flinch.* You can't harass migratory birds. It's against the law! AGAINST THE LAW! You hear me?!

Take it easy pops, *the man suggests, not unkindly.* It's just a lousy bird. Besides, Prince didn't even touch him. You all right boy? *the man gently pats the dog's side, which seems to perk up the animal's spirits; it wriggles its angular hips and wags its tail, lets out another stupid bark as if to answer its owner in the affirmative. The man bends down, clips the leash onto the dog's collar, and they retreat from the scene. The grandfather stares after them for a moment, as if contemplating whether or not to make chase. Then, suddenly—as if he were a dog himself hearing a new noise—he flinches and pivots his head to search for his grandchild.* Come here Matthew, *he beckons to the boy, waving him in for emphasis. The child strides slowly, warily toward his grandfather.*

Wasn't it beautiful? the grandfather asks the child, a hand placed gently on his shoulder. His globular earlobes are bright red, whether from excitement or the cold the child can't discern. A common loon, *the grandfather continues.* They don't usually make their way so far off the coast. I've never seen one before. Quite a sight, wasn't it?

Grandpa, I'm cold, *the child answers.* Can I have my mitten back? *He points toward the piece of wool fabric spilling out from the heel of his grandfather's left palm. The grandfather looks down at his hand and seems surprised to notice the mitten in his grasp.* Can we go home now, grandpa?

The grandfather silently kneels before the child, cups the boy's tiny, pallid hand, as if it were a wounded bird, between his larger, gloved hands, and revives it with his hot, moist breath. He gingerly slips the mitten back onto the hand. He kisses his grandson on his numb cheek. I'm sorry, Matthew. Forgive your grandfather.

Only later, snuggled up in his thermal underwear beneath the covers of the twin bed across the room from Sara (whose bad sinuses make her snore) does the boy's cheek begin to sting brightly from his grandfather's unshaven face.

"It's against the law!" Shuman repeated, luring Glassman back to the present. It wasn't an alligator, or a snake, or any other dangerous animal that threatened to harm the child. It wasn't the boy's life at all that so concerned the old man.

"Okay . . . okay," the father intoned softly, lifting an upraised hand to his waist, hoping to pacify the old man who so violently accosted them. Glassman finally caught up to his companion and touched his shoulder lightly, reluctantly, with a palm, as if Shuman were a strange dog he feared might bite. It seemed to Glassman as if a switch in the old man's brain had suddenly flipped, turning him into a raving lunatic. It was, indeed, a side of Shuman that Glassman had never seen before, even though thinking of it as merely a "side" seemed altogether inadequate.

"It's okay, Mr. Shuman," Glassman cooed. "It's okay." He could feel the man's enraged heat rise through his thin shirt at his bony shoulder. A ropy, blue vein protruded from his temple. Had it been there before? Glassman wondered. Still livid, Shuman seemed willfully oblivious to Glassman's presence.

"It's not enough you've destroyed ninety percent of the swamp sparrows' habitat!?" he continued. "Now you come here, here to the refuge to finish them off!?"

"Mr. Shuman! . . . Irving!" the young editor now shouted. He decided to take a more aggressive tack, jolt Shuman from his fevered rantings. He wasn't even making sense now.

"Bobby, come along! Let's keep walking," the mother urgently instructed her son. Neither she nor her husband said anything further. They just wanted to get away from the crazy old man. A smart idea, Glassman conceded. He kept his hand on Shuman's shoulder as the family walked briskly away, not to comfort him now, but to hold him back in case he decided to chase after the poor people. Thankfully, Shuman didn't attempt to give chase, but kept his eyes fixed on them for several moments as they made their way around the observation tower.

"Mr. Shuman, are you all right?" Glassman asked in a calmer voice. He stood directly in front of Shuman, both hands now on the old man's shoulders, intentionally obstructing his line of sight toward the family off into the distance, headed toward their car. He hoped, thereby, to interrupt the man's manic reverie. "Is there anything I can do for you, Mr. Shuman?"

The old man began to shake his head slowly, then finally looked Glassman directly in the eyes, a rheumy gaze that pierced Glassman's surface and startled him. The young editor felt exposed, vulnerable. His insides churned. He reflexively jostled the old man's shoulders, then dropped his hands and turned his eyes away for a moment to collect himself. The old man's stare cut Glassman to the quick: the frustrated disorientation, the angry fear, the loneliness. Glassman knew—only fleetingly, but he knew—what it was like to slip loose from his familiar skin, to become someone else entirely, someone terrified and alone.

"No, there's nothing to do," Shuman answered in the calm,

albeit slightly raspy, voice Glassman recognized. He seemed to be back to his old self and Glassman was relieved. As the old man continued to shake his head, though, Glassman could sense him growing ever so slightly angry once again. His lips began to purse tightly against the surface of his dry teeth.

"It's just that people," Shuman continued, "people, goddamnit... they always have to go and ruin things."

Glassman suddenly heard the low rumble of thunder from the north. He glanced toward the noise, above the stand of sparsely clothed cypress trees in the nearby swamp; he saw a dark blanket slowly rolling down to cover them. It was time to go home. Reaching this silent agreement, they briskly made their way toward their cars just as heavy drops began to fall like gunshot all about them, lifting up dust on the trail. A solitary great blue heron pushed off its powerful legs and took to the air, beating its enormous wings slowly as it made its way west, deeper into the Everglades. Perhaps it knew a dry place amid the sawgrass to wait out the storm.

Shuman didn't say a word the whole way back to the lot. Was he angry at him? Glassman wondered. Had he somehow let the old man down? Had he been disrespectful? It seemed to Glassman that they had reached some sort of breaking point, that if he didn't say something quickly, now, before Shuman opened his car door and sputtered away, he might never again see the old man. Might never again see his grandfather.

Yes, Glassman felt almost certain now that Shuman was his grandfather. The layering upon layering of coincidences were one thing, but Shuman's outburst—coupled with Glassman's haunting recollection that the outburst triggered—stripped away nearly every cautious layer of doubt from the young editor's mind. The scene that had taken shape in his mind was too vivid to be the mischievous workings of his imagination. It was surely real, Glassman felt. That is, the scene had actually transpired between a grandfather and a grandson in Lackawanna. Glassman wondered how many additional memories of Abe lay dormant in his memory, how many were growing restless, prone at any moment to arise and stomp fiercely across his mental screen.

"I'm sorry . . . you know . . . about what happened, Mr. Shuman. . . . I'm sorry about everything." It was the only thing Glassman could think of to say.

"It's not your fault son." Shuman now consoled Glassman. "I'm sorry you had to see me behave that way. I promised I wouldn't allow myself to get that way in front of you. It's not something you should have to see and I'm sorry." Shuman paused at his open door, wiped a drop of rain or sweat off his brow. "It's just like what I said . . . what I said before our walk. . . ."

A booming thunder-clap suddenly shook the very ground and startled Glassman. *"Shit!"* he cried out fearfully. By the time he came to his senses, Shuman had already shut his door and was driving off slowly. Again, the old man had abruptly made himself scarce.

What did Shuman—for he would await permission, await the old man's irrevocable confirmation, to call him otherwise—mean when he referred to what he had said before their walk? He had said a lot of things before they started walking. Another peal of thunder, this time with a flash of lightning, crackled threateningly close, like attenuated radio static blaring. Glassman urgently swung open his car door and sealed himself inside. The rain beat down heavily now. A heavier rain than any Glassman could remember. The thick, deafening drops pounded against the roof and hood of the Toyota, which seemed to rock ever so slightly on its shocks. Glassman started the car and turned the wipers on their fastest setting, but thick, translucent sheets of water coated the windshield as soon as they were wiped away. He would have to sit out the storm, at least its most intense phase. He wondered how far Shuman had gotten, and hoped that he found a safe place to pull off the road.

Feeling vulnerable still, Glassman locked the doors, then reclined his seat the closest it would go to horizontal. The pinprick design on the car's ceiling distorted his depth perception. Disoriented, he lifted his hand, touched the ceiling and gained his bearings.

"Solitude ruins a man," he uttered to himself. The words came to his lips involuntarily, words he couldn't hear, though, over the metallic din of the storm. He tried again, louder—"solitude ruins a man!"—but still he could only hear the pounding rain. Finally, he desperately shouted the words as if he were drowning and thought that words could save him. SOLITUDE RUINS A MAN . . . IT DEVOURS YOU LIKE A CANCER!!! DEVOURS YOU!! SOLITUDE!!! DEVOURS!!!

Are You Talking
to Everybody, or Just
to a Few People?

The next morning after Glassman returned rain-soaked from the Everglades, he called his Uncle Ben from his office and set a date to deliver a short talk to one of Beth Sholom's havurah groups. He called his Uncle Ben because of what Shuman had told him the day before; he called because he felt it was partly his responsibility, as Weekly Books Editor for the local Jewish paper, to share his limited expertise with the community; he called because he was still on something of a high from Rebecca's news and felt that he could face a small group of twenty or so bookworms; and he called because he knew his uncle well enough to know that he wouldn't stop pestering him to deliver a free talk until he finally acquiesced. (It wasn't for nothing that the walls of Ben's study were lined with five outstanding service in fundraising plaques from the Lackawanna chapter of the United Jewish Federation.)

"Have sports jacket, will travel," Glassman announced jokingly to Rebecca as he entered their kitchen on the evening of the presentation. While she waited for him to shower and dress, she busied herself by scrubbing his coffee stain moons off their counters. She had agreed to come along for moral support. She stated her intentions casually the night before in a foamy voice as she brushed her teeth, but Glassman knew that Rebecca would never allow him to speak at such an event, unescorted. He was terribly vulnerable, she knew, especially amid his elders, who didn't recognize his vulnerability and often failed to treat him with the requisite tenderness. She would offer what protection she could.

"You look nice," she complimented him. "I love your floral tie."

"It's not . . . you know, too feminine?"

"Don't be ridiculous," Rebecca assured him. "You look like someone who doesn't have any hang-ups about his masculinity." What her comment said about the tie in question he wasn't sure. But it was too late to change.

Rebecca drove, which was unusual for them as she hated driving. Sitting there in the passenger seat ("Buckle up," his wife reminded him) somehow gave Glassman the feeling that his wife was taking him to the doctor's office to undergo a semi-serious procedure, or to the dentist to have his wisdom teeth pulled.

After some trouble punching in the correct code at the neighborhood gate ("I can never remember which one's the pound sign and which one's the star," Rebecca explained herself), they reached Dr. and Mrs. Bernard Fein's home in west Ropa. Ben had arranged for the Feins to host the talk since they lived in a fairly large home, which should have been Glassman's first warning that Ben had something slightly larger than an intimate gathering in mind. By the look of things—namely the rows of gleaming sedans parked haphazardly up and down the block, most halfway off the road onto the grass sward—one would have guessed there were over a hundred people there.

"Did you have any idea it would be this packed?" Rebecca asked.

"No idea. I guess I'm more popular than I thought." He tried to make light of the moment, but he was apprehensive. He hadn't counted on such a scene, and suddenly felt unprepared. He should have gone over his paper once more, revised the introduction for clarity, nailed down that final sentence that had dogged him rather than just abandon it as he had done.

"Just relax honey. You're going to be fine. Remember, you're the expert. They don't know anything."

"If only *they* thought I was the expert," Glassman answered.

Rebecca knew how to interpret the deep, crow's feet imprints suddenly aside his eyes, his splayed fingers through his hair, once, twice, three times. *Poor Matthew,* she thought. How did he get himself into these . . . these talks. Her husband really wasn't cut out for these engagements with his elders. In fact, he would have been much better off had he chosen a separate profession entirely, something less highly charged with familial and communal currents, something suitably subdued like law or accounting. But then, she reconsidered, would that accountant or lawyer have been Matthew? Her Matthew? Probably not.

Glassman knew enough from his phone conversations with irate readers of the *Jewish Weekly Times* that the older folks in south Florida—the very people currently crowded into the Fein's home—rarely deferred to his graduate degree and estimable position at the *Weekly*. He was just a twenty-eight year old pisher. What could he know? Themselves? They had *lived* what he purported to know. They stubbornly, almost pridefully, refused to stay current in their reading. They were history, but history that talked back. No, shouted back.

"Look at this house," Rebecca commented as they finally made their way to the home (the only parking spot they could find was a block away). She would try to get his mind off his presentation, if only for a moment.

She was right about the house. It was a gorgeous white stuccoed two-story with a Spanish style tile roof in at least three shades of red. The feathery leaves of two medium-sized Royal Poincianas swayed in the warm breeze on the front lawn. In the late spring, these trees (and others planted throughout Ropa) would be ablaze with orange-red blossoms.

"Boy those trees must be gorgeous in the spring," Rebecca continued, as if she had read his mind.

"Jeez hon', why don't *we* live out here?" It was a rhetorical question. They could never afford such new construction. Even if they could, Mary Beth Evans, their time-worn Southern Belle agent, had assured them that it was significantly hotter and wetter "out west" anyway.

"Well, time to face the enemy," Glassman joked mordantly at the front door; he stabbed at the doorbell quickly, in one motion, as if he were pulling an adhesive bandage off his forearm. WELCOME, said the mat in blue letters. A porcelain mezuzah, with hand-painted detailing in yellow and blue, apparently to match the colors of the front door and matt, was nailed aslant on the doorpost.

Their hostess, a diminutive, attractive woman of fifty or fifty-five, much younger than Glassman had expected, greeted them with effusive cheer. He noticed copies of the flyer advertising his talk on a narrow glass table bedecked with various silver pieces, THE SHOAH MUST GO ON: TRENDS IN AMERICAN JEWISH HOLOCAUST FICTION. The host then made his way over and shook his and Rebecca's hands vigorously. Dr. and Mrs. Fein (Linda, he learned) led them through the marble-floored foyer to an expansive living room, where he was to present his talk. Glassman envied the vaulted ceilings and complimented Dr. and Mrs. Fein profusely, almost covetously, on their lovely home. Several of the walls, in both the foyer and the living room, were mirrored to make the already large home seem larger, a minor touch Glassman disliked. The mirrored walls disoriented him, making him feel as if he were in a carnival fun house.

But the appointments of the home only occupied Glassman's attention for a brief moment. What demanded his attention instead were the throngs of people crammed like sardines into the Feins' living room. Only a select few, apparently, had managed to arrive early enough to secure one of the twenty or so seats on flimsy card-table chairs of various make and model. (Sofas, recliners, coffee tables, cushioned chairs and ottomans must have been stashed away somewhere to make more room.) The large majority of the guests were standing behind their more fortunate peers and around the perimeter of the room. Some were fidgeting with their watches; others had their hands crossed or on their hips. Glassman noticed one man exercising his neck in slow, three hundred and sixty degree rotations. They were restless.

The Feins had to clear the way through the crowd so that Glassman could make his way to his own lucite and metal card-table chair facing the crowd. He was certain that several of the standing guests flashed disgruntled looks at their hosts as they were forced to put their conversations on hold to make way for the speaker.

Glassman took his seat and felt immediately uncomfortable. For one thing, he couldn't see Rebecca, who decided to listen to the talk from the rear of the room rather than brave the "madding crowd," as she put it. "I'll be right back here for you," she assured him. "Break a leg sweetie." Glassman had counted on there being a lectern behind which he could stand. Without this physical barrier between himself and the audience, he felt vulnerable, exposed. The whole set up struck Glassman as an inharmonious marriage of the formal and intimate, stuck there in front of a massive audience, but sitting only five feet away from them without so much as a table in between. He considered standing to exert his authority as the expert (and, perhaps, capitalize on his considerable height), but decided against doing so. He thought it would be more awkward flipping through his crumpled pages while standing than it would be sitting down, where he could rest his pages discreetly on his lap.

Glassman knew before he uttered his first syllable that he had already failed the first test of his listeners by deciding not to speak extemporaneously. People hated to listen to someone read a talk. This he knew. Even his mother would complain about B'nai Torah's guest speakers who had the gall to simply stand up there at the lectern and read their presentations ("without even making any eye contact," she had criticized Golda Meir's niece or cousin). But speaking off the cuff demanded, at the very least, a modicum of professional confidence and/or trust in the generosity of one's audience. Glassman, at the moment, was blessed with neither.

Linda Fein, suddenly speaking beside him (standing, she only seemed a foot or two taller than Glassman in his seat), had prepared a long introduction, as effusive as her greeting at the door. Glassman gathered that she must have talked with Alten, or at least gotten her hands on his résumé, for she scrupulously described his educational training. Her tongue positively trilled over Latin and Greek phrases like magna cum laude and phi beta kappa. She went so far as to allude to his "brave, culturally confident" work at the *Collegian,* and even quoted from one of the atonement pieces, as he thought of them.

Shit, Glassman thought, *she's laying it on too thick.* He preferred short introductions, introductions that left him as little as possible to live up to. In a flurry of mental activity, he drafted options for an opening line: *I'm really not that bright folks, honest. . . . What she's not telling you, you know, is that my SAT scores, Princeton Review and all, weren't really that fabulous. . . . Well, that all shows you what a meager social life can do for the average college student.* No, Glassman thought, it was all too self-effacing. He tended toward the self-deprecatory comment, for which Rebecca continually chastised him. *Enough people will say bad things about you, Matt. You've got to learn to toot your own horn a little instead of always crashing your car into light posts.* Teenie, even less tolerant of his self-effacing tendencies, had taken to crying out the acronym "S-E! S-E!" each time he put himself down, however jokingly.

To his grandmother's mind, self-effacement was unseemly. Titles, awards, accomplishments, skills. These weren't things for which to apologize. Rather, they were to be celebrated, even touted. Glassman noticed that his grandmother, even to Rebecca's discomfort, insisted upon introducing his wife as Dr. Glassman to her friends and relatives and rolled her eyes when Rebecca dared introduce herself as a mere "teacher." It was an immigrant sensibility, he had determined. America, like Europe, wasn't egalitarian (despite what Americans liked to think), but stratified, and this was okay. You just worked your tuchus off to make sure that *you* were the one with the leather goods store, the thriving law practice, or the Dr. in front of your name. The social status. For that was the difference between Europe and America. Here, you could earn your yichus. Although there seemed to be something ruthless about it that grated against his sensibilities, who was he to deride a system that had worked so well, at least by his kin?

After Linda Fein was through, Glassman simply said thank you, cleared his throat, searching for just the right pitch to his voice, and began:

"Only within the past—"

"EXCUSE ME!" a woman's voice interrupted him from somewhere toward the back of the room. "CAN YOU SPEAK LOUDER!? WE'RE HAVING TROUBLE HEARING YOU BACK HERE!"

"AND SLOWER TOO!"a separate, male voice chimed in. Glassman could see him. The man was fortunate enough to have gotten a seat in the middle of the room. Glassman took a deep breath and tried to compose himself. They wanted slow? They wanted loud? Fine. He could manage that.

"Okay . . . can . . . everyone . . . hear . . . me?" he asked in a loud, measured voice. Most everyone nodded their approval, but Glassman was amazed to recognize still a few guests scattered throughout the room who, through hunched shoulders and a tilt of their heads, offered up only the most equivocal satisfaction with the clarity of his enunciation and the new and improved decibel level.

"As I was saying, only within the past thirty or so years—"

"MAYBE, SWEETHEART, YOU SHOULD STAND UP," Glassman heard the same woman's voice suggest, not unkindly. He was certain she thought she was doing the speaker a favor, immeasurably enhancing the efficacy of his presentation. "THEN WE'D ALL BE ABLE TO HEAR YOU BETTER," she continued.

Glassman shot himself up from his seat abruptly. He felt his composure slipping, and feared that he might lash back rudely if provoked further. But no, he remembered Shuman's manic episode at the Everglades—*STOP! STOP! STOP!*—and resolved to gather his wits, to keep himself from slipping irrevocably out of his skin.

"Okay, one more try. . . . Only within the past thirty or so years have American Jewish writers explored the Holocaust significantly in their work. One can readily enough imagine why these writers, in the wake of the catastrophe, were reluctant to—"

"EXCUSE ME!" a new male voice cut him off in mid-sentence. "ARE YOU TALKING TO *EVERYBODY* OR JUST A *FEW* PEOPLE!?"

Before Glassman, struck speechless by the man's brazenness, could think to respond, he heard a familiar voice from the rear chasten the crowd: "WHY DON'T YOU ALL STOP TALKING AND START LISTENING FOR A CHANGE AND SHOW YOUR GUEST SOME RESPECT!" Rebecca, unable to contain herself, had rushed to his defense. Unlike him, she wasn't the type of person to put up with any crap, especially crap slung at her vulnerable husband. Glassman noticed the crowd pivot their heads in unison to locate the source of the youthful voice; he himself couldn't see Rebecca.

The old man's sarcasm, as it turned out, was too caustic even for his cohorts to abide. As if to apologize for the behavior of their peer, they sat quietly through the rest of his presentation, which Glassman was fairly sure went poorly. He was flustered beyond the point of recovery and too distracted to pay much attention to what he was reading. Wishing only to get the talk over with and hightail it out of there, he plodded mechanically through his discussion of Bellow's and Malamud's elliptical, allusive treatments of the Holocaust in their work, and meandered his way through some sentences about the new works of fiction, *as courageous as they are controversial, in which a new generation of Jewish fiction writers grapple with the ongoing legacy of Holocaust, and challenge conventional approaches to thinking and writing about the atrocity.* At least this was what he thought he had written. But for all Glassman knew, he could have been reading recipes from a cookbook; he didn't even pause to punch key words and phrases, so unabsorbed was he with the content of his own speech.

What further distracted Glassman during his presentation was a man in the front row of the audience who sat completely still, arms crossed, knees spread, his back stiff in his seat, throughout the entire presentation. The man's gray eyes, beneath thick lenses and below bushy white furrowed eyebrows, were fixed angrily at him. He seemed to be about Shuman's age, but of a completely different species. The man's sizeable paunch, his pallid complexion, his heavy eyeglasses . . . all evoked a life spent mostly indoors. Not knowing the old man, Glassman entertained optimistically the possibility that this was the man's standard, neutral posture and expression. Or perhaps it was his contemplative one. Perhaps this old man was listening more attentively than Glassman was to the sentences streaming out of his mouth. But Glassman doubted it. He was no expert in body language, but he figured the best he could hope for was that the fellow, lost in his own thoughts, was angry at someone else. Several times during Glassman's mechanical recitation of his paper, he heard the man exhale sharply through his nostrils, a jet of impatient, angry air. Yes, hopefully it was just someone else who had pissed in his cereal to start off his day—the man's wife, perhaps, if she were still alive,

Finally, Glassman reached the merciful white space toward the bottom of his last page. He said thank you, received a tentative, but cordial, round of applause from the crowd, tightened his lips around his teeth and gave a short nod to return the gesture. He hoped to be on his way within minutes.

"Well," Linda Fein began, suddenly standing next to Glassman again, "that certainly was an intelligent and provocative talk," she offered charitably. Then she gestured toward him with an open palm as if she were showcasing a new car or boat on a game-show that some contestant stood the chance of winning. "I'm sure that Mr. Glassman would be happy to entertain a few questions."

"Yes, of course," he reluctantly replied.

As Glassman feared, the man who had been glaring at him began to speak in a halting, wheezy voice. The few hands scattered about him in the sky meant nothing to him. He had something to say and he was darn well going to say it.

"Vat, you s'ink, z'at your title . . . your title I von't even repeat your title . . . z'at it is cute or zamting?"

His title. Yes, Glassman had thought twice about using it, had feared it was too provocative. But the title, he decided, accurately illustrated the role that the Holocaust, the painful history, continued to play in forging the very identity of American Jews. This, at least, was what the recent novels and stories he had been reading (and trying, with limited success, to get reviewed in the *Jewish Weekly Times*) were telling him at the same time that everyone else was getting sick and tired of hearing about the suffering of the Jews and preferred to discuss other Holocausts, like the "American Holocausts" of the Middle Passage and the Trail of Tears.

His title, Rebecca thought. Why had her husband insisted upon that horrible title? And why had she allowed him to use it? She had read the draft of his presentation, just as she read everything that he wrote, and was irked by the title, as well. But she let it go, thinking that she was being supportive. Her husband didn't take criticism particularly well, especially concerning his writing, so she had let it go. But, in retrospect, it would have been wiser to make him reconsider the distasteful title. He had allowed a catchy pun to interfere with his good judgment. She should have predicted the angry response. The Holocaust survivor had asked a question that her husband would have to answer for himself. Rebecca could do nothing to protect her husband now. She stood stock still in the back of the room, mute and powerless, her jaw clenched tightly. What's more, she could feel the prickly heat of hives erupting on her neck and spreading northward toward her cheeks.

The audience shifted its gaze to Glassman as a unit, as if they were watching a tennis match between their pugnacious cohort and the speaker. They were waiting for Glassman to return the volley. "Ummm . . . well . . . I don't really think it's cute, no. That's not what I was trying to evoke in my title. I just think that it—"

"Mine muth-hair, mine fahth-hair, mine vife. All of z'em vair kilt, murchdered . . . vight in f'ont of mine eyes." The room was silent as he finished what he had to say. How many of them, Glassman wondered, had a similar tale to tell?

He didn't know how, exactly, to respond to the man's statement, but he had to say something. "Yes, I'm terribly, terribly sorry about your loss . . . but you see . . . what I'm trying to do here now is describe the aesthetic tradition of Jewish literature, and what role the Holocaust played in shaping that tradition." He had managed to articulate what he wanted to say better than he thought he would. He was talking about literature, art, not the Holocaust per se. Had this man listened to a word he was saying? Probably not. He had just chanced upon his title, which he thought was despicable, in the mailing that Ben sent to all the Havurah groups, or perhaps to the entire congregation for all Glassman knew. What Glassman had to say beyond the title of his talk was beside the point. Little wonder, then, that the man was equally unimpressed by his blatherings about aesthetic traditions and literature. Upon hearing Glassman's response to his statement, the old man swatted the nonsense down from the air between them with two outstretched hands. It was a dramatic gesture.

"Vat do you know of zuffering?" the old man challenged Glassman. "Vat do you know of loss?"

Something, Glassman silently thought. Something. But in the grand scheme of things, perhaps not much. The old man's suffering had been greater. Barbarous forces alien and unimaginable to Glassman had violently shaped the jagged contours of his life.

There was nothing he could say to this man just a few feet away, he realized. They spoke different languages.

But this wouldn't do.

Just a few feet away.

Glassman's very proximity to this aged man boggled his mind. Some ineffable force in the universe had created entirely separate worlds for the two of them. And this same force, it seemed to Glassman, had somehow thrust them together, a young American book editor and a death camp survivor. Had seen to it that these two souls collide on this designated spec of space in the universe, at this fleeting spot of time. Glassman hadn't been looking for this aged man, this relic. His energies had been spent on entirely separate salvage efforts. But here they were. No denying that. Surely there was something to extract. Some necessary knowledge, human knowledge, to glean.

Was Glassman to understand now, to understand finally, why the Holocaust was still sacrosanct to many, like his accuser seated just a few feet away? Why it was still off limits to irony, satire, humor (however mordant)? Off limits to the imagination itself?

To understand why Alten, his boss, had quashed that Glickstein review?

Matt, Alten had sounded out his name crisply to begin that ill-fated editor's meeting. *We all read this review you want to publish on that Holocaust novel, and it's just not something that's okay for the* Jewish Weekly Times. *I'm not about to give such dreck any more attention than it's already bound to get. It's a despicable novel. When there's definitive proof that Holocaust survivors actually stood on Berlin street corners after they were liberated and sold yellow stars and other such paraphernalia for profit, then he can write about it if he so chooses. But until then this novel, as you call it, is scurrilous, exploitative trash as far as I'm concerned.*

And so the review was quashed. Killed. At the time, Glassman took a certain amount of comfort in his self-righteous indignation. He was right and Alten was wrong. Sure, there *were* morally despicable works of fiction out there. Plenty of them. But the book in question wasn't exploitative. It wasn't sensationalist shlock. There was a moral purpose undergirding the scenes Alten and his cohorts found so disconcerting. Glassman was certain of this. Enough already with the redemptive, feel-good, *Schindler's List* type imaginings of the Holocaust—the by now stock horrific scenes tempered by the obligatory nod to the resiliency of the human spirit. Now *that* was despicable.

But maybe he had been wrong. Or, at least, not unequivocally in the right. His own vision, he realized now, could have been broader. But how to relate this, how to relate anything, to this intractable old man just a few feet away. *Just a few feet away.*

The young editor stood there, silent.

Fortunately for Glassman, a few other audience members broke the silence, which was becoming awkward. They piped in with a few innocuous questions. It was obvious that they were just being gracious enough to toss him a couple lobs. One man asked him simply to repeat the title of a book he had mentioned. Another asked him to recommend a recent novel to read ("if you could only read one?" the man asked, causing Glassman to ponder the extent to which the old man's question was a hypothetical one, as far as the elderly man was concerned).

Rebecca felt her hives recede, gradually. She unclenched her jaw.

After Glassman fielded these few, harmless questions, his hostess stood and asked her audience to join her in thanking Glassman once again. Following another courteous, if not exuberant, round of applause, Glassman thanked his hosts, retrieved Rebecca, and fled the home (making up a serviceable excuse about an early morning the next day) rather than enjoy the coffee, rugelach, and Russian tea cake that the Feins had put out for their guests. Rebecca told him that her stomach felt a bit cramped in any case.

"Really honey it wasn't that bad," Rebecca assured her distressed husband once they were back in the car.

"Wasn't that bad?" Glassman challenged his wife. "Wasn't that bad? Were we in the same fucking room! They ate me alive!"

"Well now you're exaggerating things. It was really only a few people. The rest of them seemed to enjoy the talk very much, although you really could slow down a bit. I even saw a couple women next to me nod their heads in agreement with what you were saying—"

"But that man," Glassman interjected. "That old man. What can I do about a man like that. What do I say to *him*? How do I talk to *him*?"

Rebecca elided the question. "You're too sensitive," she answered tangentially. She wouldn't think of critiquing his title now. "That's your problem. You can please some of the people some of the time, and . . . well, you know the expression."

Fine, Glassman thought. Maybe he was a bit thin-skinned. But Rebecca, he decided, was only being half sincere, trying to underplay the disaster that was their evening. It was a miserable talk.

He didn't care so much about the petty hecklers. These were the same people who rudely kibbitzed with one another in the middle of Rabbi Pinsker's sermon. It had flat out become too exasperating for them to attend Beth Sholom during the season when the sanctuary was packed, when a caravan of airport-like shuttle buses brandishing the logos of various retirement communities clogged up the parking lot.

But the old man still troubled him. He wished that he had handled the situation better, that he hadn't stood there mute, waiting for the audience to bail him out. At the very least, he should have approached the old man after the talk. There had to be something more to say. You couldn't let people like that just up and leave. The stakes, the human stakes, were too high. Perhaps all this searching and searching for lost souls, Glassman reflected, was a waste of valuable time and effort. Forget the relevant dead and gone. There were plenty of relevant living in his midst. If it was contact he needed, why not make it with those standing in front of his nose? He resolved not to let them flutter off into the breeze again, or disappear at the clap of thunder.

The editor loosened his tie with three jerky motions and reclined his seat close to horizontal. He put his hand over his eyes covering his vision. He felt the fingertips of a gentle hand on his thigh, comforting him. He needed to breathe . . . *breathe, breathe.*

"There there, honey," Rebecca cooed. "Relax now. It's going to be okay."

He knew what his grandmother would tell him about the evening. He could hear her very words: *I don't know why you agreed to deliver a talk without being compensated anyway. I could kill Benjamin. The synagogue has money. They could have paid you something for your trouble. You see what happens when you let people take advantage of you?*

And Teenie would have a point. But this is what Glassman wondered the whole way home in the car as he breathed deeply in, deeply out. As red-faced as he was at the Feins as he stood up to escape, why did he feel the tears well up in his eyes and his Adam's apple thicken in his throat when, nearly to the door, nearly to freedom, a separate elderly man approached him arm in arm with his female companion and said, "I'm Harry Rubenstein. This is my wife Miriam. That was a *very* provocative evening young man! Thank you."

You and your Jews. You and your old people.

I Heard the Heartbeat

Was Glassman to blame? Was it all his fault? So obsessed was he with his own poor performance at the Feins that he didn't give more than a passing thought to Rebecca's upset stomach. Such a load of damaged goods was he that he effectively kept his wife from thinking of herself for even one precious moment. He had greedily allowed her to come along to protect him without even thinking that *she* was the one who more legitimately required protection. Protection and rest. Not the stress of spending an evening as his emotional bodyguard. So was Glassman to blame?

"Noooo! Oh noooo!" Rebecca shrieked from the bathroom that night, waking Glassman from his sleep. In a flash, he was wide awake, as if he hadn't even been asleep just seconds before. It was still pitch black outside. He knew immediately what was wrong. What else could it be? He had never heard Rebecca wail before. She was experiencing, he thought, a previously untapped emotion. At least one he had never seen her experience before. It frightened him.

He rushed to the door of the bathroom. Rebecca looked up at him, tears in her eyes. Had he ever seen her cry before? She was bracing herself against the vanity, her cotton underpants just above her knees, half-soaked in blood. *Blood!*

"I'm bleeding, Matt! I'm bleeding," she cried, her terror giving way gradually to sadness. She seemed to be leaning there out of inertia more than anything else. She didn't know what else to do.

"Here, get those off," he pleaded with her, trying his best to be helpful. "Go lie on the bed. I'll call Dr. Arias's answering service."

Rebecca complied. He had the number in a card in his wallet just next to the ultrasound photograph, folded into quarters. He turned on the light, found the card easily and dialed the number, then entered their number into the machine. As he hung up the phone, gingerly, he noticed the time on the nightstand clock: 4:48 A.M.

Rebecca had grown silent. She was sitting up in the bed, bolt upright, crying softly now. She had already made her own diagnosis. "Can I get you anything?" he asked. "Are you in pain?" She shrugged. Told him she didn't want anything.

Glassman rushed to the family room to retrieve a recently purchased book.

"Here, here!" Glassman pointed frantically at a page in the center of the book as he burst back into the room. "It says that spotting's okay! Maybe everything's okay!" Glassman tried to convince Rebecca. And himself. But they both knew better. Even Troy, who Glassman just noticed, seemed to know better. He lay still on the carpet, his head half hidden in his outstretched forelegs, a mournful look on his face.

The phone suddenly rang (just as Glassman began wondering whether they should go to the emergency room) and Rebecca answered it quickly.

"I'm bleeding," he heard Rebecca explain. "No, it's much more than that . . . yes, like my period . . . more even . . . no, just blood that I can see . . . no, well maybe just a little . . . yes, I can wait . . . uh huh . . . uh huh . . . I know . . . thank you . . . see you soon."

"Well?" Glassman asked after Rebecca returned the phone to the cradle gently. "What did she say?"

"She said that I'm most likely having a miscarriage, and that there was nothing that she could do to reverse it even if it were just starting. . . ."

She said this all with complete calm. Glassman marveled at his wife's powers of recovery. She was a rock. He had always thought this about her, realized that her possession of this quality he so utterly lacked accounted in no small part for her pull over him. But he had never seen it so convincingly demonstrated.

"She said that it's not our fault. That it's increasingly common. Up to 40 percent of all conceptions, which seems sort of high to me . . . I think she might be exaggerating a little to make us feel better."

"She's a doctor, honey. She wouldn't exaggerate. Is she going to meet us at her office?" Glassman was already reaching into his drawer for his jeans.

"No, she said I could go to the emergency room, but I told her I'd rather wait until six thirty and see her in the office. I'm not really in much pain. I just have mild cramps."

Mild cramps? Wait until six thirty? Why, Glassman wondered, *so Dr. Arias can eat her Cheerios?* This was the kind of asinine etiquette that he practiced, not Rebecca. Why on earth did she say she could wait?

The hour dragged. They didn't even contemplate trying to sleep. Glassman offered to make chamomile tea. Rebecca thanked him and said that tea would be nice. He noticed that she let it grow cold in its oversized mug in front of her, but he didn't press her to drink it. They just sat silently on the futon in the family room. It struck him bitterly that only seven weeks ago or so they were sitting in the exact same position on the futon, silently holding one another's hands in precisely the same way, just after Rebecca had told him that she was pregnant.

I'm going to be a father! he had said.

He wondered whether Rebecca was suffering through the same recollection. He hoped not and didn't inquire.

Dr. Arias met them outside the locked building. Glassman was a bit surprised when she initiated a hug with Rebecca upon seeing her. He supposed he wasn't up on the latest doctor/patient etiquette. From the neck down he was healthy, preternaturally so. His Tay-Sachs test and the stitches he recently received on his brow were his first doctor's visits in quite a while. Rebecca, on the other hand, had been seeing Dr. Arias rather regularly over the past year or so. He decided it was natural and good that Arias developed warm relationships with her patients.

Rebecca didn't want Glassman to come into the room with her. Did she really want to be in there alone, or did she simply want to spare her fragile husband? Should he have protested more vehemently? Insisted upon being with her? He didn't know. In any case, she was in the examination room before he could think to challenge her professed wishes. He didn't feel there was anything he could do about it now.

Rebecca was in the examination room for less than an hour, but it seemed much longer to Glassman, who flipped mechanically through pages of *Shape* and *Working Woman*. At one point, a woman with a ponytail and dressed in what Glassman identified as pink health care clothes entered the office and greeted Glassman in subdued tones. She was probably a nurse, who had been surprised to see him, but had been surprised several times before by husbands in waiting rooms at odd hours. She knew that it was a bad sign and didn't ask questions of him. He was thankful.

The door finally clicked open and Rebecca reentered the waiting room. Dr. Arias had her arm around her as they approached.

"We lost the baby," Rebecca informed him. The news didn't rock him. What would have rocked him would have been hearing that everything was all right. "It wasn't our fault, Dr. Arias says. It was still an *early* miscarriage, even though it was sort of close to the borderline. Up to 40 percent of all conceptions end in an early miscarriage. It was already underway by the time I woke up, probably. And there was nothing we could have done even if we would have caught it earlier. She had to perform a D and C to stop the bleeding and complete the . . . removal of the . . ."

"Embryonic material," Dr. Arias helped Rebecca to explain.

Did they have to go over all the painful details now? Who insisted upon it? Arias or Rebecca? Glassman wasn't sure.

"Do you have any questions you'd like to ask me?" Dr. Arias inquired. Somehow he hadn't anticipated that she would address him. He couldn't think of any questions to ask.

Arias finally anticipated a question he might have had: "Just so you are aware, Mr. Glassman, this miscarriage shouldn't have any effect on your ability to conceive as a couple in the future and carry a baby to term."

"Oh, that's good," he answered lamely. He somehow hadn't thought of the opposite, darker possibility. He hoped that Rebecca hadn't been worrying about it.

"I'm sorry honey. I'm sorry I lost the baby," Rebecca apologized softly on the way home. She sat slouched in her seat and gripped the canvas shoulder-strap of her seat belt, as if to keep herself from sliding to the floor.

"Don't be ridiculous, sweetie. It's not your fault. You heard what Dr. Arias said. Remember, we didn't even think we could conceive for a long time. At least now we know we can conceive. That's half the battle. Right?"

But it was too early to be focusing on the bright side of things. Rebecca raised her left arm to ward off his words, then let it fall limply to her lap.

"Not now, honey," she insisted. "Please. Not now. I just lost our baby."

"It wasn't a *baby*, Rebecca. Stop calling it that!" he cried, more harshly than he had intended. He regained his composure and continued in a more soothing voice, "You heard what Dr. Arias said. It was an *early* miscarriage. It happens to 40 percent of pregnancies. It wasn't our fault. It just happens sometimes. It was just an embryo. Not even an embryo. Just some embryonic material."

"But Matt . . . Matt . . ."

"Yes? What is it honey?"

"I heard the heartbeat."

The Defender of Weak
and Victimized Pooches

S evere episodes of depression, Glassman had read, could be triggered by specific events; or one could occur out of the blue
without any precipitating event at all. The chemical imbalances in the brain could wreak their own, unassisted havoc. He had
always taken comfort in the knowledge that, at least since the shock
treatments at Saint Vincent, he could trace his especially depressed
periods to traumatic events. He took this to mean that he was less
sick than those who suffered episodes for no apparent reason. In
graduate school, just after he had started dating Rebecca, it had been
the combination of bronchitis and the antibiotics that had wiped
him out. He didn't care what the nurse said, or the thick pharmaceu-
tical handbook he had checked out of Pattee after he had recovered.
Erythromycin was largely responsible for sending him into a tail-
spin. More recently, it was the violent blow to his head at Patch Corral that had rocked him. The fog had only lifted after Rebecca shared
her happy news with him.

So of course the fog rolled back in after her miscarriage.

Could there be a more appropriate time to be disconsolate? How
could anyone gauge the appropriateness of an emotional response?

Who, if anyone, should be granted the authority to proffer such judgments? Sometimes, Glassman tried to convince himself, it was good and right to be depressed. Suffering had gotten a bad rap in America. With all the latest medications and therapies, one needn't suffer through manic or depressed episodes any longer. Drugs couldn't make your problems go away, but they would help you sail along even-keeled through the storm. *Why screw with depression in the 1990s for God's sake?* Rebecca had challenged him. This seemed to be the prevailing wisdom of the day. And there was definitely something to be said for it. Perhaps all his rationalizing about the virtues of suffering was what was truly pathological. A Jewish thing. Like the old joke went: *Why don't Jews drink? It interferes with their suffering.*

But jokes aside, he wondered whether one could ever experience exuberant, boundless joy on an even keel. Could he experience the euphoria that had characterized his spirits during the weeks just after Rebecca had told him she was pregnant? Was he willing to give this feeling up?

Plus, would his medicated mind be nearly so agile, so productive, so damn entertaining to himself, if to no one else, during his non-depressed weeks and months (at least 75 percent of the time after all)?

Could a medicated mind ever do more than just "show?"

These were the thoughts that now consumed Glassman, consumed him while he waited for Shuman to return. He desperately needed the old man now, needed to confide in the one person who intimately knew his pain. Who else would truly understand? He wouldn't burden Rebecca with his own suffering. It wouldn't be fair. She had withdrawn into her own shell for a solid week after the miscarriage, called in sick to school, had someone cover her classes. She had moped about the house in a dingy white T-shirt and gray sweatpants from her grad school days that Glassman hadn't realized she still owned. In short, she frighteningly reminded Glassman of himself for those seven days. But after the week was up—as if she had consciously allotted herself exactly one mournful week—she showered, brushed her teeth and hair, even applied a light coat of lipstick to her lovely mouth, and returned to work, returned to the world of the living. Glassman was disinclined to drag her back down to his gloomier realm through selfishly venting his pain.

This was the type of crisis during which children, Glassman knew, relied upon the experience, the kindness, the empathy, of their parents. And their grandparents if they were lucky enough to have any. He knew, however, that he wouldn't confide in his mother or in Teenie. They would be angry with him if they knew that he had spared them such vital knowledge. Yet his mother had suffered (perhaps continued to suffer, despite her protestations to the contrary) her own interior demons. And both is mother and grandmother had already suffered the untimely disappearance of a loved one. However tough they outwardly appeared, however hardened by their experience, Glassman couldn't bring himself now to contribute to their losses. Especially since he had so hoped to share happy news with them about a forthcoming addition to the Glassman-Fishbein clan.

He also couldn't quite bring himself to seek Shuman out at the Everglades. Somehow he knew that he wouldn't be there for him, and feared that the sight of that empty bench, under the interlaced branches, would be too much for him to bear. The old man had fled during a storm and would return only on his own terms. This much Glassman knew. So he waited for Shuman to call and tried the best he could, in the meantime, to stick with his routines.

He managed to go to work each day, although he shaved only every other day. It was a good thing that Alten expected so little of him. It took exceedingly little creative energy to polish up the prose of one insipid review after the other, and set up the columns of his Weekly Books page on his computer behind his closed office door. He passed Sylvia Kreiser's desk each morning and afternoon, grunted a hello, and communicated with Trish Rowan only when absolutely necessary.

He noticed Trish staring over his head one day as she dropped off his mail at his desk. The next instant, she trotted behind him to flip the pages of his calendar, a free one he had received from the World

Wildlife Fund after impassively donating a small sum. "You're two months behind," she observed perplexedly. "Jeez, you've been on a different planet lately." She was mildly irritated, Glassman knew, having already more or less purged him as a friend. He often noticed her on the phone just outside his office, fondling a Starbuck's cup in one hand, her hair tucked femininely behind the ear pressed against the receiver, speaking through a smile, probably to a confidant or some new boyfriend. She had bigger, saner fish to fry.

When he wasn't working, he moped about the house in his boxers. He slept fitfully and, more often than not, endured silent, somnambulant nights. He had taken to drinking two Dos Equis beers before bed to help him rest, but it didn't seem to work. More often, it had the opposite effect, forcing him to lurch resentfully toward the bathroom in the middle of the night to empty his bladder.

He walked Troy, who mysteriously seemed to share his sorrow, just long enough for him to do his "business," then dragged the poor cur back to the house. He allowed his gumbo limbo branches to hang over the sidewalk, in gross violation of the Ropa Gatos city ordinances, ordinances he had always viewed as semi-fascist anyway. He permitted a rich carpet-colony of yellowish green algae to reestablish itself along the sides and bottom of their swimming pool.

He still called Teenie every other day, and managed to utter a few desultory sentences, but begged out of most of their television nights. He was glad, and somewhat surprised, that Teenie didn't press him.

He didn't touch Rebecca in bed.

Rebecca had touched him a few times. She had been greeted twice with his limp and unresponsive noodle as she reached over his hip from behind; she didn't seem willing to make a third attempt. For the moment, she told him, she didn't really care about the sex. But she wouldn't start taking on all of his chores. It was enough that she had started to do most of the cooking, but she couldn't do everything she insisted.

For her part, she seemed to be coping better and better as the weeks passed. Coping almost too well, Glassman couldn't help but think.

"Maybe you're internalizing it," he finally proposed to Rebecca. Truth was, he had begun to wish that she would manifest more visible signs of grief. Something about her resilience struck him as cool, even a bit ruthless.

"I am not 'internalizing!' You think I haven't grieved!? You think I'm still not grieving!? I am! But we have to get on with it, Matt!" She paused, exhaled contemplatively through her nostrils. "I'm only twenty-seven, Matthew," she continued, softly. "We have plenty of time to have kids. Do you have any idea how lucky we are? What good does it do anyone to mope around?"

She paused once again. He wasn't sure whether she was gathering her thoughts or waiting for him to respond to her question. "You know, you're not grieving, Matt. You're obsessing. One thing's for sure. You're not yourself."

"I'm sorry."

"Well, sorry's not enough Matt. You've got to snap out of it. It's been weeks. We can't go on like this. You need to talk to somebody. I'm not . . . I'm not . . ."

"What?"

"Qualified," she answered. "I'm your wife. I can't be your doctor."

"Okay," he assured her. "If I don't snap out of it soon, I promise I'll see someone."

"One week," Rebecca told him, raising her index finger for clarity.

You're not yourself.

Maybe this *was* himself? Had she ever thought of that? Maybe this was precisely who he was. Maybe the drugs, and even just talking with a doctor, wouldn't restore him to his true self at all, but transform him into someone else entirely. All things considered, Glassman had to admit to himself, maybe this wouldn't be so bad. But still, it seemed to him that every life had its own narrative, of sorts, with its own distinct peaks and valleys. The narrative wasn't always pretty or pleasant, but it was *your* narrative and yours alone. Wouldn't mood altering drugs rob you of that story, the story of your brief but miraculous life?

Passover passed Glassman right by. He managed to feign illness on the night of the first Seder. (They hadn't been invited to a second.) He coaxed Rebecca into going to Teenie's without him. In tupperware containers, she brought back matzo ball soup, brisket, haroset, and potent slivers of horseradish. To mollify Rebecca, he nibbled on a Hillel sandwich of bitter herbs and sweet haroset before the hypnotic, blue glow of the television.

She made him matzo brei with syrup and raspberry preserves on the first two mornings of the eight day holiday (which left Glassman painfully constipated for the remaining six), and steered clear of bread, pasta, cereal, even legumes, even though some of these dietary restrictions had always seemed asinine to her (*what in the world peas have to do with yeast I'd really like to know,* she complained). Glassman was usually a stickler when it came to the Passover rules. This year he ate what Rebecca served, but otherwise didn't discriminate between what was leavened and unleavened. He knew that Kreiser looked at him aslant when he strolled into the building and tossed the remains of a half eaten bagel into her wastebasket, but he didn't care.

Glassman managed to tread water for several more weeks. The night was both his greatest friend and his worst enemy. When he managed to sleep, the hours between midnight and morning were a merciful reprieve from a day fraught with amorphous worry and despair. But when sleep eluded him, the anguish he felt during those six silent hours was far more intense than the anguish of the day. However frenetic and bustling Ropa Gatos was during daylight hours, it was hardly a city that never slept. Rather, it was asleep by nine o'clock, when practically all that could be heard was the sporadic, plaintive whistle of the Florida East Coast trains, which lumbered up and down the coast on the tracks near the Dixie Highway. When he lay in his bed awake, the entire somnolent city mocked him. Most frustratingly, he couldn't identify any pattern, or any variable, that explained his insomnia. Some nights he slept. Others he didn't.

Glassman knew that he had to stick with his routines if he was going to pull himself out of the mire. So instead of retreating home from his office to end a second miserable week, he forced himself to the gourmet Italian market that he usually frequented at least once a week. Shopping at Mascolo's, he knew, would be a true test of his fitness. Customers at Mascolo's assumed malevolence on the part of everyone else and acted accordingly. Glassman could never quite embrace the competitive protocol and usually lurched through the aisles in a funk, often forgetting what he was even there to purchase. While he proficiently selected milk cartons imprinted with the most far off sell-by date, he invariably brought home mediocre fruit—peaches mottled with caramel bruises, strawberries already exuding that overripe saccharine stench, bananas somehow both immaturely green and bearing black stripes of old age. Still, the fish and baked goods at Mascolo's outstripped the displeasure of shopping there. Pretty much every week he would splurge on yellowtail snapper, Atlantic (rather than the bland farm-raised) salmon, sushi quality tuna steaks, and, for dessert, miniature chocolate chip cannolis and Russian tea cake filled with cherries and golden raisins and covered with slivered almonds under a sugary glaze.

Given the state he had been in lately, he felt that the least he could do was get off his self-pitying ass for one evening and please Rebecca. Yellowtail snapper, a delectable local fish with soft and sweet white flesh, had become Rebecca's favorite meal when he prepared it Francese, a simple pan-frying in butter and lemon after a light flour dredging. So he drove the short distance to the store. The parking lot was far too small to accommodate the daily horde of cars and customers, but Glassman managed somehow to find a spot at the far end next to the garbage dumpster. That putrid stench, common to garbage dumpsters nationwide, it seemed to Glassman, offered him a sour greeting as he stepped from his car. Ambling toward Mascolo's entrance, he noticed a woman in a white sedan turn sharply into a spot just after it was vacated by man in a black Ford Explorer. She had, perhaps unwittingly, stolen the spot from another woman in a tan minivan, whom Glassman had noticed waiting with her blinker on before the woman in the white sedan sped past his right shoulder and took the spot from the opposite direction. Glassman had been in south Florida long enough to know that there was going to be trouble.

The woman in the minivan, a blond woman of about forty, spun her wheels and nearly rammed into the parked car before slamming on her brakes. She blared her horn in three long complaints. The woman in the parked sedan, an older woman, had just gotten out of her car and looked nonplused. *What does this crazy woman want?* Glassman imagined her thinking.

The blond woman stepped down from her minivan and slammed her door. She put both hands on her hips, jutting her elbows at angry angles.

"GET YOUR CAR OUT OF THAT SPOT LADY! IT'S MINE! MY BLINKER WAS ON! DON'T EVEN TRY TO PRETEND YOU DIDN'T SEE ME!"

This is no way to go about things, Glassman thought. She was absolutely mad. The older woman, however, did steal the spot. If she didn't see the minivan waiting, she certainly should have. Glassman tried to give the elderly the benefit of the doubt during such circumstances. They didn't see as well. Their hand-eye coordination wasn't what it used to be. They were just doing the best they could. Still, he was almost certain that some of them went about their business willfully blind and clueless. Farmisht. It seemed to work for them.

"Well," the older woman replied in a huff, "I'm certainly not getting back into my car to park somewhere else now. Not after the way you're behaving."

"You're *not!?* You're *not!?*" Glassman wasn't sure whether the younger woman said this out of sheer surprise or as a challenge to her adversary.

"YOU KNOW," she continued, "IT'S YOU OLD FUCKING JEWISH LADIES WHO ARE RUINING THIS TOWN! IF YOU ALL JUST LEFT THE REST OF US WOULD BE BETTER OFF!"

Glassman's stomach churned. He should have been in the store shopping already. Several people had passed back and forth between Mascolo's and their cars, just barely taking notice of the hubbub. Why had his feet remained planted?

"Ooo . . . ooo. The language! How dare you speak like that to me young lady! I'm taking down your license plate and reporting you to the police! *That's* what I'm doing!"

The woman, scrunching her eyebrows together quizzically, seemed unperturbed by the threat, but retreated nonetheless. She climbed back into her minivan and proceeded to back out violently, almost running over the old woman who had clomped on her thick heels behind her to memorize the plate number. It was a special order tag that advertised the Florida Panthers hockey team. Glassman noticed her purple bumper sticker that read, MY CHILD IS ON THE HONOR ROLL AT ROPA GATOS COMMUNITY MIDDLE SCHOOL. He was too overwrought to memorize the tag number.

"Seeya later gran'ma!" the woman shrieked as she sped to a vacant space at the rear of the lot.

"YOU!" the older woman shouted at Glassman, having seemingly just noticed his timid presence. She raised an index finger and pointed it at him like a gun. "You're a witness! You saw her! You heard what she said!"

"No," he pleaded as he shrank back toward his car. "I . . . I . . . I didn't see anything. I'm not a witness."

He bolted toward the entrance on the balls of his feet and waited impatiently as the automatic sliding glass doors reluctantly opened wide enough to allow him inside.

In the store at last, Glassman was promptly greeted by a clash of metal as an elderly woman banged his cart aside in the dairy aisle with her own cart, wordlessly passing him on the left. Thick folds of fat swung from underneath her biceps like globular hammocks; her hair was tinted to an enraged orange hue. He had been debating whether to buy a domestic Parmesan or spring for a costly wedge of the imported Reggiano; his fellow shopper evidently didn't have time to wait for Glassman to decide. He shouldn't have been fazed. It was common for shoppers in Mascolo's to drive their miniature carts recklessly through the cramped aisles at breakneck speed as if they were bumper cars. But the minor, uncivil gesture somehow affected him powerfully. The old woman hadn't even acknowledged his presence. She would have erased him if she could. Erased him and casually swept his ash-drift remains off the face of the planet with the blade of her hand.

He headed toward the produce section, plucking miscellaneous items from the shelves along the way. In front of tomato pyramids, he glumly observed several customers standing side-by-side, holding their ground, plucking, pressing, and replacing, plucking, pressing, and replacing tomato after tomato with a singleness of purpose that amazed Glassman. An aura of desperation hovered over those testing avocados, who worked at an even more furious clip. There weren't enough ripe ones to go around!

Peaches. Yes, he would pick out some ripe peaches for Rebecca, who loved to slice them over her cereal. Two women stood before the peach pyramid, feverishly pitching the best ones they could find into their thin plastic baggies. Glassman ripped a baggie from the enormous roll, then hesitated for a moment, unsure whether to join the ladies at the rapidly dismantling pyramid or wait for at least one of them to finish. He decided to join them. There was just enough room for another shopper between them; if he didn't fill the vacancy, someone else surely would. So he left his cart in an unobtrusive corner of the produce alcove, stepped lightly between his two fellow shoppers, barely brushing up against the elderly woman to his right, reached toward the fuzzy flesh of the first prospective peach . . .

"Excuse me boychik! We were here first. Would it kill you to wait a few minutes?"

It was all that he could take for one afternoon.

All that he could take? What had he really witnessed? Nothing in the grand scheme of things. The gnashing of metal carts, sharpened elbows and tongues. Certainly no crimes. YOU OLD FUCKING JEWISH LADIES. Was such scurrilous speech a crime? Glassman wasn't sure. It was certainly nothing compared to the cataclysmic horrors of a bloody century, the horrors witnessed by the irascible aged man, Glassman's accuser, at his ill-fated talk. But perhaps the age of tumult on a grand scale had passed. Nuclear threats, tribal skirmishes, localized atrocities. These realities would persist. It seemed to Glassman, however, that a more insidious and slow death, an anesthetized killing, threatened humankind as well in the soul-crushing incivility that had gradually become standard protocol in his new home, this densely populated swath of paved earth. Too many people, he thought. Too many people hermetically sealed from one another by their very anonymity in this throbbing foot of the continent, the simultaneous density and transiency of the human population its most salient quality. Too many people sealed from one another in their climate controlled automobiles and condominiums; sealed from one another in gated "neighborhoods" and retirement villages, designed seemingly to preclude any chance of human intercourse from within or without (no sidewalks, no central parks, pools, or stores); sealed from one another by their cell phones equipped with unlimited minutes that insured unlimited, vapid conversations that, in turn, insured that no one was ever really there where their corporeal presence happened to be at the moment, where various other tangible souls happened to be at the very same moment, but elsewhere, anywhere, anywhere but there . . .

Fuck, Glassman thought. *I'm fucking losing it. No . . . no . . . no.*

Had he intoned these final words audibly? He wasn't sure, but thought so. The mental screen that he could usually count upon to filter his manic cerebrations before they became public rantings had given way. He could have sworn that the woman who had just admonished him glanced quickly toward him to figure out what was what. He retreated a single step backwards from the fruit and lifted a hand to shield his eyes from the blinking, piercing fluorescent light.

"Are you all right, dear?" the woman asked, gazing up at him. Glassman realized that he must have looked as if he were suffering from an intense migraine. She abruptly dropped her bag of fruit on top of the dissembled pyramid, and didn't even seem to notice that one of her painstakingly selected peaches tumbled from the bag to the floor. She was visibly concerned, which frightened Glassman. "Don't take it so hard boychikele. I just didn't want you to step on my toe. I had a bunion removed this morning. Is it your head?" she asked. "Would you like an aspirin? I always carry them in—"

"No," Glassman answered resolutely. His head was fine. Fine.

He needed to get out of there. Right away! But he couldn't leave without the fish. It was the only vital ingredient he simply had to retrieve. After all, if he couldn't carry out a simple trip to Mascolo's, what good was he? So he bolted with his cart to the fish counter at the rear of the store.

"Oh, that's a real sly move mister! That's a good one, I gotta hand it to you!" a middle-aged woman at the counter sarcastically berated a thickly built man, about the same age. Her bejewelled hand stretched over the glass counter, as if to implore the fish monger to pluck the green ticket she gripped tightly between a meaty thumb and forefinger. Glassman, ripping a green ticket of his own from the red dispenser, apparently had arrived just in time to witness yet another altercation for the day.

"Fine. Fine. Just go ahead of me. I'd hate to hold you up, ma'am. I'm sure you have *really* important things to do!" Upon delivering his caustic retort, his large ears reddened to a near crimson. Glassman heard enough to know what had transpired. These squabbles at bakery and fish counters were commonplace. The waits were so long that shoppers, like this thickly built man, usually ripped their tickets from the dispensers and continued their shopping elsewhere in the store, only to return six or seven numbers late and—to the consternation of those who had aggressively waited—insist upon being served next.

The tightly clustered group of twenty or so shoppers brandishing green tickets of their own waited impatiently for the situation to resolve itself. One man gazed straight up toward the ceiling, perhaps to distract himself from the awkward scene before him. A young woman straining to carry her plastic basket—overflowing with bananas, a long loaf of bread, a glass bottle of herb-infused vinegar, and several other items Glassman couldn't see—shook her head from side to side slowly and methodically, a protracted advertisement of her disgust. A teenaged girl baring her flat midriff and navel ring flipped open her hot-pink cell phone, perhaps to explain her delay to someone who expected her.

Glassman knew Pete, the fish monger on duty. So frequently did he shop at Mascolo's, in fact, that he knew all of the fish mongers and nearly always received service with an extra touch of conviviality. Pete was built slightly with close-cropped, blonde hair beneath his red Mascolo's cap. He was a soft-spoken fellow with an incongruous, thick Boston accent, who regularly lamented the scarcity of Haddock in Florida. *Sure, I'll sell you some Chilean sea bass, but you know what would really be good with some butter and lemon . . .* Glassman liked Pete, especially after the fish monger had given him two of his four soft-shell crabs for free a couple months ago after Glassman shared his simple but scrumptious recipe (a long buttermilk soak, a thin coating of flour and cayenne pepper, and a cast iron pan).

Pete, unsurprisingly to Glassman, seemed loath to intervene in the current dispute between his customers. He just stood there impassively, his blue, bloodshot eyes darting back and forth between the antagonists; he would wait for them to iron things out. The other customers weren't so patient.

"Come on for Christ's sake!" a young man standing just beside Glassman with enormous biceps and a dark tan complained. Wearing black spandex shorts and an artfully torn, purple tank-top, he looked as if he had just come from the gym. "Screw these two idiots!" he continued. "The rest of us are waiting too, you know." Glassman's every muscle stiffened.

"I hope you don't eat with that mouth," a matronly woman chastised the muscle-bound man. She wore a long floral dress, overabundant with fabric, and kept her protective hand on her young son's shoulder. She could have been anywhere between twenty-five and fifty years old for all that her vehemently desexed appearance revealed. "You're in public you know," she continued to berate the man. "Children are present. You should watch your behavior."

"Listen lady, don't bring your fucking goody-two-shoe crap—

"STOOOOOPPPPPPP!!!" Glassman suddenly heard himself screaming at the top of his lungs, raising his clenched fists before him. During this reflexive gesture he accidentally—or at least he thought it was an accident—upended his cart. A bottle of extra virgin olive oil shattered on the hard floor, bleeding a green pool from which the crowd retreated in a giant O. Everyone except for Glassman, that is, who stood in the center of the thick pool, beside his toppled groceries. "ARE YOU ALL CRAZY?!!! . . . HAVE YOU ALL LOST YOUR MINDS?!!!"

So much for his mental screen.

He bent over and plucked the wet groceries from the floor, clutched the whole awkward mass to his chest. "HERE!" he proposed to his fellow shoppers, utterly silent and still. Assholes of every stripe they could deal with. Lunatics, evidently, threw them off their game. "YOU ALL WANT YOUR WAY RIGHT THIS INSTANT!? FINE. YOU WANT SOME CHEESE? TAKE SOME CHEESE." Glassman lobbed his triangular wedge of Reggiano at the man with the purple tank-top, who easily dodged the projectile by taking a deliberate step to the side. "WHO WANTS MILK? SPAGHETTI? CASHEWS? PICKLES? FOCACCIO?" One by one, he tossed the items high in the sky toward his fellow shoppers to the north, south, east, and west. Luckily, an alert citizen, forming a basket with both his outstretched arms, caught the glass jar of Kosher dills over his shoulder à la Willie Mays before it could shatter on the floor.

Suddenly, Glassman was out of groceries and didn't quite know what to do. Quiet pervaded the store. He could hear the bubbles percolating from the lobster tank behind the counter and the clang of a cash register's drawer slamming shut at the very front of Mascolo's. *Did they think a robbery was taking place?* Pete finally decided it was time to intervene. Time to mollify his whacked out regular who, poor guy, thought everyone *else* was crazy.

"Hey, listen, we're just gonna forget the numbers, okay?" he intoned softly, as if he were trying to talk Glassman off the edge of a ten-story building. "Listen, buddy," he addressed Glassman, still wide-eyed like a raving lunatic, "don't worry about the mess. I know you, pal. We'll get someone to mop it all up. Can I help you in the meantime? I bet you're here for some of my special Yellowtail snapper. Am I right?"

Glassman didn't answer. Turning on his oiled heels, he abandoned the mess he had made and wordlessly fled the scene, leaving sloppy green footprints behind him. A gauntlet of dazed Floridians followed his progress toward the exit with watchful, wary eyes.

"Hey, pal, come back!" he heard Pete beckon from behind. "Don't worry about the mess. Come back. Are you sure I can't help you?"

Yes, Glassman was sure. He needed to be home. Home, where it was safe.

His own neighborhood, however, proved treacherous. Somehow, his melancholy acted as a beacon to all things human and animal that might seek to prey upon him. His disease was a rich blood spilling into shark-infested waters.

He was on his morning walk with Troy. A part of his daily routine that made him feel useful, even necessary. Their Labrador needed to be exercised, after all. But Glassman, as it turned out, could no longer seek refuge even in his routines. One fearful glance at the loose German shepherd across the street told him as much. He noticed the dog before it noticed them. He was sure it was one of the two dogs that had been barking viciously at them each day from behind the chain-link fence ever since they had moved to Pine Lakes. Now it was frolicking loose across the street, chasing curly-tailed lizards—often successfully hunted in the neighborhood by cattle egrets and the larger great egrets—from the grass to the hibiscus shrubs, under which they safely disappeared. Fear gripped him with an iron fist, constricting his breath. Should he make a run for it? With Troy? Obese, slow-footed Troy? Not a chance. Dogs possessed chasing instincts. Running would be the worst thing he could do. The best thing to do, he thought, was keep still. Perhaps the dog—*that fucking dog!*—wouldn't notice them? *Shit!* Glassman thought to himself, frozen in his tracks. He knew one of those dogs, or both, would get loose sooner or later. Why hadn't he bought the pepper spray he had scribbled on several of his "Things to Do" lists strewn about the house?

The German shepherd glanced toward them from across the street. It pricked up its ears even higher and straighter than they already stood in their cropped position. It had spotted them. Then, in the next instant, it was on its way. It didn't seem in any particular hurry. It just trotted across the street toward them, seemingly out of mere curiosity. *Maybe you're a friendly dog,* Glassman thought optimistically. Plenty of dogs, he knew, put on a fierce act while they protected the boundaries of their property but, once off their own turf, would sooner lick you with their thick, sweaty tongues than attack you with their fangs.

"Nice dog . . . yes, that's a good, good boy," Glassman encouraged the shepherd as it approached. It didn't seem interested in Glassman at all, but began to sniff Troy instead, who just stood there meekly, his tail between his legs, his ears tucked down close to his cheeks, his eyebrows wrinkled in that worried expression Troy had down so well (*I think it's the economy,* Glassman would tell concerned friends for a laugh). What dog would want to bite Troy? Submissive, groveling, lethargic Troy?

"Yes, good boy. That's a nice, ugly fucking dog that shouldn't be out of its yard," Glassman cooed soothingly. For a moment, he was certain that everything would be okay.

Then, the shepherd's body language changed. It stood straighter up on its legs to stand higher above Troy, positioned itself closer to Troy's side as if taking its measure. Glassman saw the dog's hackles rise in a stripe all the way down its spine. Then, without further warning, without so much as a growl, it clamped its jaws around the back of Troy's neck, began tearing at Troy's loose flesh, whipping its locked jaw back and forth, shaking the life out of his prey.

"Noooo!" Glassman screamed impotently. Troy had begun a high-pitched yelping Glassman was certain he had never heard from him before. Troy was begging for his life. The shepherd either didn't understand Troy's submissive plea or didn't care. Glassman began KICKING, KICKING, KICKING the ferocious dog in the ribs as hard as he could. But his kicks seemed to have no effect whatsoever. The animal barely budged from the force of the blows. He might as well

have been kicking a brick wall. Troy's terrified yelping continued. Glassman was certain he saw blood—or was it just the shepherd's saliva?—wet against Troy's black neck. He took aim at the shepherd's pendulous testicles that swung underneath him and kicked at them repeatedly from behind, but couldn't land a direct hit. Or else the shepherd was simply impervious to the strikes. Fatigue began to lessen the force of Glassman's already powerless blows. Tears blurred his vision.

Then, out of nowhere, a human form was on top of the dogs. Chuck. Glassman saw him grab Troy's leash. In one motion, he quickly wrapped the leash around the shepherd's neck, who, still tearing at its yelping victim, seemed as oblivious to Chuck's presence as it was to Glassman's. *That was its fatal mistake,* Glassman would think later. *It thought it could safely ignore* both *of us.* Chuck began to tighten the leash around the beast's neck with all his might. The complex network of veins in his biceps and forearms seemed about to burst through the walls of his flesh. In just seconds, the shepherd released his grip from Troy's neck. Free, Troy tried to run, but could only lurch against the leash Chuck had wrapped around the shepherds neck, which was still attached to Troy's collar. Glassman reached toward them and managed to unclip leash from collar. Troy made a beeline for home. The shepherd struggled to turn so that it might defend itself against its assailant. But Chuck would have none of it. He had the shepherd straddled between his powerful thighs. The dog suddenly fell onto his front haunches. Its back legs gave way seconds later and it fell crooked to the sidewalk. Its bloodshot eyes rolled. All Glassman could see were its whites. His bloody mouth remained open, his tongue hung to the side. He was unconscious, Glassman realized.

Chuck showed no signs of loosening his grip.

"It's okay!" Glassman shouted. "He's unconscious! You can let go!"

Chuck stared up at Glassman with knitted eyebrows.

"FUCK THAT! This is the third time this fucking dog's gotten loose. Do you want it to get one of the kids next time!?"

Glassman didn't know how to respond. He hadn't known that the dog had been loose before. Right there, on the spot, he didn't know whether it was right to kill the dog. After the favor Chuck had done him, though, he wasn't about to argue with him. Troy would have been dead if it hadn't been for Chuck. He had saved Troy's life. Glassman hadn't proven himself capable of doing so.

Suddenly Glassman was aware of several other neighbors standing about them. He exchanged a pregnant glance with Tom Murphy, who had apparently set down a yellow jug of chlorine beside him on the asphalt. Robert Chadwick had his eyes fixed upon Chuck and his arm around the shoulder of his beautiful wife, Sylvia; she had one hand placed over her mouth. They all looked on soberly as Chuck squeezed the life out of the once fierce, seemingly indomitable, animal.

"That ought'a do it," Chuck announced brightly as he rose from the prostrate beast with the leash. He handed it to Glassman. "I'll call environmental services to pick it up. Stay away from this carcass, everybody!" he warned. Then he strolled off toward his home to make the call.

"Thanks," Glassman uttered after him, dazedly. Chuck acknowledged his neighbor's thanks by raising his hand halfway in the air, dismissively, without turning around. Glassman glanced down briefly at the dead dog and began walking home, slowly, to meet Troy who was surely crying at the front door to be let in the house.

"Troy's okay," Rebecca assured her husband, trembling on the futon, and taking only panting breaths of air. "I can see he's okay. He's just going to need stitches for one cut, but it's not bleeding anymore. Try to relax." Glassman nodded his head, but remained silent. Rebecca wrapped the quilt that they kept hung decoratively over the futon around him. She rose, walked to the kitchen, and brought back a glass of tepid water for him to drink, then put it back onto the counter before handing it to him. She paused for a moment in contemplation.

"You know, don't drink that. I'm calling the doctor. Troy can wait. You can't," she uttered matter-of-factly.

Next thing Glassman knew, he was sitting in the emergency room waiting area at Ropa General, the quilt still wrapped around him. So why was he still trembling? Panting for breath? He noticed a few other patients sitting casually on the purple vinyl chairs. They seemed to be staring at him. He was something of a curiosity, he realized. A black man wearing tan coveralls, his work clothes, was busy applying pressure with bloodied white gauze to a wound on his hand that probably needed stitching; a Latina was soothing her crying child, who had somehow suffered a bad burn that had transformed the flesh around his knee into red blotches and white, liquid welts; an elderly woman held an oxygen mask to the face of her feeble husband. What was wrong with Glassman wasn't so obvious.

Before too long (somehow, before the others who had been waiting before him), he was in an examination room sitting at the end of a padded table covered with a sheet of crisp, white paper. Butcher paper, Glassman darkly thought. Rebecca was at his side, a middle-aged bald-headed doctor, who looked Indian to Glassman, was on his other side. A nurse had already taken his temperature and blood pressure.

He was repeatedly struck by a pool cue in the face, Glassman heard a man outside his door explain to someone on the other end of his phone line. He could see him talking into the receiver behind his counter at the nurse's station.

"I'm Dr. Patel. It's nice to meet you Mr."—he glanced at the chart in his hand—"Glassman." He placed a reassuring hand, which was especially warm and dry, on Glassman's forearm. "Now, Mr. Glassman, it seems that you've had quite an exciting day for yourself now haven't you?"

We've given him fifteen stitches across the bridge of his nose, he sustained . . . let me see . . . a fracture to his ocular bone and . . .

"Y-y-yes . . . d-d-definitely." Glassman didn't know why he could only speak gibberish, why he couldn't stop trembling, why he couldn't breathe deeply, but only in short, panting inhalations and exhalations. It almost felt as if his lungs were battling, once again, the toxic smog of the San Fernando Valley. He felt especially meek. He wasn't used to being in hospitals, and suddenly felt as if he were ten years old again. If his friends on the basketball court could see him now.

. . . he's suffered ennucleation to his right eye . . . yes, ennucleation. E-N-N-U-C-L-E-A-T-I-O-N. We just transferred him to Broward County Laser Eye Surgery Center. . . . Yes, I guess it was a pretty shitty night for him down at the bar.

"I'll tell you what we're going to do," Patel said soothingly. "Your b.p., your blood pressure, is a bit low, but I'm not too worried about it. We're just going to give you a little bit of oxygen, and see how you feel after you relax here for a little while. Okay?"

"You're not going to give me drugs, are you? I don't like drugs!" Glassman warned the soft-spoken doctor.

"No, no. Don't worry. You're just suffering from mild shock. Some oxygen should bring you right back to your old self."

Terrific.

"Okay," Glassman said. Patel didn't wrap the elastic band around his patient's head, but simply placed the mask over Glassman's nose and mouth with his hand.

"Here, do you want to hold it yourself?" he asked. Glassman obediently raised his hand to the mask.

The air felt cool and clear, and almost seemed to permeate his lungs on its own accord, without the need of Glassman's inhalations, which gradually deepened. After only a few seconds, Glassman felt his breath return to normal; he saw his wedding ring that had been flickering like a lightning bug under the fluorescent light grow still as his hand rested softly on his knee. He had ceased trembling almost completely.

Glassman had heard, and never quite understood, how many elderly people allowed themselves to grow terribly dependent upon oxygen. He routinely spotted oxygen supply vans on the streets as they made their rounds to drop off the precious canisters. He eyed them suspiciously, unsure whether to view them as benevolent health care providers or opportunistic enablers. Glassman couldn't understand why people allowed themselves to get hooked on the stuff. Every breath of pure oxygen they inhaled further reduced their ability to breathe the earth's air, rendered them less and less fit for the world of the living.

But sitting there at Ropa General, breathing the pure oxygen for the first time, he suddenly realized how addictive it could be. His heart swelled with empathy.

"That's enough, I think," Glassman said as he removed the mask abruptly from his face. The delicious air frightened him.

"You can have a bit more, Mr. Glassman," Patel suggested. "Are you sure you wouldn't like to take a few more breaths?"

"Better not."

Patel wrapped the velcro sleeve tightly around Glassman's right arm. It grew tighter as he pumped. Glassman didn't particularly mind needles, but never liked having his blood pressure taken. It always felt as if his veins would burst underneath the sleeve's throttle.

Sssssss. The release of air finally relieved the pressure from his arm.

"There. That's more like it," Patel said. "Your blood pressure's 126 over 72. Perfectly normal. Let's just keep an eye on you here for another . . . oh, half hour or so?" He looked at Glassman briefly, his bushy, salt and pepper eyebrows raised, then glanced toward Rebecca.

"That'll be fine. Thank you, Dr. Patel," Rebecca answered for him.

Rebecca dropped Glassman off at home and took Troy for his stitches. There was no reason for him to come along. He should just relax at home, she insisted. Glassman obediently lay down on the futon, under the quilt, and gazed inattentively at the technicolor images that flashed through the dust-coated television screen. He had read somewhere that dust was composed largely of exfoliated human skin, which wafted about the atmosphere at all times. Which meant, Glassman deduced, that we were constantly breathing one another into our lungs. He didn't quite know what to make of this.

Rebecca found him in the same position she had left him in when she returned an hour or so later. Troy, all stitched up now with barely visible thread, his hair around the wound shaved to an abrasive stubble, crashed on the cool tile floor just underneath Glassman, who stroked poor Troy's head a few times.

"Dr. Peterson gave him a sedative. That's probably why he's so out of it," Rebecca explained.

"Oh. That's good."

"So how do you feel honey?" Rebecca stood next to him; she ran her fingers once through his hair, offering him the same canine comfort he had just offered Troy.

"I'm fine now." He did feel fine, somewhat mellowed, as if their vet had given *him* the sedative. His muscles were relaxed. Every one of them, it seemed, had been flexed to their limit through exertion and sheer stress.

"It's a good thing Chuck was around, huh?"

"I'll say," Rebecca replied. "We should really get him a gift or something. What do you think he'd like? I have no idea."

"I don't know. A subscription to *Penthouse* or something," Glassman proposed derisively, bitterly. He disapproved of the pornographic calendars Chuck hung in his garage, a naked woman with a trimmed pubis and enhanced breasts absurdly clutching some power tool January through December. Still, he had to admit that they always caught his eye when he ventured across the street.

"Why would you say something like that?" Rebecca asked perplexedly. Not angrily.

Why did he say something like that? He should be thankful, and he was thankful. If Chuck hadn't come along Troy would be dead. His dog was flatulent, lazy, and obese, but also sweet. Glassman loved Troy. *If you only treated me with such affection,* Rebecca had needled him during their first year together. Yes, he was thankful. A part of him, however, envied (even resented) Chuck's heroism. The shmuck always knew exactly what to do. He had rushed on over and, without skipping a beat, proceeded to strangle the life out of the vicious canine like it was his career or something. Like he was the official Defender of Weak and Victimized Pooches. Then, he knew exactly who to call to clean up the mess. (What the hell was "environmental services" anyway?)

Releasing the German shepherd from his death grip had never even been a consideration. In retrospect, Glassman found Chuck guilty of no transgression or misjudgment. The dog had proven himself a threat to the general health and welfare of the neighborhood. Its owners had proven themselves disastrously negligent. Did you wait for something tragic to happen so that Ropa Animal Control finally would do something other than issue official warnings and citations that had already gone ignored? No, you lay in wait and kill the animal with your bare hands as soon as the opportunity presented itself.

Where did Chuck get off being so resourceful, so effectual, so damn confident in the propriety of his actions?

Rebecca decided to change the subject under discussion. "So, honey, do you think, after all this, that it's time for you to see someone? Just to talk?"

Just to talk.

Glassman didn't know whether Rebecca actually believed that the dog attack would exacerbate his depression, that there was some connection, or if she just figured that in his mellow, post-traumatic state, his resistance to her prodding would be low.

In any case, he had decided before Rebecca even returned from the veterinarian's office that it was time to suck it up and see someone. Maybe even try a new course of drugs. Time to give pharmacology another chance. Time to punt. It was all, finally, too much for him. They either had to pull up the stakes and leave south Florida, or he had to seek professional help. One thing was for certain: they couldn't leave Florida right away, even if they wanted to. What would they do? Where would they go? Neither one of them was exactly in high demand in the work force. So, he had decided to placate Rebecca, and perhaps even begin healing himself in the bargain.

"Yes, Rebecca. Yes. Let's make a few calls tomorrow."

That night, Glassman couldn't sleep. Instead, he found himself pacing up and down the hallway. Found himself. He couldn't remember when he had gotten out of bed. That is, he couldn't remember consciously making the decision to arise and roam the halls of the house. He was just suddenly aware that that was what this person he seemed to be watching, who Glassman begrudgingly accepted could only be himself, was doing—pacing back and forth in front of the Cossack, the painting that haunted him as a child and that he for some reason asked his mother to ship down to him when he and Rebecca moved to Florida. The foreground of the canvas was dominated by a muscular horse in full gallop, its globular bloodshot eyes bulged, its dark mane a flame stirred by the wind. Smoke billowed from its nostrils. Riding the horse was a dark man (a Cossack, his mother had explained to her young son) with a military uniform, a hat without a brim and a thick mustache turned down at the corners. The dark man brandished a curved sword high above his head in a gloved hand, ready to strike, its tip already dripping blood from earlier blows. In a split second, the man's sword would descend to strike the much smaller figure crouching below, shrinking impotently away from his attacker in a tiny corner of the canvas, already grimacing on the blood-soaked snow in anticipation of the pain.

Glassman kept his eye on the painting each time he passed, as if he feared the Cossack might gallop off the canvas and strike him down in the hall. He didn't have a coherent thought in his head. Rather, his mind raced from one trivial worry to the next: the lever on the toaster oven that wouldn't stay down to enact a successful toast cycle, the dead olive tree leaves weighing down the patio screen that would tear under the pressure at any moment, an awkward night of impotence with a woman he briefly dated his sophomore year, the inane wedding toast he had made years ago at Vinnie Dechiaro's wedding in Cherry Hill that had made his friend fidget awkwardly as his Catholic bride blushed beside him. . . . *Stupid . . . stupid . . . stupid.*

He knew he was obsessing over petty, meaningless details and events, long ago forgotten by everyone else concerned, but was powerless to contain his thoughts. His brain was a car without brakes or an ignition switch, racing in fifth gear. What he needed was a safe place to crash.

The pain in his wrists told him that his fists were clenched. He felt hot tears on his cheeks. He heard his throat emit a stifled squeak, helium released from a balloon through pinched fingers. And suddenly he was in Lackawanna:

Do you want the children to hear you and wake up? Is that what you want? Was it his grandmother's words that had woken him—her whispered shouting—or the sound that must have been emanating from his grandfather Abe's throat, a prolonged whimpering, almost canine, interrupted by unintelligible mutterings. He saw a shadow repeatedly erase the sliver of light on the carpet just inside the door. They must have been in the hallway, pacing. Grandpa Abe had just a few hours ago slid the trundle out from underneath Sara's mattress; she lay just above him, breathing rhythmically. Asleep. *Come to bed right this instant Abe! Abraham? Are you listening to me? The children trusted us with Sara and Matthew for the night. Do you want me to have to call them at Lenape and have them drive back at four in the morning? Is that what you want?*

Did he want to wake up Rebecca? Is that what he wanted? He made his way back to the bedroom and lay down softly above the sheets. Through the blinds, the moonlight splintered, casting daggers onto his chest. He agonized over this fresh, terrifying vision of his grandfather. This additional piece of the puzzle that was Abraham Fishbein. It was yet another true vision, like the vision he had had at the Everglades: the drab, gray and black duck, the dopey dog giving chase. Somehow, both these episodes had hibernated for years in some dark recess of his mind, only to awaken and stretch toward the light years later. What a mystery the mind was. What a horribly awesome mystery. He tossed and turned, thrashed about like a fish on dry earth for several minutes, then settled in defeat on his back.

He could only await the mercy of dawn, and stare quietly above him at the images that leapt out from the ceiling popcorn: a muscular steed breathing smoke, a mountain aflame in green and blue, a funnel cloud of winged creatures above outstretched arms, splayed fingers.

Stop Calling Me Shuman, Son

Where had Shuman gone? Didn't he know that Glassman needed him? Why did he come out from under his rock at all if he only planned to disappear again, and then again, for weeks at a time? If he had no real intention of helping Glassman, or himself? What good could come of things if the old man refused to take that extra step and reveal himself? Not just for Glassman's sake, but for his mother's sake, and for his Aunt Janet's. And, of course, for Teenie's sake as well, for surely the old man knew that his wife was still alive. Things, of course, would never be the same between them. It was one thing for Glassman to forgive him, another thing for his wife, and there was no way the indefatigable Teenie would take Abe Fishbein back. Of this Glassman was certain. But she at least deserved an explanation. An apology.

Perhaps their last encounter at the Everglades was too much for Shuman. Perhaps he had simply snapped. Snapped again. Glassman forced himself to consider that he might never again see the old man. What would he do, in this case, with the knowledge he now possessed. Should he tell his mother? His grandmother? Rebecca? Yes, Rebecca. He would tell his wife, the one both closest to him and the furthest removed from his grandfather, the one least likely to be

226

injured by his revelation. Rebecca would know what they should do. He would tell her over dinner at Pumperdore's.

They reached the stripmall where Pumperdore's was located. Rebecca parked between a blue minivan that read LEON'S PET MASSAGE in large, red script, and an ambulance. Glassman read the word printed on the ambulance's sloping hood, ECNALUBMA. Like most of the drivers in south Florida, he was slowly becoming inured to the privately owned fleets of ambulances that sped all over the streets, sirens blaring, at all hours of the day and night.

Pumperdore's was something of a Ropa Gatos landmark. Its claim to fame was that diners ordered all of their food at a bar area, brought it to one of the formica tables, consumed said food, and when they were finished, simply told one of the four cashiers what they ate, paid, and were on their way. The honor system. Pumperdore's, no doubt, was rooked by plenty of people, but managed to make it up, and then some, by the sheer novelty of the system, which attracted quite a following, and their copious corned beef sandwiches, stacked to an obscene height, for which they were also famous.

As they entered the restaurant, Glassman could tell immediately that something was wrong. There was a throng of people near the door, but they weren't in any sort of line waiting to be seated; nor were they paying for their meals at one of the cashiers. Rather, they were all massed together in a clump looking in toward the dining room, which seemed eerily empty. Or, rather, as Glassman stood on the tips of his toes to see what it was exactly that they were looking at, there was a figure prostrate in the center of the dining room, and another crowd of onlookers spread out against the rear wall of the restaurant. Two other figures in light uniforms and latex gloves (paramedics from the ambulance, Glassman surmised) attended to the victim, a man. One paramedic, crouching behind his patient in a catcher's stance, had the man's head propped up and was applying pressure with a white cloth to a spot toward the back of the cranium. The other paramedic was kneeling beside his patient, gingerly holding a wrist to test its pulse. The paramedic with the white cloth was helping the stricken man to sit up.

"I saw the whole thing," he heard an older woman tell someone next to her. "He just fell backwards in his chair and hit his head against the corner of a table. Wham! What a sight." She shuddered as if from a sudden chill.

"Let's just go somewhere else," he heard Rebecca plead from somewhere behind him. "The paramedics are here. There's nothing *we* can do."

"Just wait a sec' honey, okay?" Glassman struggled to gain a better vantage point. Nearly the tallest person in the crowd, it wasn't too difficult for him to see over the other patrons, but he wanted to move sideways to see the man's face. Yes, it was a man . . . an older man . . .

Shuman!

Glassman seemed to recognize his grandfather more with the pit of his stomach, which suddenly dropped out from under him, than with his eyes.

"Honey, where are you going!" Rebecca asked alarmingly, but he was already pushing and shoving his way past the onlookers.

"Excuse me! Pardon me! Excuse me! I've gotta get through. I *know* him!" Glassman reasoned with the other diners, who had temporarily abandoned their brisket, meat loaf, and pastrami on their tables. A few of them muttered angry words at him ("that doesn't give you the right to trample over us!" he distinctly heard one older man protest), but he didn't care.

He finally managed to pierce through the final layer of humanity and rushed to his grandfather's side as everyone watched. Chattering noisily with one another when he and Rebecca had arrived, the crowd had suddenly grown silent. This was a new development in the drama unfolding before them. "I know him. His name is Irving Shuman!" He considered claiming him as his grandfather right then and there, but figured that the old man was in enough shock as it was. Glassman noticed a large pool of blood, some of it smeared as if from a hand or foot, on the white linoleum behind Shuman where his head had come crashing down after it collided with the corner of the table. A can of Welch's grape juice had been knocked over and still dripped from another table, Shuman's table it seemed from the current orientation of his body and the pool of blood.

"Are you all right . . . Mr. Shuman?" Glassman asked worriedly. "Is there anything I can do? Anyone I can call?" He looked into his grandfather's face and his grandfather looked at him. The old man looked . . . different. Naked. His short-sleeve shirt was pulled open, exposing a bare, pallid chest; the paramedic's gloved hand was hidden underneath a clump of the old man's hair, or toupee rather, set askew on the crown of his head; his exposed arms were coated modestly with red . . . not white, hair; he seemed slim; there was no paunch at all underneath his shirt.

Wait! Glassman thought to himself. *This isn't Shuman!*

"Stop calling me Shuman, son! My name's Harvey Katz! Who the heck *you* are I have no idea!" The injured man looked away from Glassman. He resented the young editor's presence. Glassman had somehow humiliated the man. The paramedics looked searchingly into Glassman's eyes. It was the twenty-eight year old who they were putting their money on, not the old geezer who had been eating alone and was only just regaining consciousness. Glassman knew what they were asking of him.

"No . . . no. He's right. I've made a mistake," Glassman admitted as he retreated from the scene. The paramedics began buttoning Katz's shirt for him. "A terrible, terrible mistake."

Glassman explained everything to his stunned wife on the way home, where they had decided to boil frozen pierogies for dinner. Irving Shuman wasn't just some man he had met at the office. He was his grandfather, Abraham Fishbein. Glassman was certain, even more certain as he articulated the claim for the first time. Rebecca listened to him patiently in the passenger's seat, waited for him to say everything he had to say in defense of his dubious sanity. Glassman kept his eyes on the road, but could feel the heat from her incredulous gaze trained upon him. He could picture her expression exactly: her glassy, deep brown eyes, her half-open mouth from which the femininely rounded tips of her teeth peeked, her aquiline nose flaring involuntarily, as it always did when Rebecca was agitated. He spoke quickly, firing his entire clip of ammunition before giving Rebecca the chance to fire back. *Shuman looked exactly like his grandfather, and he was about the right age, and he was a bird-watcher, and he abandoned his family, and he grew up in New York, and he was in the shmatteh business, and . . . and . . . and . . .* The evidence was circumstantial, yes, but overwhelming just the same.

After he was through presenting his case, Rebecca paused for a few moments. Glassman wasn't sure whether this was for dramatic effect, or whether he had simply left his wife speechless. A white ibis flock passed overhead. He noticed the black tips of their wings flutter over Glades as he awaited her response.

"It doesn't matter," Rebecca finally intoned in a soft voice, a calm cadence. "It doesn't matter whether he's Grandpa Abe or not. Either way, you're seeing Dr. Levin next week, like you promised. Either way, you'll need to."

Glassman silently acquiesced. How could he argue with such sound logic?

Did You Think I Wouldn't Know You . . .

Glassman arrived ten minutes late to his office the next morning to find the old man waiting for him. It was as if Shuman somehow heard Glassman cry for him at Pumperdore's. The young editor experienced a flash of déjà vu. Wasn't this, after all, how he had first glimpsed his grandfather just a matter of weeks ago? How Abe Fishbein had reappeared?

Glassman quickly took inventory of his emotions. He wasn't surprised to see his grandfather. Nor was he excited, or even relieved. No, a separate visceral stimulus made the follicles on his scalp burn. The familiarity of his own office emboldened Glassman. He made his way to his chair, behind the desk, and faced his grandfather.

"Where have you been!?" he heard himself acidly greet the old man sitting stiffly in the black, vinyl chair. His grandfather clearly hadn't expected such a hostile reception and was visibly perturbed. Glassman noticed the smile on the old man's face freeze, the corners of his mouth gradually descend as he groped for a suitable response.

"Yes, I'm sorry Matthew, I suppose it has been too long since I've been in touch." The old man fidgeted in his chair, gaining a more upright posture. He violently cleared his throat. "I'm sure, though, you've been busy yourself"—he opened a palm upright toward

Glassman as if he were presenting him a small gift—"what with your wife's condition." He clearly wished to shift to a more pleasant topic, but stumbled onto a landmine.

Glassman wouldn't spare the old man's feelings.

"We lost the baby," he announced matter-of-factly. He saw his grandfather's eyes widen with alarm, heard a barely audible groan emanate from his chafed lips. His news had caused his grandfather pain, he realized, and realized a split-second later that he didn't regret having caused such pain, but relished this small injury he had inflicted.

"You know, you were the only one we told. I hadn't even told mom and dad. I *still* haven't told them." Glassman felt his face grow hot, the muscles in his jaw clench in anger. "I really needed you again . . . and again you weren't there."

The old man lowered his eyes, bit down upon the inside of his lower lip—hard, it seemed to Glassman, as if he were testing his ability to perceive pain. Yet he didn't seem to have anything to say.

"I DON'T KNOW WHY YOU EVEN BOTHERED TO COME BACK GRANDPA!"

There! So much for Abe's dark secret!

"Grandpa?"

"Yes, *grandpa*! I know who you are. I *always* knew. You're Abe Fishbein. Teenie's husband. My grandfather. Your birds . . . your cryptic little revelations . . . your face for crying out loud. . . . How long were you going to play this game? Did you think I wouldn't know you . . . did you—"

"Matthew!" the old man interjected.

"But—"

"Matthew, get a hold of yourself!" The old man glanced behind him out the open door, fearing that someone had heard the outburst. Glassman didn't care who heard. "Now relax!" Shuman firmly, yet somehow quietly, instructed, turning toward the young editor once again. Glassman sat back in his chair and let out a slow exhale. Fine, he would wait to hear what Abe Fishbein had to say for himself.

232

"I don't know exactly how to say this," the old man began, more softly now, stroking his cleft chin pensively with a curled finger, "but . . . you see . . . it's just that . . . well, I'm *not* your grandfather. I'm not *anyone's* grandfather."

"No, you don't understand," Glassman replied in a softer tone. He had recovered from his initial anger and was ready now to yield to more complex emotions. "You don't have to worry. I'm not angry, grandpa. Not anymore. It's okay. You don't have to hide anymore. Please don't disappear again."

"Oh, gevalt. What a mess I've made of things," the old man replied, chastising himself with a slow shake of his head. "There's nothing I'd like more than to be your grandfather, Matthew. But I'm telling you I'm not him. What else can I say?"

Glassman looked deep into the old man's moist eyes. A diaphanous web of pink vessels stretched from the inside corners toward the outer rim of his hazel irises. He hadn't imagined his physical resemblance to Shuman. Of this he was certain. But Shuman didn't seem to be lying, either.

"What about the birds? What about all the stuff about you disappearing, and regretting it . . . about wanting to go back home . . . ?"

Yes, it was all true, Shuman assured the young editor. But that didn't make him Abe Fishbein. He owed the young editor a fuller explanation, he realized.

"You're not completely off track, Matthew," he began ominously. "I didn't just come to you out of the blue. I knew who you were. I knew you were Abe's grandson." He took a long pause, audibly inhaled as he gathered the thoughts he wished now to share. "You see, I did know your grandfather . . . back in Lackawanna. As a matter of fact, I showed him his first red-eyed vireo at scout camp when we were just teenagers. If anyone knew that back home they'd have yet another reason to despise me."

"But why haven't I heard of you?" Glassman inquired, skeptically. "I've never even heard the name Shuman mentioned by any—"

"I changed my name, Matthew. After I fled town once and for all. I wanted to start fresh. I fooled myself into thinking that this was possible. Fooled myself into thinking that I could simply wipe the slate clean with a new name. A new place to hang my hat. What I didn't realize, what I didn't allow myself to realize at the time, was that even then starting fresh had nothing to do with it. I was ashamed. That's why I changed my name—"

"What's your real name!" Glassman asked urgently.

"Birnbaum," the old man answered softly. "Irving Birnbaum."

Birnbaum! It took Glassman a moment to recall why the name was so familiar to him.

"Any relation to Leonard Birnbaum?" the editor asked. He could tell that the old man didn't realize that he knew Leonard. Deep fissures emerged between the old man's woolly eyebrows.

"Yes," he finally admitted. "He's my younger brother. Younger by six years. I'm afraid he probably still doesn't want anything to do with me. Just like the rest of Lackawanna."

Yes, Glassman thought. Leonard Birnbaum had almost mentioned his older brother during their walk at Edith's brunch. Glassman's grandfather wasn't the fraternity type, Leonard had told him. *He'd much rather be off by himself hiking somewhere in the woods . . . like . . .*

Like my brother, Irving!

This was the phrase on the tip of Leonard's tongue, the phrase he was only a half breath short of mentioning. Would have mentioned, Glassman was fairly certain, had he made the proper inquiry. But other questions, questions about his grandfather, were burning in his mind that day. Now, however, he wanted to know all there was to know about Irving Birnbaum, seated before him.

"Why?" Glassman inquired. "Why do you think your brother, why do you think Lackawanna, doesn't want anything to do with you? What happened?"

And so Birnbaum told him his story . . .

He was a widower with no children. He hadn't really wanted to marry in the first place. He wanted to go to college, where he could study his birds. But his parents could only afford tuition for one of their sons, and certainly weren't going to throw it down the drain on the one who wanted to study ornithology. Leonard was brighter anyway, Birnbaum admitted. So he stayed in Lackawanna and helped keep his father's wholesale clothing outlet afloat. The hours were long but the work was easy. He coasted along for years, married Annette Silverman not because he particularly loved her, or because she particularly loved him even, but because they were both rather plain looking and nearing their thirties. Marrying one another seemed like the only logical thing for either one of them to do.

Birnbaum had far less of a reason to leave Annette some fifteen years later. It wasn't another woman, he assured Glassman from across the table. Or another man on her end, for that matter. He wasn't a cuckold, however amenable he would have been to such a fate. All and all they lived a comfortable life. Perhaps too comfortable. Children might have made all the difference, he conjectured. Might have united them behind a common, lofty purpose. But Annette was unable to conceive. She had been heartbroken by her doctor's diagnosis, was convinced that her barrenness was to blame for their growing estrangement. But it was more than that. Or, rather, less than that. Put simply, Annette's mild idiosyncrasies, which he had actually found endearing during their first years together, slowly began to grate against his nerves. She hummed Cole Porter tunes, not so much off-key but off-tempo, while she did the ironing; she softly passed gas underneath the cotton sheets while she slept; she affected a cloying sweetness, as if she were meeting a puppy, when introduced to strangers; she laboriously peppered her sentences with ill-chosen Yiddish words and phrases, routinely confused *yachneh* for *yachsen*, *oysgedart* for *oysgematert*.

Gradually, her physical appearance began to repel him. She relished peanut brittle, devoured the sweet, jagged shards as she puttered about the house, and went from zaftig to fat by their tenth anniversary. More irksome, however, was her pug nose. It was actually the envy of many of her friends, but its slightly upturned orientation forced him to look half-way up her dark nostrils every time he faced her. He didn't know how many more days he could stand to look at that nose. So he left. Just up and left. Left his job and left his wife.

235

Fled town altogether to start anew in the Florida sticks, alone. Only recently had Florida's human inhabitants begun creeping northward, north of West Palm, north of Jupiter, Hobe Sound, Stuart, and Port St. Lucie, as if to flush him out of hiding.

"I left Annette," Birnbaum reiterated. "Left her for no good reason. And so it was my fault. I've always known it was my fault."

"What?" Glassman asked. "What happened to her?" He fearfully anticipated the answer, as if Annette's fate, long ago decided, somehow still hung in the balance.

"She killed herself," Birnbaum explained bluntly. "Oh, they said it was an accident, that she mistakenly forgot to light the oven, received a telephone call that distracted her and left the gas on, or some narishkeit like that . . . but I knew better. Everyone knew better."

"I'm sorry," Glassman uttered. And he was sorry. Sorry for Annette, mostly. Yet thankful, as well. Thankful that his grandmother was made of stronger stuff than poor Annette. Teenie was such an indomitable presence, such an outright force, that Glassman had never even really felt sorry for her. Her very being repelled pity.

He didn't know what to think of this old man before his desk now. His head was aswim with too much information. It was difficult enough adjusting himself to the stark reality that Shuman was actually Birnbaum, not Fishbein, not his grandfather; he struggled mightily to assimilate the more complex details of Birnbaum's tragic past. This old man before him was now a stranger, only not quite strange enough for Glassman's comfort. His story was eerily similar to his grandfather's. They had both up and left, abandoned the ones who loved them, the ones who depended upon them. His grandfather was sick, though. Ill for years. Birnbaum didn't appear to have any such excuse for his misanthropy. He was something of an obverse reflection of his grandfather Abe, it seemed to Glassman. The person Abe easily could have been had his wiring just been given one final adjustment—and, by implication, the person Glassman could potentially become.

Birnbaum, however, was more than a cautionary tale. He was a life. A sad life at that. In many respects a life poorly led. Glassman understood why Birnbaum had been so reticent to divulge the details of his past. Why he was such an elusive character. He had behaved reprehensibly toward his wife. He *was* to blame for her death, and it was appropriate that he suffered so many years later. Still, his wife was gone. What remained of her, it seemed to Glassman, sat before him now. This tattered network of nerves and bones and organs stubbornly performing their vital functions. Annette Silverman's legacy, such as it was. She was gone, but her recalcitrant husband was sitting there before him, like a defendant awaiting a verdict.

Guilty, he could pronounce, and be done with Birnbaum forever, who most assuredly awaited Glassman's rebuff. The old man was nothing to him, after all. He wasn't a relative. He wasn't Glassman's responsibility. But somehow, Glassman knew, the last several weeks had altered this tidy formula and rendered Birnbaum's culpability for his wife's tragic demise, his guilt or innocence, wholly beside the point. However errantly, Birnbaum and Glassman had nudged their way into one another's lives. Yes, Birnbaum was a living presence in his life now. And the living, like the dead, made certain inexorable demands.

"Why, Mr. Birnbaum?" Glassman heard himself inquire. "Why did you start up with me? Of all people. I never even lived in Lackawanna. What could you possibly want with me?"

Why did he first seek Glassman out in his office? All that business about his journal—the journal he hadn't mentioned since their first meeting—was obviously a pretense. Reading it to the young book editor was a necessary step toward some goal rather than the goal itself.

Birnbaum's mouth began to form around the first word of an answer, a word he swallowed rather than spoke. It seemed to Glassman that he feared the inadequacy, perhaps the implausibility, of his answer. Finally, he began:

"The truth is, Matthew . . . the truth is I'm lonely from time to time. That's all. It's as simple as that. And I knew that Lackawanna wasn't really there for me anymore. Abe would have been there for me, though. But he's gone, isn't he?" It didn't seem to be a rhetorical question. It was as if Birnbaum wanted him to shout *NO, Abraham*

Fishbein wasn't gone. But Glassman couldn't tell him this, so Birnbaum continued:

"See that's the difference between your grandfather and me. He disappeared, whether of his own volition or not, and if he reappeared one day, all of Lackawanna would welcome him back. But, me, I just left, and everyone said good riddance. Abe was the only one I even said goodbye to. It was just a few years later that he vanished. I had to find out about it on the local news. His disappearance was so strange it made headlines all the way down here."

Of his own volition or not. . . . Glassman had been convinced that Shuman was his grandfather, convinced, in turn, that Abe Fishbein had fled Lackawanna of his own will, however misguided or even delusional. But now that Shuman was Birnbaum, not Fishbein, the long dormant, darker scenarios—the more likely scenarios— bloomed once again in his mind.

"Anyway," Birnbaum continued, "when I saw your name in the paper outside Publix and put it together that you were Abe's grandson . . . well . . . I just had to see you. . . . And it seemed to me . . . that first time I visited you . . . it seemed to me that you . . . like your grandfather . . . like me . . . also knew something of loneliness."

Glassman nodded his head slowly. Surrounded by family he was anything but lonesome. But lonely? Yes, he knew something of loneliness.

This Your Mother Knows
Nothing Of

B *RRIIIINNG!*
      "Don't answer it, Matt," Rebecca advised him over her orange juice. "It's just somebody trying to sell us something. They'll hang up when the machine answers." Glassman envied Rebecca's attitude toward the phone. *It's a luxury,* she would opine. *You shouldn't feel any obligation to answer it.* While Rebecca's philosophy made good sense to him, he couldn't bring himself, hard as he tried, to allow a phone within his reach to go unanswered. One of his many weaknesses.

"Is this a Mr. Matthew Glassman?" a nondescript female voice inquired after he said hello.

"Yes, that's me," Glassman answered reluctantly. Her sterile, nearly inflectionless query smacked of the unsolicited sales call.

"I'm a registered nurse in the intensive care unit of Mercy Hospital in Deerpoint . . ." The expression on Glassman's face froze.

"Who is it?" Rebecca asked, apprehensively. Glassman raised a finger to quiet her.

"Your grandmother, Martina Fishbein, was brought into the emergency room by a fire rescue ambulance at six twenty-five A.M. . . . you're listed on her records as her closest blood relative." *Fire rescue?*

"YesyesIamwhatisit?" Glassman spat out urgently.

"Mr. Glassman, your grandmother suffered a stroke sometime this morning. She called 911"—she *called 911, a good sign*—"and the ambulance brought her here at six twenty-five A.M."

"How bad is it? Come on, tell me!"

"When the paramedics reached her, she was suffering numbness and loss of vision on her right side. She's now in stable condition. The doctors are monitoring her blood pressure very carefully and seem to have it under control. She's cognizant. Her speech is somewhat garbled—"

"Is she going to recover?" He could tell that the nurse was reading off a doctor's chart. He wanted to hear in her own, less scripted, words the extent of the bad news. She was a registered nurse. She must have known more.

"I'm sorry, I really can't give you any information regarding her prognosis. You'll have to speak with one of her doctors. A doctor-r-r-r . . . Prager, her personal physician, has been paged and will be here shortly. She *is* in stable condition, Mr. Glassman." This was, he inferred, the best news on the chart and the nurse was kind enough to emphasize it for him.

"It's Grandma, isn't it?" Rebecca shouted after Glassman, who had dropped the phone somewhere in the vicinity of its cradle and rushed to the bedroom.

"Yeah. She had a stroke . . . OH FUCKING JESUS A STROKE! . . . but it sounds like she might be okay!" Glassman yelled from the bedroom as he buttoned his shorts. He grasped the straps of both his sandals with one hand and rushed barefoot to the garage past Rebecca, who stood in the hall, waiting for him to emerge. "I'll call you as soon as I know more!"

"Are you sure you don't want me to come with you?" Rebecca asked from the garage door. "I can be ready in two minutes."

"No, stay here! You can answer the phone . . . make calls or something."

Had anyone called his mother yet? He hadn't thought to ask the nurse. Should Rebecca call? He was too frazzled to think clearly about this or anything else. Only one thing was for certain. He had to get to the hospital.

"I'll call you as soon as I get to Mercy and find out what's what."

"STOP!!" Rebecca screeched too late. *BAM!* Glassman knew immediately what he had done. He had rammed the Corolla right into the garage door. It didn't occur to him that it was closed. He reached up and pressed the remote control clipped to the car's visor hard with a thumb; he unclenched his teeth.

COULDN'T YOU OPEN THE FUCKING GARAGE?!" he yelled stupidly at Rebecca out his window.

It seemed to take forever for the door to lift. He felt the roof of his car scrape against it as he backed out too soon. Rebecca scurried out to the driveway after him in her robe. "RELAX!" she shouted between cupped hands. "RELAX!"

How he managed to navigate his car from his home to the hospital five miles away he would never know. As he turned into the parking lot, it occurred to him that he couldn't remember anything in between the time he left the house and turned into the hospital's lot. Had he taken the 95 or Federal? His mind had just been wandering from one potential scenario to the next. Everything would be fine: *It was just a warning sign for us,* Dr. Prager would reassure him once he arrived. Or, no, a sober emergency room doctor in scrubs would be waiting outside Teenie's room with the bad news: *I'm sorry we did everything we could. She just took a sudden turn for the worse.* But some part of his brain had successfully driven the car. That mysterious automatic pilot inside of him had seen him through the crisis thus far.

He parked as close as he could to the overhang that read EMERGENCY in red letters. They would be able to direct him, he figured, to the intensive care unit. *Critical care . . . intensive care . . . emergency care.* What distinguished them from one another? What did it mean that Teenie was in intensive care?

He approached the first person he saw in a uniform, a triage nurse taking a man's blood pressure. "Excuse me! Where's the intensive care unit? I need to get there right now!"

The nurse, sensing Glassman's alarm, removed her stethoscope from her ears with only the mildest trace of annoyance. She pointed with an outstretched arm. "Go through those doors sir and take the elevator to the third floor. There'll be a nurse at the station just to the right of the elevator when you get off."

He thanked the nurse behind him as he burst through the doors. *Were there any stairs?* he wondered as he looked around. The five on the ceiling above elevator had remained lit for ten seconds . . . fifteen seconds . . . twenty seconds . . .

"Ooooooooh," Glassman heard a woman moan from a nearby room. "Oooooooh," she moaned again.

"Now come on. You can make it up here to the bed now can't you?" a woman, probably a nurse, asked sternly, unsympathetically, Glassman judged. He walked a few steps toward the noise and saw them. The black woman had somehow made it onto the bed and lay in a fetal position. "Oooooooh," she moaned, then began to whimper. The poor woman was in great pain. She clutched her belly with her hand. *Abdominal? Or maybe something female?* Glassman speculated. She didn't seem to have any external injury. A man's shirt just barely hung on her ample frame. Her flesh was coated with silvery-gray ash. Glassman couldn't help but notice an exposed dark aureole of a breast, drooping against her arm.

He heard the chime of the open elevator, and rushed to secure it, slipping briefly on the linoleum before gaining traction. He shared the ride with an elderly man on a stretcher, lying on his side with a short, ludicrously diaphanous robe tied in the back. A Latino with a faint mustache and wearing green scrubs escorted the patient. "We'll have you up there rápido, Mr. Hoffman. In a jiffy. Just hang in there chief," he urged the man. Mr. Hoffman remained silent and still. Glassman admonished himself for being repulsed by the intricate webbing of varicose veins, in various shades of purple, on the man's spindly, sparsely haired legs.

"I'm Matthew Glassman," he explained breathlessly to the nurse behind the counter. "I just talked with someone on the phone about fifteen minutes ago? My grandmother's here, right? Teenie . . . Martina Fishbein?"

"Yes, Mr. Glassman. She's in room eighteen, down the hall." The nurse leaned over the counter and pointed his finger back down the hall in the direction from which Glassman came. "She's in stable condition, and she's alert. You can go in and see her now. I'll tell the doctor that you're here."

"Oh, okay." Glassman was slightly surprised that his presence merited the doctor's attention. But he supposed he was the closest blood relative. His mother, he knew, would be on a flight as soon as she could find a seat. But for now, *he* was the closest blood relative. *He* was the one who needed to ask the doctors all of the urgent questions, if only to let them know that this patient of theirs—one of a hundred or so local elderly who had probably suffered a stroke on this particular day—mattered to several loved ones, mattered deeply. They had better pull out all the stops, spare no expense to treat Teenie Glassman. There were legions of worried friends and family looking over their shoulders.

A patient's care shouldn't hinge upon such issues, Glassman mused. A life was a life was a life. Each one no more or less precious than the other. *Everyone can feel love, Matthew. Everyone,* his mother had told him.

But doctors were human, and susceptible to all the usual human pressures. Just because lives were in their hands didn't mean they didn't slack off, or play favorites, or go that extra yard, or make mistakes, or make the brilliant diagnosis from time to time. It was his duty, he thought, to make sure his grandmother's doctors were operating sharply, at their peak. He brainstormed questions he should ask as he made his way to his grandmother's room. He took a deep breath and exhaled sharply. At least until his mother arrived on the scene, he had to call upon all his reserves.

He had to be the rock.

"Grandma!?" he uttered upon seeing her, almost as a question. For he scarcely recognized Teenie. She was slightly inclined from the waist up, restive rather than relaxed. Her left hand worried the edge of a pale blue hospital blanket. An IV was taped just above her wrist. Glassman's eyes followed the thin, clear tube to the stainless steel stand and the small sack of clear fluid dripping . . . dripping . . . dripping. Her eyes. *Her eyes.* He had always thought her eyes were blue, but now her irises seemed a washed-out gray. The only colors standing out prominently on her face were the thin red oval borders demarcating outer from inner eyelids, the purple of her puffed pillows underneath, and the liver-islands that seemed to surface overnight, bespeckling her cheeks and forehead with their jagged, irregular coastlines. Her right eyebrow, faint as it was, hung lower over her upper eyelid, and even her right eye socket itself seemed positioned slightly lower than the left. Her lower lip drooped to the side as well into a half frown, which would have been comical had it been affected voluntarily. He noticed a pool of saliva between Teenie's pallid inner lip and gums.

She looked, it occurred to him, like one of the countless before-and-after shots plastic surgeons advertised in the local yellow pages, except that the after side of her face looked only slightly better than the before side. He wondered to what extent it was the stroke that accounted for her beaten down appearance, and to what extent this was just the way eighty-six looked without makeup and under the unforgiving glare of fluorescent lighting.

It came to him as something of a relief that to the best of his recollection he had never laid eyes upon her face in its natural state. She didn't apply her makeup too thickly, like several of her friends in his estimation, but never left the house without enhancing, concealing, or augmenting her features with various shades of color. She frequently, in fact, reapplied her lipstick in his presence with the aid of a small, ornate pewter mirror, variations of which all of his female relatives in south Florida seemed to own. The mirror had a rustic scene forged on its back side, goats and chickens and straw-thatched shanties.

"Oh, it's . . . so good . . . to see you . . . dear," his grandmother greeted him. Her voice was halted, and slightly laborious, but not especially garbled. He was relieved. Her eyes moistened; a tear trickled down her right side onto her hospital gown. No doubt about it. His presence had made her cry. Suddenly, he felt his own tears threaten and just barely managed to fight them back.

Some rock.

For the first time in his life, his grandmother looked tiny to him. Two of her could have fit lengthwise in the bed. The small white-sheeted mattress dwarfed her frame. As her feet protruded under the sheets several feet from the end of the bed, Glassman sat there facing her, just beyond the reach of the metal bars upraised on each side to prevent her from rolling off. He had never thought of her as a small person, but it struck him then that she couldn't have been five feet from head to toe. People didn't call her Teenie for nothing, he supposed. But truth be told, it had never really occurred to him before that people had taken to calling her Teenie because the nickname suited her diminutive frame.

He reached up and took her hand in his lightly. "You look well, grandma. Really. You're going to be okay," he reassured her, although he really didn't know for certain whether this was the case.

"Oh . . . I . . . know," she replied not altogether convincingly.

The arch in his grandmother's left brow informed him that someone had entered the room. He turned around, rose, and saw a fairly young woman in a white coat. Her name was stitched in script in blue thread just above the gentle rise of her breast: *Dr. Patricia Sullivan, M.D. Neurology.*

"Hello, I'm Dr. Sullivan." She reached out her hand and Glassman shook it. "I was the neurologist on call when Mrs. Fishbein arrived You're Mrs. Fishbein's . . ."

"Grandson," Glassman filled in the blank for Dr. Sullivan. "Matt Glassman."

"Well, Mr. Glassman, we've already talked with your grandmother, but let me explain to you what happened and what's going on."

She seemed very up-front. He was the closest blood relative and wanted to know the details. Everything.

This was a relatively new dispensation, Glassman thought. It wasn't always like this between doctors, patients, and their relatives. He remembered his father telling him about the terrible fight he had had with his father, Grandpa Morty, while his mother, Pearl, was dying in Lackawanna's hospital. The doctors wanted to perform one final surgery, one last ditch attempt to excise as many cancerous cells as they could manage while still leaving just enough vital organ behind. So they exhorted. But his father, mild-mannered under normal circumstances, would have none of it.

She's dying, right?! I mean come on. Right?! You've already told us she's dying. It sounds to me like you just want to put her through yet another painful surgical procedure as some kind of experiment—

Stanley! Morton had interrupted his son. *How dare you accuse the doctor of something like that. Now apologize right this instant!* Morton came from a generation, Teenie's generation, that didn't think to question the judgment, and certainly not the motives, of medical doctors.

Glassman's father didn't apologize. They didn't perform the procedure. Pearl died a few days later.

"Your grandmother came in with significant numbness on her right side, and loss of vision in her right eye. Some difficulty with her speech also," he suddenly heard Dr. Sullivan explain.

Glassman snapped to, knitted his brows together and crossed his arms, forcing himself to concentrate deeply on what Dr. Sullivan was telling him. This was no time to zone out. It was time to live in the present, not the past. "We performed a CAT scan right away to see what we were dealing with. We had to rule out a hemorrhagic stroke, and we did. That's good news." Dr. Sullivan briefly placed her fingertips on his forearm. "What she suffered looks like a minor ischemic stroke, a bit worse than a TIA, a transient ischemic attack, but I think she's going to be okay. We put her on a TPA"—she pointed to the IV with her pen—"right away, and that's lowered her blood pressure and alleviated most of her symptoms already . . ."

Dr. Sullivan suddenly grasped Teenie's right hand, as if sidetracked. "Do you still feel this pressure?" she asked Teenie in a slightly higher pitch than she had been addressing him. His grandmother nodded. Sullivan proceeded to poke gently various locations up and down Teenie's right leg, frame, and arm, and Teenie nodded at all the appropriate times. Dr. Sullivan then covered his grandmother's left eye with her clipboard. "Can you follow this light?" Her pen, evidently, doubled as a small flashlight. Glassman saw his grandmother's eye follow the dot of light back and forth. Then the doctor shined the light directly into Teenie's eye briefly, then once more. Checking for dilation, Glassman supposed. His grandmother seemed to pass the test.

"Very nice," Dr. Sullivan said. Glassman smiled at his grandmother, who seemed to smile slightly, if slightly askew, as well.

"We're still waiting on her family doctor," she addressed Glassman once again. "He should be here shortly. What we'll probably do is put her on ticlopidine to preclude any future episodes. It's a platelet inhibitor that helps prevent blood clots. We'll also want to do an angiography, maybe a magnetic resonance angiography, to determine where, exactly, the trouble is. We'll go over all the options with you a bit later. . . . I think we can expect a fairly complete, and quick, recovery. Your grandma will be here, though, for at least a few days. We want to keep an eye on her. Okay?"

"Yes, thank you doctor," Glassman replied. It sounded like she knew what she was doing.

"Any questions?"

"Ummm"—she seemed to have answered most of his questions— "no, not right now. Grandma?" Did his grandmother have any questions? Teenie shrugged. No. Dr. Sullivan smiled and left the room.

"So grandma, it sounds good, don't you think?" he asked her a bit too exuberantly, trying to buoy her spirits. She shrugged again. Glassman supposed that just after you had a stroke, you weren't likely to be immediately thankful that it wasn't a worse one.

"How . . . are *you* . . . doing?" she asked him. *How was he doing?* The question threw him. Yes, she hadn't seen him in weeks. He had missed Passover by fabricating some lame excuse; he hadn't visited her for *Law & Order* night in over a month; he only muttered a few lugubrious words when he managed dutifully to call. But at a time like this, what did it matter how *he* was doing?

His grandmother must have been petrified. Waking up in the middle of the night numb, unable to see out of her right eye! She was no fool. She knew it was a stroke. She probably thought that it was all over. *When your time's up, your time's up.* That was her philosophy about death and dying. It was a good one to have, Glassman thought. It probably took the edge off. There was nothing you could do, so why worry about it? *When your time's up, your time's up.* Maybe she didn't worry much. Her health, after all, could have been a lot worse. She was one of those ideal elderly that the HMO's could stomach, which was to say she didn't suffer from anything inefficiently terminal, a combination they especially dreaded. She just needed a few procedures now and again.

"Grandma?" he asked vacuously. He suddenly, selfishly, needed to be reassured of her presence.

"Yes . . . dear . . ."

"Grandma?" he asked again, then again. "Grandma?" Another question seemed to make its way from his stomach, up his throat, to the tip of his tongue—further than it had ever traveled before. Perspiration beaded like pinpricks on his forehead. The hair on his forearms tingled.

"Yes, what is it?" A pregnant pause. A deep breath. *How are* you *doing?* she had asked him. . . .

"Do you think Grandpa Abe killed himself? Did he kill himself? Is that what happened?" Glassman asked more audibly, at a lower register. "Please tell me."

It was a scenario that he could not remember ever entertaining seriously, that he had somehow long ago banished from his mind. A separate narrative somehow obtained . . .

All Teenie could do was watch her husband withdraw further and further within himself. He brooded more and more, silently sulked throughout the house each night when he should have been sleeping. Whole weeks would go by and it would dawn upon her that they hadn't exchanged more than one or two desultory sentences over the breakfast

248

table. He stopped playing golf at Willow Woods completely. Refused to go to shul on Saturdays. He began to spend practically all of his free time on his farkuckt birds. They were all he had time for anymore. On the weekends, he watched them with his binoculars at various undisclosed locales in the nearby Pocono woods.

And so, finally, he left. . . .

To tell you the truth, Barb, *Teenie had told Glassman's mother over the long distance wires to Los Angeles,* your father hasn't really been here anyway. Not for a very long time. *And this was the last thing Teenie wished to say about the matter, or about Abe Fishbein period.*

Abe had left. He had abandoned Teenie. Abandoned Lackawanna. . . .

Straining on the tips of her toes, Teenie grasped the too-light Bausch & Laumb case from the top shelf and immediately knew that Abe had taken his binoculars. A chill ran down her spine. God in Heaven! *Teenie cried.* Abe is gone!

Abe had fled. He had taken his binoculars and fled. These were the details he had gleaned over the years.

Or was it, rather, the story that had been painstakingly administered to him by Teenie, by his mother, like a bittersweet medicine? A story intended not to condemn Abe, but, maybe, to comfort, to protect, the heir to his legacy. Abe hadn't been abducted. He hadn't killed himself. Abe had left. . . .

But neither Leonard nor Irving Birnbaum had been so sure. And neither was Glassman.

That terrifying night in the hallway. The angry Cossack glaring down at him as he paced. The hot tears on his face. Glassman knew the fiery agony of wakefulness. A fire to smother no matter the cost, no matter what else would be extinguished in the bargain.

Do you think Grandpa Abe killed himself? Did he kill himself? Is that what happened? Did the police find him dead somewhere?

He needed to know. Now.

Another pregnant pause. The question hovered in the air between them. Had she heard what he had asked her? She must have . . .

"Do you . . . think it was . . . strange . . . your Grandpa Abraham and I . . . only had your mother and your Aunt . . . Janet?"

What was his grandmother talking about? What did his mother and Aunt Janet have to do with what he had asked her?

"No," he answered. "Why would I think that was strange?"

"Ehh," she shrugged her shoulders. "Some people thought . . . it was strange . . . we didn't . . . try for . . . a boy . . . thought something . . . was wrong."

"Well, it was none of their business anyway," Glassman answered. Why was his grandmother telling him this?

"Something *was* . . . wrong," she continued. She placed her hand, the one with the IV just above the wrist, on Glassman's forearm to secure his attention. "Before . . . Abraham went . . . to Europe during the war"—*yes, grandpa Abe fought in World War II*, Glassman reminded himself—"we . . . did . . . try to have a . . . baby . . . a son." Teenie took a few deep breaths.

"It's all right grandma. You don't have to tell me all this now." Was she delirious? "I'm sorry I upset you. Just relax." But Teenie tightened her grip on his arm. She had something to say.

"Four times . . . four times"—her eyes welled up—"I lost . . . our baby. The last time . . . the last time . . . it was a . . . a"—Teenie groped for the right word, or simply steeled herself so that she might utter it—"stillborn. . . . I asked the . . . doctor to tell me . . . was it a boy or . . . a girl. He wouldn't . . . tell me. . . .

"It was a relief then . . . when Abraham had . . . to go. Terrible I felt . . . that I felt . . . like that . . . but I was . . . broken. I didn't . . . want to . . . try . . . again."

"That's perfectly understandable," Glassman tried lamely to comfort her. Why had he opened his big fat mouth? Why did everything have to be about *him*? His grandmother was lying in a hospital bed for crying out loud.

"Sha . . . sha . . . listen"—she lifted her hand from his forearm and raised a finger—"when your grandfather . . . came back . . . we had . . . your mother. I . . . was so frightened . . . the

250

whole . . . time . . . but she . . . was fine. Then . . . we had your Aunt Janet. And then . . . well . . . then . . . genug . . . enough."

Glassman thought that his grandmother had reached the end of her story. But something also told him that she had one more thing to say, perhaps the way her chest abruptly rose upon a short intake of breath. "My father, may he rest in peace . . . your great-grandfather Lionel . . . who you never knew . . . buried the baby in the cemetery . . . but didn't tell me . . ."

Teenie must have noticed the disapproving furrow in his brow, because she promptly defended her father. "No, Matthew . . . he only wanted to spare me . . . the hurt. He was a good father. . . . I didn't see the stone . . . almost covered over by grass and weeds . . . until twenty years later or so . . . by accident . . . when I was trying to help Noma Dinner find one of her cousins. . . .

"'Baby Fishbein Died 1940' is all it says."

It struck Glassman as improbable that his grandmother didn't know for twenty years that her baby was buried in the cemetery. He couldn't help himself from probing, "How did you miss the stone for all those years that you visited the Fishbein plot? Or the Glassman plot? Where was the baby buried, anyway?"

"Yes," Teenie answered with a raised eyebrow. "That's it, you see. They weren't . . . allowed to bury the baby in either of the . . . family plots. It wasn't allowed. He's in the corner of the cemetery . . . underneath the messy sycamore tree that sheds its paper skin and leaves . . . all by himself. . . . I don't like that . . . but who am I to argue with the law?" *He?* Glassman took note of the male pronoun Teenie used to refer to her lost baby, but didn't know what, if anything, to make of it.

She placed her hand back, lightly, on his forearm.

"This your mother knows nothing of." She looked at him through glassy eyes and the hint of a smile. Glassman lowered his gaze.

He had received his answer.

"You should probably rest now," he told her. He felt that he needed to get out of there. He needed some air. And his grandmother probably did need to rest. "I'm going to go home, make some calls, get a book or something. I'll be back in a couple hours. I'm sure the doctor wants you to rest." Teenie nodded. He kissed her on the cheek and exited the room, looking back to see her once again, nodding slowly still, as if from inertia, a curious knowing expression, albeit somewhat aslant, on her face.

We had to lavage him 'cause he swallowed some cocaine, he heard a nurse tell her coworkers as he waited for the slow elevator to rise from the first floor.

And then we took his boots off and, like, fifteen packets of cocaine fell on the floor. Laughter. *And then he points to 'em and says, those aren't my boots!* More laughter.

Before leaving the hospital, he called Rebecca from the pay phone just inside the glass doors. He wanted to let her know that Teenie was okay, and wanted her to tell his mother the same. Rebecca answered the phone on the first ring. She already knew about Teenie's fairly good condition from Glassman's mother, who had, evidently, been informed about the stroke as well and had just spoken to Dr. Sullivan. Both of Glassman's parents were flying in to West Palm on an afternoon flight. They had given Rebecca the flight details. Yes, she told them, she and Matthew would be there to pick them up.

"Good," Glassman told Rebecca. His mother and father were coming down. There was so much now he wanted to tell them. "I love you, Rebecca."

Rebecca told him to drive home carefully. She loved him too.

Glassman walked out the glass doors of the emergency room and climate control gave way to Florida's balmy, moist breath. For a healthy person, he mused, he had certainly spent a lot of time lately in hospitals.

On the drive home, he played back his grandmother's words as if it were a recording he would always have at his disposal. It was almost as if he were hearing the words for the first time, right there on the interstate. He had been so concerned by the apparent strain she was under as she delivered her curious answer to his query that he hadn't absorbed fully what she had revealed to him. What her curious countenance betrayed . . .

She knew!

It struck him like a thunderbolt. She knew about Rebecca's miscarriage. Why else would she have told him what she had told him? What sense would it have made if she hadn't known about Rebecca. It was a special message, a gift, just for him.

Do you think Grandpa Abe killed himself?

He had asked too much of his grandmother with this question. Even if she knew the answer, she wouldn't tell him. And it wasn't because she resented Abe. At least not anymore, Glassman knew. It wasn't that she couldn't stand to hear the name of the scoundrel who had abandoned her. Abandoned her one way or the other. Rather, she now guarded his grandfather's illness, his pain, under lock and key, because it was Abe's property. It wasn't hers to share. She was only its custodian. *Right? Wrong? Wrong? Right? It was both and neither. It was just her way,* Glassman reflected. Her pain, however, *her* pain she could offer her grandson. It was his for the taking. Free of charge . . . practically. He could have it. Make what use of it he could. Tsum glik, tsum shlimazel, as his grandmother would say. For better or for worse.

Do you think grandpa Abe killed himself? He would probably never know the answer to this burning question, the answer he thought he needed so desperately to know. But he had been wrong about that, he now realized. He had migrated to Florida to retrieve something essential, something that had been tangible and abundant in Lackawanna, like its rich anthracite buried deep in the earth. Teetering over a dangerous precipice, he had hoped to achieve some primal point of balance among his dwindling elders, Lackawanna's survivors. An errant impulse? Glassman didn't think so. He had simply been sidetracked by the too tantalizing promise of his grandfather, Abe Fishbein, in the flesh, come back to save him. Well, given Birnbaum's eery emergence, who could blame him? But his grandfather, like Lackawanna itself, was irretrievable. He could accept this now. It was time to forgo nostalgia. Even Lackawanna's anthracite, Glassman reminded himself, had been overmined, depleted. It was time to mourn the loss of his grandfather—for one way or the other he was lost—and say goodbye to Lackawanna.

Yet, no. Not goodbye exactly. For what did Lackawanna mean, anyway? This American homeland of the Fishbein and Glassman tribe. Nothing that Glassman didn't have now in abundance, before his very eyes. He had Rebecca; he had his grandmother and a host of distant and not-too-distant relatives; he had Birnbaum; he had his neighbors in Pine Lakes; he had his colleagues at the *Jewish Weekly Times* and its plethora of readers (he could still redeem himself at work, he knew); he had the Everglades and the ocean. In short, he had achieved contact with the Florida earth and an electric current of human souls. For you couldn't have one without the other—the natural world divorced from the social, or vice-versa. They were inextricably connected. This was the lesson Birnbaum had taught him. There *was* a community in south Florida. It was a community vastly different than Lackawanna, but a community nonetheless. A place, at the very least, to make a start. And perhaps . . . perhaps this was enough for now.

A Vision of Feathers

I'm calling with some bad news," Teenie ominously greeted her
grandson over the phone line. . . .

It had been three months since Teenie's stroke, and they
had been a good three months—for Glassman and for his grandmother. Teenie, as Dr. Sullivan prognosticated, had made a complete recovery. She just had one more pill now to ingest over her
breakfasts of Melba toast, cantaloupe, and hot water with lemon,
one more set of water exercises to perform in the shallow end of her
overheated pool. To celebrate her recovered health and good spirits,
Glassman and Rebecca hosted a brunch for the first time and invited
as many of Glassman's Lackawanna relatives and friends as they
could fit into their house. They went "overboard," as Teenie harshly
praised afterwards. Edith and Ben, Ellen and Herbie, Mildred and
Nat, Ruth Spitz, and various and sundry Fishbeins, Dinners, Bassoffs, Truckers, Wolfs, Gelbs, Popkins, and Bornsteins crammed
gamely around the kitchen table, the edge of the family room futon,
the wobbly card-table on the patio, and, mostly, in a line of knees
across the slate ledge before the faux fireplace.

Irving Birnbaum attended the brunch as well. After telling his
grandmother to take a deep breath, Glassman told his grandmother

all about Birnbaum's emergence and convinced her that welcoming him back into the Lackawanna fold was the right thing to do. He had anticipated a stronger resistance from Teenie, but his grandmother seemed oddly excited about Birnbaum's emergence. She easily persuaded the rest of Lackawanna-south to be welcoming to Irving. A forty-year, largely self-imposed exile for his wrongs was plenty punishment enough.

At Glassman's brunch, Birnbaum sat directly in the middle of the line of knees across the slate ledge, between Teenie and Uncle Herbie. Glassman was glad that Birnbaum accepted the invitation, for he knew that the old man needed more by way of companionship than what he could provide alone. Birnbaum, perhaps, realized this as well. In fact, unless Glassman was mistaken, Birnbaum and his grandmother sat closer to one another than was absolutely necessary, the fabric of their clothes just touching shoulder to shoulder, thigh to thigh.

Birnbaum, along with twenty of his contemporaries, balanced on his lap a heavy plate of smoked fish, a sesame bagel and kugel, and a generous wedge of cantaloupe. He joined with them as they all toasted Teenie's health, the family room a motley assortment of inexpensive ceramic mugs filled with "coffee" (read: decaf), upraised and clinking.

Glassman, like Teenie, had also begun a course of medication. A very, very low dosage, the balding, bespectacled, and eminently likeable Dr. Gould had assured him. Glassman had to admit to Rebecca that the small pills didn't turn him into a zombie as he had feared. The medication only sanded away the sharpest, most dangerous of his edges. He was still Glassman. Ever Glassman. And, for the first time, this didn't seem like such a harsh fate.

Rebecca and he had even started trying once again to conceive. Dr. Arias had given Rebecca a clean bill of health just before the brunch. Rather than resign themselves to a long cycle of effortful copulation, they had resolved not to allow their reproductive efforts to affect their lovemaking. No fertility kits, no rigid schedules to take advantage of ovular receptiveness, no conception-friendly positions.

They would let nature take its course. Life, they assured themselves, would find a way.

Not such a harsh fate to be Glassman.

This is what he was thinking as he held forth at his brunch . . . *More coffee Aunt Edith? . . . Can I get you something while I'm up, Mildred? . . .* what he was thinking as Nat Siegel, engorged after his third bagel, finally relinquished his plate for him to clear, as he scraped the last stray egg noodle from one of the plates into the sink's disposal with a fork, as he faintly heard through the kitchen window his Uncle Ben (on the patio now where everyone retired to digest) retell his favorite joke . . . *Why do Jewish wives have sex with their eyes closed? They can't stand to see their husbands having a good time. . . .* and as he heard Ruth Spitz return the volley . . . *Why don't I ever hear you when you have your orgasm? the husband asks his wife. Because you're never there, she answers.* Not such a harsh fate to be Matthew Glassman, he thought as he filed upside down the last of the juice glasses in the top rack of the dishwasher, laughing softly at Ruth's joke. The warm fingertips of Rebecca's fingers on both his elbows, the briefest touch of her warm lips just below his ear, sent a shiver of surprise up his spine.

Hand in hand, they walked out to the patio to join their guests, who would stay for another two hours enjoying the cool breeze and one another's company under the patio screen. For these two splendid hours, Glassman and Rebecca, as they mingled separately, glanced giddily toward one another from various locations on the patio, as if they were teenagers conspiring toward some mischief later that afternoon.

The future seemed full of promise . . .

So what was this bad news his grandmother now had for him?

"It's okay, grandma. Go ahead. Tell me."

Teenie sighed regretfully, then told him that Ruth Spitz had passed away during the night. "They think she had a heart attack in her sleep," she explained.

"Oh, jeez grandma. I'm so sorry. Are you okay?"

"Yes, yes." Teenie shrugged off the suggestion to the contrary. "I'm happy for Ruth. She was failing in the end, so God finally just took her. I'll tell you, Matthew, that's the way to go." Glassman agreed.

But poor Ruth. As soon as he got off the phone with his grandmother, he remained stock still on the edge of the bed and gathered up his earliest memory of Ruth, as if it were a valuable gem he feared losing. She was in her fifties or so, lying on a chaise lounge by the pool at Willow Woods. A small piece of white plastic, like two teaspoons melded together, shielded her eyes from the sun. She wore a brown one piece bathing suit with white piping, cut high up her thigh; her flesh was as brown practically as the sun freckles on her chest. *How's the little marshmallow?* she asked him as she sat up to greet him by the pool, reaching for her soft crinkly pack of menthol cigarettes. Poor Ruth.

And poor Teenie. It was no picnic being his grandmother's age, if only because she had to witness the precipitous decline of all her contemporaries. Glassman hadn't truly absorbed this defining reality of his grandmother's existence until he moved to Florida and began speaking to her every other day or so. It seemed like there was always a funeral from which she had just returned, or had to prepare for, or regretted not being able to attend. Most of the burials, after all, were miles away in Lackawanna, which was no longer fit for the living but, evidently, remained the preferred place in which to be caught dead.

I'm next. I'm next. Was it possible that this thought didn't go through his grandmother's mind every time she said her final goodbyes to her Lackawanna cronies? Especially now, after her stroke.

There was no need for Rebecca to cancel class and join him at Ruth's funeral, Glassman assured his wife. She had only met Ruth a handful of times, after all. He would pray for them both, pay both their respects to Ruth's son.

Birnbaum, for his part, surprised Glassman over the phone when he asked him for directions to the cemetery in Pompano Beach.

"She was an awfully nice lady," Birnbaum told him, as if to defend his decision to attend the funeral. It was an explanation that more than sufficed, and Glassman didn't attempt to dissuade his old friend. It was a big step for Birnbaum. Yet he wondered at the old man's motivations. Who, really, did Birnbaum wish to mourn? Who did he wish to comfort?

Beth David was a large swath of green grass and cement bordered on every side by busy and treacherous four-lane streets. Immediately, it struck Glassman as a somewhat too highly efficient funeral factory. Before he and Birnbaum even made their way into one of the four receiving rooms to pay their condolences to Ruth's son, Arthur, they waited patiently with Teenie and the rest of Ruth's mourners against the walls of the large, darkly carpeted foyer. Three separate funeral parties coursed out the hall between them and made their way back toward the parking lot, where three separate hearses led three separate vehicle snakes to three separate burials on the grounds. Plenty of people, Glassman thought, must have gotten confused on a regular basis and followed wrong hearses to wrong burials.

At the grave side at last, Glassman reached into the pocket of his suit jacket and unearthed, almost magically, a plain black kippah. There was always a kippah to be found in the breast pocket of Glassman's only suit, which gave some indication of how infrequently he wore the traditional blue pinstripe, and for what occasions. Gold block letters stamped small inside the kippah read, "Property of Temple Beth Israel, Lackawanna, Pennsylvania, Donated by Louis and Sophia Trucker."

Glassman placed the Lackawanna kippah precariously atop his head and listened to Ruth Spitz's eulogy. The man giving the eulogy (who worked for the funeral home and knew only as much about Ruth as her son, Teenie, and the thirty or so friends and family members who managed to outlive her had revealed to him that morning) struck Glassman as competent and kind enough. It seemed to him that the old man did the best he could under the circumstances. He reviewed the highlights of her life, glancing down at cue cards from time to time, and emphasized her love for her family and friends in slow, measured cadences. He needed to stretch the limited material he had to work with into a respectably long eulogy. Well, what was the man to do?

"He's used this one before," Glassman heard one woman he didn't know complain to the person standing beside her.

"Shhhh!" the reply.

"I'm telling you I recognize it!"

"Shhhh!"

The eulogy didn't matter much to his grandmother, he thought. Looking down at her next to him, he knew that Teenie was lost in her own thoughts. She leaned over her walker, supporting most of her weight with her still strong arms. On the surface, she appeared to be examining her shoes. She began to cry softly.

It was more difficult to read Birnbaum's emotions, who stood to his other side just as impassively as Glassman himself stood. The old man stretched his arm in front of Glassman and handed Teenie a dry tissue, which she wordlessly accepted.

They recited the Mourner's Kaddish, sprinkled some dirt on Ruth's simple wood coffin, then slid her into a low second-story shelf next to her late husband, who had passed away five years ago, before Glassman and Rebecca moved to Florida.

Not bad, Glassman thought of Ruth's new surroundings. *Better than in the scorching, Florida earth, under hundreds of pounds of sandy dirt.*

"Are you doing okay, grandma?" he finally asked.

"Well, I'm not doing so hot. But it'll all come out in the wash. . . . It'll all come out in the wash." She lifted a hand from her walker and blotted her eyes with the limp tissue as if stanching the flow of blood.

Looking out over the gray-capped sea of mourners, it occurred to Glassman that he was by far the youngest person in attendance. Other than Arthur Spitz, who must have been twenty or so years older than Glassman, all the mourners had to be in their seventies, at the very least. A generation was almost wholly absent in Florida, Arthur's generation, the sons and daughters of the Jewish aged. How many more years could these elders hold on? In five, ten, maybe fifteen years at the most, Glassman knew—as his elders surely knew—all of the mourners surrounding him now would be gone themselves. Vanished. And who would replace them in south Florida? Who would enjoy their tidy condominiums? Their manicured gardens and grass? Not their Jewish children, evidently, who would scatter themselves across the west in more fashionable retirement locales. No, instead the Dominicans, Argentinians, Cubans, Jamaicans, Brazilians, Haitians, Trinidadians . . . the new Americans, would live here, along with increasing numbers of African Americans, as well—like the two black men in caps and blue jumpsuits who stood silently and almost invisibly beyond the shoulder of the elderly eulogist, waiting unobtrusively until it was time to seal Ruth Spitz in her shelf, until it was time to take care of their death business—these were the ones who would occupy the space formerly taken up by Glassman's relatives.

This was okay, he reflected. Sad, in its own way, but okay.

After the short service, the small funeral party dispersed toward the parking lot only to congregate once again at Ruth Spitz's small apartment at Cypress Ponds, which her son would surely sell. The mirror in the foyer was carefully soaped, according to custom. It was no time for vanity. Teenie had somehow beaten them to the apartment and was busy giving directives to Maria, whose services Teenie evidently secured for the luncheon. Upon Teenie's exacting instructions, Maria proceeded to arrange four circular metal trays of cold cuts, crisp vegetables, pasta and potato salads on the rectangular dining room table. Glassman approached and offered to help remove the plastic wrap that covered each tray.

Glassman stayed longer than he had anticipated. He didn't feel much like eating, but nibbled on a dry turkey sandwich (asking for mayonnaise somehow seemed inappropriate given the occasion) while listening to several stories about Ruth he hadn't heard before. She and Teenie had gotten suspended from Lackawanna High when they were caught smoking cigarettes in the girl's bathroom. She spearheaded an unsuccessful campaign sometime in the early seventies to quash Willow Woods's policy of men's only Sundays on the golf course. That Tuesday was women's day didn't suffice as far as she was concerned since more than half of the girls now worked during the week just like the men. True, Ruth herself never worked outside the home, but she volunteered every Wednesday and Thursday afternoon at the Jewish home, where her parents had both resided for a short time before passing away within three months of one another. There, she coordinated card games and bingo for a growing contingent of her parents' friends. Sometimes she just sat and talked with whomever beckoned toward her from across the expansive common room. *Ruthie dear . . . Ruthie . . . come over and kibbitz with me, won't you? Ruthie . . .*

Glassman could imagine the desperate pleas, the pleas Ruthie had answered. For Glassman had been to Lackawanna's Jewish home once to visit his great-grandfather Herschel with his parents and Sara. On their way to Herschel's room down the long, hard hallway, Glassman had heard these pleas echo from three or four of the shared rooms. *Barbie? Barbie? Is that you? . . . Stanley Glassman! Stanley . . . Stanley . . .* Several excited elders had recognized his wayward, west coast parents. It took them nearly an hour to reach his great-grandfather's room some thirty yards down the hall.

When Glassman was finally ready to leave, he looked around for Birnbaum and Teenie so that he could say goodbye. He found them alone in the living room, away from the food, talking softly with one another on the low, wooden mourner's chairs. They seemed engrossed in their conversation. Something told Glassman not to interrupt them, so he paid his respects once again to Ruth's relatives and departed silently.

It was already late afternoon, rush hour, by the time Glassman was on the interstate. The highway was heavily congested. Yet somehow Glassman didn't mind today. He was moving at least. Moving upon this river of steel flowing slowly northward. He was one person among thousands and thousands obdurately wending their way toward their destinations. A river of commitments made and commitments honored. Day after day after day. It was glorious.

Then he saw them. A vision of feathers. A conspiracy between his eyes and his mind tricked him into thinking they were pigeons at first glance. But they weren't pigeons. Decidedly not pigeons. It was a dazzling sight. One to share, not hoard. The heel of his palm automatically moved toward his horn to alert his fellow commuters, but, for safety's sake, he checked the impulse; he didn't want to cause an accident. The enormous salt and pepper wings, the fleshy prehistoric heads pointed westward. They flew in low formation over Glassman's windshield. One bird seemed almost to glance the roof of a dusty truck trailer on the southbound side with the black fingertip of a wing. Ten of them flying in V formation, vigorously beating their broad wings against an easterly gust that rattled Glassman's window. He was relieved to see the birds cross over the highway safely, to see the feathered squadron rise and dip, and rise once again, gradually gaining altitude in the azure sky. Miraculous forces somehow drew them westward, toward the sawgrass and cypress of the Everglades, toward the orange yolk that was the sun dripping off the edge of the earth. Like Glassman, the wood storks were headed home.

Library of American Fiction
The University of Wisconsin Press Fiction Series

Marleen S. Barr
Oy Pioneer! A Novel

Dodie Bellamy
The Letters of Mina Harker

Melvin Jules Bukiet
Stories of an Imaginary Childhood

Andrew Furman
Alligators May Be Present: A Novel

Merrill Joan Gerber
Glimmering Girls: A Novel of the Fifties

Rebecca Goldstein
The Dark Sister

Rebecca Goldstein
Mazel

Jesse Lee Kercheval
The Museum of Happiness: A Novel

Alan Lelchuk
American Mischief

Alan Lelchuk
Brooklyn Boy

Curt Leviant
Ladies and Gentlemen, The Original Music of the Hebrew Alphabet *and*
    Weekend in Mustara: *Two Novellas*

David Milofsky
A Friend of Kissinger: A Novel

Lesléa Newman
A Letter to Harvey Milk: Short Stories

Mordecai Roshwald
Level 7

Lewis Weinstein
The Heretic: A Novel

wrinkled pgs 10/15 RC

BOCA RATON PUBLIC LIBRARY, FLORIDA

3 3656 0338816 8

Furman, Andrew, 1968–
Alligators may be present

MAY   2005